Henry Taylor

Philip van Artevelde

A Dramatic Romance

Henry Taylor

Philip van Artevelde
A Dramatic Romance

ISBN/EAN: 9783337348663

Printed in Europe, USA, Canada, Australia, Japan

Cover: Foto ©Andreas Hilbeck / pixelio.de

More available books at **www.hansebooks.com**

IN TWO PARTS.

BY HENRY TAYLOR.

"Dramatica Poesis est veluti Historia spectabilis."
BACON DE AUGMENTIS.

SIXTH EDITION.

LONDON:
CHAPMAN AND HALL, 193, PICCADILLY.
1862.

ROBERT SOUTHEY.

THIS Book, though it should travel far and wide
  As ever unripe Author's quick conceit
  Could feign his page dispersed, should nowhere meet
A friendlier censor than by Greta's side,
  A warmer welcome than at Skiddaw's feet.
Unhappily infrequent in the land
  Is now the sage seclusion, the retreat
Sacred to letters: but let this command
Fitting acknowledgment,—that time and tide
  Saw never yet embellish'd with more grace
Outward and inward, with more charms allied,
  With honours more attended, man or place,
Than where by Greta's silver current sweet
Learning still keeps one calm sequester'd seat.

ADVERTISEMENT TO THE THIRD EDITION.

In the Advertisement to the Second Edition of this Work, published three months after the first, it was stated that the one differed from the other only in one or two trifling insertions, in the correction of some faults which had been pointed out in periodical publications, and in the alteration of a few lines here and there, made for the most part with a view to consolidate the rhythm. In the years which have since elapsed there has been ample time for revision, and though some of the more material defects, being what may be called structural, are so incorporated with the whole as to be beyond the reach of correction; yet the Author trusts that much improvement has been effected by the removal of blemishes that lay on the surface. One or two short scenes have been introduced also where they seemed to be wanted for purposes either of connection or separation.

NAPLES, *January*, 1841.

ADVERTISEMENT TO THE SIXTH EDITION.

In publishing the Sixth Edition the Author wishes to add, that he has been indebted to the critical discernment and true poetic feeling of Professor Heimann, the German translator of the Work, for suggestions which have been of great value to him in the renewed revision of it.

MORTLAKE, *April*, 1852.

PREFACE.

As this work, consisting of two Plays and an Interlude, is equal in length to about six such plays as are adapted to representation, it is almost unnecessary to say that it was not intended for the stage. It is properly an Historical Romance, cast in a dramatic and rhythmical form. Historic truth is preserved in it, as far as the material events are concerned—of course with the usual exception of such occasional dilatations and compressions of time as are required in dramatic composition.

This is, perhaps, all the explanation which is absolutely required in this place; but as there may be readers who feel an inclination to learn something of an author's tastes in poetry before they proceed to the perusal of what he has written, I will take the opportunity which a preface affords me of expressing my opinions upon two or three of the most prominent features in the present state of poetical literature; and I shall do so the more gladly because I am apprehensive that without some previous intimations of the kind, my work might occasion disappointment

to the admirers of that highly coloured poetry which
has been popular in these latter years. If in the
strictures which, with this object, I may be led to
make upon authors of great reputation, I should
appear to be wanting in the respect due to prevalent
opinions,—opinions which, from the very circumstance
of their prevalence, must be assumed to be partaken
by many to whom deference is owing,—I trust that
it will be attributed, not to any spirit of dogmatism,
far less to a love of disparagement; but simply to the
desire of exercising, with a discreet freedom, that
humble independence of judgment in matters of taste,
which it is for the advantage of literature that every
man of letters should maintain.

My views have not, in truth, been founded upon
any predisposition to depreciate the popular poetry of
the times. It will always produce a powerful impression upon very young readers, and I scarcely think
that it can have been more admired by any than by
myself, when I was included in that category. I have
not ceased to admire this poetry in its degree; and the
interlude which I have inserted between these plays
will show, that, to a limited extent, I have been
desirous even to cultivate and employ it: but I am
unable to concur in opinion with those who would
place it in the foremost ranks of the art: nor does
it seem to have been capable of sustaining itself quite
firmly in the very high degree of public estimation in
which it was held at its first appearance and for some
years afterwards. The poetical taste to which some
of the popular poets of this century gave birth, appears

at present to maintain a more unshaken dominion
over the writers of poetry, than over its readers.

These poets were characterised by great sensibility
and fervour, by a profusion of imagery, by force and
beauty of language, and by a versification peculiarly
easy and adroit, and abounding in that sort of melody
which, by its very obvious cadences, makes itself most
pleasing to an unpractised ear. They exhibited, therefore, many of the most attractive graces and charms
of poetry—its vital warmth not less than its external
embellishments; and had not the admiration which
they excited tended to produce an indifference to
higher, graver, and more various endowments, no one
would have said that it was, in any evil sense, exces-
sive. But from this unbounded indulgence in the
mere luxuries of poetry, has there not ensued a want
of adequate appreciation for its intellectual and
immortal part? I confess that such seems to me
to have been both the actual and the natural result;
and I can hardly believe the public taste to have
been in a healthy state whilst the most approved
poetry of past times was almost unread. We may now
perhaps be turning back to it; but it was not, as far
as I can judge, till more than a quarter of a century
had expired, that any signs of re-action could be
discerned. Till then, the elder luminaries of our
poetical literature were obscured or little regarded;
and we sate with dazzled eyes at a high festival of
poetry, where, as at the funeral of Arvalan, the torch-
light put out the star-light.

So keen was the sense of what the new poets

possessed, that it never seemed to be felt that anything was deficient in them. Yet their deficiencies
were not unimportant. They wanted, in the first
place, subject-matter. A feeling came more easily
to them than a reflection, and an image was always
at hand when a thought was not forthcoming. Either
they did not look upon mankind with observant eyes,
or they did not feel it to be any part of their vocation
to turn what they saw to account. It did not belong
to poetry, in their apprehension, to thread the mazes
of life in all its classes and under all its circumstances,
common as well as romantic, and, seeing all things, to
infer and to instruct : on the contrary, it was to stand
aloof from everything that is plain and true ; to have
little concern with what is rational or wise ; it was to
be, like music, a moving and enchanting art, acting
upon the fancy, the affections, the passions, but
scarcely connected with the exercise of the intellectual
faculties. These writers had, indeed, adopted a tone
of language which is hardly consistent with the state
of mind in which a man makes use of his understanding. The realities of nature, and the truths which
they suggest, would have seemed cold and incongruous,
if suffered to mix with the strains of impassioned
sentiment and glowing imagery in which they poured
themselves forth. Spirit was not to be debased by
any union with matter, in their effusions ; dwelling,
as they did, in a region of poetical sentiment which
did not permit them to walk upon the common earth
or to breathe the common air.

Writers, however, whose appeal is made so exclusively to the excitabilities of mankind, will not find it possible to work upon them continuously without a diminishing effect. Poetry of which sense is not the basis,—sense rapt or inspired by passion, not bewildered or subverted,—poetry over which the passionate reason of Man does not preside in all its strength as well as all its ardours,—though it may be excellent of its kind, will not long be reputed to be poetry of the highest order. It may move the feelings and charm the fancy; but failing to satisfy the understanding, it will not take permanent possession of the strong-holds of fame. Lord Byron, in giving the most admirable example of this species of poetry, undoubtedly gave the strongest impulse to the appetite for it. Yet this impulse is losing its force, and even Lord Byron himself repudiated, in the latter years of his life, the poetical taste which he had espoused and propagated. The constitution of this writer's mind is not difficult to understand, and sufficiently explains the growth of his taste.

Had he united a philosophical intellect with his peculiarly poetical temperament, he would probably have been the greatest poet of his age. But no man can be a very great poet who is not also a great philosopher. Whatever Lord Byron's natural powers may have been, idleness and light reading, an early acquisition of popularity by the exercise of a single talent, and an absorbing and contracting self-love, confined the field of his operations within narrow limits. He was in knowledge merely a man of Belles-lettres; nor does he appear at any time to have betaken himself to such studies as would have tended to the cultivation and discipline of his reasoning powers or the enlargement of his mind. He had, however, not only an ardent and brilliant imagination, but a clear understanding, and the signs both of what he had and of what he wanted are apparent in his poetry. There is apparent in it a working and moulding spirit, with a want of material to work up,—a great command of language, with a want of any views or reflections which, if unembellished by imagery or unassociated with passionate feelings, it would be very much worth while to express. Page after page throughout his earlier poems, there is the same uninformed energy at work upon the same old feelings; and when at last he became conscious that a theme was wanting, it was at a period of life when no man will consent to put himself to school; he could change his style and manner, but he could not change his moral and intellectual being, nor extend the sphere of his contemplations to subjects which were alien in *spirit* from those with which he had been hitherto, whether in life or in literature, exclusively conversant: in short, his mind was past the period of growth; there was (to use a phrase of Ben Jonson's) an *ingeni-stitium*, or wit-stand: he felt, apparently, that the food on which he had fed his mind had not been invigorating; but he could no longer bear a stronger diet, and he turned his genius loose to rove over the surface of society, content with such light observations upon life and manners as any acute man of the world might collect upon his travels, and conscious that he could recommend them to attention by such wit, brilliancy, dexterity of phrase, and versatility of fancy, as no one but himself could command.

His misanthropy was probably, like his tenderness, not practical, but merely matter of imagination, assumed for purposes of effect. But whilst his ignorance of the better elements of human nature may be believed to have been in a great measure affected, it is not to be supposed that he knew of them with a large and appreciating knowledge. Yet that knowledge of human nature which is exclusive of what is good in it, is, to say the least, as shallow and imperfect as that which is exclusive of what is evil. There is no such thing as philosophical misanthropy; and if a misanthropical spirit, be it genuine or affected, be found to pervade a man's writings, that spirit may be poetical as far as it goes, but being at fault in its philosophy, it will never, in the long run of time, approve itself equal to the institution of a poetical fame of the highest and most durable order.

These imperfections are especially observable in the portraitures of human character (if such it can be called) which are most prominent in Lord Byron's works. There is nothing in them of the mixture and modification,—nothing of the composite fabric which Nature has assigned to Man. They exhibit rather passions personified than persons impassioned. But there is a yet worse defect in them. Lord Byron's conception of a hero is an evidence, not only of scanty materials of knowledge from which to construct the ideal of a human being, but also of a want of perception of what is great or noble in our nature. His heroes are creatures abandoned to their passions, and essentially, therefore, weak of mind. Strip them of the veil of mystery and the trappings of poetry, resolve them into their plain realities, and they are such beings as, in the eyes of a reader of masculine judgment, would certainly excite no sentiment of admiration, even if they did not provoke contempt. When the conduct and feelings attributed to them are reduced into prose, and brought to the test of a rational consideration, they must be perceived to be beings in whom there is no strength except that of their intensely selfish passions,—in whom all is vanity; their exertions being for vanity under the name of love or revenge, and their sufferings for vanity under the name of pride. If such beings as these are to be regarded as heroical, where in human nature are we to look for what is low in sentiment or infirm in character ?

How nobly opposite to Lord Byron's ideal was that conception of an heroical character which took life and immortality from the hand of Shakspeare :—

> " Give me that man
> That is not passion's slave, and I will wear him
> In my heart's core; aye, in my heart of heart."

Lord Byron's genius, however, was powerful enough to cast a highly romantic colouring over these puerile creations, and to impart the charms of forcible expression, fervid feeling, and beautiful imagery, to thoughts in themselves not more remarkable for novelty than for soundness. The public required nothing more; and if he himself was brought latterly to a sense of his deficiencies of knowledge and general intellectual cultivation, it must have been more by the effect of time in so far maturing his very vigorous understanding than by any correction from without. No writer of his age has had less of the benefits of adverse criticism. His own judgment and that of his readers have been left equally without check or guidance; and the decline in popular estimation which he has suffered for these last few years may be rather attributed to a satiated appetite on the part of the public than to a rectified taste: for those who have ceased to admire his poetry so ardently as they did do not appear in general to have transferred their admiration to any worthier object.

Nor can it be said that anything better, or indeed anything half so good, has been subsequently produced. The poetry of the day, whilst it is greatly inferior in quality, continues to be like his in kind. It consists of little more than a poetical diction, an arrangement of words implying a sensitive state of mind, and therefore more or less calculated to excite corresponding associations, though, for the most part, not pertinently to any matter in hand; a diction which addresses itself to the sentient, not the percipient, properties of the mind, and displays merely symbols or types of feelings which might exist with equal force in a being the most barren of understanding.

It may be proper, however, to take a distinction between the ordinary Byronian poetry, and that which may be considered as the offspring, either in the first or second generation, of the genius of Mr. Shelley. Mr. Shelley was a person of a more powerful and expansive imagination than Lord Byron, but he was inferior to him in those practical abilities which (unacceptable as such an opinion may be to those who believe themselves to be writing under the guidance of inspiration) are essential to the production of consummate poetry. The editor of Mr. Shelley's posthumous poems apologises for the publication of some fragments in a very incomplete state by remarking how much " more than every other poet of the present day, every line and word he wrote is instinct with peculiar beauty." Let no man sit down to write with the purpose of making every line and word beautiful and peculiar. The only effect of such an endeavour will be to corrupt his judgment and confound his understanding. In Mr. Shelley's case, besides an endeavour of this kind, there seems to have been an attempt to unrealise every object in nature, presenting them under forms and combinations in which they are never to be seen through the mere medium of our eye-sight. Mr. Shelley seems to have written under the notion that no phenomena can be perfectly poetical, until they shall have been so decomposed from their natural order and coherency as to be brought before the reader in the likeness of a phantasma or a vision. A poet is, in his estimation, (if I may venture to infer his principles from his

practice,) purely and pre-eminently a visionary. Much
beauty, exceeding splendour of diction and imagery,
cannot but be perceived in his poetry, as well as
exquisite charms of versification ; and a reader of
an apprehensive fancy will doubtless be entranced
whilst he reads : but when he shall have closed the
volume and considered within himself what it has
added to his stock of permanent impressions, of
recurring thoughts, of pregnant recollections, he
will probably find his stores in this kind no more
enriched by having read Mr. Shelley's poems, than
by having gazed on so many gorgeously coloured
clouds in an evening sky. Surpassingly beautiful
they were whilst before his eyes ; but forasmuch
as they had no relevancy to his life, past or future,
the impression upon the memory barely survived
that upon the senses.

I would by no means wish to be understood as
saying that a poet can be too imaginative, provided
that his other faculties be exercised in due proportion
to his imagination. I would have no man depress
his imagination, but I would have him raise his
reason to be its equipoise. What I would be understood to oppugn is the strange opinion which seems
to prevail amongst certain of our writers and readers
of poetry, that good sense stands in a species of
antagonism to poetical genius, instead of being one of
its most essential constituents. The maxim that a poet
should be " of imagination all compact," is not, I think,
to be adopted thus literally. That predominance of the
imaginative faculty, or of impassioned temperament,

which is incompatible with the attributes of a sound understanding and a just judgment, may make a rhapsodist, a melodist, or a visionary, each of whom may produce what may be admired for the particular talent and beauty belonging to it : but imagination and passion thus unsupported will never make a poet in the largest and highest sense of the appellation :—

> "For Poetry is Reason's self sublimed ;
> 'Tis Reason's sovereignty, whereunto
> All properties of sense, all dues of wit,
> All fancies, images, perceptions, passions,
> All intellectual ordinance grown up
> From accident, necessity, or custom,
> Seen to be good, and after made authentic ;
> All ordinance aforethought, that from science
> Doth prescience take, and from experience law ;
> All lights and institutes of digested knowledge,
> Gifts and endowments of intelligence
> From sources living, from the dead bequests,—
> Subserve and minister."*

Mr. Shelley and his disciples, however,—the followers, (if I may so call them) of the PHANTASTIC SCHOOL, labour to effect a revolution in this order of things. They would transfer the domicile of poetry to regions where reason, far from having any supremacy or rule, is all but unknown, an alien and an outcast; to seats of anarchy and abstraction, where imagination exercises the shadow of an authority, over a people of phantoms, in a land of dreams.

In bringing these cursory criticisms to an end, I must beg leave to warn the reader against any expectation that he will find my work free either from

* MS.

the faults which I attribute to others, or from faults
which may be worse, and more peculiarly my own.
The actual works of men will not bear to be measured
by their ideal standards in any case; and I may
observe, in reference to my own, that my critical
views have rather resulted from composition than
directed it. If, however, I have been unable to avoid
the errors which I condemn, or errors not less censur-
able, I trust, that, on the other hand, I shall not be
found to have deprived myself, by any narrowness or
perversity of judgment, of the advantage which the
study of these writers, exceptionable though they
be, may undoubtedly afford to one who, whilst duly
taking note of their general defects, shall not have
closed his mind to a perception of their particular
excellences. I feel and have already expressed, a
most genuine and I hope not an inadequate admiration for the powers which they respectively possess;
and wherever it might occur to me that the exercise
of those powers would be appropriate and consistent,
I should not fail to benefit by their example to the
extent of my capabilities. To say, indeed, that I
admire them, is to admit that I owe them much;
for admiration is never thrown away upon the mind
of him who feels it, except when it is misdirected
or blindly indulged. There is perhaps nothing which
more enlarges or enriches the mind than the dis-
position to lay it genially open to impressions of
pleasure from the exercise of every species of talent;
nothing by which it is more impoverished than

the habit of undue depreciation. What is puerile, pusillanimous, or wicked, it can do us no good to admire; but let us admire all that can be admired without debasing the dispositions or stultifying the understanding.

LONDON, *May*, 1834.

INTRODUCTION.

In the fourteenth century the Flemish towns were the most opulent and considerable in Europe; and of these, Ghent and Bruges were, in size, wealth, and population, perhaps scarcely inferior even to Venice. They were of right subject to the Earl of Flanders, and in ordinary times he exercised by his bailiffs the powers of sovereignty in them: but they had secured various franchises and immunities, which they guarded with jealousy, and which, when need was, they rose in arms to defend. On such occasions they were seldom all joined in a league together; for the trading interests of several of them were in some respects opposite, and some would generally remain subject to the Earl, and at war, therefore, with those which leagued against him.

These towns were not only asunder one from another, but each one was commonly divided by parties within itself. The towns consisted each of various crafts or guilds, as the weavers, the fullers, the clothiers, the mariners, &c., and some of these crafts were occasionally well affected towards the Earl, at the same time that others were disposed to rebellion. But the chief opposition was between the rich inhabitants and the poor. The rich wished for peace and repose; the poor were eager for war, which, in that age, when most men were warlike, was perhaps the best trade that a poor man could follow. When therefore any of these towns was in rebellion, there was generally a peace-faction within it, which rose or fell in importance according to the varying circumstances of military success or failure.

In the year 1381, the inhabitants of Bruges made themselves friends with Lois, Earl of Flanders, and under the countenance of his authority, which they purchased, began to cut a channel which would have opened to them a direct communication with the river Lis, the navigation of which was otherwise only accessible to them by passing through Ghent. Ghent was, however, by no means willing to lose her exclusive possession or control of the navigation up the Lis. Like the "*Crowning City*" of more ancient days, "*the harvest of the river was her revenue.*"

"There was at this time in Ghent a burgess called John Lyon, a sage man, cruel, hardy, subtle, and a great enterpriser, and cold and patient enough in all his works." This John Lyon (the Flemish name is Heins, but it is thus Englished) was a dismissed officer of the Earl, and he took the opportunity of the discontent occasioned by the proceedings of the Earl and the people of Bruges, to revive an old usage of Ghent, by which all the disaffected were accustomed to form themselves into a corps, distin-

guished by white hoods, and subordinated to one
ruler. Such a corps was now formed, and John Lyon,
being chosen their chief, conducted a party of them
to attack the pioneers from Bruges who were digging
at the Lis. But the pioneers retreated, and desisted
without fighting.

The professed object of forming the corps was
accomplished therefore; "but notwithstanding that,
John Lyon did not abandon his office, but the White-
Hoods went daily up and down the town, and John
Lyon kept them still in that state, and to some he would
say secretly, 'Hold you well content; eat and drink,
and make merry, and be not concerned at any thing
you spend; for hereafter such shall pay you as will
not now give you one penny.'"

For men thus organised and thus disposed, a fresh
cause of quarrel was easily to be found. "In the
same week that John Lyon had been thus at Deinse,
to have met with the pioneers of Bruges, there came
many out of the Franc of Ghent, to complain to them
that had then the rule of the law, and said, 'Sirs, at
Erclo, near here, which is within the Franchise of
Ghent, there is one of our burgesses in the Earl's
prison, and we have desired the Earl's bailiff there to
deliver him; but he hath plainly answered that he
will not deliver him, which is evidently against the
privilege of this town of Ghent; and so thereby your
privileges will be by degrees broken, which have
hitherto been so nobly and so highly praised, and
besides that, so well kept and maintained that none
durst break them, and that the most noble Knight

of Flanders considered it an honour to be a burgess of Ghent.' Then they of the Law answered and said, that 'they would write to the bailiff desiring that the burgess may be delivered; for truly his office extendeth not so far as to keep our burgess in the Earl's prison.' And so they wrote to the bailiff for the deliverance of the burgess who was in prison in Erclo.—The bailiff answered, 'What needeth all these words for a mariner? Say,' quoth the bailiff, who was named Roger d'Auterne, 'to them of Ghent; that though he were ten times richer than he is, he shall never go out of prison unless my lord the Earl command it. I have power to arrest, but I have no power to deliver.' "

They of Ghent were ill content with this answer, and complained loudly to the Earl, who agreed to release the prisoner and redress their grievances, on condition that the White-Hoods should be disbanded. But John Lyon maintained that it was only by keeping up the White-Hoods that they would ever have any security for their privileges; and in spite of all the Earl's remonstrances, the White-Hoods increased in number and were formed into companies with captains over them. The Earl then sent his bailiff to Ghent with two hundred men, to seize and execute John Lyon and other captains. This brought on an encounter in the market-place, where the bailiff was slain and the Earl's banner torn in pieces by the White-Hoods.

Such was the beginning of a war which continued for several years between the Earl of Flanders and the town of Ghent, and in which the principal towns on the part of the Earl were Bruges, Oudenarde, Dendermonde, Lisle, and Tournay; and those on the part of Ghent were Damme, Ypres, Courtray, Grammont, Poperinguen, and Messines:—A war which in its progress extended to the whole of Flanders, and excited a degree of interest in all the civilised countries of Europe for which the cause must be sought in the state of European communities at the time. It was believed that entire success on the part of Ghent would bring on a general rising almost throughont Christendom, of the Commonalty against the Feudal Lords and men of substance. The incorporation of the citizens of Paris known by the name of "the Army with Mallets," was, according to the well-known chronicler of the period, "all by the example of them of Ghent." Nicholas le Flamand deterred them from pulling down the Louvre, by urging the expediency of waiting to see what success might attend the Flemish insurgents. At Rheims, Chalons on the Marne, at Orleans, Beauvoisin, the like designs were entertained. "The rebellion of the Jacquerie," says Froissart, "was never so terrible as this was likely to have been." Brabant, Burgundy, and the lower part of Germany, were in a dangerous condition; and in England Wat Tyler's rebellion was contemporaneous and not unconnected with what was going on in Flanders.

I have related by way of introduction, the origin of the war,—not that the incidents in which it originated are immediately connected with those of my play, which opens at a later period, after the death of John Lyon; but because I have wished (as much as in so small a compass may be) to give those of my readers who may require it, a notion of the temper of mind which prevailed in Flanders towards the end of the fourteenth century.

PHILIP VAN ARTEVELDE.

PART THE FIRST.

"No arts, no letters, no society,—and, which is worst of all, continual fear and danger of violent death, and the life of Man, solitary, poor, nasty, brutish, and short."

LEVIATHAN, Part I. c. 18.

B

DRAMATIS PERSONÆ.

———◆———

MEN OF GHENT.

PHILIP VAN ARTEVELDE.
PETER VAN DEN BOSCH,
SIR GUY, LORD OF OCCO, } *Leaders of the White-Hoods.*
PETER VAN NUITRE,
FRANS ACKERMAN,
VAN AESWYN, *Squire to Sir Guy of Occo.*
HENRY VAN DRONGELEN, *Page to Van Artevelde.*
FATHER JOHN OF HEDA, *a Monk, formerly Preceptor to Van Artevelde.*
VAN RYK,
VAN MUCK, } *Deans of two of the Crafts.*
UKENHEIM, *a Citizen.*
SIR SIMON BETTE,
SIR GUISEBERT GRUTT, } *Wealthy Citizens.*
MYK STEENSEL,

MEN OF BRUGES.

THE EARL OF FLANDERS.
SIR WALTER D'ARLON.
GILBERT MATTHEW.
SIR ROBERT MARESCHAULT, *and others.*

WOMEN.

ADRIANA VAN MERESTYN.
CLARA VAN ARTEVELDE, *Sister of Philip Van Artevelde.*

The SCENE is laid sometimes at GHENT, sometimes at BRUGES, or in its neighbourhood.

PHILIP VAN ARTEVELDE.

PART THE FIRST.

ACT I.

SCENE I.—*A Street in the Suburbs of Ghent.*

The LORD OF OCCO, *meeting* SIR SIMON BETTE *and* SIR
GUISEBERT GRUTT.

OCCO.

Sir Guisebert Grutt, and, by my faith, I think
Sir Simon Betté too!   Pray you pardon me ;
I thought that you were sped upon your mission
To treat for peace at Bruges ?

SIR SIMON.

Sir, in good time.
We'd have a word with you before we go.
You are a noble born, my Lord of Occo ;
And let me tell you, many marvel much
To find a gentleman of so great worth
A flatterer of the Commons.

SIR GUISEBERT.

Yea, my lord :
It looks not well when nobles fall away

B 2

One from another.   That the small-crafts here
Should lift their hands against their natural lord
Is but the plague and sorrow of the time,
Which we, that are of credit, must abide :
But ne'er till now a gentleman of name
Was found amongst their leaders.

OCCO.

                              Oh, dear sirs,
I could remind you how your sometime selves
Bore less goodwill toward the Earl's affairs
Than spurs your errand now; and if to you
Pardon be promised, I would fain be told
Why not to me as well.

SIR GUISEBERT.

                    Truly, why not?
To whoso merits it 'twill freely fall;
So give us leave to make a good report
Of how you stand affected.   'Twere your wisdom.

OCCO.

Kind sirs, I thank you; you shall say, so please you,
That I am not of them that evermore
Cry out for war, and having not a hope
Of the Earl's mercy, act as desperate men;
For were I sure the multitude met pity,
It would not then behove me to stand out
For my particular ransom,—though, to say truth,
The Earl should do himself but little service
Were he to deal too hardly with us all.

SIR SIMON.

'Tis fairly spoken, sir.   When we come back,
Bringing conditions with us as we trust,
We'll look for aid from you amongst the Commons.

For truly there are here a sort of crafts
So factious still for war and obstinate,
That we shall be endanger'd.   Suing for peace
Is ever treason to the White-Hoods.   Well,
We'll look for your support.

OCCO.

      God speed you, sirs.
To fair conditions you shall find me friendly.

[*Exeunt* SIR SIMON BETTE *and* SIR GUISEBERT GRUTT.
VAN AESWYN *comes forward.*

AESWYN.

My lord, were those that parted from you here
The worshipful negociators?

OCCO.

       Ay!
Would they had passed the windmills—how they
  crawl!—
And met no babbling burghers on their way.

AESWYN.

What! you have made an overture?

OCCO.

       Not so:
I've flung my line, and yonder pair of hooks
Are aptly baited to ensure me one;
But compromised I am not,—no, nor will be,
Till it be seen if yet my suit may thrive
With yon fair frozen dew-drop: all that's left
To represent Van Merestyn's hot blood.

AESWYN.

'Tis said she is but backwardly inclined
To any of her swains.

OCCO.

                 Such wealth as hers
Makes a maid whimsical and hard to please.
She that can have her will, be what it may,
Is much to seek to settle what it shall be.
The damsel must be tried; for if she yield,
The charier must I be, whilst times permit,
Of the good town's goodwill.   Her lands lie all
Within the Franc of Ghent.   Send Berckel to her,
And bid him say I wait upon her leisure.

SCENE II.—*The House Van Merestyn.*

ADRIANA VAN MERESTYN, *and* CLARA VAN ARTEVELDE.

CLARA.

I do not bid thee take him or refuse him ;
I only say, think twice.

ADRIANA.

             But once to think,
When the heart knows itself, is once too much.

CLARA.

Well ; answer what you will ; no, yes—yes, no ;
Either or both ; I would the chance were mine ;
I say no more ; I would it were my lot
To have a lover.

ADRIANA.

           Yours ? why there's Sir Walter.

CLARA.

Sir Walter? very good ; but he's at Bruges.
I want one here.

ADRIANA.

On days of truce he comes.

CLARA.

I want one every day.   Besides, the war
Will never slacken now ; a truce to truces.
And though on moonless, cloud-encompass'd nights,
He will, in his discretion, truce or none,
Hazard a trip, yet should he be discover'd,
Mild Van den Bosch would pat him on the head,
And then he'd come no more.   But ponder well
What you shall say ; for if it must be ' no '
In substance, you shall hardly find that form
Which shall convey it pleasantly.

ADRIANA.

                              In truth,
To mould denial to a pleasing shape
In all things, and most specially in love,
Is a hard task ; alas ! I have not wit
From such a sharp and waspish word as ' no '
To pluck the sting.   What think you I should say ?

CLARA.

A colourable thing or two ; as thus :
My lord, we women swim not with our hearts,
Nor yet our judgments, but the world's opinions ;
And though I prize you dearly in my soul
And think you of all excellence compounded,
Yet 'tis a serious and unhappy thing
To hear you spoken of : for men protest
That you are cruel, cowardly, and cold,
Boastful, malicious ; envious, spiteful, false,

A bull in ire, an ape in jealousy,
A wolf in greediness for blood.

ADRIANA.

                              No more?
Am I to use no courtesies but these?

CLARA.

No more?   Yes, plentifully more! where was I?
This for your mind's repute.   Then for your person,
(Which for my own particular I love)
'Tis said that you are strangely ill to look at;
Your brow as bleak as winter, with a fringe
Of wither'd grass for hair, your nose oblique,
Pointing and slanting like a dial's hand.
They say the fish you had your eyes of laugh'd
To see how they were set, and that your mouth
Grows daily wider, bandying of big words.
All which imaginations, good my lord,
Grossly as they may counterfeit defect
Where worth abounds, are yet so noised abroad
That in despite of that so high esteem
In which I hold you, I'm constrain'd to say
I'd sooner wed your scullion than yourself.

ADRIANA.

Thanks for your counsel; cunning is the maid
That can convert a lover to a friend,
And you have imp'd me with a new device.
But look! Is this—no, 'tis your brother's page.

CLARA.

All hail to him! he is my daily sport.
Of all things under heaven that make me merry,

It makes me merriest to see a boy
That wants to be a man. ✓

ADRIANA.

His want fulfill'd,
He will not be the worse; 'tis well for them
That have no faults but what they needs must leave.

Enter the Page.

CLARA.

How now, Sir Henry! whither away, brave knight?

PAGE.

I'm coming but to pay my duty here;
The Lady Adriana lets me come.

CLARA.

I wish thy master knew it.

PAGE.

So he does;
He tells me to come too.

CLARA.

Alas, poor man!
Hath he no eyes?

PAGE.

What mean you, Mistress Clara?

CLARA.

Why, when our pages steal away our loves,
Tell gardeners to keep blackbirds.   Look you here—
Seest thou this drooping melancholy maid;
What hast thou done?

PAGE.

Who, I? it was not I.

CLARA.

Who was it then ?   Well—'kissing goes by favour'—
So saith the proverb; truly, more's the pity !
Yet I commend your prudence, Adriana,
For favouring in place of men and monsters
This pure and pretty child.   I'll learn from you;
And if, when I have kiss'd my pug and parrot,
I have the matter of a mouthful left,
For fear of waste that's worse I'll spend them here.

PAGE.

I would advise you to be more discreet.

CLARA.

Soho ! and wherefore ?   Oh ! so old you are !
Full fifteen summers elder than your beard,
And that was born last week— before its time.
I told you, Adriana, did I not,
Of the untimely birth ?   It chanced o' Wednesday,
By reason of a fright he gave his chin,
Making its innocent down to stand on end
With brandishing of a most superfluous razor.

ADRIANA.

You told me no such tale ; and if you had,
I should not have believed you ; for your tongue
Was ever nimbler in the track of sport
Than fits for hunting in a leash with truth.
Heed her not, Henry, she is full of slanders.

CLARA.

Ay, no one marks me.   I but jest and lie,
And so must go unheeded.   Honest times !
Slanders and jests have lost the ear o' the World !
But do I slander him to say he's young ?

PAGE.

I am almost as old as you.

CLARA.

           I grant thee;
But we are women when boys are but boys.
God gives us grace to ripen and grow wise
Some six years earlier. I thank heaven for it ;
We grow upon the sunny side o' the wall.

PAGE.

Methinks your wisdom grows o' the windy side,
And bears but little fruit.

CLARA.

           What! malapert!
It bears more fruit than thou hast wit to steal,
Or stomach to digest. Were I thy tutor,
To teach thee wisdom, and beheld such store
Of goodly fruitage, I should say to thee,
' Rob me this orchard.' Then wouldst thou reply,
' Five feet three inches stand I in my shoes,
And yet I cannot reach to pluck these plums,
So loftily they flourish!' God ha' mercy,
Here comes the knight upon an ambling nag.
Now, Adriana!

ADRIANA.

           I am sore perplex'd.
What shall I say?

CLARA.

           My counsel you have heard,
And partly slighted, wherefore seek to better ;
Take we direction from our full-grown friend.
Henry, a knight will presently be here

To ask our Adriana's hand in marriage :
What shall she answer?

PAGE.

Let her say—'My lord,
You are the flower of Flemish chivalry,
But I have vow'd to live and die a maid.'

CLARA.

A goodly vow!   God give her grace to make it,
If it be not too troublesome to keep.
But he's no more the flower of Flemish knights,
Than thou the pearl of pages.   Adriana,
Bethink you of your answer and be ready,
Lest he surprise you and you speak the truth.

ADRIANA.

Prithee, what truth ?   There's nothing to be hidden.

CLARA.

Except, except—yes, turn your face away,
That so informs against you.   Here he comes.

Enter the LORD OF OCCO.

OCCO.

Fairest of ladies ! an unworthy knight
Does homage to your beauty.

ADRIANA.

Good my lord,
I am beholden to your courtesy
That gives to this poor semblance such a name.
But here is one by whose associate charms
And kindly converse I am brighten'd ever,—
A daughter of the House of Artevelde.

OCCO.

Fair damsel, I am happy in the fortune
Which shines upon me from two spheres at once.

CLARA.

Fair sir, I thank you for your courtesy.
No lady lives in Ghent with ears to hear,
Who has not heard recounted night and day
The exploits of Lord Occo.

OCCO.

          On my soul.
I blush to hear it said ; though true it is
I have perform'd what little in me lay
To bring renown to Flemish chivalry.
I give to God the glory ; and next Him
'Tis due to her whose charms would kindle valour
In the most coldest heart of Christendom.

CLARA.

Whoe'er inspired your valour, your exploits
Must give that lady high pre-eminence.
Three hundred men at arms, I think it was,
You freely fell upon with sword in hand,
After the storming of the Fort at Sas,
And not a soul survived ?

OCCO.

          Your pardon, lady ;
Some other trifle's in your thoughts ; at Sas
There is no fort, and they who perish'd there
Were but three hundred peasants who were burn'd
By firing of a barn to which they'd fled.

CLARA.

Ah, was it so ?   At Zeveren then surely—

OCCO.

What happen'd there too, was of no account.

CLARA.

Oh, pardon me; the modesty which still
Accompanies true valour, casts in shade
Your noble actions.   I beseech you tell
What came to pass at Zeveren.

OCCO.

            The town
Was taken by surprise.

CLARA.

           Ay, true, and then
The garrison that made themselves so strong
Within the convent's walls—

OCCO.

           At Zeveren
There was no garrison.

CLARA.

            You say not so?
How false is Fame!   I'm certain I was told
Of a great slaughter in the convent there.

OCCO.

True; a proportion of the sisterhood
Met with mishap.   But, lady, by your leave
We'll treat of other things.   Haply you know not
The usages of war, and scarce approve
Proceedings which its hard necessities
Will oft-times force upon us warriors.
A softer theme were meeter, and there's one
On which I burn to speak.

CLARA.

Alack, alack!
Then I am gone ; soft speeches please mine ear,
As do soft pillows—when I fain would sleep.
But what's the time of day?   Come hither, Henry :
We walk by high examples in this world ;
Let's to the poultry-yard and win our spurs.
Give you good day, my lord.
                                    [*Exeunt* CLARA *and* Page.
OCCO.
                         A merry lady
Your friend appears ; but now that she is gone,
I must entreat your hearing for a word
Of graver import—grave, if aught imports
The life or death of this poor heart of mine.
A burning fiery furnace is this heart;
I waste like wax before a witch's fire,
Whilst but one word from thee would make earth heaven,
And I must soon be nothing or a god !
There's an unutterable want and void,
A gulf, a craving, and a sucking in,
As when a mighty ship goes down at sea.
I roam about with hunger-bitten heart,
A famine in my bosom—a dry heat,
A desperate thirst, and I must glut it now,
Or like a dog by summer solstice parch'd
I shall go mad.

ADRIANA.

O no, my lord, your pardon ;
You flatter me or else deceive yourself ;
But, so far as I may, I yield you thanks,
Lamenting that I cannot be so grateful
As you may think I ought.

OCCO.

                 Nay, lady, nay :
Deem that I 've been tormented long enough
And let this coyness have a timely end.

ADRIANA.

I am not coy, and plainly now to speak
(When aught but plainness should be less than just)
I cannot be your wife.

OCCO.

             And wherefore so ?
It is not that your nature is unloving ;
You will not tell me that ?

ADRIANA.

             I 've told you all
Which it can profit you to know.

OCCO.

                Ah ! now
I see it clearly ; there's some smooth-tongued knave
Has been before me,—yea, some wheedling minion,
With song and dance and lute and lily hands,
Has wriggled into favour, I the while
Fighting hard battles to my neck in blood.
Tell me in honesty if this be sooth :
If it be not, in charity say No.

ADRIANA.

In charity I never will speak more
With you, Sir Guy of Occo,
Nor till I see a sign of gentle blood,
Or knightly courtesy in one so bold,
Will I again hold converse, or with him,
Or any that abets him.   This to me !   [Exit.

OCCO.

Thanks, gentle lady !   Thanks, kind, loving soul !
I am instructed ; there came out the truth ;
Those flashing eyes could hold it in no longer.
They are as plain to read as are the stars
To him who knows their signs.   Would that I knew
The name of him who thrusts himself between us,
And what star rules him in the house of life !
Who rides this way and waves that long salute ?
Philip Van Artevelde, as I'm a knight !
Then no more need I knowledge of the stars.

SCENE III.—*The Stadt-House.*

Enter MYK STEENSEL, *followed by several* Burghers.

MYK.

And who is Van den Bosch, resolve me that :
I say, sirs, who is he to lay on taxes ?

FIRST BURGHER.

Or Ackerman, or Launoy, who are they ?

MYK.

I say, sirs, if our goods be not our own,
Better our natural liege lord should have them
Than thus to render them to John or Peter.

SECOND BURGHER.

Why, look you, sirs, our case stands simply here :
The Earl of Flanders is a valiant lord,
And was a gracious master, till the Devil,
Who never sleeps, awaken'd them of Bruges

C

To dig about the Lis to turn the water.
But what, sirs,—we have fought enough for that.

MYK.

Why still the more we fight the more we lose;
For every battle that our White-Hoods win
But gives a warrant to this Van den Bosch
To spoil us of our substance.——Welcome, sirs.

Enter two Deans of the Crafts.

FIRST DEAN.

Friends, have ye heard the news?

MYK.

I know not, sir;
If the news be, we owe the White-Hoods pay
For giving us a hosier for our liege,—
'Tis old, sir, old.

SECOND DEAN.

No, this is what you'll owe them;
A ready market for your rats and mice.
Corn is already risen cent. per cent.,
Though many question if the news be true.
Our John of Launoy's slain, with all his men,
And the Earl's troops possess the Quatre-Metiers.

MYK.

There's a fair end to our supplies from Brabant.
But how came this to pass?

SECOND DEAN.

'Twas briefly thus:
Beside Nivelle the Earl and Launoy met.
Six thousand voices shouted with the last,
'Ghent the good Town! Ghent and the Chaperons
     Blancs!'

But from that force thrice-told there came the cry
Of ' Flanders with the Lion of the Bastard !'
So then the battle join'd, and they of Ghent
Gave back and open'd after three hours' fight,
And hardly flying had they gain'd Nivelle,
When the Earl's vanguard came upon their rear
Ere they could close the gate, and enter'd with them.
Then all were slain save Launoy and his guard,
Who barricaded in the minster tower
Made desperate resistance, whereupon
The Earl wax'd wrothful and bade fire the church.

FIRST BURGHER.

Say'st thou?   O sacrilege accursed !   Was't done?

SECOND DEAN.

'Twas done,—and presently was heard a yell,
And after that the rushing of the flames !
Then Launoy from the steeple cried aloud
' A ransom !' and held up his coat to sight
With florins filled, but they without but laugh'd
And mock'd him, saying, ' Come amongst us, John.
And we will give thee welcome ; make a leap ;
Come out at window, John.'—With that the flames
Rose up and reach'd him, and he drew his sword,
Cast his rich coat behind him in the fire,
And shouting ' Ghent, ye slaves !' leapt freely forth.
When they below received him on their spears.
And so died John of Launoy.

FIRST BURGHER.

> A brave end.
'Tis certain we must now make peace betimes ;
The city will be starved else—Will be, said I ?

Starvation is upon us : want and woe
Stand round about and stare us in the face ;
And what will be the end ?

MYK.

             Believe me, sirs,
So long as Van den Bosch bears rule in Ghent,
You'll not have peace ; for well wots he no terms
That spare his life will pacify the Earl.
Sirs, if we make no peace but with the will
Of them whose heads must answer it, woe to us !
For we must fight for ever ; sirs, I say,
We must put down this Van den Bosch, and up
The men that with the Earl stand fair and free,
Who shall take counsel for the city's weal.

BURGHERS.

Truly we must.

MYK.

          Then, friends, stand fast by me,
And as we're all agreed to give no denier
Of this five hundred marks, I will speak out,
And let him know our minds.

Enter VAN DEN BOSCH, FRANS ACKERMAN, *and the* LORD OF
    OCCO, *with a retinue of* White-Hoods.

VAN DEN BOSCH.

Good morrow, worthy friends ; good morrow, all !
'Tis a sweet sight to look on, in these times,
A score of true and trusty friends to Ghent
So fresh and hearty and so well provided.
Ah, sirs, you know not, you, who lies afield
When nights are cold, with frogs for bed-fellows ;
You know not, you, who fights and sheds his blood,

And fasts and fills his belly with the east wind !
Poor souls and virtuous citizens they are !
'Tis they that keep the franchises of Ghent.
But what ! they must be fed ; they must have meat !
Sirs, have ye brought me these five hundred marks
That they demanded ?

MYK.

    Master Van den Bosch,
Look round about ; as many as stand here
Are of one mind, and this is what they think :
The company of White-Hoods, sometime past,
Were, as thou say'st, brave citizens and true,
And they fought stoutly for our franchises :
But they were afterward as beasts of prey,
That, tasting blood, grow greedy and break loose
And turn upon their keepers : so at length
The city, like a camp in mutiny,
Saw nothing else to walk her streets unharm'd
But these your free-companions.   They at will
Enter'd our houses, lived upon our means
In riotry, made plunder of our goods,
Lay with our wives and daughters ; and if once
Some hardy fool made bold to lift his hand
For safeguard of his own, he met his death.
Now this we have resolved to bear no longer,
Nor will we give our substance so to feed
The lewd excesses of your company.

VAN DEN BOSCH.

How now, Myk Steensel ! thou art bold of tongue ;
I marvel thou shouldst speak so like a traitor
In presence of such honest, virtuous men,

As these thou seest about me.   How can I,
Think you, give warranty that some good soul,
Inflamed with anger at thy foolish speech,
May not cut out thy tongue and slit thy nose
For uttering of such treasons—how, indeed?

MYK.

Thou think'st by this to hound thy pack upon me ;
But know, thy reign is o'er, and I defy thee.
Thy brother Launoy with his men-at-arms
Will never answer to thy bidding more ;
And if thou dare do violence to me,
Thou shalt be fain to take as long a leap
As his was at Nivelle.

VAN DEN BOSCH.

Oh, ho ! my masters !
'Tis this then that emboldens you, this tale
Brought by Van Borselen, who ran away
Before the fight began, and calls it lost
That so his cowardice should stand excused ;
For which his false report and foul desertion
I have already had him gibbeted.
Bring not yourselves, I pray you for your honours,
With the like nimbleness to a grave i' the air.
I say, sirs, bring me these five hundred marks,
And that or ere to-morrow's sun go down—
Five hundred marks—I'll bate you not a scute.
Ye slothful, hide-blown, gormandising niggards !
What ! all must starve but you, that lie a-bed
And lack a day of fast to purge your grossness.
What, know ye who I am ?   Are ye awake ?
Or sleeping off the wine of yesternight,

And deeming this some tustle with your wives
For pulling of a blanket here or there !
Five hundred marks—begone, and bring the money.

MYK.

Begone we will.   Let's to our homes, my friends.
And what we'll bring thee thou shalt know betimes
Nor wait the setting of to-morrow's sun.
Not gold, sir, no, nor silver, be thou sure,
But what shall best befit a brave man's hand.

[*Exeunt* MYK *and the* Burghers; *manent* VAN DEN BOSCH,
OCCO, *and* FRANS ACKERMAN.

VAN DEN BOSCH.

Ye see, sirs, how the knaves take heart and rail
On this mishap.

OCCO.

I saw both that and more ;
Our White-Hoods look'd like very renegades,
As though they knew not which to fear the most,
Thy rod and gallows-tree, or the Earl's bailiff.
Trust me, we're falling fast to pieces, Peter.

VAN DEN BOSCH.

My lord of Occo, thou hast judged aright.
But what can I ?   Our chiefs drop one by one ;
Launoy, too truly, perish'd at Nivelle ;
Le Clerc lies leaning up against a hedge
(Till some one dare go bury him), at Chem ;
Thy cousin fell with Launoy.   Now, Van Nuitre
And Lichtenvelde are good for men-at-arms,
But want the wit to govern a great town.
And I am good at arms, and want not wit ;
But then I'm sore suspected of the rich,

By reason of my rudeness, and the fruit
Which that same gallows-tree of mine hath borne;
And to say truth, although my wit be good,
It hath a fitter range without the gates,
In ordering of an enterprise, than here.
The city leans to peace for lack of leading,
And we must put a head upon its shoulders.

OCCO.

Hast thou bethought thee of a man that's wise,
And fit to bear this rule ?

VAN DEN BOSCH.

       Why, there be such ;
Though one that's wise would scarce be wise to take it.
What think'st thou, Frans ? And thou, my lord of Occo?
Know ye a man that, being wise, were willing ?

ACKERMAN.

There is no game so desperate which wise men
Will not take freely up for love of power,
Or love of fame, or merely love of play.
These men are wise, and then reputed wise,
And so their great repute of wisdom grows,
Till for great wisdom a great price is bid,
And then their wisdom do they part withal:
Such men must still be tempted with high stakes.

OCCO.

Tempt them and take them ; true, there be such men ;
Philip Van Artevelde is such a man.

VAN DEN BOSCH.

That is well thought of. Let us try him then.

SCENE IV.—*The House Van Merestyn.*

ADRIANA VAN MERESTYN *and* CLARA VAN ARTEVELDE.

CLARA.

So you've dismiss'd the Lord of Occo ?

ADRIANA.

Yes.

CLARA.

How many suitors have you discharged this morning ?

ADRIANA.

How many ?

CLARA.

Yes.　Was not my brother here ?

ADRIANA.

He saw me through the lattice, and stayed his horse
an instant under the window.

CLARA.

Was that all ?

ADRIANA.

Yes—no—yes—I suppose so.

CLARA.

Oh that maids would learn to speak the truth, or else
to lie becomingly !

ADRIANA.

Do *I* not lie becomingly ?—Well, 'tis from want of
use.　What should I say ?

CLARA.

What say ?　Had my sworn friend so question'd me,
And I been minded, maugre our sworn friendship,
To coil my thoughts up in my secret self,

I with a brave and careless hardihood
Had graced the disavowal of my love.

ADRIANA.

But did I say I loved him not?   Oh, God!
If I said that, I say since truth was truth
There never was a falsehood half so false.
I say I love him, and I say beside
That but to say I love him is as nothing;
'Tis but a tithe and scantling of the truth!
And oh! how much I love him what can tell?
Not words, not tears—Heaven only knows how much;
And every evening when I say my prayers,
I pray to be forgiven for the sin
Of loving aught on earth with such a love.

CLARA.

Well, God forgive you! for you answer now
Like a true maid and honest though a sinning.
But tell me, if that's mention'd in your prayers,
For how much love has *he* to be forgiven?

ADRIANA.

Alas! I know not.

CLARA.

Nay, but you can guess.

ADRIANA.

Oh! I have guess'd a thousand times too oft.
And sometimes I am hopeful as the spring,
And up my fluttering heart is borne aloft
As high and gladsome as the lark at sunrise;
And then, as though the fowler's shaft had pierced it,
It comes plumb down with such a dead, dead fall.

CLARA.

And all the while is he, I nothing doubt,
As wayward and as love-sick as yourself.

ADRIANA.

He love-sick!   No—it may be that he loves me;
But if he loves me 'tis with no love-sickness.
His nerves are made of other cord than mine;
He saunters undisturb'd along the Lis,
For ever angling as he used to do.
And when he told me he must come to-night,
And that he then would lay a burden down
Which he had borne in silence all-too-long,
His voice was strong and steady, calm and clear,
So that I doubted if it could be love
That then was in his thoughts.

CLARA.

               Oh! much the doubt!
But this was what I knew had come to pass,
When answering with your vacant no and yes,
You fed upon your thoughts and mark'd me not.

ADRIANA.

But honestly, think you it must be love
He comes to speak of?

CLARA.

              Why, 'tis either that,
Or else to tell you of what fish he caught.

ADRIANA.

Oh, do not tease me; for my heart is faint
With over-fulness of its expectations.

CLARA.

Nay, if your love's so lamentable sick,
Nurse it yourself; I'll go.

ADRIANA.

                    With all my heart.
You're too light-headed for my company.

CLARA.

Is it with all your heart? then I'll not go;
Or else I'll take you with me.   Come along;
Your bower lacks tendance; it is strewn with leaves;
The autumn winds have broken in, alas!
And many a flower is hanging down its head
Since the rude kissing of those wild intruders.
Come, come with me; the dew is on the grass;
The snails are running races on the walks;
And at this merry pace, an inch an hour,
We shall o'ertake some laggard.   Snail, good day!
I like you well, but will not marry you.
I'll tell you why.   Your eyes are in your horns.

SCENE V.—*The House Van Artevelde.*

PHILIP VAN ARTEVELDE *and* FATHER JOHN of HEDA.

ARTEVELDE.

I never look'd that he should live so long.
He was a man of that unsleeping spirit,
He seem'd to live by miracle: his food
Was glory, which was poison to his mind
And peril to his body.   He was one
Of many thousand such that die betimes,
Whose story is a fragment, known to few.
Then comes the man who has the luck to live,
And he's a prodigy.   Compute the chances,
And deem there's ne'er a one in dangerous times

Who wins the race of glory, but than him
A thousand men more gloriously endow'd
Have fallen upon the course ; a thousand others
Have had their fortunes founder'd by a chance,
Whilst lighter barks push'd past them ; to whom add
A smaller tally, of the singular few
Who, gifted with predominating powers,
Bear yet a temperate will and keep the peace.
The world knows nothing of its greatest men.

FATHER JOHN.

Had Launoy lived he might have pass'd for great,
But not by conquests in the Franc of Bruges.
The sphere, the scale of circumstance, is all
Which makes the wonder of the many.   Still
An ardent soul was Launoy's, and his deeds
Were such as dazzled many a Flemish dame.
There'll some bright eyes in Ghent be dimm'd for him.

ARTEVELDE.

They will be dim and then be bright again.
All is in busy, stirring, stormy motion,
And many a cloud drifts by and none sojourns.
Lightly is life laid down amongst us now,
And lightly is death mourn'd : a dusk star blinks
As fleets the rack, but look again, and lo !
In a wide solitude of wintry sky
Twinkles the re-illuminated star,
And all is out of sight that smirch'd the ray.
We have not time to mourn.

FATHER JOHN.

                              The worse for us !
He that lacks time to mourn, lacks time to mend.

Eternity mourns that.   'Tis an ill cure
For life's worst ills, to have no time to feel them.
Where sorrow's held intrusive and turn'd out,
There wisdom will not enter, nor true power,
Nor aught that dignifies humanity.
Yet such the barrenness of busy life!
From shelf to shelf Ambition clambers up
To reach the naked'st pinnacle of all,
Whilst Magnanimity, absolved from toil,
Reposes self-included at the base.
But this thou know'st.

ARTEVELDE.

                    Else had I little learn'd
From my much learn'd preceptor.

Enter the Page.

                                   What, Sir Page!
Hast thou been idling in the market-place?
Canst tell whose chattels have been sold to-day
For payment of the White-Hoods?

PAGE.

                              Sir, I cannot;
'Tis at the house Van Merestyn I've been
To see the Lady Adriana.

ARTEVELDE.
                    Her!
Well, and what said the damsel?

PAGE.

                              Sir, not much;
For Mistress Clara was her visiter,
And she said everything; she said it all.

ARTEVELDE.

What was it that ye spake of?

PAGE.

              When I came
The talk was all of chivalry and love.
And presently arrived the Lord of Occo.

ARTEVELDE.

And what was talk'd of then?

PAGE.

              Oh! still the same.
The ladies praised him mightily for deeds
Whose fame, they said, effulgent far and wide,
Eclipsed Sir Roland and Sir Oliver.

ARTEVELDE.

Now, Father, mark you that; hearts soft as wax
These damsels would be thought to bear about,
Yet ever is the bloodiest knight the best!

FATHER JOHN.

It is most true.   Full many a dame I've known
Who'd faint and sicken at the sight of blood,
And shriek and wring her hands and rend her hair
To see her lord brought wounded to the door;
And many a one I've known to pine with dread
Of such mishap or worse,—lie down in fear,
The night-mare sole sad partner of her bed,
Rise up in horror to recount bad dreams
And seek to witches to interpret them,—
This oft I've known, but never knew I one
Who'd be content her lord should live at home
In love and christian charity and peace.

ARTEVELDE.

And wherefore so?　Because the women's heaven
Is vanity, and that is over all.
What's firiest still finds favour in their eyes;
What's noisiest keeps the entrance of their ears.
The noise and blaze of arms enchants them most:
Wit, too, and wisdom, that's admired of all,
They can admire—the glory, not the thing.
An unreflected light did never yet
Dazzle the vision feminine.　For me,
Nor noise nor blaze attend my peaceful path;
Nor, were it otherwise, should I desire
That noise and blaze of mine won any heart.
Wherefore it is that I would fain possess,
If any, that which David wept,—a love
Passing the love of women.

FATHER JOHN.

　　　　　　　　Deem you not
There may be one who so transcends her sex
In loving, as to match the son of Saul?

ARTEVELDE.

It may be I have deem'd or dream'd of such.
But what know I?　We figure to ourselves
The thing we like, and then we build it up
As chance will have it, on the rock or sand:
For thought is tired of wandering o'er the world,
And home-bound fancy runs her bark ashore.

Enter an Attendant.

ATTENDANT.

Sir, here is Master Van den Bosch below
Desires to speak with you.

ARTEVELDE.

To speak with me!
I marvel on what errand Van den Bosch
Can seek Van Artevelde.   Say I attend him.
Will you not stay?

FRIAR JOHN.

No, no, my son; farewell!
The very name of men like Van den Bosch
Sends me to prayers.

SCENE VI.—*The Market-place, at the entrance of the Clothiers' Hall.*

The Provost of the Clothiers *with several principal* Burghers *and the* Chaplain *of that craft.*

PROVOST.

Him! did ye say?   Choose him for Captain? So!
Then look about you in the morning, friends,
For ye shall find him stirring before noon;
The latest time o' the day is twelve o' the clock;
Then comes he forth his study with his book,
And looking off and on like parson preaching,
Delivers me his orders.

A BURGHER.

Nay, Provost, nay;
He is a worthy and a mild good man,
And we have need of such.

CHAPLAIN.

He's what you say;
But 'tis not mildness of the man that rules
Makes the mild regimen.

D

PROVOST.

Who's to rule the fierce ?
' I prithee, Van den Bosch, cut not that throat ;
' Roast not this man alive, or for my sake,
' If roast he must, not at so slow a fire ;
' Nor yet so hastily impale this other,
' But give him time to ruminate and foretaste
' So terrible an end.'   Mild Philip thus
Shall read his lecture of humanity.

CHAPLAIN.

Truly the tender mercies of the weak,
As of the wicked, are but cruel.   Well ;
Pass we within ; the most of us are here,
And Heaven direct us to a just conclusion !
                              [*Exeunt all but two* Burghers.

FIRST BURGHER.

The scaffold, as I see, is newly wet ;
Who was the last that suffer'd ?

SECOND BURGHER.

                              What, to-day?
I know not; but the brave Van Borselen's blood
(God rest his soul !) can scarcely yet be dry,
That suffer'd yesterday.

FIRST BURGHER.

                              For treason, was't not ?

SECOND BURGHER.

Ay ; the treason of the times ; the being rich ;
His wealth was wanted.

FIRST BURGHER.

                              Hath he not an heir ?

SECOND BURGHER.

A bold one if he claim the inheritance.
Come, pass we in.

SCENE VII.—*The House Van Artevelde.*

ARTEVELDE *and* VAN DEN BOSCH.

ARTEVELDE.

This is a mighty matter, Van den Bosch,
And much to be revolved ere it be answer'd.

VAN DEN BOSCH.

The people shall elect thee with one voice.
I will ensure the White-Hoods, and the rest
Will eagerly accept thy nomination,
So to be rid of some that they like less.
Thy name is honour'd both of rich and poor;
For all are mindful of the glorious rule
Thy father bore, when Flanders, prosperous then,
From end to end obey'd him as one town.

ARTEVELDE.

They may remember it—and, Van den Bosch,
May I not too bethink me of the end
To which this people brought my noble father?
They gorged the fruits of his good husbandry,
Till drunk with long prosperity, and blind
With too much fatness, they tore up the root
From which their common weal had sprung and flourish'd.

VAN DEN BOSCH.

Nay, Master Philip, let the past be past.

D 2

ARTEVELDE.

Here on the doorstead of my father's house
The blood of his they spilt is seen no more.
But when I was a child I saw it there ;
For so long as my widow-mother lived
Water came never near the sanguine stain.
She loved to show it me, and then with awe,
But hoarding still the purpose of revenge,
I heard the tale—which like a daily prayer
Repeated to a rooted feeling grew—
How long he fought, how falsely came like friends
The villains Guisebert Grutt and Simon Bette,—
All the base murder of the one by many.
Even such a brutal multitude as they
Who slew my father—yea, who slew their own,
(For like one had he ruled the parricides)
Even such a multitude thou'dst have me govern.

VAN DEN BOSCH.

Why, what if Jacques Artevelde was kill'd ?
He had his reign, and that for many a year,
And a great glory did he gain thereby.
And as for Guisebert Grutt and Simon Bette,
Their breath is in their nostrils as was his.
If you be as stout-hearted as your father,
And mindful of the villanous trick they play'd him,
Their hour of reckoning is well nigh come.
Of that, and of this base false-hearted league
They're making with the Earl, these two to us
Shall give account.

ARTEVELDE.

They cannot render back

The golden bowl that's broken at the fountain,
Or mend the wheel that's broken at the cistern,
Or twist again the silver cord that's loosed.
Yea, life for life, vile bankrupts as they are,
Their worthless lives for his of countless price,
Is their whole wherewithal to pay their debt.
Yet retribution is a goodly thing,
And it were well to wring the payment from them
Even to the utmost drop of their heart's blood.

VAN DEN BOSCH.

Then will I call the people to the Square
And speak for your election.

ARTEVELDE.

                              Not so fast.
Your vessel, Van den Bosch, hath felt the storm :
She rolls dismasted in an ugly swell,
And you would make a jury-mast of me
Whereon to spread the tatters of your canvas.
And what am I ?—Why I am as the oak
Which stood apart far down the vale of life,
Growing retired beneath a quiet sky.
Wherefore should this be added to the wreck ?

VAN DEN BOSCH.

I pray you, speak it in the Burghers' tongue ;
I lack the scholarship to talk in tropes.

ARTEVELDE.

The question, to be plain, is briefly this :
Shall I, who, chary of tranquillity,
Not busy in this factious city's broils
Nor frequent in the market-place, eschew'd
The even battle,—shall I join the rout ?

VAN DEN BOSCH.

Times are sore changed I see; there's none in Ghent
That answers to the name of Artevelde.
Thy father did not carp nor question thus
When Ghent invoked his aid.   The days have been
When not a citizen drew breath in Ghent
But freely would have died in Freedom's cause.

ARTEVELDE.

With a good name thou christenest the cause.
True, to make choice of despots is some freedom,
The only freedom for this turbulent town,
Rule her who may.   And in my father's time
We still were independent, if not free;
And wealth from independence, and from wealth
Enfranchisement will partially proceed.
The cause, I grant thee, Van den Bosch, is good;
And were I link'd to earth no otherwise
But that my whole heart centred in myself,
I could have toss'd you this poor life to play with,
Taking no second thought.   But as things are,
I will revolve the matter warily,
And send thee word betimes of my conclusion.

VAN DEN BOSCH.

Betimes it must be; for some two hours hence
I meet the Deans, and ere we separate
Our course must be determined.

ARTEVELDE.

                              In two hours,
If I be for you, I will send this ring
In token I have so resolved.   Farewell.

VAN DEN BOSCH.

Philip Van Artevelde, a greater man
Than ever Ghent beheld we'll make of thee,
If thou be bold enough to try this venture.
God give thee heart to do so.   Fare thee well.

[*Exit* VAN DEN BOSCH.

ARTEVELDE.

Is it vain-glory which thus whispers me
That 'tis ignoble to have led my life
In idle meditations—that the times
Demand me, echoing my father's name?
Oh! what a fiery heart was his! such souls
Whose sudden visitations daze the world,
Vanish like lightning, but they leave behind
A voice that in the distance far away
Wakens the slumbering ages.   Oh! my father!
Thy life is eloquent, and more persuades
Unto dominion than thy death deters;
For that reminds me of a debt of blood
Descended with my patrimony to me,
Whose paying off would clear my soul's estate.

Enter CLARA.

CLARA.

Was some one here?   I thought I heard you speak.

ARTEVELDE.

You heard me speak?

CLARA.

            I surely thought I heard you,
Just now, as I came in.

ARTEVELDE.

            It may be so.

CLARA.

Was no one here then?

ARTEVELDE.

No one, as you see.

CLARA.

Why then I trust the orator your tongue
Found favour with the audience your ears;
But this poor orator of mine finds none,
For all at once I see they droop and flag.
Will you not listen? I've a tale to tell.

ARTEVELDE.

My fairest, sweetest, best beloved sister!
Who in the whole world would protect thy youth
If I were gone?

CLARA.

Gone! where? what ails you, Philip?

ARTEVELDE.

Nowhere, my love. Well, what hast thou to tell?

CLARA.

When I came home, on entering the hall
I stared to see the household all before me.
There was the steward sitting on the bench
His head upon his hands between his knees.
In the oak chair old Ursel sate upright
Swaying her body—so—from side to side,
Whilst maids and varlets stood disconsolate round.
What cheer? quoth I. But not a soul replied.
Is Philip well? Yea, madam, God be praised.
Then what dost look so gloomy for, my friend?
Alack a-day, the stork! then all chimed in,

The stork, the stork, the stork! What, _he_ is sick?
No, madam; sick!—he's gone—he's flown away.
Why then, quoth I, God speed him; speaking so
To raise their hearts, but they were all-too-heavy.
And, Philip, to say truth, I could have wish'd
This had not happen'd.

ARTEVELDE.

　　　　　I remember now,
I thought I miss'd his clatter all night long.

CLARA.

Old Ursel says the sign proved never false
In all her time,—and she's so very old!
And then she says that Roger was esteem'd
The wisest stork in Ghent, and flew away
But twice before—the first time in the night
Before my father took that office up
Which proved so fatal in the end, and then
The second time, the night before he died.

ARTEVELDE.

Sooner or later, something, it is certain,
Must bring men to their graves. Our every act
Is death's forerunner. It is but the date
That puzzles us to fix. My father lived
In that ill-omen'd office many a year,
And men had augur'd he must die at last
Without the stork to aid. If this be all
The wisest of his tribe can prophesy,
I am as wise as he. Enough of this.
Thou hast been visiting thy friend to-day,—
The Lady Adriana.

CLARA.

I come thence:
She is impatiently expecting you.

ARTEVELDE.

Can she with such impatience flatter one
So slothful and obscure as Artevelde?

CLARA.

How mean you?

ARTEVELDE.

Clara, know I not your sex?
Is she not one of you?   Are you not all,
All from the shade averse? all prompt and prone
To make your idol of the million's idol?
Had I been one of these rash White-Hood chiefs
Who live by military larceny,
Then might I well believe that she would wait
Impatiently my coming.

CLARA.

There you're wrong;
She never loved the White-Hoods.

ARTEVELDE.   .

She were wise
In that unloving humour to abide:
To wed a White-Hood, other ills apart,
Would put in jeopardy her fair possessions.
Fatal perchance it might be to her wealth;
Fatal it surely would be to her weal.
Farewell her peace, if such a one she loved.

CLARA.

Go ask her, Philip,—ask her whom she loves,

And she will tell you it is no such man.
Why go you not?

ARTEVELDE.

My mind is not at ease.
Yet I am going—to my chamber now,
Where let me own an undisturb'd half hour
Of rumination ;—afterward to her.

SCENE VIII.—*The Market-place in front of the Stadt-House.*

Enter two of VAN DEN BOSCH'S *Officers, dragging a* Burgher *between them, and followed by an* Executioner *with an axe, and a crowd of* Citizens. *A scaffold is seen at a distance.*

FIRST OFFICER.

Where hast thou put it?

BURGHER.

What?   Put what—put what?

SECOND OFFICER.

A few last words—where is it?

BURGHER.

Mercy! what?

FIRST OFFICER.

Oh, very well!   Come, clap his thumb in a winch.

BURGHER.

No need of that—what is it that ye seek?

FIRST OFFICER.

Van Borselen's head.   'Twas sticking on that spike
At nine last night.   Who took it thence but thou?

BURGHER.

I never touch'd it.

SECOND OFFICER.

Thou art next of kin,
And rightfully shouldst fill his vacancy.

FIRST OFFICER.

Thy head to his stands in a just succession.
Besides, they are as like as are two cherries.
Bring him away.

SECOND OFFICER.

Friend with the axe, come on.

[*Exeunt all but two* Citizens.

FIRST CITIZEN.

When will this end?

SECOND CITIZEN.

When Van den Bosch...

FIRST CITIZEN.

Hush! Hush!

SCENE IX.—*The Entrance-Hall of the House Van Merestyn.*

Enter ARTEVELDE, *with* Attendants.

ARTEVELDE.

Bear thou these letters to my steward; say
That messengers must straight proceed with them
To Grammont and elsewhere, as superscribed;
And should mishap occur to any one
Upon the road, which is not over free,
I charge me with ten masses for his soul.
(*To another*) My service to the noble Lord of Occo;
I thank him for his counsel and will weigh it.

(*To the rest*) I will return alone.   If any come
To seek me at my house, entreat their stay.

[*They withdraw, and a* Waiting-Woman *enters.*

This, if I err not, is the pretty wench
That waits upon my lady.   What, fair maid !
Thy mistress, having comeliness to spare,
Hath given thee of it.   She's within I think,
Or else wert thou a truant.

WAITING-WOMAN.

Sir, she is.

ARTEVELDE.

Acquaint her then that I attend her leisure.

[*Exit* Waiting-Woman.

There is but one thing that still harks me back.
To bring a cloud upon the summer day
Of one so happy and so beautiful,—
It is a hard condition.   For myself
I know not that the circumstance of life
In all its changes can so far afflict me
As makes anticipation much worth while.
But she is younger,—of a sex beside
Whose spirits are to ours as flame to fire,
More sudden and more perishable too ;
So that the gust wherewith the one is kindled
Extinguishes the other.   Oh she is fair !
As fair as Heaven to look upon ! as fair
As ever vision of the Virgin blest
That weary pilgrim, resting by the fount
Beneath the palm and dreaming to the tune
Of flowing waters, duped his soul withal.
It was permitted in my pilgrimage

To rest beside the fount beneath the tree,
Beholding there no vision, but a maid
Whose form was light and graceful as the palm,
Whose heart was pure and jocund as the fount
And spread a freshness and a verdure round.
This was permitted in my pilgrimage
And loth am I to take my staff again.
Say that I fall not in this enterprise—
Yet must my life be full of hazardous turns,
And they that house with me must ever live
In imminent peril of some evil fate.

[A pause.

Danger from foes—that is a daylight danger—
Danger from tyrants—that too is seen and known—
But envious friends and jealous multitudes....
In dusk to walk through a perpetual ambush....

[A pause again.

Still for myself, I fear not but that I,
Taking what comes, leaving what leave I must,
Could make a sturdy struggle through the world.
But for the maid, the choice were better far
To win her dear heart back again if lost,
And stake it upon some less dangerous throw.

Re-enter Waiting-Woman.

WAITING-WOMAN.

My mistress, sir, so please you, takes her walk
Along the garden terrace, and desires
That you'll go forth to meet her.

ARTEVELDE.
                                   For if fate
Had done its best to single out a soul
Most form'd for peaceful virtues——ah ! I come.

SCENE X.—*A Garden.*

ARTEVELDE *and* ADRIANA.

ARTEVELDE.

I have some little overstaid my time.
First let me plead for pardon of that trespass.

ADRIANA.

I said to Clara when the sun went down
Now if—though truly 'tis impossible—
He come not ere yon blushing cloud grows gray,
His promises are no more worth than bubbles.
And look how gray it is !

ARTEVELDE.

           A hectic change.
The smiling dawn, the laughing blue-eyed day,
The graybeard eve incessantly pass on,
Fast fleeting generations born of time
And buried in eternity—they pass
And not a day resigns its little life
And enters into darkness, that can say
' Lo ! I was fair, and such as I have been
My issue shall be.   Lo ! I cast abroad
Such affluence of glory over earth,
That what had been but goodly to the sight
Was made magnificent, what had been bare
Show'd forth a naked beauty—in all this
Was I thus rich, and that which I possess'd
To-morrow shall inherit.'   False as hope !
To-morrow's heritage is cloud and storm.

ADRIANA.

Oh! what a moody moralist you grow!
Yet in the even-down letter you are right;
For Ursel, who is weatherwise, says always
That when the sun sets red with the wind south
The morrow shall be stormy.   What of that?
Oh! now I know; the fish won't take the bait.   ·
'Tis marvellous the delight you take in fishing!
Were I to hang upon a river's edge
So tediously, angling, angling still,
The fiend that watches our impatient fits
Would sometime tempt me to jump headlong in.
And you—you cannot quit it for a day!
Have I not read your sadness?

ARTEVELDE.

Have you so!
Oh! you are cunning to divine men's thoughts.
But come what may to-morrow, we have now
A tranquil hour, which let us entertain
As though it were the latest of its kind.

ADRIANA.

Why should we think it so?

ARTEVELDE.

Sweet Adriana,
I trust that many such may come to you;
But for myself, I feel as if life's stream
Were shooting o'er some verge, to make a short,
An angry and precipitate descent,
Thenceforward much tormented on its way.

ADRIANA.

What can have fill'd you with such sad surmises?
You were not wont to speak despondently.

ARTEVELDE.

Nor do I now despond.   All my life long
I have beheld with most respect the man
Who knew himself and knew the ways before him,
And from amongst them chose considerately,
With a clear foresight, not a blindfold courage,
And, having chosen, with a steadfast mind
Pursued his purposes.   I trained myself
To take my place in high or low estate
As one of that scant order of mankind.
Wherefore, though I indulge no more the dream
Of living as I hoped I might have lived,
A life of temperate and thoughtful joy,
Yet I repine not, and from this time forth
Will cast no look behind.

ADRIANA.

               Oh Artevelde ;
What change hath come since morning !   Oh ! how soon
The words and looks which seem'd all confidence,
To me at least—how soon are they recalled !
But let them be—it matters not ; I, too,
Will cast no look behind—Oh, if I should,
My heart would never hold its wretchedness.

ARTEVELDE.

My gentle Adriana, you run wild
In false conjectures ; hear me to the end.
If hitherto we have not said we loved,
Yet hath the heart of each declared its love
By all the tokens wherein love delights.
We heretofore have trusted in each other,
Too wholly have we trusted to have need

E

Of words or vows, pledges or protestations.
Let not such trust be hastily dissolved.

ADRIANA.

I trusted not.   I hoped that I was loved,
Hoped and despair'd, doubted and hoped again,
Till this day, when I first breathed freelier,
Daring to trust—and now—Oh God, my heart!
It was not made to bear this agony—
Tell me you love me, or you love me not.

ARTEVELDE.

I love thee, dearest, with as large a love
As e'er was compass'd in the breast of man.
Hide then those tears, beloved, where thou wilt,
And find a resting-place for that so wild
And troubled heart of thine; sustain it here,
And be its flood of passion wept away.

ADRIANA.

What was it that you said then?   If you love,
Why have you thus tormented me?

ARTEVELDE.

                              Be calm;
And let me warn thee, ere thy choice be fixed,
What fate thou mayst be wedded to with me.
Thou hast beheld me living heretofore
As one retired in staid tranquillity:
The dweller in the mountains, on whose ear
The accustom'd cataract thunders unobserved;
The seaman who sleeps sound upon the deck
Nor hears the loud lamenting of the blast
Nor heeds the weltering of the plangent wave,—
These have not lived more undisturb'd than I:

But build not upon this ; the swollen stream
May shake the cottage of the mountaineer
And drive him forth ; the seaman roused at length
Leaps from his slumber on the wave-wash'd deck ;
And now the time comes fast when here in Ghent
He who would live exempt from injuries
Of armed men, must be himself in arms.
This time is near for all,—nearer for me :
I will not wait upon necessity
And leave myself no choice of vantage ground,
But rather meet the times where best I may,
And mould and fashion them as best I can.
Reflect then that I soon may be embark'd
In all the hazards of these troublesome times,
And in your own free choice take or resign me.

ADRIANA.

Oh Artevelde, my choice is free no more.
Be mine, all mine, let good or ill betide.
In war or peace, in sickness or in health,
In trouble and in danger and in distress,
Through time and through eternity I'll love thee ;
In youth and age, in life and death I'll love thee,
Here and hereafter, with all my soul and strength.
So God accept me as I never cease
From loving and adoring thee next Him ;
And oh, may He pardon me if so betray'd
By mortal frailty as to love thee more.

ARTEVELDE.

I fear, my Adriana, 'tis a rash
And passionate resolve that thou hast made :
But how should *I* admonish thee, myself

E 2

So great a winner by thy desperate play.
Heaven is o'er all, and unto Heaven I leave it.
That which hath made me weak shall make me strong,
Weak to resist, strong to requite thy love;
And if some tax thou payest for that love,
Thou shalt receive it from Love's exchequer.
Farewell; I'm waited for ere this.

ADRIANA.

                Farewell.
But take my signet-ring and give me thine,
That I may know when I have slept and waked
This was no false enchantment of a dream.

ARTEVELDE.

My signet-ring, I have it not to-day:
But in its stead wear this around thy neck.
And now, my Adriana, my betrothed,
Give Love a good night's rest within thy heart
And bid him wake to-morrow calm and strong.

SCENE XI.—BRUGES.—An Apartment in the Palace of the
Earl of Flanders.

The EARL and SIR WALTER D'ARLON.

D'ARLON.

I marvel, my good lord, you take that knave
So freely to your counsels.

EARL.

              Treason done
Against my enemies secures him mine.
His countrymen of Ghent can ne'er forgive him;

Which knowing, he will therefore cleave to me.
Besides, he learns the minds of men toward me
Here and in Ghent, how each man stands affected.
For this and other serviceable arts,
Not out of friendship, do I show him favour.
Have you not seen a jackdaw take his stand
On a sheep's back, permitted there to perch
Less out of kindness to so foul a bird
Than for commodious uses of his beak?
As to the sheep the jackdaw, so to me
Is Gilbert Matthew; from my fleece he picks
The vermin that molest me.—Here he comes!

Enter GILBERT MATTHEW.

Well, honest Gilbert, are the knights not gone?

GILBERT.

Not yet, my lord; they urge in lieu of lives
The forfeiture of sundry burgages
To fill your coffers.   I denied them roundly.

EARL.

I bid thee not!

GILBERT.

        Lives, lives, my lord, take freely;
But spare the lands and burgages and moneys.
The father dead, shall sleep and be forgotten;
The patrimony gone,—that makes a wound
That's slow to heal; heirs are above-ground ever.

EARL.

Well, be it so.

GILBERT.

       The knights wait here without.

They ask an audience of leave, and bring
A new adherent.

EARL.

Give them entrance, Gilbert.

GILBERT MATTHEW *goes out, and returns with* SIR SIMON BETTE *and* SIR GUISEBERT GRUTT.

SIR SIMON.

This audience we made bold to crave, my lord,
To advertise your highness that our friend
Of whom we spake, the valiant Lord of Occo,
Has come here at great hazard in disguise
To show how matters now proceed in Ghent.

EARL.

He shall be welcome.   Does he wait?

SIR SIMON.

                  He does;
And with your highness' leave I'll bring him to you.

[*Exit.*

EARL.

Think'st thou he may be steadied?

GILBERT.

                At this time
He has great power to do your highness service;
And your free pardon for all past misdeeds,
And promise of preferment, will do much
To make him wholly yours.

EARL.

              Well, well, so be it.
'Tis no such urgent need we have of him;
But if he be so contrite, it is well.

Re-enter SIR SIMON BETTE *with* Occo.

You're a bold man, my Lord of Occo, you
That have so long borne arms against your liege,
Without safe-conduct to have ventured here.

OCCO.

My sole safe-conduct is the good intent
I bear to your affairs, my noble lord ;
Nought else impell'd me hither, and nought else,
I trust, is needed for my safe return.

EARL.

Thou shalt return in safety.   Say, what news
Bring'st thou from Ghent?

OCCO.

My lord, Peace, peace ! is there
The only cry, except with desperate chiefs,
Who are so weak that fair conditions now
Would draw their followers from them to a man.

EARL.

Our proffer of conditions is made known
Already to our good Sir Simon Bette
And Guisebert Grutt.

SIR GUISEBERT.

My lord is pleased to grant
Indemnity to all save some three hundred ;
The list to be hereafter named by him
And dealt with at his pleasure.

OCCO.

This is well!
These terms are just and merciful indeed !
But then they must be proffer'd presently.
You know, my lord, the humour we of Ghent

Have still indulged—we never cry for peace
But when we're out of breath; give breathing-time,
And ere the echo of our cry for peace
Have died away, we drown it with War! war!
Even now the faction hopes to be redeem'd
By a new leader, Philip of Artevelde.

EARL.

Ha! Artevelde? that name is ominous.
Whenever sunshine has come near my house
An Artevelde has cast his shadow there.
I have not heard the name of Artevelde
Since that usurper Jacques died the death.
This Philip then was in his infancy.
What is he made of? Of his father's metal?
A dangerous man, in truth, sirs, if he be.

GILBERT.

Oh fear him not, my lord; his father's name
Is all that from his father he derives.
He is a man of singular address
In catching river-fish. His life hath been
Till now, more like a peasant's or a monk's
Than like the issue of so great a man.

OCCO.

Yet is his name so worshipp'd of the people,
That were the time and scope permitted him
To grow expert, some danger might come of him.
Wherefore 'twere well to note him on your list.

EARL.

Let him be noted. Think you, then, Sir Guy,
That they'll accept our terms, or still hold out?

OCCO.

Let these good knights make instant speed to Ghent
And call the burghers to the market-place;
Then let to-morrow, at their bidding, wear
The aspect of to-day, and all will prosper.
Take them whilst yet Nivelle is in their thoughts.

EARL.

You counsel well.   Prepare, sirs, to depart;
We'll have the terms engross'd and send you them.
Farewell, my lord; farewell, Sir Simon Bette;
Sir Guisebert Grutt, farewell.—We'll send you them.

> [*Exeunt the* EARL, GILBERT MATTHEW, OCCO, *and* SIR SIMON
> BETTE. *As* SIR GUISEBERT GRUTT *is following, he is detained
> by* D'ARLON.

D'ARLON.

One word, fair sir.

SIR GUISEBERT.

My good lord, at your pleasure.

D'ARLON.

I have a foolish errand in your town.
There is a damsel . . . . . . but your head is white;
You will not heed me.

SIR GUISEBERT.

Pray proceed, my lord,
I have not yet forgotten how in youth
A damsel's love, amongst the amorous,
Was more than bed of down or morning posset.

D'ARLON.

In brief, kind sir, conveyance hence to Ghent
Is what I crave.   Methinks amongst your train,
And habited like them, I well could pass
And no one mark me.

SIR GUISEBERT.

             Sir, you're free to try ;
And if our friends should still be uppermost
You will risk nothing.   Should the faction reign,
You shall do well to keep your secret close
And make your best speed back.

D'ARLON.

                Leave that to me.

ACT II.

SCENE I.—GHENT.   *The House Van Artevelde.*

VAN ARTEVELDE *and* VAN DEN BOSCH.

VAN DEN BOSCH.

When they were brought together in the Square,
I spake.   I told them that they lack'd a chief;
For though they saw that dangers compass'd them,
Amongst their captains there was none could win
The love of all, but still some guild or craft
Would stone him if they might.   I bade them think
How Jacques Artevelde from humblest state
Had borne this city up to sovereign sway,
And how his son had lived aloof from strife,
To none bore malice, and wish'd well to all.
With that they caught thy name and shouted much;
And some old men swore they remember'd well
In the good times of Jacques Artevelde,
When they were young, that all the world went right,

And after he was dead, that they grew old ;
And wenches who were there, said Artevelde
Was a sweet name and musical to hear.
In brief, for these and other weighty reasons
They were resolved to choose thee for their chief.
But 'Soft! my friends,' quoth I ; 'ye know not yet
How he inclines to that you'd put upon him ;
He hath no friends and favourites to reward ;
He hath no adverse faction to repress ;
Of what avail to him were power and office ?
But nathless we'll entreat him.'   'Bring him here,'
Was then the cry.   'More meet it were, my friends,'
Quoth I, 'that we go seek this noble youth ;
On such high worth we humbly should attend,
And not expect such worth should wait on us.'
To this they gave assent, and will be here
So soon as the outlying crafts are muster'd.

ARTEVELDE.

Good ! When they come I'll speak to them.

VAN DEN BOSCH.

                              'Twere well.
Thou canst not miss to please them in this mood.
The trial will be after, when they flag
And want a long spur-rowel in their bellies.
Thou lack'st experience to deal with men ;
Thou must take counsel.

ARTEVELDE.

                    I will hear it always.
But yet my task methinks were easy learnt.

VAN DEN BOSCH.

Canst learn to bear thee high amongst the commons ?

Canst thou be cruel?   To be esteem'd of them,
Thou must not set more store by lives of men
Than lives of larks in season.

ARTEVELDE.

Be it so.
I can do what is needful.   Where, I pray you,
Abide the messengers of peace from Bruges?

VAN DEN BOSCH.

They lodg'd last night i' the Clothiers' Square.   God's
    blood!
They thought their houses not so safe, belike.

ARTEVELDE.

Why thought they that?

VAN DEN BOSCH.

They enter'd by that quarter;
And near Sir Simon's, which they reach'd the first,
I had provided some pick'd men to meet them;
But, spite my cautions, they brake forth too soon,
And that with howls that Bruges itself might hear.

ARTEVELDE.

So the knights took the warning?

VAN DEN BOSCH.

They drew back
And gallop'd to the Square, the while their train
Stood fast and fought; and it is worthy note
That one amongst them shouted in the fray
The D'Arlons' war-cry, whence he may be known
Of that lord's following, and wherefore here
We well may guess.

ARTEVELDE.

Had *he* been slain 'twere well :
Had others been 'twere not.   If I rule Ghent,
No man shall charge me that his life or goods
Are less secure than mine, so he but keep
The laws that I have made.   Believe me, Peter,
Thy scheme of rule is too disorderly.
Thy force still spends and not augments itself.
To make the needy and the desperate thine,
Thou gav'st them up the plunder of the rich ;
Now these, grown desperate and needy too,
Raise up a host against thee ;—whereupon,
No spoil remaining, thy good friends depart.

VAN DEN BOSCH.

God's curse go with them !

ARTEVELDE.

Like enough it may.
They've carried it about these five long years ;
They took it with them to the peasant's hut,
They took it with them to the burgher's stall,
A roving curse it followed at their heels,
And like enough it will abide amongst them.

VAN DEN BOSCH.

Hark ! here they come.
                    [*Shouts of* ' Artevelde !' *are heard from without.*
                    Out, out ! and show thyself.

Scene II.—*The Street in front of Van Artevelde's House.*

Van Artevelde *and* Van den Bosch.   *The Multitude below.*

ARTEVELDE.

My friends, I thank you for the good respect
In which you hold me ; sirs, I thank you all.
You say that for the love you bore my father,
You and your predecessors, you'd have me
What he was once,—your captain.   Verily
I think you do not well remember, sirs,
The end of all the love ye bore my father.
He was the noblest and the wisest man
That ever ruled in Ghent; yet sirs, ye slew him ;
By his own door, here where I stand, ye slew him ;
What then am I to look for from your loves ?
If the like trust ye should repose in me,
And then in like wise cancel it,—my friends,
That were an ill reward.

SEVERAL BURGESSES.

Nay, Master Philip !

ARTEVELDE.

Oh sirs ! I know ye look not to such end,
Nor may it be yourselves that bring it round ;
But he who rules must still displeasure some,
And he should have protection from the many
So long as he shall serve the many well.
Sirs, to that end his power must be maintain'd ;
The power of peace and war, of life and death,
He must have absolute.   How say ye, sirs ?

Will ye bestow this power on me ? if so,
Shout 'Artevelde,' and ye may add to that,
' Captain of Ghent,'—if not, go straightway home.

[*All shout* ' Artevelde, Captain of Ghent!'

ARTEVELDE.

So be it.
Now listen to your Captain's first command.
It has been heretofore the use of some
On each cross accident, here or without,
To cry aloud for peace.   This is most hurtful.
It much unsettles brave men's minds, disturbs
The counsels of the wise, and daunts the weak.
Wherefore my pleasure is and I decree
That whoso shall but talk of terms of peace
From this time forth, save in my private ear,
Be deem'd a traitor to the town of Ghent
And me its Captain; and a traitor's death
Shall that man die.

BURGESSES.

He shall, he shall, he shall.
We'll kill the slave outright.

ARTEVELDE.

No: mark me further.
If any citizen shall slay another
Without my warranty by word or sign,
Although that slayer be as true as steel,
This other treacherous as Iscariot's self,
The punishment is death.   *[A pause.*
Ye speak no word.
What do we fight for, friends ? for liberty?
What is that liberty for which we fight?

Is it the liberty to slay each other?
Then better were it we had back again
Roger d'Auterne, the bailiff.   No, my friends,
It is the liberty to choose our chief
And bow to none beside.   Now ye choose me,
And in that choice let each man be assured
That none but I alone shall dare to judge him.
Whoso spills blood without my warranty,
High man or low, rich man or poor, shall die.

BURGESSES.

The man shall die; he shall deserve to die;
We'll kill him on the spot, and that is law.

ARTEVELDE.

Hold, hold, my friends! ye are too hasty here.
You shall *not* kill him; 'tis the headsman's part,
Who first must have my warrant for his death.

BURGESSES.

Kill him who likes, the man shall die; that's law.

ARTEVELDE.

What further knowledge of my rules ye need
Ye peradventure may obtain, my friends,
More aptly from my practice than my speech.
Now to the Stadt-House—bring the litter, fellows—
And there the deans of crafts shall do me homage.

VAN DEN BOSCH.

Ho! stand apart.   Bring in the litter, varlets.
Now sirs, let's hear your voices as you go.
          [*Exeunt, with shouts of* 'Artevelde!'

SCENE III.—*The House Van Merestyn.*

SIR WALTER D'ARLON *and* CLARA VAN ARTEVELDE. *She is
engaged in binding up his arm, which is wounded.*

CLARA.

False knight, thou com'st to see thy ladye love
And canst not stay thy stomach for an hour
But thou must fight i' the street. Thy hungry sword—
Could it keep lent no longer? By my faith,
Thou shall do penance at thy lady's feet
The live-long night for this.

D'ARLON.

     God's mercy! lady!
'Twere a sharp trial, one man to keep lent
Whilst all around kept carnival; the sin
Was in the stomachs of your citizens:
But I will do the penance not the less.

CLARA.

Come, come! confess thyself; make a clean breast.
Thou'dst vow'd a vow to some fair dame at Bruges
To kill for her dear love a score of burghers.
Nay, it is certain—never cross thyself—
Hold up this arm—alas! there was a time
When knights were true and constant to their loves
And had but one a-piece—an honest time;
Knights were knights then; God mend the age, say I!
True as the steel upon their backs were they
And their one lady's word was gospel law.
Would I had lived a hundred years ago!

D'ARLON.

Could you live backward for a hundred years,

F

And then live on a hundred years to come,
You'd not find one to love you truelier
Than I have loved.

CLARA.

What, what ! no truer knight ?
A seemly word forsooth !   Hast many more such ?
No truer knight ?—'Tis thus you great lords live
With flatterers round you all your golden youth,
And know yourselves as much as I know Puck—
Your heads so many bee-hives ; honey'd words
Swarm in your ears, and other from your mouth
Go buzzing out to ply for sweets abroad ;
And so your summer wastes, till some cold night
The cunning husbandman comes stealthily
And there is fire and brimstone for my lords !
Hold up this arm—let go my hand, I say—
Am I to tie thy bandage with my teeth ?

Enter ADRIANA.

ADRIANA.

My lord—good heaven !   Your arm—I fear you're hurt.

CLARA.

Hold, hush !   I'll answer for thee.   Merely a scratch ;
A scratch, fair lady,—that, and nothing more ;
It gives us no concern ; 'twas thus we got it:
Riding along the streets of this good town,
A score of burghers met us, peaceful drones—
Saying their prayers, belike ; howe'er that be,
The senseless men were rapt in such abstraction
They heeded not our lordship ; whereat we,
Unused to such demeanour, shook ourselves,
And prick'd them with our lance ; a fray ensued,

And lo! as we were slaying some fourteen
That stay'd our passage, it pleased Providence,
Of whom the meanest may be instruments,
Thus gently to chastise us on the arm,
Doubtless for some good cause, tho' what, we know not.

ADRIANA.

My lord, you know her; she is ever thus,
Still driving things against you to your face,
And when you're gone, if I should chance let fall
A word, or but a hint of censure, as—
My Lord of Arlon is too rash, too hot,
Too anything—

CLARA.

She sighs and says, too true.

ADRIANA.

No verily.　But why, my lord, come here
At all this hazard only to be rail'd at?

CLARA.

Yes, tell us why.

D'ARLON.

Behold the very cause.

Enter ARTEVELDE.

ARTEVELDE (*as he enters*).

Let my guard wait without.

CLARA.

His guard!　What's this?

ARTEVELDE.

My Lord of Arlon, God be with your lordship!
And guide you upon less adventurous tracks
Than this you tread.　I'll speak with you anon:

F 2

My Adriana! victim that thou art!
Thy lover should have been some gentle youth
In gay attire, with laughter on his lips,
Who'd nestle in thy bosom all night long,
And ne'er let harness clink upon thine ears,
Save only in romaunt and roundelay.
Such is what should be, and behold what is!
A man of many cares new taken up,
To whom there's nothing more can come in life
But what is serious and solicitous:
One who betakes him to his nuptial bed,
His thoughts still busy with the watch and ward,
And if his love breathe louder than her wont,
Starts from his sleep, and thinks the bells ring backwards:
A man begirt with eighty thousand swords,
Scarce knowing which are in the hands of friends
And which against him; such a sort of man
Thy lover is—his fate for life or death
Link'd to a cause which some deem desperate.
Such is Van Artevelde, for he is now
Chief Captain of the White-Hoods and of Ghent.

CLARA.

Nay! is it even so!

ARTEVELDE.

Even so it is.

ADRIANA.

And thou art captain of these savages!
And thou wilt trample with them through the blood
Of fellow-men, alas it may be, too,
Of fellow-citizens—for what care they?
And thou who wert a gentle-hearted man,
Must lead these monsters where they will!

ARTEVELDE.

Not so.
I purpose but to lead them where *I* will.

ADRIANA.

Then they will turn upon thee; never yet
Would they endure a chief that cross'd their humour.

ARTEVELDE.

That is the patience they've to learn from me.
The times have tamed them, and mischance of late
Has forced an iron bit between their teeth,
By help whereof I hope to rein them round.

CLARA.

Oh, they will murder thee!

ARTEVELDE.

It may be so.
But I hope better things—yet this is sure,
That they *shall* murder me ere make me go
The way that is not my way for an inch.

ADRIANA.

'Alas! and is it come to this!—Oh God!

ARTEVELDE.

This I foresaw, and things have fallen out
No worse than I forwarn'd thee that they might.
What must be, must.   My course hath been appointed;
For I feel that within me which accords
With what I have to do.   The field is fair,
And I have no perplexity or cloud
Upon my vision.   Every thing is clear.
And take this with thee for thy comfort too—
That man is not the most in tribulation
Who, resolute of mind, walks his own way,

With answerable skill to plant his steps.
Men in their places are the men that stand,
And I am strong and stable on my legs;
For though full many a care from this time forth
Must harbour in my head, my heart is fresh,
And there is but one trouble touches it,
That this portends a troubled fate for thee.

ADRIANA.

For me?—Oh never vex thy heart for that;
Nor think of me so all unworthily,
Nor fancy for me fears I have not—No,
I'll follow thee through sunshine and through storm;
I will be with thee in thy weal and woe,
In thy afflictions, should they fall upon thee,
In thy temptations when bad men beset thee,
In all the perils which must now press round thee,
And, should they crush thee, in the hour of death.
If thy ambition, late aroused, was that
Which push'd thee on this perilous adventure,
Then *I* will be ambitious too,—if not,
And it was thy ill-fortune drove thee to it,
Then I will be unfortunate no less.
I will resemble thee in that and all things
Wherein a woman may; grave will I be
And thoughtful, for already it is gone—
God's blessing on my earlier years bestowed,
The clear contentment of a heart at ease.
All will I part with to partake thy cares,
Let but thy love my lesser joys outlast.

ARTEVELDE.

The last of love for thee were last of all

That through this passage of mortality
Lights on my soul to heaven.   All will be well.
Much happiness shall be thy portion yet.
Love will be with thee, breathing his native air,
And peace around thee, thro' the power of love.
But bring me through the business of this day —
My lord, your pardon ; we consume your time,
Which, I'm constrain'd to say, is short in Ghent.
I hitherto have welcomed you amongst us,
And kept the secret of your sojourns here ;
So doing, partly for respect to you,
And partly for her sake, this foolish girl's,
My pretty Clara's, who will let me say
I had not pleased her else ; but now, my lord,
As you have heard, I hold an office here
With duties appertaining, and must needs
(With sorrow for your sudden going hence)
Make offer of my passport,—good till sunset.

D'ARLON.

If no discourtesy is meant by this
I have but to depart.

CLARA.

Depart ! and wherefore ?

ARTEVELDE.

There's nothing meant but honour, nothing else,
Howe'er to rude appearances enforced.
When there is peace between the Earl and Ghent
'Twill be a joy to me to see again
The gallant Lord of Arlon ; till that time
We meet not, save in hostile ranks opposed,
Or captive, I in Bruges or he in Ghent.

D'ARLON.

Sir, it is not for me to say you nay
In your own town, with not a man to back me ;
Nor would I willingly distrust your word
That all is honourably meant ; for else
I scarce should miss to find a future time
For fair requital.

ARTEVELDE.

On my faith, my lord,
I love you and respect you.

D'ARLON.

'Tis enough.
Then I depart in peace.

CLARA.

Depart ! what's this ?
What's all the coil about ?   Depart ! aye truly,
That's when I bid him, not an instant sooner.
Dismiss him thus, and bid him come no more !
Then what becomes of me ?   Oh, I'm a child !
I'm to be whipp'd for crying after him ?
But let me tell thee, Philip, I'm the child
Of Jacques Artevelde—So look well to it.
An injury to myself I might forgive,
But one to D'Arlon—
                              [*Bursting into tears.*
Sir, think twice upon it,
Lest you should lose a sister unawares.

D'ARLON.

Nay Clara, nay, be not so troubled.

ARTEVELDE.

There—
You see the humour she is of, my lord ;

But be my sins confess'd, the fault is mine.
An orphan sister and an only one,
What could I less but let her have her will
In all things possible ?   An easy man
She still has found me, and knows nothing yet
Of opposition to her high commands.
You, if you e'er should take her to yourself,
May teach her better doctrine.   Patience, Clara,
Patience, my love ; nor let this knight discern
His future trials thus presignified
In rain and lightning ; let him not, my love.

CLARA (weeping).

When will he come again ?

ARTEVELDE.

                    When peace comes, dearest ;
We'll make him welcome then to bower and hall,
And thou shalt twine a garland for his brow
Of olive and of laurels won from me.

D'ARLON.

Be pacified, sweet Clara ; dry your tears.
He but deals with me as he has the right
And deems himself in duty bound.   Such things
Shall jar no string between us.

ARTEVELDE.

                    Nobly said.
I leave her in your hands, and hope your aid
For bringing her to reason.

D'ARLON.

                    I entreat
One word in private with you ere we part.

ARTEVELDE.

Take in my sister, Adriana—go,
Impart to her a portion of that strength
Which there is in thee—teach her to subdue
Her woman's wilfulness.

[Exeunt ADRIANA *and* CLARA.

D'ARLON.

　　　　　　　　　　My errand here
Is not so wholly idle as no doubt
Thou deem'st it.　I would first have warn'd thee off
The office which, with most unhappy haste,
Already thou hast clutch'd.　That being vain,
I next would bid thee to beware false friends.
Look that there be no treason in thy camp;
I may not now say more; but be assured
'Twill be thy life thou fight'st for.

ARTEVELDE.

　　　　　　　　　　Noble D'Arlon!
It is a grief to me that we should meet
In opposition thus.　I will look round,
And profit by thy warning if I may.
Trust me 'twould irk my heart no less than thine,
(And may this show in all my acts hereafter,)
To enter in alliance with foul play
For any earthly meed.　Sir, fare you well.

D'ARLON.

Whenso' the choice and noblest of my friends
Are bid to memory's feast, then, Artevelde,
The place of honour shall be thine.　Farewell.

[Exit.

Enter the Captain *of* ARTEVELDE'S *Guard.*

CAPTAIN.

Sir, there's a messenger from Van den Bosch

Who craves to see you instantly : another
Says the Lord Occo waits your leisure.

ARTEVELDE (*after a pause*).
                                        Ha !
Lord Occo, saidst thou ? tell me, what of him !

CAPTAIN.
He waits your leisure, sir.

ARTEVELDE.
                              And when comes that ?
He shall *not* wait my leisure.   And what more ?

CAPTAIN.
Sir, Van den Bosch would see you.

ARTEVELDE.
                                        It is well :
I will attend the Lord of Occo first,
And Van den Bosch shall find me at my house
Some half hour hence.   How look we, sir, abroad ?

CAPTAIN.
The citizens are trooping to the Stadt-House.
'Tis said Sir Simon and Sir Guisebert pass
From door to door incessantly.

ARTEVELDE.
                                  To beg ?

CAPTAIN.
To gain a strong attendance.

ARTEVELDE.
                              Wo the while !
A bear, a fiddle, and a pair of monkeys,
Had sped the service better.

CAPTAIN.

Both mean and notable, and rich and poor,
Have they solicited, assuring all
That when it shall be heard what terms of peace
Are offer'd, they will hug the messengers
That after painful travail for their love
Have brought them such good news.

ARTEVELDE.

I'll swear they will.
But what ?   Thou look'st not over cheerily ;
Think'st thou the knights have made some way then, ha?

CAPTAIN.

The deacons of eight crafts have sided with them,
And many of the aldermen.

ARTEVELDE.

Ay, truly ?

CAPTAIN.

And all the men of lineage.

ARTEVELDE.

That's as thou hearest.

CAPTAIN.

The citizens pass'd by me in the street
By scores and hundreds, and of them I saw
The greater part, 'twas plain, would stand against us.

ARTEVELDE.

Build up, and then pull down, and then build up,—
And always in the ruins some are—Well ?

CAPTAIN.

And I'm afeard, though loth I am to think it,

A few amongst your guard have fallen off
At seeing us outnumber'd thus.

ARTEVELDE.

Is't so ?
Why, wherefore should I wish that it were not ?
The more faint hearts fall off the better, sir ;
So fear shall purge us to a sound condition.

SCENE IV.—*The Dwelling-house of the Lord of Occo.*

OCCO *and* VAN AESWYN.

OCCO.

The mariners, then, are for us ?

AESWYN.

They are ours.

OCCO.

And these are of the curriers that thou bring'st me ?

AESWYN.

The deacons of that craft—they're backward still :
They're ever harping upon Artevelde,
Who told their worships when they did him homage
If his poor humour govern'd, nothing else
But leathern jerkins should be worn in Ghent.

OCCO.

We'll deal with them the same as with the fullers ;
So bring them in.

[*Exit* VAN AESWYN.

Well done, Sir Curriers !
These precious moments must be given to you !
The devil curry you for senseless boors !

Re-enter VAN AESWYN *with the two* Craftsmen.

Good-morrow, masters—Ha ! my valued friend,

Jacob Van Ryk; and if my eyes see true,
Master——

AESWYN.

Van Muck.

OCCO.

                    Tush, tush, sir! tell not me.
Have I forgotten my old friend Van Muck,
Or any of my friends?—though time is short,
And we must scant our greetings.   Worthy sirs,
We're in a perilous predicament,
And I should take no step without advice.
Rash were it, and a tempting Providence,
Should I proceed without consulting you.
We see, sirs, we must see—we can't but own,
That we have no choice left us but of peace
Or else destruction.   It is come to that.
Then if we must be subject to the Earl,
I will confess I'm not so subtle-witted
To see much difference 'twixt this hour and that,
The going over to him now at once
With flesh upon our bones, or holding back
Till famine wastes it or steel hacks it off:
I see no difference.

VAN MUCK.

Truly, sir, nor I.

OCCO.

Aye, but there is a difference, my friends,
Which I forgot.   For, hark you in your ear!
Those who go over but when all go over,
If they escape from pains and penalties,
Can scarcely claim much merit with the Earl;
But they who find a guidance for themselves,

Who take a step or two before the herd,
Whilst the will's free, who lead and do not follow—
These men have claims ; they have a right to say,
Reward us for our voluntary service ;
Nor will they be unanswer'd, that I know :
' First serve the first,' is what they say at Bruges.

VAN RYK.

'Tis a good proverb, sir, for early men,
And we have ne'er been slack in things of credit ;
But we have scruples here.   We see it thus :
If we should but shout peace with half the town,
The Earl would scarce distinguish us from others ;
If, on the other hand, we use our weapons
Against our friends, they'd call us renegades,
And blacken us for false and treacherous knaves.

OCCO.

Why look ye now ; too surely, should ye shout,
And fail in action, 'twere no singular service ;
There's no great guerdon were deserved by that ;
The clerkships of the wards (which after peace
Must be new filled) would not be won by shouts :
But where's the treachery ?   My worthy friends,
Look at the matter simply as it is :
Here is a town beleaguer'd in such wise
That it must needs surrender upon terms :
Then come a knot of desperate-minded men,
Who, deeming the rendition gives them up
To punishment, make head against the rest :
These think no shame to say that all must die
To save their one—two—three—half-dozen heads
From certain hazards.   Why, if fall they must

And they would rather 'twere by steel than cord,
Let them assail us and let us be men.
Are we not free to choose twixt peace and war?
They—they it is that are so treacherous—they,
Who would betray a city to destruction
For private and particular ends of theirs.
Then let us rally round the public weal
And link our names with that.

VAN RYK.

It must be own'd
The city's weal doth loudly call upon us;
But some of us there are who recently
Swore fealty to Artevelde.

OCCO.

What then?
That was but for the war—not knowing then
That it was ended by your deputies
And peace concluded: answer not so idly.
Swore ye not fealty to the Earl before?
Come, come, my friends—we're all as one, I see;
And let me tell you that the whole of Ghent,
Almost the whole, is minded like yourselves.
Strange is it men shall meditate and muse
In secret all alike, and show no sign
Till a blow's struck, and then they speak it out,
And each man finds in each his counterpart;
And, as a sluice were open'd, all shall rush
To find the self-same level, and pour on
To the same end.   But I forgot, my friends;
We have to think of what particular mark
Should first be aim'd at when the blow is struck.

VAN RYK.

So please you, sir, a cast at Van den Bosch
Were not amiss, methinks.

OCCO.

Well shot, Van Ryk ;
But yet not quite the bull's eye.

VAN MUCK.

By the mass,
He's shot the bull he had his horns of—Ha !
What will Dame Oda say to thee ?

VAN RYK.

Come, come !
If that's our archery, Frans Fleisch for thee.

OCCO.

My friends, we'll settle all such scores at will.
But is not Ghent more precious than our wives ?
And who debauches her ?   When she was fain
To creep into her long-left lord's embrace,
Who came at night and whistled her away ?
This is the aggravation that most stirs
The choler of the Earl.   The other chiefs,
Men that by accidents and long degrees
Became entangled in rebellion,—them
He can forgive ; but he that plunged plump in
And so new troubled what was settling down,
This is the man that he has mark'd for death :
Whoso brings down that head has hit a mark
That's worth five hundred florins.   Ha ! my friends !
Who strikes a good stroke with his sword for this ?

[*A pause.*

Van Artevelde must die, you understand me.

[*A pause again.*
G

VAN RYK.

Why, if he must, he must, and there's an end.

OCCO.

The Earl must have his life ; who hath the guerdon
Is not material save to them that get it ;
But truly were the money on my head,
And I as sure to die as Artevelde,
I'd rather that such men as you should have it,
Than see it snatch'd by luck ; when die we must,
'Tis better that thereby good men should thrive
Than snatchers.

VAN RYK.

         Saving your displeasure, sir,
'Tis said good men ne'er thrive but by good deeds.
Now, were it but the slaying Van den Bosch,
Or Peter Nuitre, or Frans Ackerman,
There's husbands, widows, orphans, all through Ghent,
Would say the deed was good : but Artevelde
Has, as it were, a creditable name,
And men would say we struck not for revenge,
But only lucre, which were scandalous ;
And also, sir—

OCCO (*to a* Serving-man, *who enters*).

         What, sirrah ?—speak—what now ?

                [*The* Serving-man *whispers him.*

Van Artevelde ! he is not coming here ?
Not now—not now ?

SERVING-MAN.

         Now, instantly, my lord.

OCCO.

Masters, I wish you both good-day—good-day.

God prosper thee, Van Ryk—Van Muck, farewell.
Why op'st thou not the door, thou villain groom ?
Think'st thou the burgesses have time to lose ?
Farewell at once, sirs—not to keep you longer
When things are all so stirring in the town ;
You're needed at your posts, I know ; farewell.

VAN RYK.

My lord, as touching these five hundred florins—

OCCO.

Just as ye will, sirs—any way ye please ;
I bid God speed you, and so fare you well.

VAN RYK.

If you would take four hundred from the five,
And set the residue on Van den Bosch,
His head I'd bring you in for that much money,
And Ackerman's for love and pure good-will.

VAN MUCK.

And sir, as touching Artevelde—

OCCO.

                                   Nay, nay,
I will not press it further.

VAN MUCK.

                          If the florins—

OCCO.

Peace on your lives, he's here !

Enter VAN ARTEVELDE.

ARTEVELDE.

My Lord of Occo, at your pleasure.   Ha !
Attended, too, as I could wish to see you ;
I'd not desire to see a friend of mine

G 2

Better accompanied,—no, nor a foe
Better encounter'd than by men like these.
Jacob Van Ryk, my father loved you much :
No man knew better, Jacob, than my father,
Who were the worthiest to be loved and trusted ;
And I, thou seest, have mounted to his seat.
How the old times come back upon me now !
I was a very little prating child
When thou wert wonted to attend my father
Home from the Stadt-House : it was always thou
Whom he would choose from them that brought him
        home
To ask thy company ; and in thine arms
He oft would put me for his more repose,
For I was stillest there.   Times change, Van Ryk ;
Years shift us up and down ; but something sticks ;
And for myself, there's nothing as a man
That I love more than what a child I loved.
Honest Van Muck, thy hand—thou look'st abash'd—
Ah, thou bethink'st thee of thy little debt,
The money that I lent thee for the close.
Why, what of that, man ?   Didst thou ever hear
An Artevelde would hurt his friend for gold ?
Thy debt is cancell'd—think no more upon it ;
Thou shalt look boldly upward in the world
And care for no man.   I will settle that
This instant with a writing.

OCÇO.

                By your leave,
The burgesses are tarried for elsewhere ;
They are incontinently going hence ;

You will forgive their haste, they cannot stay;
Open the doors.   Good-day, sirs, once again.

VAN MUCK.

Master Van Artevelde, I'm more your debtor
Than ever I was yet.   The Lord requite you,
And keep you in your perils near at hand!

VAN RYK.

Master Van Artevelde, God bless you, sir!
And give you grace to know and to discern,
And read men's hearts,—the gift your father had.
Look for your friends amongst the commons ever;
An' 'twere not for Lord Occo standing here,
I'd bid you trust in ne'er a Lord of Ghent.

[Exeunt the Craftsmen.

ARTEVELDE (after a pause).

These are ambiguous knaves.

OCCO.

True craftsmen both!

Ever suspicious of nobility.

ARTEVELDE.

That am I not.   You had some news to tell,
So your lieutenant said.

OCCO.

Intelligence

Has reach'd me of the terms the Earl will offer:
A guarantee of franchises and rights,
Conditional on some three hundred of us
Being deliver'd over to his mercy.

ARTEVELDE.

Of whom then is this number?

OCCO.

They must be
Whomso' the Earl may please to name hereafter.
The lists are written out, though not divulged ;
But, what is worthiest note, upon the file
Your name appears not.

ARTEVELDE.

By my faith, that's strange !
But are these tidings certain ?

OCCO.

Beyond doubt.

ARTEVELDE.

How came you by them, if they be so certain ?

OCCO.

They're rumour'd—very confidently rumour'd.
I had them also from my spies at Bruges ;
A most sagacious spy—he saw the lists ;
He never yet deceived me—there's no doubt.

ARTEVELDE.

And what do you advise, if this be truth ?

OCCO.

Why, if the town be obstinately bent
On making peace, my counsel to yourself,
Whose life peace places not in jeopardy,
Would be to leave the forward part to us,
Whose only hope of safety is resistance ;
So that, if we should fall, you still may stand,
Whatever turn things take. And bear in mind,
If there be danger, and the crafts turn on us,
To throw yourself among the mariners ;
There's none of all the crafts so wholly with us.

ARTEVELDE.

With which of us, my lord?

OCCO.

With one and all.

ARTEVELDE.

Aye, say you so?   And my part, as you think,
Is to hold back and see you play the game.
My apprehension of a leader's part
Is different from this.   I ask'd your counsel,
And I have not unprofitably heard it:
Now I will give you mine, and be you pleased
To profit in like sort, lest worse befall you.
I too have had my spies upon the watch,
And what they brought me sounded in my ears
A note of warning link'd with names well known,
Now known for traitors' names.   I hereupon
Took order for a numerous company,
Selected for their hardihood and faith,
To be for ever close upon the heels
Of these same traitors at all guild-assemblies
And use their weapons on a sign from me.
Which matters recommending to your notice,
My counsel to you is to stay at home.

[Exit.

Enter VAN AESWYN.

AESWYN.

My lord, Sir Guisebert Grutt is much impatient,
And sends one message on another's heels
To ask why tarry you?

OCCO.

I am not well.

AESWYN.

But they are setting forth immediately ;
The market-place is full to overflowing.

OCCO.

Hark ye ! he knows it all.

AESWYN.

Van Artevelde ?

OCCO.

Knows every thing.

AESWYN.

And what is to be done ?

OCCO.

I'm ill at ease ; I know not ; what think'st thou ?

AESWYN.

If he but knew it half an hour too soon,
His knowledge is of small account.

OCCO.

God's death !

But I am ignorant how long he's known it—
How many he has practised with and gain'd—
How many may have falsely seem'd to swerve
By his direction, only to delude
And so embolden me to my destruction.
I would this hour were past !

AESWYN.

Resolve on something ;
Take one part or the other, lest it pass,
And leave you ruin'd both ways.

OCCO.

Ruin'd ! Ruin'd !

He told me if I ventured to the meeting
His followers should slay me.

AESWYN.

                      Yours may him ;
'Tis a fair challenge, let us fight it out.

OCCO.

Why that is bravely said.   Then be it so.
Thou shalt have warranty to fight it out ;
And if we're beaten, I shall stand prepared
To fly to Bruges with such as choose to follow.
And hark you ! we will not go empty-handed ;
We'll take a prize that's worth a good town's ransom,—
A damsel whom thou wot'st of.   Pick me out
Ten of the sturdiest of my body-guard,
Van Truckler and Van Linden at their head ;
Bid them have horses saddled, and a litter.
Shouldst thou be worsted in the market-place
I will be nigh thee to protect thy flight
Till thou mayst reach the gates.   God prosper thee !
[*Exit.*

AESWYN.

The dastard ! when the service is of danger
The follower must lead, and venture all
For him that ventures nothing.   Are we fools ?

SCENE V.—*The House Van Artevelde.*—ARTEVELDE *in a suit of armour, reclining in a window-seat. The* Page *is standing by him.*

ARTEVELDE.

Not to be fear'd—Give me my sword !   Go forth,
And see what folk be these that throng the street.
[*Exit the* Page.

Not to be fear'd is to be nothing here.
And wherefore have I taken up this office,
If I be nothing in it?   There they go.

[Shouts are heard.

Of them that pass my house some shout my name,
But the most part pass silently; and once
I heard the cry of ' Flanders and the Lion.'

Re-enter Page.

PAGE.

The knights that newly have arrived from Bruges
Pass down the street, my lord, and many with them.

ARTEVELDE.

Give me my cloak and dagger!   There, enough—
Thy service is perform'd.   Go to thy sports,
But come not near the market-place to-day.

[Exit Page.

To be the chief of honourable men
Is honour; and if dangerous, yet faith
Still binds them faster as the danger grows.
To be the head of villains,—what is that
But to be mind to an unwholesome body—
To give away a noble human soul
In sad metempsychosis to the brutes,
Whose carrion, else exanimate, but gains
A moment's life from this, then so infects
That altogether die the death of beasts.

[A pause.

These hands are spotless yet—
Yea, white as when in infancy they stray'd
Unconscious o'er my mother's face, or closed
With that small grasp which mothers love to feel.
No stain has come upon them since that time—
They have done nothing violent—

Of a calm will untroubled servants they,
And went about their offices, if here
I must not say in purity, in peace.
But he they served,—he is not what he was.

[*A party pass the window, and a voice cries,* 'The Lion for Flanders.'

That cry again !
Sir knights, ye drive me close upon the rocks,
And of my cargo you're the vilest bales,
So overboard with you !   What, men of blood !
Can the son better auspicate his arms
Than by the slaying of who slew the father ?
Some blood may flow because that it needs must,
But yours by choice—I'll slay you, and thank God.

Enter VAN DEN BOSCH.

VAN DEN BOSCH.

The common bell has rung ! the knights are there ;
Thou must come instantly.

ARTEVELDE.

I come, I come.

VAN DEN BOSCH.

Now, Master Philip, if thou miss thy way
Through this affair, we're lost.   For Jesus' sake
Be counsell'd now by me ; have thou in mind—

ARTEVELDE.

Enough, I need not counsel ; I'm resolved.
Take thou thy stand beside Sir Simon Bette,
As I by Grutt ; take note of all I do,
And do thyself accordingly.   Come on.

SCENE VI.—*The exterior of the Stadt-House. Two external flights of stone stairs meet in a landing-place or platform, midway in the front of the building and level with the first floor. On this platform appear* SIR GUISEBERT GRUTT, *with the aldermen of sundry guilds and the deans of the several crafts of butchers, fishermen, glaziers, and cordwainers. Also* VAN ARTEVELDE, VAN DEN BOSCH, FRANS ACKERMAN, VAN NUITRE, *and others of their party.* SIR GUISEBERT GRUTT *descends some steps, and meets* SIR SIMON BETTE, *as he is coming up from the street.*

SIR GUISEBERT (*aside to* SIR SIMON BETTE).

God's life, sir! where is Occo?

SIR SIMON.
                                        Sick, sick, sick.
He has sent word he's sick and cannot come.

SIR GUISEBERT.

Pray God his sickness be the death of him!

SIR SIMON.

Nay, his lieutenant's here, and has his orders.

VAN DEN BOSCH (*aside to* ARTEVELDE).

I see there's something that hath staggered them.
Now push them to the point. [*Aloud.*] Make way
    there, Ho!

ARTEVELDE (*coming forward*).

Some citizen hath brought this concourse here.
Who is the man, and what hath he to say?

SIR GUISEBERT.

The noble Earl of Flanders of his grace
Commissions me to speak.

[*Some* White-Hoods *interrupt him with cries of* 'Ghent,' *on which there is a great tumult, and they are instantly drowned in the cry of* 'Flanders.'

ARTEVELDE.

What, silence! peace!
Silence, and hear this noble Earl's behests,
Deliver'd by this thrice puissant knight.

SIR GUISEBERT.

First will I speak—not what I'm bid to say,
But what it most imports yourselves to hear.
For though ye cannot choose but know it well,
Yet by these cries I deem that some of you
Would, much like madmen, cast your knowledge off,
And both of that and of your reason reft
Run naked on the sword—which to forefend,
Let me *remind* you of the things ye know.
Sirs, when this month began ye had four chiefs
Of great renown and valour,—Jan de Bol,
Arnoul le Clerc, and Launoy and Van Ranst :
Where are they now? and what be ye without them?
Sirs, when the month began ye had good aid
From Brabant, Liege, St. Tron, and Huy and Dinant:
How shall they serve you now?   The Earl sits fast
Upon the Quatre-metiers and the Bridge:
What aid of theirs can reach you?   What supplies?
I tell you, sirs, that thirty thousand men
Could barely bring a bullock to your gates.
If thus without, how stand you then within?
Ask of your chatelain, the Lord of Occo ;
Which worthy knight will tell you—

ARTEVELDE (*aside to* VAN DEN BOSCH).

Mark you that?
Then aloud to SIR GUISEBERT.] Where is this chatelain, your
    speech's sponsor?

SIR GUISEBERT.

He's sick in bed; but were he here, he'd tell you
There's not provision in the public stores
To keep you for a day.   Such is your plight.
Now hear the offer of your natural liege.
Moved to compassion by our prayers and tears,
Well aided as they were by good Duke Aubert,
My Lady of Brabant and Lord Compelant—
To whom our thanks are due,—the Earl says thus:
He will have peace, and take you to his love,
And be your good lord as in former days;
And all the injuries, hatreds, and ill-will
He had against you he will now forget,
And he will pardon you your past offences,
And he will keep you in your ancient rights;
And for his love and graces thus vouchsafed
He doth demand of you three hundred men,
Such citizens of Ghent as he shall name,
To be deliver'd up to his good pleasure.

VAN DEN BOSCH.

Three hundred citizens!

ARTEVELDE.

Peace, Van den Bosch.
Hear we this other knight.   Well, worthy sir,
Hast aught to say, or hast not got thy priming,
That thus thou gaspest like a droughty pump?

VAN DEN BOSCH.

Nay, 'tis black bile that chokes him.   Come, up with it!
Be it but a gallon it shall ease thy stomach.

SEVERAL CITIZENS.

Silence!   Sir Simon Bette's about to speak.

SIR SIMON.

Right worthy burgesses, good men and rich!
Much trouble ye may guess, and strife had we
To win his Highness to this loving humour;
For if ye rightly think, sirs, and remember,
You've done him much offence—not of yourselves,
But through ill guidance of ungracious men.
For first ye slew his bailiff at the cross,
And with the Earl's own banner in his hand,
Which falling down was trampled under foot
Through heedlessness of them that stood about.
Also ye burn'd the castle he loved best
And ravaged all his parks at Andrehen,
All those delightful gardens on the plain:
And ye beat down two gates at Oudenarde,
And in the dike ye cast them upside down:
Also ye slew five knights of his, and brake
The silver font wherein he was baptised.
Wherefore it must be own'd, sirs, that much cause
He had of quarrel with the town of Ghent.
For how, sirs, had the Earl afflicted you
That ye should thus dishonour him? 'tis true
That once a burgess was detain'd at Erclo
Through misbehaviour of the bailiff; still
He hath deliver'd many a time and oft
Out of his prisons burgesses of yours
Only to do you pleasure; and when late
By kinsmen of the bailiff whom ye slew,
Some mariners of yours were sorely maim'd,
(Which was an inconvenience to this town)
What did the Earl? To prove it not his act
He banish'd out of Flanders them that did it.

Moreover, sirs, the taxes of the Earl
Were not so heavy, but that, being rich,
Ye might have borne them; they were not the half
Of what ye since have paid to wage this war;
And yet had these been double that were half,
The double would have grieved you less in peace
Than but the half in war.   Bethink ye, sirs,
What were the fowage and the subsidies
When bread was but four mites that's now a groat?
All which considered, sirs, I counsel you
That ye accept this honourable peace,
For mercifully is the Earl inclined,
And ye may surely deem of them he takes
A large and liberal number will be spared,
And many here who least expect his love
May find him free and gracious.   Sirs, what say ye?

ARTEVELDE.

First, if it be your pleasure, hear me speak.
                    [*Great tumult, and cries of* ' Flanders.'
What, sirs, not hear me? was it then for this
Ye made me your chief captain yesternight,
To snare me in a trust, whereof I bear
The name and danger only, not the power?
                              [*The tumult increases.*
Sirs, if we needs must come to blows, so be it;
For I have friends amongst you who can deal them.

SIR SIMON (*aside to* SIR GUISEBERT).

Had Occo now been here! but lacking him
It must not come to that.

SIR GUISEBERT.

                         My loving friends,
Let us behave like brethren as we are,

And not like listed combatants.   Ho, peace!
Hear this young bachelor of high renown,
Who writes himself your captain since last night,
When a few score of varlets, being drunk,
In mirth and sport so dubbed him.   Peace, sirs! hear
    him.

ARTEVELDE.

Peace let it be, if so ye will; if not,
We are as ready as yourselves for blows.

ONE OF THE CITIZENS.

Speak, master Philip, speak, and you'll be heard.

ARTEVELDE.

I thank you, sirs; I knew it could not be
But men like you must listen to the truth.
Sirs, ye have heard these knights discourse to you
Of your ill fortunes, telling on their fingers
The worthy leaders ye have lately lost:
True, they were worthy men, most gallant chiefs;
And ill would it become us to make light
Of the great loss we suffer by their fall:
They died like heroes; for no recreant step
Had e'er dishonour'd them, no stain of fear,
No base despair, no cowardly recoil:
They had the hearts of freemen to the last,
And the free blood that bounded in their veins
Was shed for freedom with a liberal joy.
But had they guess'd, or could they but have dream'd
The great examples which they died to show
Should fall so flat, should shine so fruitless here,
That men should say 'For liberty these died,
Wherefore let us be slaves,'—had they thought this,

H

Oh, then, with what an agony of shame,
Their blushing faces buried in the dust,
Had their great spirits parted hence for heaven!
What? shall we teach our chroniclers henceforth
To write that in five bodies were contained
The sole brave hearts of Ghent! which five defunct,
The heartless town, by brainless counsel led,
Deliver'd up her keys, stript off her robes,
And so with all humility besought
Her haughty lord that he would scourge her lightly!
It shall not be—no, verily! for now,
Thus looking on you as ye stand before me,
Mine eye can single out full many a man
Who lacks but opportunity to shine
As great and glorious as the chiefs that fell.—
But lo! the Earl is mercifully minded!
And surely if we, rather than revenge
The slaughter of our bravest, cry them shame,
And fall upon our knees, and say we've sinned,
Then will my lord the Earl have mercy on us,
And pardon us our letch for liberty!
What pardon it shall be, if we know not,
Yet Ypres, Courtray, Grammont, Bruges, they know;
For never can those towns forget the day
When by the hangman's hands five hundred men,
The bravest of each guild, were done to death
In those base butcheries that he called pardons.
And did it seal their pardons, all this blood?
Had they the Earl's good love from that time forth?
Oh, sirs! look round you lest ye be deceived;
Forgiveness may be spoken with the tongue,
Forgiveness may be written with the pen,

But think not that the parchment and mouth pardon
Will e'er eject old hatreds from the heart.
There's that betwixt you been which men remember
Till they forget themselves, till all's forgot,
Till the deep sleep falls on them in that bed
From which no morrow's mischief knocks them up.
There's that betwixt you been which you yourselves,
Should ye forget, would then not be yourselves;
For must it not be thought some base men's souls
Have ta'en the seats of yours and turn'd you out,
If in the coldness of a craven heart
Ye should forgive this bloody-minded man
For all his black and murderous monstrous crimes?
Think of your mariners, three hundred men,
After long absence in the Indian seas
Upon their peaceful homeward voyage bound,
And now, all dangers conquer'd as they thought,
Warping the vessels up their native stream,
Their wives and children waiting them at home
In joy, with festal preparation made,—
Think of these mariners, their eyes torn out,
Their hands chopped off, turn'd staggering into Ghent,
To meet the blasted eye-sight of their friends?
And was not this the Earl? 'Twas none but he!
No Hauterive of them all had dared to do it,
Save at the express instance of the Earl.
And now what asks he? Pardon me, sir knights;
[*To* GRUTT *and* BETTE.

I had forgotten, looking back and back
From felony to felony foregoing,
This present civil message which ye bring:
Three hundred citizens to be surrendered

Up to that mercy which I tell you of—
That mercy which your mariners proved—which steep'd
Courtray and Ypres, Grammont, Bruges, in blood!
Three hundred citizens,—a secret list—
No man knows who—not one can say he's safe—
Not one of you so humble but that still
The malice of some secret enemy
May whisper him to death—and hark—look to it!
Have some of you seem'd braver than their fellows,
Their courage is their surest condemnation;
They are marked men—and not a man stands here
But may be so.—Your pardon, sirs, again!

                             [*To* GRUTT *and* BETTE.

You are the pickers and the choosers here,
And doubtless you're all safe, ye think—ha! ha!
But we have pick'd and chosen, too, sir knights—
What was the law for I made yesterday—
What! is it you that would deliver up
Three hundred citizens to certain death?
Ho! Van den Bosch! have at these traitors—ha—

                            [*Stabs* GRUTT *who falls.*

VAN DEN BOSCH.

Die, treasonable dog—is that enough?
Down, felon, and plot treacheries in hell.

                             [*Stabs* BETTE.

> [*The* White-Hoods *draw their swords, with loud cries of* 'Treason,'
> 'Artevelde,' 'Ghent,' *and* 'The Chaperons Blancs.' *A citizen
> of the other party, who in the former part of the scene had
> unfurled the* Earl's *banner, now throws it down and flies; several
> others are following him, and the* Aldermen *and* Deans, *some
> of whom had been dropping off towards the end of* Artevelde's
> *speech, now quit the platform with precipitation.* VAN AESWYN
> *is crossed by* VAN DEN BOSCH.

VAN DEN BOSCH.

Die thou, too, traitor.

                             [*Aiming a blow at him.*

ARTEVELDE (*warding it off*).

Van den Bosch, forbear.
Up with your weapons, White-Hoods ; no more blood.
These only are the guilty who lie here.
Let no more blood be spilt on pain of death.
Sirs, ye have nought to fear ; I say, stand fast ;
No man shall harm you ; if he does, he dies.
Stand fast, or if ye go, take this word with you,
Philip Van Artevelde is friend with all ;
There's no man lives within the walls of Ghent
But Artevelde will look to him and his,
And suffer none to plunder or molest him.
Haste, Van den Bosch ! by Heav'n they run like lizards !
Take they not heart the sooner, by St. Paul
They'll fly the city, and that cripples us.
Haste with thy company to the west wards,
And see thou that no violence be done
Amongst the weavers and the fullers—stay—
And any that betake themselves to pillage
Hang without stint—and hark—begone—yet stay ;
Shut the west gate, postern and wicket too,
And catch my Lord of Occo where you can.
Stay—on thy life let no man's house be plundered.

VAN DEN BOSCH.

That is not to my mind ; but what of that ?
Thou'st play'd the game right boldly, and for me,
My oath of homage binds me to thee.

ARTEVELDE.

Well,
Thou to thy errand then, and I myself
Will go from street to street through all the town,

To reassure the citizens ; that done
I'll meet thee here again.   Form, White-Hoods, form :
Range ten abreast ; I'm coming down amongst you.
You Floris, Leefdale, Spanghen, mount ye here,
And bear me down these bodies.   Now, set forth.

> [*The* White-Hoods, *by whose shouts of ' Artevelde for Ghent' the
> latter part of the scene has been frequently interrupted, now join
> in a cry of triumph, and carry him off on their shoulders.*

ACT III.

Scene I.—*Night.   A Wood in the vicinity of Bruges.*

The Lord of Occo *and* Followers.

OCCO.

No more than half a league to Bruges ? then halt,
And let the men of arms be drawn together
Where the ground's open.   Berckel, ride thou on
And hail the warders on the walls ; make known
That for the love which we have shown the Earl
We're driven forth of Ghent, and humbly crave
His hospitality.

> [*To* Van Aeswyn, *who enters.*

Where is the lady ?

AESWYN.

They've dropp'd behind some furlong with the litter.

OCCO.

Keep thou beside her, lest she should prevail
To make the varlets speak.   Let none approach

After we pass the gates but men of mine,
Nor ever let the litter be unclosed.
Now, if we're all in order, march we on.

SCENE II.—*A Banquetting Hall in the Stadt-house at Bruges.
—Tables are spread, and the* EARL OF FLANDERS, *the* HASE
OF FLANDERS, *with several* Lords, Knights, *and* followers
of the EARL, *are entertained by the* Mayor *of Bruges and the*
Aldermen.

EARL.

Sir Mayor, we thank you ; 'tis a royal feast.

MAYOR.

My gracious lord, the supper is but poor ;
Very exceeding poor the supper is ;
And yet the most we can ; your humble hosts,
Being but meagre citizens God wot,
Can but purvey your highness what they have,
A very sorry supper.

ALDERMAN.

True indeed.
Yet if your highness please to cast it up,
A thousand florins—

MAYOR.

Hold thy peace, Van Holst ;
The minstrels twang their cat-gut.

EARL (*aside to the* HASE).

In good time.
If aught could make me cast my supper up,
'Twere to taste further of their courtesies.
Soho, sir minstrel ! what hast got to sing !

VAN HOLST.

That matter has been cared for, please your highness ;
We knew your highness had a skilful ear,
And 'twas not every poesy would please you.
This is a ditty craftily conceited,
Trump'd up as 'twere extempore for the nonce ;
He was no tavern cantabank that made it,
But a squire minstrel of your highness' court.
So—sing, sir minstrel—there you have it—ah !
Fal-lal—the very thing—the tune's ' Green Sleeves.'

THE MINSTREL SINGS.

The little bird sat on the greenwood tree,
And the sun was as bright as bright could be ;
The leaf was broad, the shade was deep,
The Lion of Flanders lay fast asleep.

The little bird sang, ' Sir Lion arise,
For I hear with my ears and I see with my eyes,
And I know what I know, and I tell thee this,
That the men of Ghent have done something amiss.'

From his lair the Lion of Flanders rose,
And he shook his mane and toss'd up his nose ;
' Ere a leaf be fallen or summer be spent,'
Quoth he, ' if God spare me, I'll go to Ghent.'

' For a little bird sang and I dream'd beside
That the people of Ghent were puff'd up with pride ;
And I had been far over hill and dale
And was fast asleep, and they trod on my tail.'

Ere a leaf was fallen the lion he went,
And growl'd a growl at the gates of Ghent ;
But they bended low when they saw him awake,
And said that they trod on his tail by mistake.

The little bird sat on the bush so bare,
And the leaf fell brown on the lion's lair ;
The little bird pick'd a berry so red,
And dropp'd it down on the lion's head.

' Sir Lion awake, and put out your claws,
And lift your chin from your tawny paws ;
My ears are smaller than yours, but more
I hear than you, and worse than before.'

The lion stirr'd and awoke with a snort,
And swell'd with rage till his breath came short;
'Ere the brown leaf meet with the flake of snow
On the roundabout stair, to Ghent I'll go.

' For a little bird sang, and I dream'd as well,
That the people of Ghent were as false as hell;
Coming by stealth when nought I fear'd,
They trod on my corns and pull'd my beard.'

Ere a snow-flake fell the lion he went,
And roar'd a roar at the gates of Ghent;
The gates they shook though they were fast barr'd,
And the warders heard it at Oudenarde.

At the first roar ten thousand men
Fell sick to death—he roar'd again,
And the blood of twenty thousand flow'd
On the bridge of Roone, as broad as the road.

Wo worth thee, Ghent! if, having heard
The first and second, thou bidest the third!
Flat stones and awry, grass, potsherd and shard,
Thy place shall be like an old churchyard.

EARL.

A singular good song, and daintily accompanied with
the music. Give him three florins, and a denier for the
lad withal.

VAN HOLST.

Your highness is too bountiful. He made it not
himself. 'Twas your highness's serjeant-minstrel that
made it. The making and mending of it together was
seven days and nights, bating twelve hours for sleeping,
and four hours for eating, and five minutes for saying
his prayers. Drinking never stopped him, for still the
more he drank, the more he made of it. And he ranted
and sang, an' it like your highness, that it would have
pleased you to hear him; for being that the song was
made in honour of your highness, he said he could
sing it a thousand times over and think better of it
every time.

EARL.

It is good poesy—marry and good prophecy too.
Hark ye, master mayor; I have some whit repented me
that I was wrought upon by those old Knights of Ghent
to proffer terms of such easy acquittance.

MAYOR.

When your highness is graciously pleased to give
away your advantages, it is not for such as I to say you
do wrong; but every man in Bruges, that is well
affected to your highness, said that three hundred heads
was too little.

EARL.

By my faith they said true; and Gilbert Matthew
told me no less; but I was persuaded by the old
Knights. I was too easy with them. Where is Gilbert
Matthew?

GILBERT.

Here, my lord.

EARL.

Come hither, Gilbert. I have bethought me, Gilbert,
I almost sinn'd against true chivalry
To let yon rabble off.

GILBERT.

Your highness says it.

EARL.

Thoud'st tell me 'twas not by thy counsel,—well.

GILBERT.

As many heads of each insurgent craft
Would not have been denied. A hundred nail'd
Like weasels to the gates of each wall'd town
Thorough the States of Flanders—that had been

A warning wholesome and significant
To the good towns.

EARL.

A salutary caution.
I would the bargain were to make again.
Why, so now! who comes here? the good Sir Walter.

Enter SIR WALTER D'ARLON.

D'Arlon, I never see thee but with joy.
What new adventure hast thou been upon?
We miss thee oft at court, but thy return
Is ever with new honours at thy heels.
What captives follow thee to Bruges to-night?
Or hast thou turn'd base metal into gold,
And bring'st their ransoms?—either way is well.

D'ARLON.

My lord, I come alone.

EARL.

Why, still thou'rt welcome.

D'ARLON.

Yet there is something following at my heels
Which hardly shall your highness in like sort
Make welcome here.

EARL.

Why, say'st thou? what is that?

D'ARLON.

Ill rumours, my good lord.

EARL.

And of what import?

D'ARLON.

The rebels are alive again and fresh.

The messengers of peace lie stabb'd to death
Upon the steps i' the market-place.

EARL.

>   Not so!
It cannot be,—D'Arlon, it must be false.

D'ARLON.

I fear, my lord, it will not so be found.

EARL.

Nay, nay,—so stripped of every thing—so bare
As we had made them—scarce a leader left,
And those that were so wild and scant of skill!

D'ARLON.

That were an ugly breach if not repair'd.
They've made young Artevelde their chief.

EARL.

>   God help them!
A man that as much knowledge has of war
As I of brewing mead!   God help their souls!
A bookish nursling of the monks—a meacock!

D'ARLON.

My lord, I'm fearful you mistake the man.
If my accounts be true, the life he's led
Served rather in its transit to eclipse
Than to show forth his nature; and, that pass'd,
You'll now behold him as he truly is,
One of a cold and of a constant mind,
Not quicken'd into ardent action soon,
Nor prompt for petty enterprise; yet bold,
Fierce when need is, and capable of all things.

EARL.

And hath he slain the knights?

D'ARLON.
　　　　　　With his own hand.

EARL.

I tell thee it is false; it cannot be.
Thou, Gilbert Matthew, how think'st thou o' the tale?

GILBERT.

My lord, it may be there's some stir at Ghent,
Which rumour, floating like a mist before,
Augments to this.

EARL.

　　　　　Thou deem'st it to be nothing.

GILBERT.

I deem of Ghent as of a fly in winter
That in a gleam of sunshine creeping forth
Kicks with stiff legs a feeble stroke or two
And falls upon its back.　My lord, 'tis nothing.

EARL.

Gilbert, thy wisdom never was at fault.
Thou art a comfortable councillor.
Sirrah, what tidings?

　　　　　　　　[To an Attendant who enters.

ATTENDANT.

　　　　　Sir, the Lord of Occo
Came with his men at arms before the walls.
Apprised that he was driven forth of Ghent,
The warders have admitted him, and here
He waits your pleasure.

EARL.

　　　　　Bid him in at once.
He comes like confirmation.　Oh Ghent! Ghent!
Oh ye ungracious people!

Enter the LORD OF OCCO.

Speak, Sir Guy.

Out with the worst, for I have guess'd it all.
Fame was here first as breathless as you are.

OCCO.

'Tis the worst fortune ever yet befel me
To be the bearer of this heavy news.
Our friends are slain, the White-Hoods hold the town,
And he, the homicide whose bloody hand
Despatch'd the peaceful knights, is lord of all.

EARL.

Oh that unhappy people! hear me, God!
Hear me ye host of heaven, and all good men!
If e'er I lift the wine-cup to my lips,
If ever other than a soldier's bed
Contain me, or if any pleasant sport
Inveigle off my heart while that town stands,
May I be driven from my royalties
To dwell with beasts like him that sinned of old!
Rise, sirs, and feast no more.   My Lord of Occo,
Such entertainment as such times afford
We'll give you.   Bid my chamberlain see to it.
Adieu, sirs; when the walls of Ghent lie flat
Our revel we resume.

D'ARLON.

Leave *me*, my lord,
The entertainment of your friends from Ghent.
My house will hold them.—[*Aside.*] Grant me this, my
    lord;
They need a supervisor.

EARL.

　　　　Good ;—Sir Guy,
Sir Walter D'Arlon is your host at Bruges.
Adieu, sirs ; come to council in the morning
You that are of it.　Stand aside, Sir Minstrel—
What, are you blind?　Good night, good night, adieu.

SCENE III.—*A Chamber in the* LORD OF ARLON's *House.* ADRIANA
　　VAN MERESTYN, *and three* Attendants *in the* LORD OF OCCO's
　　livery.

ADRIANA.

Where have ye brought me, Sirs?　What house is this?
Nay, must I ask for ever?　Wilt not speak?
Nor thou, nor thou?　If ye are bid be dumb,
But say ye are so and I'll ask no more.

FIRST ATTENDANT.

Madam, we are.

ADRIANA.

　　　　Who bid you?—Not a word?
If you're afraid to tell me, make a sign.
Was it the Lord of Occo?

　　　　　　　[*First* Attendant *shakes his head.*

　　　　'Twas not he.
Then whosoe'er enjoined it, send him here ;
Entreat him were it but for courtesy
To come to me.　He that hath tied your tongues
May loose them, or may hold his own unfettered.
I pray thee send him ; thou art not so rude,
To guess thee by thy mien, as this so slight,
So slender service to deny me—no—
Or else thou wear'st a mask.

　　　　[*The first* Attendant *goes out. She turns aside from the others.*

                              Befriend me now,
Heart, head, and tongue ; be bold, be wise, be ready !
Oh for some potion that for one hour's space
Should make me twice myself !

                    Enter VAN AESWYN.

        AESWYN (*to the* Attendants).
                              Depart the chamber.
                              [*Exeunt the* Attendants.

                    ADRIANA.
Master Van Aeswyn !

                    AESWYN.
                    Madam !

                    ADRIANA.
                              It is thou
That thus abusest me !

                    AESWYN.
                    I, Madam !   No.
I have done nothing ; if a wrong there be,
It lies with others ; I have but obeyed
Whom I am bound to serve.

                    ADRIANA.
                              Alas ! thy guilt
Is but more abject, being ministrant
Unto another's, and thyself no less
Accountable to Heaven.   His lust and greed
Whom thou abettest thou dost make thine own,
And nothing gett'st but wages of thy service
To pay thy sin.   What ! is't not shame on shame !
Thou puttest thine immortal soul to sale
For profit of another, thy reward
Being the sorry guerdon of a squire

With blot and stain of such addition vile
Of countenance and favour, bred of guilt,
As he that uses thee may please to show thee:
Favour, that coming from so soiled a source,
And for such soil of service, if well weighed,
Less of reward than punishment should taste,
And less of honourable show should wear,
Than show of reprehension.   Thou to stamp
A gentle name with stigma of such deeds!
Oh curse of bad men's hire!

AESWYN.

      Nay, madam, nay;
'Tis not for hire, neither for countenance:
But I have taken service with this lord,
And by the law of arms—

ADRIANA.

      What law is that?
'Tis not the law of God, nor yet above it.

AESWYN.

An honest squire is bound by plighted faith,
And by the law of arms, to execute
His lord's behests.

ADRIANA.

     Though they be base and foul?
Oh Sin! what thread or filament so fine
Of casual consent, of compact void,
Slipt in betwixt ' God save you ' and ' good morrow,'
That's not a warrant of authority
To bind a man to thee! to thee, glib Sin!
But Virtue! where is that indissolute chain
Which to thy anchored mandaments eterne

I

The floating soul shall grapple!   Law of arms!
Grant 'twere that law supernal it is not,
Yet dost thou break it : for all wrongs to women
Stand in its code denounced.

AESWYN.

                     By all that's just,
The deed misliked me from the first; three times
I prayed his lordship to bethink himself
What quittance he should hazard and what blame,
In wronging of so rich and good a lady;
But still he said the Earl should bring him through
Let come what might; insisting that by law
You were in wardship, and His Grace might grant
Your hand to whom was fittest.

ADRIANA.

                     Oh blind craft!
Oh frail inventions of humanity!
Me shall no earthly prince nor potentate
Toss like a morsel of his broken meat
To any supplicant.   Be they advised
I am in wardship to the King of Kings;
God and my heart alone dispose of me.

AESWYN.

Madam, I would it were so.

ADRIANA.

                     Say besides
The Earl should cast the mantle of his power
Over thy master, what shall cover thee,
That canst not borrow greatness for the cloak
Of evil deeds, from naked, manifest shame?
Lo, here I stand in jeopardy and fear,

Weak, trembling, sick at heart, and wearied so
With perturbation, and with pain so racked,
That I have lost my patience, and for hours
Have pray'd for God's deliverance through death ;
Yet rather would I, yea, far rather, live
A dateless life of anguish such as this ;
Rather live out my reason thus, and twist
For restless years upon a bed-rid couch
With the sole sense of dotage and distress
Than change with thee and take upon my soul
Thy forfeiture, and lodge within my breast
That worm of memory which to-day shall breed,
And which upon thy death-bed shall not die,
But being of the soul, shall be immortal !
Go—God forgive thee ! for not mine the heart
That would invoke a curse.

AESWYN.

                       Lady, I swear
I bore a part not willingly in this ;
And could I, without ruin of my fortunes, ·
Do aught that should redeem it——

ADRIANA.

                       For thy fortunes
Trust them to me.

Enter one of the Attendants.

ATTENDANT.

            My lord is at the gate,
And asks for you.   ·   [*Exit.*

ADRIANA.

            I say, trust them to me ;
Do to thyself the justice to renounce

I 2

This false knight's service, and to me one act
Of loyalty : seek out with instant haste
The Lord of Arlon ; tell him I am here
In tribulation, and beseech his aid,
And bid him by the love he bears his lady,
To grant it me with speed.   Wilt thou do this ?

AESWYN.

Madam, I will.

ADRIANA.

                    Go now then to thy lord,
Lest he suspect thy tarriance.   I, meanwhile,
Will to the inner chamber make retreat,
Where I shall watch and pray till shall be seen
The issue of thine errand.   Hark ! they call thee.

SCENE IV.—*An Ante-chamber in the Earl's Palace.*

SIR WALTER D'ARLON *and* GILBERT MATTHEW.

GILBERT.

No sooner had his highness reach'd the palace
Than he sends back for me.

D'ARLON.

                    And me the same.

GILBERT.

His highness is not happy.

D'ARLON.

                    That is likely ;
But have you any private cause to think it?

GILBERT.

I have observed that when he is not happy
He sends for me.

D'ARLON.

And do you mend his mood?

GILBERT.

Nay, what I can. His highness at such times
Is wishful to be counsell'd to shed blood.

D'ARLON.

'Tis said that he is counsell'd oft to that.

GILBERT.

It is my duty to advise his highness
With neither fear nor favour. As I came,
The bodies of three citizens lay stretch'd
Upon the causeway.

D'ARLON.

How had they been kill'd?

GILBERT.

By knocking on the head.

D'ARLON.

And who had done it?

GILBERT.

The officers that walk'd before the Earl
To make him room to pass. The streets were full,
And many of the mean-crafts roam'd about
Discoursing of the news they heard from Ghent;
And as his highness pass'd they misbehaved,
And three were knock'd upon the head with staves.
I knew by that his highness was not happy.
I knew I should be sent for.

Enter an Usher *from an inner chamber.*

USHER.

Ho! Master Gilbert Matthew to his highness.

[*Re-enters the chamber, followed by* GILBERT MATTHEW.

D'ARLON.

There's some men of their bloody counsels boast,
As though the heart were difficult to harden.

Enter an Attendant.

ATTENDANT.

My lord, a gentleman has come in haste
To seek you.   I inform'd him you were here
In waiting on his highness, but he still
Insisted you would see him, did you know
The matter and its urgency.

D'ARLON.

His name?

ATTENDANT.

Van Aeswyn.

D'ARLON.

What! Sir Guy of Occo's squire?

ATTENDANT.

The same, my lord.

D'ARLON.

Yes, yes, the man I know,
But not the matter that he hath with me ;—
Unless it be some difference with my steward
About his quarters.   Bring me where he waits.

SCENE V.—*A Chamber in the Earl's Palace.*

The EARL *and* GILBERT MATTHEW.

EARL.

And thus, if all that we have heard be true,
Last night's ill news this morning somewhat betters.
There's reason to surmise these granaries
Were not destroy'd by chance, and the same hand
Which did us this good service may do more.
Meantime we'll pray Duke Aubert and the bishop
To let no victual pass their lands to Ghent.

GILBERT.

You shall do well, my lord. I know that people.
No poison works so wastingly amongst them
As a low diet—yea, it brings them down.
There'll be a hundred thousand mouths in Ghent
Gaping like callow jackdaws. Ah! I know them.
The men of battle are full feeders all;
By the strong hand they live, and help themselves
With griping of the rest. When famine comes,
'Tis worse to those, seeing that theretofore
They were too gross of body, worse to these,
For they were pinch'd already.

EARL.
That is true.

GILBERT.

Yea, sir, I know the White-Hoods. Wait awhile,
And when they feel the vulture in their gut
They shall be busy whetting of their beaks.

Wait till they hunger, and not two in Ghent
Shall be of one opinion.

EARL.

In God's time
Distress shall breed dissensions as thou say'st.
We'll trust to that, and therefore have great heed
To block them out from access of provision.
The country is well wasted thereabouts,
And what they get must travel far to reach them.
We must shut up the roads from Liege and Brabant.

Enter the LORD OF ARLON.

D'ARLON.

My lord, I do beseech you make me quit
Of Occo for my guest, and give us leave
For instant combat.

EARL.

Walter, art thou mad?
What is thy quarrel with the Lord of Occo?
He is since yesterday, with thy good leave,
Our very worthy friend.

D'ARLON.

My lord, my lord,
He is since yesterday, if not before,
The very lewdest villain that was e'er
A blur and stain to knighthood.

EARL.

Say'st thou so?
What are thy reasons?

D'ARLON.

With a violent hand
He carried off from Ghent a noble lady,

Whose honour he attempted yesternight
Beneath my roof: and here on her behalf,
And on my own, your highness I entreat
That you give order to have lists prepared,
Where I may meet the miscreant spear to spear,
And do God's will upon him.

EARL.

        Soft, my son;
I'll have no fighting for a private cause
Till Ghent be down.   I cannot spare a spear,
And this were but a childish cause at best
For breaking one.   The honest dames of Ghent
Have scarce deserved protection at our hands;
And when the time shall come, as come it will,
That Ghent is storm'd and sack'd, they'll have no more
Than their deserts: free quarters shall they give
To lusty knight, hot squire, and man at arms.
Shall they not, Gilbert?

GILBERT.

        Sir, the dames of Ghent
Must look for worse than what your highness hints.

EARL.   ·

Why then my Lord of Occo sinn'd not much
To seize occasion by the forelock,—ha?

GILBERT.

My lord, he did but what was just and right.

D'ARLON.

Peace, Master Gilbert Matthew—stand apart;
I seek an audience direct and free,

No craft of juggling renegade betwixt
To interpose, and toss me to and fro
The words that please him or that please him not.
My lord, you know what service I have done,
And with what voluntary heart, not bound
By duty or allegiance to bear arms,
For in my native land the while was peace.
I scarce am call'd a man, and service yet
I count by years, nor leave a winter out.
I was the nursling of your camp, my lord,
And play'd with weapons, ere my hands had strength
To lift an iron basnet to my head.
The war-horse neigh'd to see me when my legs
His breadth of back bestrided scarce aslope,
And rarely hath it been from that time forth
That I have housed when men at arms were mounted.
This it befits not me to say, my lord,
Save for the just conclusion: I entreat
That if it square not with your purposes
To grant the combat which I claim with Occo,
I then have leave to fold my banner up,   ,
And quit your camp.

EARL.

          Come, Walter, come, you're idle;
When cause and opportunity are rife
For reasonable fighting, we might well
Dispense with all knight-errantry.   Enough;
See the moon out, and if thy humour hold
It shall have way; the next that shines, I trust,
Shall cast upon the batter'd walls of Ghent
A thorough light.

D'ARLON.

And if I live to see it
I'll claim the combat.   Fare you well, my lord.
                                        [*Exit.*

EARL.

Was ever man, with denizens for foes
And foreigners for friends, so plagued as I !
My bravest knight would cast away his life
To do me a disservice, with more zeal
Than he was used to serve me with : denied,
Straight he shall tell me he was born elsewhere
And owes me no allegiance.

GILBERT.

                          By your leave,
I could not wish your highness better fortune,
Than that the fools you count amongst your friends
Were number'd with your foes,—or with the dead.

Enter Attendant.

ATTENDANT.

According to the summons, please your highness,
The Lords are met in council.

EARL.

                          I shall come.
Attend me, Gilbert, when the board breaks up,
And thou shalt know the issue.   Come to dinner.
And sirrah, tell the butler that to-day
I shall drink brandy.   From all use of wine
I'm interdicted by a sacred vow,
Till Ghent's submission free me.   May't be soon !

ACT IV.

SCENE I.—GHENT.—*The platform at the top of the steeple of St. Nicholas' Church.—Time, day-break.*

ARTEVELDE.

There lies a sleeping city.   God of dreams!
What an unreal and fantastic world
Is going on below!
Within the sweep of yon encircling wall
How many a large creation of the night,
Wide wilderness and mountain, rock and sea,
Peopled with busy transitory groups,
Finds room to rise, and never feels the crowd!
—If when the shows had left the dreamers' eyes
They should float upward visibly to mine,
How thick with apparitions were that void!
But now the blank and blind profundity
Turns my brain giddy with a sick aversion.
—I have not slept.   I am to blame for that.
Long vigils, join'd with scant and meagre food,
Must needs impair that promptitude of mind,
And cheerfulness of spirit, which in him
Who leads a multitude, is past all price.
I think I could redeem an hour's repose
Out of the night that I have squander'd, yet.
The breezes, launch'd upon their early voyage,
Play with a pleasing freshness on my face.
I will enfold my cloak about my limbs

And lie where I shall front them;—here, I think.

[*He lies down.*

If this were over——blessed be the calm
That comes to me at last!   A friend in need
Is nature to us, that when all is spent,
Brings slumber——bountifully——whereupon
We give her sleepy welcome——if all this
Were honourably over——Adriana—

[*Falls asleep, but starts up almost instantly.*

I heard a hoof, a horse's hoof I'll swear,
Upon the road from Bruges,—or did I dream?
No! 'tis the gallop of a horse at speed.

VAN DEN BOSCH (*without*).

What ho! Van Artevelde!

ARTEVELDE.
Who calls?

VAN DEN BOSCH (*entering*).
'Tis I.

Thou art an early riser, like myself;
Or is it that thou hast not been to bed?

ARTEVELDE.
What are thy tidings?

VAN DEN BOSCH.
Nay, what can they be?

A page from pestilence and famine's day-book;
So many to the pest-house carried in,
So many to the dead-house carried out.
The same dull, dismal, damnable old story.

ARTEVELDE.
Be quiet; listen to the westerly wind,
And tell me if it bring thee nothing new.

VAN DEN BOSCH.

Nought to my ear, save howl of hungry dog
That hears the house is stirring—nothing else.

ARTEVELDE.

No,—now—I hear it not myself—no—nothing.
The city's hum is up—but ere you came
'Twas audible enough.

VAN DEN BOSCH.

          In God's name what?

ARTEVELDE.

A horseman's tramp upon the road from Bruges.

VAN DEN BOSCH.

Why then be certain, 'tis a flag of truce!
If once he reach the city we are lost.
Nay, if he be but seen, our danger's great.
What terms so bad they would not swallow now?
Let's send some trusty varlets forth at once
To cross his way.

ARTEVELDE.

          And send him back to Bruges?

VAN DEN BOSCH.

Send him to hell—and that's a better place.

ARTEVELDE.

Nay, softly, Van den Bosch; let war be war,
But let us keep its ordinances.

VAN DEN BOSCH.

                    Tush!
I say, but let them see him from afar,
And in an hour shall we, bound hand and foot,
Be on our way to Bruges.

ARTEVELDE.

Not so, not so.
My rule of governance has not been such
As e'er to issue in so foul a close.

VAN DEN BOSCH.

What matter by what rule thou may'st have govern'd?
Think'st thou a hundred thousand citizens
Shall stay the fury of their empty maws
Because thou'st ruled them justly?

ARTEVELDE.

       It may be
That such a hope is mine.

VAN DEN BOSCH.

     Then thou art mad,
And I must take this matter on myself. [*Is going.*

ARTEVELDE.

Hold, Van den Bosch; I say this shall not be.
I must be madder than I think I am
Ere I shall yield up my authority,
Which I abuse not, to be used by thee.

VAN DEN BOSCH.

This comes of lifting dreamers into power.
I tell thee, in this strait and stress of famine,
The people, but to pave the way for peace,
Would instantly despatch our heads to Bruges.
Once and again I warn thee that thy life
Hangs by a thread.

ARTEVELDE.

   Why, know I not it does?
What hath it hung by else since Utas' eve?

Did I not by mine own advised choice
Place it in jeopardy for certain ends?
And what were these?   To prop thy tottering state?
To float thee o'er a reef, and, that perform'd,
To cater for our joint security?
No, verily; not such my high ambition.
I bent my thoughts on yonder city's weal;
I look'd to give it victory and freedom;
And working to that end, by consequence
From one great peril did deliver thee—
Not for the love of thee or of thy life,
Which I regard not, but the city's service;
And if for that same service it seem good
I will expose thy life to equal hazard.

VAN DEN BOSCH.

Thou wilt?

ARTEVELDE.

  I will.

VAN DEN BOSCH.

    Oh, Lord! to hear him speak,
What a most mighty emperor of puppets
Is this that I have brought upon the board!
But how if he that made it should unmake?

ARTEVELDE.

Unto His sovereignty who truly made me
With infinite humility I bow!
Both, both of us are puppets, Van den Bosch;
Part of the curious clock-work of this world,
We scold and squeak and crack each other's crowns;
And if by twitches moved from wires we see not,
I were to toss thee from this steeple's top,

I should be but the instrument—no more—
The tool of that chastising Providence
Which doth exalt the lowly and abase
The violent and proud: but let me hope
There's no such task appointed me to-day.
Thou passest in the world for worldly wise :
Then seeing we must sink or swim together,
What can it profit thee, in this extreme
Of our distress, to wrangle with me thus
For my supremacy and rule?   Thy fate,
As of necessity bound up with mine,
Must needs partake my cares : let that suffice
To put thy pride to rest till better times.
Contest—more reasonably wrong—a prize
More precious than the ordering of a shipwreck.

VAN DEN BOSCH.

Tush, tush, Van Artevelde ; thou talk'st and talk'st,
And honest burghers think it wondrous fine.
But thou might'st easilier with that tongue of thine
Persuade yon smoke to fly i' th' face o' the wind
Than talk away my wit and understanding.
I say yon herald shall not enter here.

ARTEVELDE.

I know, sir, no man better, where my talk
Is serviceable singly, where it needs
To be by acts enforced.   I say, beware,
And brave not mine authority too far.

VAN DEN BOSCH.

Hast thou authority to take my life?
What is it else to let yon herald in
To bargain for our blood ?

K

ARTEVELDE.

Thy life again !
Why what a very slave of life art thou!
Look round about on this once populous town;
Not one of these innumerous house-tops
But hides some spectral form of misery,
Some peevish pining child and moaning mother,
Some aged man that in his dotage scolds
Not knowing why he hungers, some cold corse
That lies unstraightened where the spirit left it.
Look round and answer what thy life can be
To tell for more than dust upon the balance.
I too would live—I have a love for life—
But rather than to live to charge my soul
With one hour's lengthening out of woes like these,
I'd leap this parapet with as free a bound
As e'er was school-boy's o'er a garden wall.

VAN DEN BOSCH.

I'd like to see thee do it.

ARTEVELDE.

I know thou wouldst;
But for the present be content to see
My less precipitate descent; for lo!
There comes the herald o'er the hill.

[*Exit.*

VAN DEN BOSCH.

Beshrew thee !
Thou shalt not have the start of me in this.

[*He follows, and the scene closes.*

SCENE II.—*The House Van Artevelde.*

URSEL, VAN RYK, *and* VAN MUCK.

URSEL.

He will be here for his breakfast anon.

VAN RYK.

And call you this his breakfast?

URSEL.

An ounce of horseflesh and half an oaten cake. It is his only meal; and if I were to make it larger, he would ne'er look at it.

VAN MUCK.

Why we ourselves fare better.

VAN RYK.

I fare somewhat better, and for thee, thou wouldst make a famine where there was none. No more than this morsel of meat in four-and-twenty hours!

URSEL.

No more; and if he hath been abroad, 'tis more than likely that he shall bring home some little child, or some sick woman to share it with him.

VAN RYK.

It is wonderful how stout he is withal. Some men shall but bite their nails and their belly's full.

VAN MUCK.

There is a difference in men; I might eat the four hoofs of an ox and my stomach should droop you, look you, and flap you, look you, like an empty sail. Here he comes.

K 2

Enter ARTEVELDE.

ARTEVELDE.

A herald, sirs, is coming here from Bruges.
To horse, Van Muck, to horse, with Swink and Kloos,
And any other of thy readiest men,
And bring him safely in.   What ails thee, man?

VAN MUCK.

Sir, saving your displeasure, Swink and Kloos
Against your express orders, and despite
Of much I said myself, have eat their horses.

ARTEVELDE.

Thou sayest not so ; God's vengeance on their stomachs!
Next horse they kill, my cook shall serve it up,
And melt the shoes for sauce.
To horse thyself, then, with what men are mounted,
And see that no mishap befal the herald.

VAN MUCK.

Sir, at your pleasure.

ARTEVELDE.

                    And beware, Van Muck.
Some there may be of evil-minded men
Who would do outrage to the city's honour,
And harm the herald.   Look thou keep him safe.

VAN MUCK.

Sir, safe he shall be, whosoe'er would harm him.

[*Exit.*

CLARA *enters, but remains behind.*

ARTEVELDE.

And now, Van Ryk, I have a charge for thee.
Thou in the porch of Old St. Nicholas' Church

Art to mount guard beside the postern-gate
Which leads upon the stair that climbs the steeple.
Betake thee thither, and until I come,
Inward or outward let none pass the wicket.
[*Turning to* CLARA.]   How fares my sister? nay—come
hither, Clara.

CLARA.

No nearer, Philip, for I breathe contagion.

ARTEVELDE.

What, com'st thou from the hospital?

CLARA.

Straight thence.
God help me for a pestilent little fool!
I tend the sick from weary day to day,
Though Heaven has set its face against a cure,
And they that should have thank'd me for my pains
Will never more speak word.

ARTEVELDE.

Thou heed'st not that.
No, I am certain 'tis for no man's thanks
That thou hast toil'd; and let them live or die,
Thou hast thine own reward.
Much hast thou merited, my sister dear,
Since these disastrous times have fallen upon us.
In easier hours it may be I had cause
This time or that, to wish thy boldness less,
Though trusting still that time, which tempers all,
Would bring thee soberer thoughts and tame thy heart.
What time to tardy consummation brings,
Calamity, most like a frosty night
That ripeneth the grain, completes at once.
But now that we're alone,——not gone, Van Ryk?

VAN RYK.

Sir, to speak freely, had it been your pleasure
To put me to a service of more action,
I had not sham'd the choice; for though I'm old,—

ARTEVELDE.

Tut, tut, Van Ryk; 'twill come, the time will come,
And action to thy heart's content thou'lt have.

[Exit VAN RYK.

Now render me account of what befel,
Where thou hast been to-day.

CLARA.

It is but little.
I paid a visit first to Ukenheim,
The man who whilome saved our father's life,
When certain Clementists and ribald folk
Assail'd him at Malines. He came last night,
And said he knew not if we owed him aught,
But if we did, a peck of oatmeal now
Would pay the debt, and save more lives than one.
I went. It seem'd a wealthy man's abode;
The costly drapery and good house-gear
Had, in an ordinary time, betokened
That with the occupant the world went well.
By a low couch, curtain'd with cloth of frieze,
Sat Ukenheim, a famine-stricken man,
With either bony fist upon his knees,
And his long back upright. His eyes were fix'd
And mov'd not, though some gentle words I spake:
Until a little urchin of a child
That call'd him father, crept to where he sat
And pluck'd him by the sleeve, and with its small
And skinny finger pointed: then he rose,

And with a low obeisance, and a smile
That look'd like watery moonlight on his face,
So pale and weak a smile, he bade me welcome.
I told him that a lading of wheat-flour
Was on its way, whereat, to my surprise,
His countenance fell, and he had almost wept.

ARTEVELDE.

Poor soul! and wherefore?

CLARA.

That I soon perceived.
He pluck'd aside the curtain of the couch,
And there two children's bodies lay composed.
They seem'd like twins of some ten years of age,
And they had died so nearly both together
He scarce could say which first: and being dead,
He put them, for some fanciful affection,
Each with its arm about the other's neck,
So that a fairer sight I had not seen
Than those two children, with their little faces
So thin and wan, so calm, and sad, and sweet.
I look'd upon them long, and for a while
I wish'd myself their sister, and to lie
With them in death as they did with each other;
I thought that there was nothing in the world
I could have lov'd so much; and then I wept.
And when he saw I wept, his own tears fell,
And he was sorely shaken and convulsed,
Through weakness of his frame and his great grief.

ARTEVELDE.

Much pity was it he so long deferred
To come to us for aid.

CLARA.

It was indeed.
But whatsoe'er had been his former pride,
He seem'd a humbled and heart-broken man.
He thank'd me much for what I said was sent;
But I knew well his thanks were for my tears.
He look'd again upon the children's couch,
And said, low down, they wanted nothing now.
So, to turn off his eyes,
I drew the small survivor of the three
Before him, and he snatched it up, and soon
Seemed quite forgetful and absorbed.   With that
I stole away.

ARTEVELDE.

There is a man by fate
Fitted for any enterprise of danger.
Alas! of many such I have the choice.
Well; next thou passedst to the hospital?

CLARA.

With Father John; but here he comes himself,
Doubtless to bring you tidings of the sick.

Enter FATHER JOHN OF HEDA.

ARTEVELDE.

What cheer, good father?

FATHER JOHN.

Heavy is my cheer;
What else but heavy, when from day to day
I see still more of suffering sinking men
Pass to the chok'd church-yard.

ARTEVELDE.
                                    Truly the sight
Must needs bring on a heaviness of cheer.
I am to blame to think of that no sooner.
Who waits?   Too many things conspire—who waits?

Enter Steward.

Repair thee to the captains of the guards,
And give my orders that from this time forth
No funerals be allow'd till after dark.

                                    [*Exit* Steward.

And so the sickness spreads?

FATHER JOHN.
                                    It spreads apace.
Since Egypt's plagues did never rage disease
So sore, and so invincible by art,
So varied in its forms, and in its signs
So unintelligibly strange : in some
The fever keeps its course from first to last;
In others intermits : here suddenly
The patient's head is seized with racking pains ;
Then shift they to his chest, with change as quick,
Then to his loins, and strangury succeeds,
With clammy sweat, hard breathing, and hot thirst ;
The intervals of pain, if such there be,
Afford him no repose, but he is still
Dejected, restless, of a hopeless mind,
Indifferent to all incidents and objects,
Or in his understanding too confused
To see or apprehend them : first the face
Is red and flush'd, with large and fiery eyes ;
Then is it dropsical and deathy pale.
Sometimes such shudderings seize upon the frame

That the bed shakes beneath it, and with that
The breath is check'd with sobbings as from cold ;
Then comes a thick dark crust upon the lips,
And tongue, and teeth ; the fatal hiccough next.
Some die in struggles and strong agonies ;
Some in a lethargy ; whilst others wake
As from a dream, shake off the fit, look round,
And with collected senses and calm speech
Tell the by-standers that their hour is come.

ARTEVELDE.

It is a dismal malady, and this,
Like all our thousand miseries beside,
Demands a remedy that kills or cures.
What wild beasts' yells are these ?
                    [*Tumult and shouting without. The* Page *enters.*
                                        Henry, what news ?

PAGE.

The man from Bruges, escorted by Van Muck,
Is coming here, with crowds of people wild
To hear what message he may bring.   Van Muck
Forbids that any word should pass his lips
Till he have speech of you.

ARTEVELDE.
                            Van Muck is right.

PAGE.

But oh ! you never saw such wrathful men !
They'll tear them both to pieces.

ARTEVELDE.
                                Have no fear.
Van Muck will make his way.   Aye, here they come.

Enter VAN MUCK *and* VAN AESWYN.

What! this the messenger? now by the rood!
Either mine eyes are treacherous as himself,
Or else I see a follower of that false
Dishonour'd knight, and perjured knave, Van Occo.
How is it, if he dares to send thee here,
That thou hast dared to come?

AESWYN.

       Under your favour
The Lord of Occo——

ARTEVELDE.

      Grant me but a day
After the siege—Furies and Fates!—one day,
To hunt that poisonous reptile to his hole
And stamp my heel upon his recreant neck!
What dost thou here?

AESWYN.

      I come not here from him,
For since he made his war upon a damsel,
I have renounced his service; more than that,
I to the Lord of Arlon did that errand
Which wrought to her deliverance.

ARTEVELDE.

       Aha!
I crave your pardon. I had heard 'twas you,
Though it escaped me. Tell your tale; but first
What tidings of that lady?

AESWYN.

      She remains
By her own will, sir, in the knightly hands
Of my good Lord of Arlon.

ARTEVELDE.

Say no more;
Elsewhere I would not wish her.

[*The tumult increases without, and* ARTEVELDE'S *name is called repeatedly.*

Let me now
Dismiss this noisy and impatient herd
That throng my doors, and then—ho! hark ye, steward,
Conduct Van Aeswyn to my private chamber.

[*Exeunt all but* ARTEVELDE *and* CLARA.

My Clara, we have here a busy day;
Perhaps I shall not see thee, love, again
Till after night-fall; but I will not lose
Thy good-night kiss, so give it to me now.

CLARA.

Philip, there's something in your thoughts . . . but no—
I will not tease you—there—good night—Adieu.

[*Exit* CLARA. *The clamour without increases.* ARTEVELDE *passes into an external gallery, which overlooks the street, and is heard addressing the people.*

ARTEVELDE.

Hence to the Stadt-house, friends; I'll meet you there,
And either bring the messenger himself,
Or tell you of his tidings: hence—begone.

[*The people disperse.*

Van Occo, thou art in thine own despite
The mainstay of my hope. I have within
Assurance strong as destiny that I,
And I alone, a mission have from Heaven
To execute God's justice upon thee. .
And Adriana! Through the storm-rent cloud
A glorious light upon thy figure falls
Which walks the waters, stately and serene,
And beckons me, and points what course to keep.

SCENE III.—*Before the Stadt-House, as in the last Scene of the Second Act.—The people assemble.* FRANS ACKERMAN *and* PETER VAN NUITRE *in front.*

ACKERMAN.

'Tis certain something hath befallen him.

VAN NUITRE.

But where?   He might be found, if so it were.

ACKERMAN.

Hast sought him at Jozyne's estaminet?

VAN NUITRE.

There, and at every lodgment in the city.
Old mother Van Den Bosch was confident
He went forth early to Van Artevelde's.

ACKERMAN.

Sure nothing can have happen'd to him there.

VAN NUITRE.

That's what I doubt.   The best will have their failings.
They were not in such unison of mind
As might have been desired.

ACKERMAN.

                               I cannot think it.
But this day's business shall no farther go
Until the truth appear.   Soft! now he comes.

[VAN ARTEVELDE *enters. There is a dead silence. He walks, slowly and with a mournful appearance, up the steps of the platform.*

ARTEVELDE.

Are we all here?

ONE FROM THE CROWD.

                          What's left of us is here,
Our bones.

ARTEVELDE.

We're wasted in the flesh, 'tis true ;
But we have spirits left.   We all are here.

ACKERMAN.

I will say nay to that.   Where's Van Den Bosch ?

ARTEVELDE.

Silence ! Frans Ackerman ; we want not him.

ACKERMAN.

Then I demand if he be dead or living.

ARTEVELDE.

He lives.

ACKERMAN.

Where is he, then ?

ARTEVELDE.

Where all shall be
Who seek, by mutiny against their chief,
To do unlawful deeds.   What ask ye more ?
He is arrested and confined.

ACKERMAN.

What cause
For this proceeding hath that brave man given ?

ARTEVELDE.

If, as his friend, thou ask wherein he erred,
I'll tell it to this people and to thee,—
Not, mark you me, as rendering account,
For that were needless,—but of free good-will.
Sirs, Van Den Bosch insisted, in despite
Of all dissuasion, all authority,
The messenger from Bruges should be waylaid

And put to death—yea, nothing less would serve,—
That so the tidings which I'm here to tell
Might never reach your ears.　To place restraint
Upon this obstinate humour, and give scope
To your deliberations, for awhile
He is in duress.　Are ye well content?

MANY VOICES.

Content, content.　The tidings, what are they?

ARTEVELDE.

Frans Ackerman, thou hear'st what cause constrained
Me, much reluctant, thus to use thy friend.
Art thou content?

ACKERMAN.

　　　I am.

ARTEVELDE.

　　　　　So far is well.
And we set forth unanimous, to end
I trust no otherwise.　Fair sirs of Ghent!
Van Aeswyn, the ambassador from Bruges,
Comes with credentials from the earl, to show
What mind he bears toward you.　Bitterer words
Did never Christian man to Christians send.
But we are fallen, my friends, and vain it were
For us to quarrel with the proud man's scorn.
Then to the matter take ye heed alone,
And trouble not your hearts for aught beside.
He will admit you to no terms but these,—
That every man and woman born in Ghent
Shall meet him on the road, half way to Bruges,
Bare-footed, and bare-headed, in their shirts,
With halters on their necks, and there kneel down,

And place their lives and chattels at his mercy.
This if ye do not now, he's sworn an oath
That he will never hearken to you more,
But famine shall consume you utterly,
And in your desolate town he'll light a flame
That shall not be extinguished.   Speak your minds.
Will ye accept the proffer'd terms, or no?

BURGHERS.

Give us your counsel.   Tell us what is best.

ARTEVELDE.

What can I say?   You know that as you are
You cannot live.   Death opens every door,
And sits in every chamber by himself.
If what might feed a sparrow should suffice
For soldiers' meals, ye have not wherewithal
To linger out three days.   For corn, there's none;
A mouse imprison'd in your granaries
Were starved to death.   And what then should I say?
Why truly this: that whatsoe'er men's plight
There is a better and a worser way,
If their discretion be not overthrown
By force of their calamities.   Three things
Ye have to choose of.   You may take his terms,
And go with halters round your necks to Loo.
You will be then his servants and his wealth,
The labourers of his vineyard; and I deem,
Although a haughty lord he be and cruel,
That he will have the sense to spare his own,
When vengeance hath been fed.   I say I deem
That when the blood of those that led you on
And of their foremost followers hath flowed,

He will be satiate and stay his hand.
If this to try be your deliberate choice,
I will not say that ye be ill-advised.
How are ye minded?   Let your Deacons speak.

[*The people speak in consultation with each other and with the* Deacons.

DEACON OF THE MARINERS.

We of the mariners' craft approve the counsel.

DEACON OF THE CORDWAINERS.

There's nothing better can be done.

DEACON OF THE FULLERS.

Agreed.

Our craft was never forward in the war.

DEACON OF THE WEAVERS.

But, Master Philip, said you not three ways
There were to choose of?   Tell us what remains.

ARTEVELDE.

You may have patience and expect the close.
If nothing else seem fit, betake yourselves
Unto your churches; at the altar's foot
Kneel down and pray, and make a Christian end,
And God will then have mercy on your souls.
This is the second way.

DEACON OF THE WEAVERS.

And what the third ?

ARTEVELDE.

If there be found amongst you men whose blood
Runs not so chilly yet as thus to die,
Then there's this third way open—but not else.
That they whose plight is best and hearts are stout
Be mustered suddenly, equipped and armed;

L

That with our little left of food and wine
The sumpter beasts be laden for their use ;
That then they follow me : to-morrow's eve
Should find us knocking at the gates of Bruges,
And then we'd strike a stroke for life or death.
This is the third and sole remaining course.
Choose of the three.

MANY VOICES.

Choose for us, Master Philip :
You are more wise than we.

ARTEVELDE.

If by my choice
Ye will abide—a soldier's death for me !

A GREAT MANY VOICES.

To Bruges, to Bruges ; a venture forth to Bruges.

ARTEVELDE.

Why yet, then, in our embers there is life !
Let whosoe'er would follow me, repair
To the West Port.   Five thousand will I choose
From them that come, if there should be so many :
And when night falls, we'll sally from the gates.

MANY CITIZENS AGAIN.

For Bruges ! for Bruges ! 'tis gallantly resolved.

ARTEVELDE.

Then fare ye well, ye citizens of Ghent !
This is the last time you will see me here,
Unless God prosper me past human hope.
I thank you for the dutiful demeanour
Which never—no not once—in any of you
Have I found wanting, though severely tried
When discipline might seem without reward.

Fortune has not been kind to me, good friends;
But let not that deprive me of your loves,
Or of your good report.   Be this the word;
My rule was brief, calamitous—but just.
No glory which a prosperous fortune gilds,
If shorn of this addition, could suffice
To lift my heart so high as it is now.
This is that joy in which my soul is strong,
That there is not a man amongst you all
Who can reproach me that I used my power
To do him an injustice.   If there be,
It is not to my knowledge; yet I pray him,
That he will now forgive me, taking note
That I had not to deal with easy times.

FIRST CITIZEN.

Oh, Master Philip, there is none—not one.

SECOND CITIZEN.

Most justly and most wisely you have ruled us.

ARTEVELDE.

I thank you, sirs; farewell to you, once more.
Once more, farewell.   If I return to Gheut,
A glory and dominion will be your's
Such as no city since the olden time
Hath been so bold to conquer or to claim.
If I return no more—God's will be done!
To Him and to His providence I leave you.

[*He descends.   The people come round him, seizing his hands, and
crying confusedly,* "God bless you, Master Philip!   God
be with you!"

Nay, press not on me, friends; I see ye weep,
Which ye did never for your past mischances.
But ye shall be disburthen'd of your griefs
The rather than dishearten'd by these tears;
Or else should I reprove them—so—farewell!

L 2

SCENE IV.—*The Vestibule of the Church of St. Nicholas.—At the extreme end of it,* VAN RYK *is seen keeping guard over the door which gives access to the church tower.—In front,* CLARA *appears, followed at a little distance by* VAN AESWYN.

CLARA.

Still he pursues me ; but I will not bear it.
How now, Sir Squire ? whom seek you ?

AESWYN.

                With your leave,
I have an errand for your private ear.

CLARA.

My private ear ! I have no private ear !
My ears will not be private.

AESWYN.

            I beseech you
To pardon my presumption.

CLARA.

           Well, what then ?
It is not past forgiveness ; no, no, no,
I freely pardon you.

AESWYN.

          I thank you, madam ;
And were I but permitted to speak out
All that he bade me say—

CLARA.

          That he ! what he ?

AESWYN.

The Lord of Arlon, madam.

CLARA.

          Lord of what ?

AESWYN.

Sir Walter, Lord of Arlon.

CLARA.

Oh! Sir Walter,—
Sir Walter D'Arlon—a good knight, they say:
He sent his service, did he?—a good knight.—
I knew him once—he came to Ghent—oh God!
I'm sick—the air is hot, I think—yes hot!
I pray you pardon me—we get no rest
In this beleaguer'd town—no anything—
This is the time of day I use to faint;
But I shall miss to do it for this once;
So please you to proceed.

AESWYN.

There's here a bench:
If you'll be seated: for you look so pale . . . .

CLARA.

No, I can stand—I think—well then, I'll sit.
So now, your errand?

AESWYN.

The Lord of Arlon, madam,
Imparted to me that of all the griefs
That Fortune had dealt out to him, was none
So broke his spirit as the cruel thought
That you in some sort must partake the woes
Of this so suffering city: he could ne'er
Lay lance in rest or do a feat of arms
But this reflection stung him to the heart,
And each success in which he might have triumph'd
Was turn'd to bitterness,—seeming nought else
But injury to his love.   Thus is he now
A man whose heart resents his handiwork,
And all his pleasure in the war is poison'd.

CLARA.

Alas, poor D'Arlon! but I cannot help him.

AESWYN.

Himself thinks otherwise; he bade me say
That he implores you to fly hence to him.

CLARA.

No, never, never.

AESWYN.

And his aunt at Bruges,
The prioress, will have you in her care
Till it shall please you to permit his suit.

CLARA.

I tell thee, never.   I a fugitive!
Whilst Philip lives and holds the city out,
Nor pestilence nor famine, fire nor sword,
Nor evil here nor good elsewhere divides us.
Much may he lose, and much that's far more worth,
But never this reliance.

AESWYN.

With your leave,
I would make bold to ask you if your absence
In these extremities might not rejoice
Rather than grieve him.

CLARA.

No, sir, you mistake,
Knowing nor him nor me: we two have grown
From birth on my side, boyhood upon his,
Inseparably together, as two grafts
Out of the self-same stock; we've shared alike
The sun and shower and all that Heaven hath sent us;
I've loved him much and quarrell'd with him oft,
And all our loves and quarrels past are links
That no adversity shall e'er dissever.

And I am useful, too ; he'll tell you that ;
We Arteveldes were made for times like these ;
The Deacon of the Mariners said well
That we are of such canvas as they use
To make storm-stay-sails.   I have much in charge,
And I'll stand by him and abide the worst.

AESWYN.

Then must I tell Sir Walter that you never—

CLARA.

Alas, poor D'Arlon ! did I then say ' never ? '
It is a most unkindly sounding word.
Tell him to ask me when the siege is raised.
But then he shall not need ; he can come hither.
But tell him—of your knowledge, not from me—
The woman could not be of nature's making
Whom, being kind, her misery made not kinder.

AESWYN.

The thought of that may solace him.   Farewell.

CLARA.

Farewell.   I mount the tower to look abroad.
After your conference at noon, they say,
My brother arm'd himself and bade his horse
Be ready harness'd in his mail complete ;
And though you keep his secret, I surmise
There's something may be seen from this church tower.

AESWYN.

Nothing to come from Bruges.

CLARA.

But yet I'll look.

[*She approaches the door of the Tower, and perceives* VAN RYK, *who
plants himself before her.*

VAN RYK.

You cannot pass, my lady.

CLARA.

How! not pass?

VAN RYK.

The door is lock'd; your brother keeps the key:
And I am station'd here with strict command
To suffer none to pass.

CLARA.

How could they pass,
If what thou say'st be true? thou hast the key.

VAN RYK.

Upon my faith I have it not, my lady.

CLARA.

A courteous usage for a lady this!
But hither comes my prince of spies, the Page,
To tell what's doing in the market-place.

Enter Page.

PAGE.

Here is a brave adventure! here's a feat!
Here is a glorious enterprise afoot!

CLARA.

What is it? tell us true.

PAGE.

Illustrious lady!
The name of Artevelde shall live for ever!
For Master Philip leads five thousand men
This very night to storm the gates of Bruges.

CLARA.

Thou dost not say it?

PAGE.

True as written book.

CLARA.

There's matter then for Flanders to discourse of,

There's cause for Ghent to tremble or rejoice,
And liberty for me; if Philip goes
I have no business here.

AESWYN.

               Most surely none;
And you will now betake yourself to Bruges?

CLARA.

Nay, nay, sir, not so fast; gain Philip first,
And then come back to me and take your chance.
              [Exeunt CLARA, VAN AESWYN, *and* Page.

Enter VAN ARTEVELDE, *who advances to the door of the Tower
where* VAN RYK *is stationed.*

ARTEVELDE.

How fares our friend within? set ope the door.

VAN RYK.

Oh, Sir! you must not enter; he is mad.
I would not give a denier for the life
Of any that should enter now; he's arm'd,
And rages like a man possess'd by devils.

ARTEVELDE.

Whence tak'st thou that conclusion?

VAN RYK.

                    For three hours
He strove and shouted as though fifty fiends
Were doing battle on the narrow stair:
He flung his body with such desperate force
Against the door, that I was much in doubt
Whether the triple bars had strength to hold it.
Then—God be merciful! the oaths and curses!
Faster they came than I could tell my beads.

ARTEVELDE.

But all is silent now.

VAN RYK.

The last half-hour
I have not heard him.

ARTEVELDE.

Open me the door.

VAN RYK.

Surely you will not enter?

ARTEVELDE.

Nay, I must.
We must be friends again. His aid is wanted.

VAN RYK.

He will assault you ere a word be spoken.

ARTEVELDE.

He is a hasty man; but we must meet.

VAN RYK.

Then I will enter with you.

ARTEVELDE.

No, Van Ryk;
I seek his confidence; a show of force
Were sure to baffle me. I go alone.

VAN RYK.

For mercy's sake forbear. Should you go in,
Or you or he will ne'er come out alive.

ARTEVELDE.

Nay, nay, thou know'st not with what winning ways
I can sleek down his wrath. Stand fast below
I charge thee, and let no intrusive step
Trouble my conference with Van Den Bosch.

SCENE V.—*The Platform at the top of the Steeple.—As in
the First Scene in this Act.*

VAN ARTEVELDE, *and* VAN DEN BOSCH.

ARTEVELDE.

He has been drunk with anger, and he sleeps.
Lest he be not the soberer for his doze
I shall do well to strip him of his weapons.
Come, courtier, from thy house—come from thy case,
Thou smooth and shining dangler by the side
Of them that put thee to a deadly use:
Thou art dismiss'd.

[*He lays aside the dagger.*

And come thou likewise forth,
Thou flashing flourisher in the battle field;
Gaudy and senseless tool of sovereignty,
Up to thy shoulders thou shalt reek in blood,
And 'tis but wiping thee to make thee clean,
So poor a thing art thou!—there—get thee gone—

[*He lays aside the sword.*

Now that he's stingless I may stir him up.
Ho! Van Den Bosch! arouse thee; what, thou sleep'st;
Why, here's a sluggard!—up, thou lubberly sot!
Get thee afoot; is this a time to sleep?
Up, ere I prod thee with my sword—up, slug!
Up, drowsy clod—why, now I think thou wak'st.

VAN DEN BOSCH.

What noisy villain's this?—Van Artevelde!

ARTEVELDE.

Nay, never grope and fumble for thy weapons;
They are convey'd away.

VAN DEN BOSCH.

     Oh! bloody villain,
And wilt thou murder me unarm'd?

ARTEVELDE.

      Out! out!
More like to whip thee for thy fond conceit.
I tell thee, man, a better friend than I
Thou'st not been bless'd with for this many a year.
When all is known to thee, thyself shalt say
That a more friendly deed was never done thee
Than this of mine—the shutting of thee up.

VAN DEN BOSCH.

Philip of Artevelde, I say thou liest—
Give me my sword again.   I say thou liest—
Give me my dagger and my sword—thou liest—
Thou art a caitiff and a lying knave,
And thou hast stolen my dagger and my sword.

ARTEVELDE.

Nay, softly, friend.

VAN DEN BOSCH.

    I'm robb'd, I'm robb'd, I'm plunder'd—
I'm plunder'd of my weapons—of my sword.
Give me my sword again, thou liar, thou!
I'm plunder'd of my dagger and my sword.
Give me my sword, thou robber, or I'll kill thee.

ARTEVELDE.

Do that, and thou shalt need thy sword no longer.

VAN DEN BOSCH.

Thou coward, wilt thou give me back my sword?

ARTEVELDE.

There—take it, and the devil give thee good on't!

Now that thou hast it, mayhap thou'lt be brought
To leave thy bellowing and listen. Hark!

VAN DEN BOSCH.

I have thee now, Van Artevelde, I have thee.
Ha, ha! I have my sword—I have thee now.

ARTEVELDE.

And if thou hadst thy senses and thine ears
It were a better having for the nonce.
Wilt thou be still and listen to me?

VAN DEN BOSCH.
                No.
Thou art a liar. Draw thy sword and fight.

ARTEVELDE.

I give thee back thy lie, and take thy challenge.
To mortal proof we'll put it, if thou wilt,
But not by instant combat. Three days hence,
I pledge my word to answer thy demand,
And I will show thee reasons why no sooner.

VAN DEN BOSCH.

A murrain on thy reasons! draw thy sword.

ARTEVELDE (*draws his sword and flings it from him*).
I'll fight thee when I please, and not before.

VAN DEN BOSCH.

Art thou a coward? wherefore wilt not fight?

ARTEVELDE.

There is a time for all things. Here I stand,
Unarm'd before thee, and I will be heard.
That which so much thou tak'st to heart, was done
Purely to save thy credit, much indeed
Endanger'd by thy wilfulness and haste.

I would have done myself no less offence
To do thee so much service.   Say thine arm
Had cut me off the messenger from Bruges.
Ghent hears the rumour—magnifies at once
The untold terms to unconditional peace,
And mad with rage for comfort thus repell'd,
Had turn'd upon thee to thine overthrow.
But listen what instead I've brought to pass :
The terms were told,—such sanguinary terms
As we had cause to look for ; on that ground
I moved the people to a last attempt
Of desperate daring, and we go to-night,
Five thousand men, to seek the earl at Bruges.
Now, Peter Van Den Bosch, give ear to me :
Thy mouth has been, this many a day, stuff'd full
Of vengeance dire denounced against this earl.
The blood of Heins, of Launoy, and Van Ranst,
(True friends of thine if truth and friendship be !)
Sinks in the ground, nor honour'd nor avenged
Save by the mouthing of an idle threat.
Dead men and living, vows after vows sent up
In hot succession to the throne of Heaven,
Deep ravage done amongst thy native fields,
Strange tortures suffer'd by thy countrymen,
Call thee with common voice to turn thy wrath
To just account ;—and is it come to this,
That for the matter of but one day's feud
With one tried friend that never did thee hurt,
Thou canst forget all else, and put thy cause
To imminent hazard at the utmost verge
Of all its fortunes and its ultimate hope !
If so, I cry thee mercy ; I mistook thee ;

For I had counted on thy aid to-day
To do the things that thou so oft hast threaten'd.

VAN DEN BOSCH.

Van Artevelde, I never yet forgave
So deep an injury as thou hast done me;
But seeing how things bear, I'll pass it by,
Until this last adventure have an end.
Then shalt thou reckon with me for the past.

ARTEVELDE.

For that I stand prepared. Meanwhile I pray thee,
Let needful harmony subsist between us;
Nor let the common welfare feel this feud.
Take thou thy charge in this day's work; come down
And I will give it thee. From me thou'lt find
All fit observance.

VAN DEN BOSCH.
I will take my charge.

ACT V.

SCENE I.—*The field of Merle, in the environs of Bruges.*

VAN ARTEVELDE, VAN DEN BOSCH, VAN RYK, VAN MUCK,
and others.

ARTEVELDE.

Not a step farther; give the word to halt,
And send the waggons here; we can't be better.
God grant that hither they may come to seek us!
Here is the fighting ground, and there the slough

In which they needs must perish should they yield.
We can't be better.

VAN DEN BOSCH.

Let it then be here.
I've probed the slough.

ARTEVELDE.

That I did too ; 'tis deep.

VAN DEN BOSCH.

He is a taller man than you or I,
That finds the bottom with his head above.

ARTEVELDE.

It is an hour to sunset.

VAN RYK.

Nay, 'tis more.

ARTEVELDE.

A little more, Van Ryk.   I would to God
The sun might not go down upon us here
Without a battle fought !

VAN DEN BOSCH.

If so it should,
We pass a perilous night.

ARTEVELDE.

A nipping night,
And wake a wasted few the morrow morn.

VAN MUCK.

We have a supper left.

ARTEVELDE.

My lady's page
If he got ne'er a better should be wroth,

And burn in effigy my lady's steward.
For us and for one supper 'twill suffice ;
But he's a skilful man at splitting hairs
That can make two on't.

VAN RYK.

           Aye, or leave behind
A breakfast in his dish.

ARTEVELDE.

          We break our fast
Elsewhere to-morrow.   I pray God the saint
Whose feast they celebrate to-night at Bruges,
May steep them well in wine.   If Ukenheim
Get undiscover'd in, we shall not miss
To profit by his skill.

VAN DEN BOSCH.

          We'll hope the best ;
But if there be a knave in power unhang'd,
And in his head a grain of sense undrown'd.
He'll be their caution not to—

ARTEVELDE.

          Van den Bosch,
Talk we of battle and survey the field,
For I *will* fight.   Let stakes be driven in
Amongst the rushes at the nether end
Of this morass.   Van Ryk, look thou to that.
And thou, Van Muck, unload the victual here ;
Then tilt the waggons up behind the stakes,
And pierce them for cross-bows.   A horse for me,
That I may know the ground.   And now, friends all,
Let's to our charges.   Ere the red sun sink
Behind yon city, Ghent is lost or saved.

                    M

SCENE II.—*An open tent erected for public entertainment in the Market-place of Bruges.—Boisterous songs, and other sounds of riot and jollity are heard on all sides. Within the tent a miscellaneous company are drinking, and amongst them is* UKENHEIM, *in the dress of a Mariner of Bruges.*

UKENHEIM.

I pray you pledge me in this, to our better acquaintance.

LUNYZ.

At your service, sir. What say'st thou, Jan Trickle? Is not this the right way? Is not this the narrow road? Knew'st thou ever a Saint's day more seemly celebrated? Dost see what a devotion there is to it!

TRICKLE.

I see very many righteous gentlemen very drunk. But my wife says, were they at church it should be more seemly.

KROOLKHUYS.

Bah! didst ever know a man's wife that liked him to be drinking without her to help?

TRICKLE.

Mine is a rare helpmate.

LUNYZ.

Let the Church speak. Father Swillen, is not this as it should be?

FATHER SWILLEN.

My son, and worthy burgesses, and beloved brethren! Of the present solemnity, I will deliver my opinion according to the canons. Wine is to be used *cum abstinentiâ et temperantiâ*, for the recovery of the sick,

the consolation of the dying, and the healing of a
wounded spirit.   It is also to be used in honour of our
Lady of Bolayne on this the day of her festival.   But
the presence of a priest is needful herein, for the
preventing of abuses, and the showing of a proper
example.   [*Drinks.*

TACKENHAM (*advancing from the farther end of the tent*).

Father Swillen——friend, if I knocked you down I
ask your pardon——Father Swillen——sirs, give me
place, for I must see the Father——Father Swillen, I
look upon you to be one man of a thousand—I will go
on my knees to you—I look upon you to be the oracle
of God—I look upon you to be the invisible oracle of
God—for there you are, and I see you not.—I can
stand,—I say I can stand—but here I kneel down, and
I will not rise unless you stretch forth your hand to
me and raise me up—and this is the view I take of our
duties as Christian men—all which is submitted to your
better judgment, and I would that all men paid their
dues to the Church.

FATHER SWILLEN.

God requite you, my son! for their salvation,—for
their salvation—nothing else.

LUNYZ (*looking out into the Market-place*).

Here is a minstrel twiddles with the strings of his
cithern.   Now we shall hear a song.

THE FOLLOWING SONG IS SUNG TO A VULGAR TUNE.

> Who mounts the merry-go-round with me,
>   Who mounts the merry-go-round?
> 'Tis I, I, I,—and who be ye
>   That would mount the merry-go-round?

A blacksmith I,—spearheads as good
    As e'er from Bordeaux came,
I've made and would in Ghentsmen's blood
    Be bold to dip the same.

Who mounts the merry-go-round with me,
    Who mounts the merry-go-round?
'Tis I, I, I,—and who may'st be,
    That would mount the merry-go-round?

A cutler I,—as true a blade
    As ever Ebro steel'd
Is this I've made, nor will't be stay'd
    By any Ghentsman's shield.

Who mounts the merry-go-round with me,
    Who mounts the merry-go-round?
'Tis I, I, I,—and now let us see
    Who mounts the merry-go-round.

A barber I,—and well appear'd
    My handicraft, for when
A Ghentsman's beard I shortly shear'd,
    It never grew again.

Who mounts the merry-go-round with me,
    Who mounts the merry-go-round?
'Tis I, I, I,—and a priest was he
    That would mount the merry-go-round.

A Ghentsman of his wounds lay sick,
    And shall I be saved? he cried;
I gave him a kick, bade him ask old Nick,
    And he should be satisfied.

KROOLKHUYS.

I 'faith he sings like a nightingale. No more thank
you,—I cannot—cannot . . . well, if I must . . . [drinks].
'Tis a charming lullaby, and the sentiment very tender
and soothing. Let us all do as we would be done by,
God bless us!
                                                    [Falls asleep.

[Suddenly is heard from the Market-place a loud cry of
    'To arms! To arms!'

UKENHEIM (starting up and drawing his sword).

To arms? what! the men of Ghent come to us?
What! the scarecrows from Ghent! To arms! to
arms! out and down with them! to arms! to arms!

KROOLKHUYS (*waking*).

Why how is this? the men of Ghent! what ho!
give me my coat of proof.

UKENHEIM.

Let cowards stay behind.   To arms! to arms!

[*They rush out confusedly.* TACKENHAM *creeps from under the
table, where he had remained in a reclining posture.*

TACKENHAM.

To arms! I look upon Father Swillen to be an
oracle, and it were to be wished that all men paid the
Church her dues.

SCENE III.—*The Palace.*

THE LORD OF OCCO *and* GILBERT MATTHEW.

GILBERT.

His Highness will be here anon.   Sir Guy,
Freely accept the combat for the morrow.
Count on my speed.   There's not a man in Bruges
Who has outlived the day I wish'd him dead.
The threads of many destinies I hold,
Unknown to them they bind for life or death,
And I am punctual as the planet stars.
A winter's night, as long as nights are now,
Is worth an age.

OCCO.

One doubt detains me still.
The earl, if ever it were known, would—

GILBERT.

Hark!
'Tis over, that.   He loves him now no more.

For every philtre that can make men love,
I know the secret of an antidote.
I've warn'd him of those private ties in Ghent.
Enough.   I've dosed him.

OCCO.

Well, it shall be done.

GILBERT.

I will provide thee hands.

OCCO.

You shall not need.
I have already sent for two tried men,—
Italians ; they are practised hands and fit.

GILBERT.

I have you then ; 'tis Erclo and Romero.

OCCO.

The same.

Enter the EARL.

EARL.

What shouting's this I hear abroad ?

OCCO.

The revellers, my good lord ; they pitch the bar,
And shoot with cross-bows for a prize.   My lord,
At noon to-morrow, if his heart but hold,
I'll meet Sir Walter D'Arlon.

GILBERT.

In good truth
But are these shouts of revel ?   Hark, again !
They cry, ' to arms.'

EARL.

By heaven I think 'tis that.
And hear ye not the bells ? They're ringing backwards.

OCCO.

'Tis an alarm.

Enter the LORD OF ARLON, SIR ROBERT MARESCHAULT,
and others.

EARL.

Well, D'Arlon, what is this?

D'ARLON.

The men of Ghent, my lord, the men of Ghent.

EARL.

What, here?

D'ARLON.

Two miles aloof they make a stand.

EARL.

What, are they mad?

D'ARLON.

I think not mad, my lord.
But desperate.

EARL.

My friends, 'tis all as one.
Now shall this war be gloriously ended,
And famine, that was tedious, be o'erta'en.
Bring out my banner, summon all to arms,
Then forth and fight them.

GILBERT.

Please you, sir, to say
How many they may number.

SIR ROBERT.

At a guess
About five thousand.

GILBERT.

May they move, or stand?

SIR ROBERT.

Since they were first descried they have not stirr'd.

EARL.

Forth with my banner ; out with horse and foot.
Sir knights, we muster in the Market-place.
Bring me my armour, ho !

GILBERT.

                              My lord, one word,
Ere yet the knights depart.   These men are few,
But they are desperate ; famine-bitten are they,
But alway are the leanest wolves most brave
To break the fold.   Sir, let us not be rash ;
Our men-at-arms are somewhat flush'd with drink,
And may be ill to guide.   Sir, think upon it.
Fight them to-morrow.   Let them sleep to-night
In winter's lap, beneath the ragged tent
Of a December's sky.   When morning breaks
You'll see them lying upon yon hill-side
As dead and sapless as the last month's leaves.
Give them this night.

THE HASE OF FLANDERS.

                    Nay, nay, they'll think we fear them.

GILBERT.

Think they their will ; whate'er they think of that
They shall unthink to-morrow.

EARL.

                              By my faith
I know not, Gilbert, but thou may'st have reason.
The winter's night is sure to thin their ranks
Of fighting men ; and if they're scantly stored

With victual, which is probable to think,
They shall endure it worse.

Enter the Mayor *in haste.*

MAYOR.

    My lord, my lord,
The crafts fly forth by thousands from the gates,
Unorder'd and unled.

EARL.

    Who kept the gates?
How came they open? Walter, haste thee, haste!
And bring the madmen back.
        [*Exit* D'ARLON.
    How came they open?

MAYOR.

A simple mariner avouch'd, my lord,
That he had heard your Highness's own mouth
Give out the order.

EARL.

    Hang the slave! he lied.

MAYOR.

Why so the warders thought, and had not done it,
But that the people, being much inflamed,
Menaced their lives.

Enter a Squire.

SQUIRE.

    Sir Walter, sir, sends word
The town is almost emptied. He entreats
Your Highness will not look to bring them back,
Which is past hope, but sound at once to arms,
And send them leaders that are gone unled.

EARL.

Now, Gilbert, we must forth.

GILBERT.

Aye, go we forth.
Fifty to five, we surely must do well,
Though peradventure, for the sparing lives
We might have done more wisely.

EARL.

Sirs, be sudden ;
And when you're mounted in the Market-place,
I'll give you there your charges.   Sound to horse.

SCENE IV.—*The Field of Merle, as in the First Scene.*

VAN ARTEVELDE, VAN RYK, VAN MUCK, *and others.*

ARTEVELDE.

See'st thou yon sweeping section of the road
That leads by Ecdorf to the eastern gate ?
My eyes are strain'd, but yet I thought I saw
A moving mass of men.

VAN RYK.

I thought so too.
When I had held mine eyes a minute fixed,
As in a morsel of dry moulder'd cheese,
I thought I could descry a tumbling movement.

ARTEVELDE.

Who hath the longest and the clearest sight
Of all our men ? go bring him.   Nay, stop, stop,
I think we shall not need him : now, look there.
By Heaven, they come ! they come !   Ha ! Van den
       Bosch !

Enter VAN DEN BOSCH.

I give you joy! by Heaven, we have our wish.

VAN DEN BOSCH.

Yea, sir, they come, and now betide what may,
We'll mix the Evil One a mess for supper
In yonder darksome pool.

ARTEVELDE.

        A ruddier tinge
Than ever evening cast, shall warm its waters,
Or ere yon sun be down.   What ho! Van Serl,
Serve out the victual all—but first to prayers.
We will be shriven first, and then we'll sup,
And after that we'll cut a road to bed,
Be it in Bruges or in a better place.
Van Ryk, abide thou here, and bring me word
If any man approach by other ways;
And when the foremost of the troop we see
Have past yon broken wall, then sound thy horn,
And I will send thee forces wherewithal
To keep thy post.   There's food behind the carts
Whereof partake with them I'll send thee.

VAN RYK.

               Nay,
I shall want nothing, sir.

ARTEVELDE.

        I tell thee, eat,
Eat and be fresh.   I'll send a priest to shrive thee.
Van Muck, thou tak'st small comfort in thy prayers;
Put thou thy muzzle in yon tub of wine.
Now, Van den Bosch, or ere the sun go down,
We'll know Heaven's will.

VAN DEN BOSCH.

              Have with thee, Artevelde!
Thou art a brave and honourable man,
And I would have thee know that should we fall,
Either or both, I bear thee now no grudge ;
And so may Heaven forgive my many sins,
As I do thee.

ARTEVELDE.

        Why, thou art now thyself;
With heart and hand we'll fall upon the foe,
And do the work like brothers. Come thy ways.

        [*Exeunt all but* VAN RYK *and* VAN MUCK.

VAN RYK.

Van Muck, I prithee step along the path
That rounds the hill, and mark if on that side
Aught may be stirring.

VAN MUCK.

        Aye, and if there be,
I'll shout, and hail thee.

                 [*Exit.*

Enter ARTEVELDE's Page.

VAN RYK.

        Why, my little man,
How cam'st thou hither? 'tis no place for thee !
What, cam'st thou with the army?

PAGE.

        No, from Bruges.

VAN RYK.

What took thee there ?

PAGE.

        I went with Mistress Clara
Who sojourns with the Prioress of St. Anne
Till all be over.

VAN RYK.

And with her, my boy,
Thou shouldst have stay'd.

PAGE.

What! in a convent?   No—
I think not when a battle is toward.
Besides the Prioress was all on edge
To hear of what befalls her sister's son,
Sir Walter D'Arlon being forth ; so me
They charged to keep good watch and bring them word
How he shall fare ; but by my halidom
I will not run of errands now ; I'll fight.

VAN RYK.

God's mercy on the knight thou fall'st upon !
Nay, nay, content thee ; couch thee by yon carts,
And dream not thou of fighting.

PAGE.

Is it true
That half an hour will bring the battle on ?

VAN RYK.

Less time than that.   Thou see'st how fast they come.
But now we scarce distinguish'd if they moved,
And now upon the skirts of yonder mass,
I can discern them, single man by man.

PAGE.

Canst thou descry the pennons of the knights
That lead them ?

VAN RYK.

Truly, I perceive not one ;
I do but see a multitude of heads ;

No banner, pennon, nor a mounted man.
If any knight be there he comes afoot.

PAGE.

The Lord of Arlon surely must be there.
He's always with the foremost.

VAN RYK.

                If he be,
His pennon is not.

PAGE.

             Nay, but look again;
I see some knights that gallop up behind,
And pennons now come streaming on the road,
Betwixt the town and them.

VAN RYK.

               Good faith, 'tis true.
Thou hast sharp eyes.

PAGE.

            And there—upon the bridge—
Whose is that pennon?

VAN RYK.

            Presently I'll tell thee;
I cannot yet distinguish.   Come this way
And we shall see them better.   Through the gap.

SCENE V.—*Another part of the Field.*

VAN ARTEVELDE *and others.*

ARTEVELDE.

Their cross-bow shafts have touch'd us on that side,
And ours fly large.   We're dazzled by the sun.
Bid Van den Bosch give gently back and back,
And wind them round the slough; I'll hover here;

And soon as he have turn'd his back o' the sun,
Let him stand fast and shoot. Thou hast thine errand ;
Let it not cool.   And you, sirs, follow me.

SCENE VI.—*Another part of the Field.*

The LORD OF ARLON *and* GILBERT MATTHEW.

GILBERT.

How came they thus?   My lord, I needs must say,
A soldier's courage, not a leader's skill,
Has placed them here.

D'ARLON.

Skill ! what can skill avail ?
Could skill have made men sober that were drunk !
The meanest archer with his senses whole
Would not have rush'd to stare the sun i' the face
As these have done ;—but nothing could withhold them.

GILBERT.

They will not long hold out.

D'ARLON.

I prithee fly,
And tell the earl to send us succours up.
I'll keep them steady, if I can, till then.

SCENE VII.—*Another part of the Field.*

VAN ARTEVELDE's Page *following an* Archer.

PAGE.

Stay, hearken.

ARCHER.

Faith of my body ! what is here ?

A mannikin at arms? Why clutch you me?
If you're afraid, why came you out?

PAGE.

                       Take that,
For saying I'm afraid.

ARCHER.

                Ho! we are slain
With buffet of a mighty man of war!
Well, thou hast metal; what is thy will with me?

PAGE.

I am thy captain's page and bidden to ask
Where D'Arlon fights.

ARCHER.

              So; stop, then; with your eye
If you can follow forth yon dry stone wall
Down to the hollow, and where further on
Again it rises, you shall see a crowd
Of fighting men, and in the midst of them
The pennon of the Lord of Arlon flies—
By Heaven! But I think no—a minute since
It there was flying, but I think 'tis down.

[Exit Page.

Enter VAN ARTEVELDE, with Followers from the one side, and
    VAN RYK <i>with</i> Followers <i>from the other.</i>

ARTEVELDE.

How is't with you? On our side all is well.
One half their host is founder'd in the swamp,
The other full in flight.

VAN RYK.

              On our side too
They all have fled; but further down the field
The D'Arlon still stands fast.

ARTEVELDE.

                    Set on,—set on—
Make for the spot.   But hurt ye not that knight.

SCENE VIII.—*A Street in Bruges.*—*It is Night.*—*The* EARL OF
    FLANDERS *and* SIR ROBERT MARESCHAULT *enter, preceded
    by* Attendants *bearing torches.*

EARL.

What succours we can find I'll lead myself.
Was ever such disaster! madmen first,
And cowards after!

Enter a Soldier *in haste.*

SOLDIER.

                    Fly, my lord! fly, fly!
The gates are lost; they're now within the walls.

EARL.

Why say they are, and must I therefore fly?
Make for the market-place; we'll rally there
Whoever will be rallied.—Pass we on—
Lights to the market-place!

Enter another Soldier.

SOLDIER.

                    Is't you, my lord?
Oh! not that way! the men of Ghent are there.
Fly, fly, my lord!

EARL.

                    The men of Ghent are where?

                                        N

SOLDIER.

I' the market-place, my lord.

EARL.

What, there already!

SIR ROBERT.

Put out your lights.

EARL.

Aye, truly, now all's lost.
Put out your lights, good fellows all, and fly.
Save me you cannot, and you may yourselves.

[*The lights are extinguished.*

Which way to turn I know not.

SIR ROBERT.

Down the street
I see the flash of cressets that come hither;
Hence, in God's name! Here, varlet, doff thy cloak,
And give it to my lord.

EARL.

Throw mine i' the gutter,
Or it might else betray thy life; get hence;
But if thou fallest in the enemy's hands,
Have a good tongue, and say not thou hast seen me.
Adieu, Sir Robert; each the other hazards
By holding thus together.

SIR ROBERT.

Sir, farewell.   [*Exit.*

[*The* EARL, *left alone, knocks at the door of a house; a window
is opened above, and a woman looks out.*

WOMAN.

Who's he that knocks?

EARL.

A much endanger'd man.

WOMAN.

We're all endanger'd on such nights as these;
I cannot let thee in.

EARL.

Nay! I beseech thee!

WOMAN.

Art thou a man-at-arms?

EARL.

Truly I am.

WOMAN.

Then get thee gone; they'll ransack every house
To hunt out men-at-arms. Go, get thee gone.

EARL.

I have no arms upon me.

WOMAN.

Get thee gone.

EARL.

I am the Earl of Flanders.

WOMAN.

Good my lord!
O mercy! my good lord, and is it you?
Woe's me! I'll ope the door. The many times
That alms were given me at your lordship's gate,
And I to hold you haggling here! Woe's me!

[*She descends and opens the door.*

Come in, my gracious lord ; up yonder steps
You'll find a cock-loft and a couch of straw ;
Betwixt the mattress and the boards lie flat,
And you may well be hidden.   Here are lights !
Come in, come in.

[They enter the house.

Enter VAN MUCK, *followed by several* Men of Ghent.
He knocks at the door.

VAN MUCK.

No answer?   Nay then, knock me in this door.

[The woman opens it.

WOMAN.

Why, gentlemen, you would not sure molest
A widow and her children.

VAN MUCK.

Who's within ?

WOMAN.

Three helpless orphans ; as I hope for mercy,
No soul beside.

VAN MUCK.

Wilt take thy oath of that ?

WOMAN.

I pray God strike me dead upon the threshold
If any be within but my three babes,
Myk, Lodowyk, and Jan.

VAN MUCK.

Why as we came
We saw a man go in.

WOMAN.

Good sir, good sir,
You are deceived ; there was no man at all.

'Twas I look'd out and emptied down a bucket.
A man! God help us! no.

VAN MUCK.

                    Go in and see.
                    [*Some of the men enter the house*

WOMAN.

Walk in, good gentlemen, walk in and welcome;
You see my humble house : one room below,
And one above.   Sir, will you not walk in?

VAN MUCK.

No, no; I'll keep the door.

WOMAN.

                    These times, sweet sir,
Are hard for widow'd women and their babes.
                    [*The* Men *come out again.*

ONE OF THE MEN.

'Tis as she says : three children are asleep
In the cock-loft, and there is none beside.

VAN MUCK.

Good even to you, dame.   Friends, follow me.
                    [*Exeunt* VAN MUCK *and his* Men.

WOMAN.

Beshrew your hearts, ye filthy dogs of Ghent!
The devil catch you by the throat! for once
You've miss'd your game.   Ah, my sweet lord, away!

SCENE IX.—*The Market-place of Bruges.—In front,* VAN
ARTEVELDE, *with* CLARA *and* D'ARLON. *Next,* UKENHEIM,
FRANS ACKERMAN, VAN NUITRE, *and other* Leaders. *Behind
them are crowds of armed* Followers *and* Attendants, *bearing
torches ; of whom some companies march off from time to time
under orders from their* Captains, *and others remain keeping
guard over prisoners and spoil.*

ARTEVELDE.

War hath dealt hardly with the noble D'Arlon ;
Him gold not ransoms, and to stricter bonds
A captive knight was never yet consign'd.

[*Turning to his* Followers.

Van Muck returns not.   Who amongst you all
Hath eye of lynx and leveret's foot to speed
Through all the town with inquisition sure,
And leave no corner of a house unsearch'd.
Where is Van Ryk?

UKENHEIM.

He left us at the gates.

ARTEVELDE.

True, true, despatch'd by me upon an errand ;
He will be here anon.   Then, Ukenheim,
Go thou, with such assistance as thou wilt,
Upon the quest, through every lane and street.
Take him, if possibly ye can, alive.
Evil and folly hath he wrought against us,
But never treason ; he had wrong'd us less
But for the renegades that gave him counsel.
Bring forth the Lord of Occo.

[Occo *is brought forward bound.*

So, my lord !

Enter VAN MUCK *and his party.*

VAN MUCK.

A prisoner, sir, we bring ; 'tis Gilbert Matthew.

ARTEVELDE.

And not the earl?

VAN MUCK.

              'Tis said that he's escaped,
And ta'en the road to Lisle.   He lay some space
Hid in a hovel till the search went by,
And then he fled away.

ARTEVELDE.

              Long must thou wait,
Earl, ere thou see thy heritage again !
Bring Gilbert Matthew forth.   [*He is brought in bound.*

          So, Gilbert Matthew !

GILBERT.

Young upstart, what wouldst thou with Gilbert Matthew ?

ARTEVELDE.

Be patient, sir ; you'll know it.   Where art thou,
Frans Ackerman ?   Ere midnight let me see
A hundred waggons on their way to Ghent,
Loaden with corn and wine.   At dawn send forth
To Damme and Sluys, and empty out their stores
For a fresh convoy.   Have me men prepared
To ride to Ypres, Courtray, Cassel, Bergues,
To Poperinguen, and to Rousselaere,
And bid the mayor and burghers of each town
Send me its keys.   Well met, bold Van den Bosch !

Enter VAN DEN BOSCH, *with followers.*

Well met at Bruges, my brethren in arms!
As ye were brave, so be ye temperate now.
Let not the small-crafts suffer.   Spare their blood,
For they but followed in the train of power,
And many wish'd us in their hearts no ill.
To all shall plunder plentifully flow
Out of the coffers of the rich; but him
That spills a foreigner's or craftsman's blood
I mulct of all his share, and, this night past,
The price (not willingly so long postponed,
But needfully for this tumultuous night)
Of all blood-guiltiness is paid in blood.
Take heed of what I say; ye ought to know
For good or ill my promises are kept.
The debt of vengeance which is due to Ghent
You shall behold acquitted where you stand.
                    [*Turning to* OCCO *and* GILBERT MATTHEW.
Look, Van den Bosch, upon your former friends,
And tell me what's their due.

                    VAN DEN BOSCH.

                              In this world, death,
And after that let Satan tend his own.
I should commend their bodies to the rack,
But that I'm loth so long to keep their souls
Out of hell-fire.
                    OCCO.
                    Thy heart was ever hard;
But, Artevelde, *thou* wilt not stain thy hands
By killing in cold blood two helpless men!
If thou'rt a soldier, do not such a deed.

Soldiers by soldiers in the field are slain,
Not murder'd in the Market-place.

ARTEVELDE.

　　　　　　　　　I grant thee.
And if the name of soldier can be claim'd
By both or one of you, ye shall not die.
Bring forth the friar.　　*[A Friar is brought forward.*

　　　　　　　Save you, holy Father!
Say in the face of these two 'that stand here,
That which thou said'st to me.

FRIAR.

　　　　　　　　　Sir, it was this:
Here in the hospital expired but now
Of many wounds a Florentine, by name
Romero, who, repentant ere his death,
Confess'd to me that he received a bribe
From Gilbert Matthew and Sir Guy of Occo,
To kill the Lord of Arlon, for some spite
That each had to him.

OCCO.

　　　　　　Miscreant, he lied!
Whoe'er procured him, it was never I.
Master Van Artevelde, my Lord of Arlon,
Believe not I would sin in such a sort.
Have mercy on a miserable man!　*[Falls on his knees.*

Oh God! there's some mistake, or else he lied.

GILBERT.

How say'st thou that he lied?   Sirs, it is true
I with this craven beggarly companion—
Of whose accompliceship to do the deed,

And not the deed itself, I speak with shame—
I with this caitiff truly did conspire,
For good and ample reasons, to remove
Sir Walter D'Arlon from this troublesome world.
Such chances as no prudence could forefend
Have baulk'd my purpose, and I go myself.
Wherefore, sirs, God be with you!   To the block!
What are ye dreaming of, ye sluggish hinds?

ARTEVELDE (signing to the men-at-arms, who lead out
GILBERT MATTHEW).

Aye, Gilbert, God forgive thee for thy sins!
Thou steppest statelily the only walk
Thou hast to take upon this solid earth.
Full many a better man less bravely dieth.
Take forth the other too.

OCCO.

            Stop: hear me yet.
If through pretext of justice I am doom'd,
What justice is it that believes not me,
And yet believes such villains as Romero
And Gilbert Matthew!   Find a credible tongue
To testify against me ere you strike.

Enter VAN RYK, conducting ADRIANA, who throws herself into
the arms of VAN ARTEVELDE. He supports her, and
addresses himself to OCCO.

ARTEVELDE.

Lo! here a witness! look upon this face,
And bid death welcome.   Lead him to the block.

ADRIANA.

Oh, spare him; speak not now of shedding blood,

Now, in this hour of happiness!   Oh, spare him!
Vengeance is God's, whose function take not thou!
Relent, Van Artevelde, and spare his life.

ARTEVELDE.

Not though an angel plead.   Vengeance is God's;
But God doth oftentimes dispense it here
By human ministration.   To my hands
He render'd victory this eventful day
For uses higher than my happiness.
Let Flanders judge me from my deeds to-night,
That I from this time forth will thus proceed,
Justice with mercy tempering where I may:
But executing always.   Lead him out.
                                        [Occo *is led out.*

Now, Adriana, I am wholly thine.

END OF THE FIRST PART.

The curtain falls upon the fancied stage,
The tale half told: here rest thee, reader sage;
Pause here and trim thine intellectual light,
Which, more than mine, shall make my meanings bright.
That ancient writer whose romantic heart
Loved war in every shape, —its pride, its art,
Its shows, appurtenance,—whose page is still
The theatre of war, turn where we will,—
That old historian, of whose truthful text
I dog the heels,—me whither leads he next?
To dark descents he guides me; sad and stern,
Him following forth, the lesson that I learn,

That in the shocks of powers so wild and rude,
Success but signifies vicissitude ;
That of that man who seeks a sovran sphere,
The triumph is the trial most severe.
And yet in times so stormy, in a land
Where Virtue's self held forth a bloody hand
To greet arm'd Justice,—in such times as these
Still woman's love could find the way to please.
Thus in the tissue of my tale, herein
By records not unvouch'd, again I spin,
As heretofore, an interwoven thread
Of feminine affection fancy-fed.

—Rest thee a space : or if thou lov'st to hear
A soft pulsation in thine easy ear,
Turn thou the page, and let thy senses drink
A lay that shall not trouble thee to think.
Quitting the heroine of the past, thou'lt see
In this prefigured her that is to be,
And find what life was hers before the date
That with the Fleming's fortunes link'd her fate.
This sang she to herself one summer's eve,
A recreant from festivities that grieve
The heart not festive ; stealing to her bower,
With this she wiled away the lonely evening hour.

THE LAY OF ELENA.

He asked me had I yet forgot
  The mountains of my native land?
I sought an answer, but had not
  The words at my command.
They would not come, and it was better so,
For had I utter'd aught, my tears I know
Had started at the word as free to flow.

But I can answer when there's none that hears;
And now if I should weep, none sees my tears;
And in my soul the voice is rising strong,
That speaks in solitude,—the voice of song.

Yes, I remember well
  The land of many hues,
Whose charms what praise can tell,
  Whose praise what heart refuse?
Sublime, but neither bleak nor bare,
Nor misty, are the mountains there,—
Softly sublime, profusely fair!
Up to their summits clothed in green,
And fruitful as the vales between,

They lightly rise,
And scale the skies,
And groves and gardens still abound,
For where no shoot
Could else take root,
The peaks are shelved and terraced round;
Earthward appear, in mingled growth,
The mulberry and maize,—above
The trellised vine extends to both
The leafy shade they love.
Looks out the white-walled cottage here,
The lowly chapel rises near;
Far down the foot must roam to reach
The lovely lake and bending beach;
Whilst chestnut green and olive grey
Chequer the steep and winding way.

A bark is launch'd on Como's lake,
A maiden sits abaft;
A little sail is loosed to take
The night wind's breath, and waft
The maiden and her bark away,
Across the lake and up the bay.
And what doth there that lady fair,
Upon the wavelet toss'd?
Before her shines the evening star,
Behind her in the woods afar
The castle lights are lost.
What doth she there? The evening air
Lifts her locks, and her neck is bare;
And the dews, that now are falling fast,

May work her harm, or a rougher blast
   May come from yonder cloud,
And that her bark might scarce sustain,
So slightly built,—and why remain,
   And would she be allowed
To brave the wind and sit in the dew
At night on the lake, if her mother knew?

Her mother sixteen years before
The burthen of the baby bore;
And though brought forth in joy, the day
So joyful, she was wont to say,
In taking count of after years,
Gave birth to fewer hopes than fears.
   For seldom smiled
   The serious child,
And as she passed from childhood, grew
More far-between those smiles and few,
   More sad and wild.
And though she loved her father well,
  And though she loved her mother more,
Upon her heart a sorrow fell,
  And sapped it to the core.
And in her father's castle, nought
She ever found of what she sought,
And all her pleasure was to roam
Among the mountains far from home,
And through thick woods, and wheresoe'er
She saddest felt to sojourn there;
And oh! she loved to linger afloat
On the lonely lake in the little boat.

It was not for the forms,—though fair,
Though grand they were beyond compare,—
It was not only for the forms
Of hills in sunshine or in storms,
Or only unrestrained to look
On wood and lake, that she forsook
    By day or night
      Her home, and far
    Wandered by light
      Of sun or star.
It was to feel her fancy free,
  Free in a world without an end,
With ears to hear, and eyes to see,
  And heart to apprehend.
It was to leave the earth behind,
And rove with liberated mind,
As fancy led, or choice, or chance,
Through wildered regions of romance.
And many a castle would she build;
And all around the woods were filled
With knights and squires that rode amain
With ladies saved and giants slain;
And as some contest wavered, came,
With eye of fire and breath of flame,
A dragon that in cave profound
Had had his dwelling underground;
And he had closed the dubious fight,
But that, behold! there came in sight
A hippogriff, that wheeled his flight
Far in the sky, then swooping low,
Brings to the field a fresher foe:

1

Dismay'd by this diversion, fly
The dragon and his dear ally ;
And now the victor knight unties
The prisoner, his unhoped-for prize,
  And lo ! a beauteous maid is she,
Whom they, in their unrighteous guise,
  Had fasten'd naked to a tree !

Much dreaming these, yet was she much awake
To portions of things earthly, for the sake
Whereof, as with a charm, away would flit
The phantoms, and the fever intermit.
Whatso' of earthly things presents a face
Of outward beauty, or a form of grace,
Might not escape her, hidden though it were
From courtly recognition ; for with her
Nature's credentials in a peasant's face
Awarded him pre-eminence of place :
Give but a handmaid majesty of mien
The handmaid rose in station to a Queen.
Devoted thus to what was fair to sight,
She loved too little else, nor this aright,
And many disappointments could not cure
This born obliquity, or break the lure
Which this strong passion spread : she grew not wise
Nor grows : experience with a world of sighs
Purchased, and tears and heart-break have been hers,
And taught her nothing : where she erred she errs.

Be it avowed, when all is said,
She trod the path the many tread ;—

o

She loved too soon in life; her dawn
Was bright with sunbeams, whence is drawn
A sure prognostic that the day
Will not unclouded pass away.
Too young she loved, and he on whom
Her first love lighted, in the bloom
Of boyhood was, and so was graced
With all that earliest runs to waste.
Intelligent, loquacious, mild,
Yet gay and sportive as a child,
With feelings light and quick, that came
And went, like flickerings of flame;
A soft demeanour, and a mind
Bright and abundant in its kind,
That, playing on the surface, made
A rapid change of light and shade,
Or if a darker hour perforce
At times o'ertook him in his course,
Still sparkling thick like glow-worms show'd
Life was to him a summer's road,—
Such was the youth to whom a love
For grace and beauty far above
Their due deserts, betray'd a heart
Which might have else perform'd a loftier part.

First love the world is wont to call
The passion which was now her all.
So be it called; but be it known,
    The feeling which possess'd her now
Was novel in degree alone;
Love early mark'd her for his own;

Soon as the winds of heaven had blown
Upon her, had the seed been sown
  In soil which needed not the plough ;
And passion with her growth had grown,
  And strengthen'd with her strength, and how
Could love be new, unless in name,
Degree, and singleness of aim ?
A tenderness had filled her mind
Pervasive, viewless, undefined ;—
As keeps the subtle fluid oft
Its secret, gathering in the soft
And sultry air, till felt at length
In all its desolating strength,
So silent, so devoid of dread,
Her objectless affections spread ;
Not wholly unemploy'd, but squander'd
At large where'er her fancy wander'd ;
Till one attraction, one desire
Concentred all the scatter'd fire ;
It broke, it burst, it blazed amain,
It flash'd its light o'er hill and plain,
O'er earth below and heaven above,—
And then it took the name of love.

How fared that love ? the tale so old,
So common, needs it to be told ?
Bellagio's woods, ye saw it through
From first accost to last adieu ;
Its changes, seasons, you can tell,—
At least you typify them well.
First came the genial, hopeful spring,

With bursting buds and birds that sing,
And fast though fitful progress made
To brighter suns and broader shade.
Those brighter suns, that broader shade,
They came, and richly then array'd
Was bough and sward, and all below
Gladdened by summer's equal glow.
What next? a change is slowly seen,
  And deepeneth day by day
The darker, soberer, sadder green
  Prevenient to decay.
Yet still at times through that green gloom,
As sudden gusts might make them room,
  And lift the spray so light,
The berries of the mountain-ash,
Arching the torrent's foam and flash,
  Waved gladly into sight.
But rare those short-lived gleamings grew,
And wore the woods a sicklier hue ;
Destruction now his phalanx forms
'Mid wailing winds and gathering storms ;
And last comes Winter's withering breath,
Keen as desertion, cold—cold as the hand of death !

Is the tale told ? too well, alas !
Is pictured here what came to pass.
So long as light affections play'd
Around their path, he loved the maid ;
Loved in half gay, half tender mood,
By passion touch'd, but not subdued ;
Laugh'd at the flame he felt or lit ;

Replied to tenderness with wit;
Sometimes when passion brightlier burn'd,
Its tokens eagerly return'd,
Then calm, supine, but pleased no less,
Softly sustain'd each soft caress.
She, watching with delight the while
His half-closed eyes and gradual smile,
(Slow pleasure's smile, how far more worth,
More beautiful than smiles of mirth!)
Seem'd to herself when back she cast
A hurried look upon the past,
  As changed from what she then had been,
As was the moon, who having run
Her orbit through since this begun,
  Now shone apparent Queen.
How dim a world, how blank a waste,
A shadowy orb how faintly traced,
Her crescent fancy first embraced!
How fair an orb, a world how bright,
How fill'd with glory and with light
Had now reveal'd itself to sight!
A glory of her essence grown,
A light incorporate with her own!

Forth from such paradise of bliss
Open the way and easy is,
  Like that renown'd of old;
And easier than the most was this,
For they were sorted more amiss
  Than outward things foretold.
The goddess that with cruel mirth

The daughters and the sons of earth
Mismatches, hath a cunning eye
In twisting of a treacherous tie;
Nor is she backward to perceive
That loftier minds to lower cleave
With ampler love (as that which flows
From a rich source) than these to those;
For still the source, not object, gives
The daily food whereon love lives.
The well-spring of his love was poor
Compared to hers: his gifts were fewer;
The total light that was in him
Before a spark of hers grew dim;
Too high, too grave, too large, too deep,
Her love could neither laugh nor sleep—
And thus it tired him; his desire
Was for a less consuming fire:
He wish'd that she should love him well,
Not wildly; wish'd her passion's spell
To charm her heart, but leave her fancy free;
To quicken converse, not to quell;
He granted her to sigh, for so could he;
But when she wept, why should it be?
'Twas irksome, for it stole away
The joy of his love-holiday.
Bred of such uncongenial mood
At length would some dim doubt intrude
If what he felt, so far below
Her passion's pitch, were love or no.
With that the common day-light's beam
Broke in upon his morning dream,

And as that common day advanced
His heart was wholly unentranced.

What follow'd was not good to do,
    Nor is it good to tell;
The anguish of that worst adieu
Which parts with love and honour too,
    Abides not,—so far well.
The human heart can not sustain
Prolong'd inalterable pain,
And not till reason cease to reign
Will nature want some moments brief
Of other moods to mix with grief;
Such and so hard to be destroy'd
That vigour which abhors a void,
And in the midst of all distress,
Such nature's need for happiness!
And when she rallied thus, more high
Her spirits ran, she knew not why,
Than was their wont in times than these
Less troubled, with a heart at ease.
So meet extremes; so joy's rebound
Is highest from the hollowest ground;
So vessels with the storm that strive
Pitch higher as they deeplier dive.

Well had it been if she had curb'd
These transports of a mind disturb'd;
For grief is then the worst of foes
When, all intolerant of repose,
It sends the heart abroad to seek

From weak recoils exemptions weak ;
After false gods to go astray,
Deck altars vile with garlands gay,
And place a painted form of stone
On Passion's abdicated throne.

Till then her heart was as a mound
Or simple plot of garden ground
    Far in a forest wild,
Where many a seedling had been sown,
And many a bright-eyed floweret grown
    To please a favourite child.
Delighted was the child to call
    The plot of garden-ground her own ;
Delighted was she at the fall
Of evening mild when shadows tall
Cross-barr'd the mound and cottage wall,
    To linger there alone.
Nor seem'd the garden flowers less fair,
Nor loved she less to linger there,
When glisten'd in the morning dew
Each lip of red and eye of blue ;
And when the sun too brightly burn'd
Towards the forest's verge she turn'd,
Where stretch'd away from glade to glade
A green interminable shade ;
And in the skirts thereof a bower
Was built with many a creeping flower,
For shelter at the noon-tide hour ;
And from the forest walks was heard
The voice of many a singing bird,

With murmurs of the cushat-dove,
That tell the secret of her love:
And pleasant therefore all day long,
From earliest dawn to even-song,—
Supremely pleasant was this wild
Sweet garden to the woodsman's child.—
The whirlwind came with fire and flood
And smote the garden in the wood;
All that was form'd to give delight
Destruction levell'd in a night;
The morning broke, the child awoke,
And when she saw what sudden stroke
The garden which she loved had swept
To ruin, she sat down and wept.
Her grief was great, but it had vent;
Its force, not spared, was sooner spent;
And she bethought her to repair
The garden which had been so fair.
Then roam'd she through the forest walks,
Cropping the wild flowers by their stalks,
And divers full-blown blossoms gay
She gather'd, and in fair array
Disposed, and stuck them in the mound
Which had been once her garden-ground.
They seem'd to flourish for awhile,
A moment's space she seem'd to smile;
But brief the bloom, and vain the toil,
They were not native to the soil.
That other child, beneath whose zone
Were passions fearfully full-grown,—
She too essay'd to deck the waste

Where love had grown, which love had graced,
With false adornments, flowers not fruit,
Fast-fading flowers, that strike not root,—
With pleasures alien to her breast,
That bloom but briefly at the best,
The world's sad substitutes for joys
To minds that lose their equipoise.

On Como's lake the evening star
    Is trembling as before;
An azure flood, a golden bar,
There as they were before they are,
But she that loved them—she is far,
    Far from her native shore.
No more is seen her slender boat
Upon the star-lit lake afloat,
With oar or sail at large to rove,
Or tether'd in its wooded cove
'Mid gentle waves that sport around
And rock it with a gurgling sound.
Keel up, it rots upon the strand,
Its gunwale sunken in the sand,
Where suns and tempests warp'd and shrank
Each shatter'd rib and riven plank.
Never again that land-wreck'd craft
Shall feel the billow boom abaft;
Never, when springs the freshening gale,
Take life again from oar or sail:
Nor shall the freight that once it bore
Again be seen on lake or shore.

A foreign land is now her choice,
    A foreign sky above her,
And unfamiliar is each voice
    Of those that say they love her.
A prince's palace is her home,
And marble floor and gilded dome,
Where festive myriads nightly meet,
Quick echoes of her steps repeat.
And she is gay at times, and light
From her makes many faces bright;
And circling flatterers hem her in,
Assiduous each a word to win,
And smooth as mirrors each the while
Reflects and multiplies her smile.
But fitful were her smiles, nor long
She cast them to that courtly throng;
And should the sound of music fall
Upon her ear in that high hall,
The smile was gone, the eye that shone
So brightly, would be dimm'd anon,
And objectless would then appear
As stretch'd to check the starting tear.
The chords within responsive rung,
For music spoke her native tongue.

And then the gay and glittering crowd
Is heard not, laugh they ne'er so loud;
Nor then is seen the simpering row
Of flatterers, bend they ne'er so low;
For there before her where she stands,
The mountains rise, the lake expands;

Around the terraced summit twines
The leafy coronal of vines;
Within the watery mirror deep
Nature's calm converse lies asleep;
Above she sees the sky's blue glow,
The forest's varied green below,
And far its vaulted vistas through
A distant grove of darker hue,
Where mounting high from clumps of oak
Curls lightly up the thin gray smoke;
And o'er the boughs that over-bower
The crag, a castle's turrets tower—
An eastern casement mantled o'er
    With ivy, flashes back the gleam
Of sun-rise—it was there of yore
She sate to see that sun-rise pour
Its splendour round—she sees no more,
      For tears disperse the dream.

Thus seized and speechless had she stood,
Surveying mountain, lake, and wood,
When to her ear came that demand
Had she forgot her native land?
'Twas but a voice within replied
She had forgotten all beside.
For words are weak and most to seek
    When wanted fifty-fold,
And then if silence will not speak,
Or trembling lip and changing cheek,
    There's nothing told.
But could she have reveal'd to him

Who question'd thus, the vision bright
That ere his words were said grew dim
 And vanish'd from her sight,
Easy the answer were to know
 And plain to understand,—
  That mind and memory both must fail,
  And life itself must slacken sail,
And thought its functions must forego,
And fancy lose its latest glow,
 Or ere that land
Could pictured be less bright and fair
To her whose home and heart are there!
That land the loveliest that eye can see
The stranger ne'er forgets, then how should she!

. . .

—Cease the soft sounds, the mellow voice is mute,
And quivers to a close that plaintive lady's lute.—
Pass we to matters masculine; to strains
Where weightier themes may pay the reader's pains.
Again disclose we counsels of the wise,
Deeds of the warlike:—let the Curtain rise.

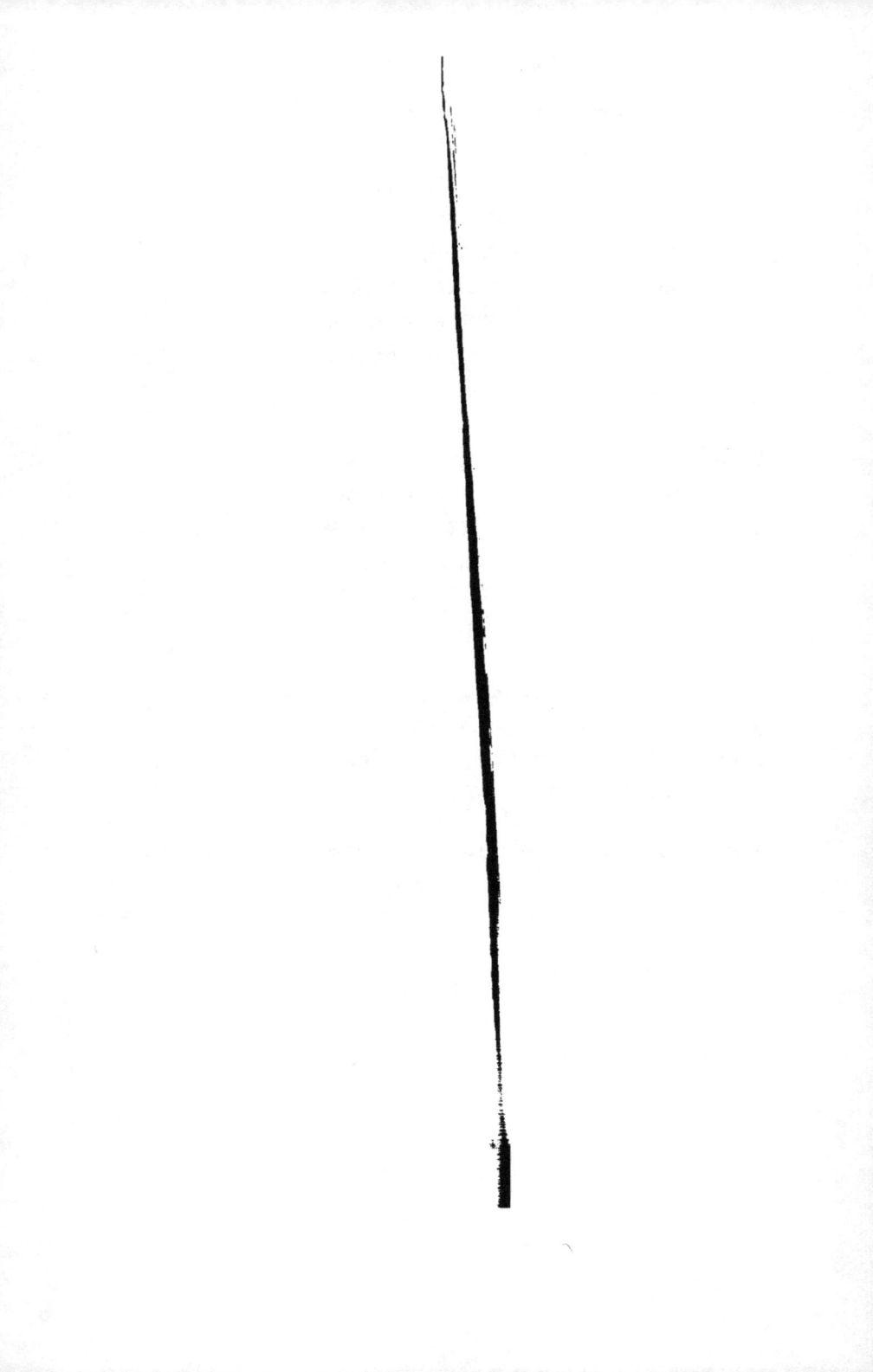

PHILIP VAN ARTEVELDE.

PART THE SECOND.

" Oh Lord. what is thys worldys blysse,
    That changeth as the mone!
My somer's day in lusty May
    Is derked before the none."
                        THE NOT-BROWNE MAYD.

" I say, ye Commoners, why were ye so stark mad,
    What frantyk frensy fyll in youre brayne;
Where was youre wit and reason ye shuld have had?
    What willfull foly made yow to ryse agayne
Yowre naturall lord?"
                        SKELTON.

DRAMATIS PERSONÆ.

(SECOND PART.)

——◆——

MEN OF FLANDERS.

PHILIP VAN ARTEVELDE, *Regent of Flanders.*

PETER VAN DEN BOSCH.

VAN RYK.

VAN MUCK.

VAUCLAIRE, } *in command at Ypres.*
ROOSDYK,

FATHER JOHN OF HEDA.

A PAGE *of Van Artevelde's.*

A FRIAR.

VAN STOCKENSTROM, } *Citizens of Ypres.*
VAN WHELE,

The Burgomaster and divers Burgesses of Ypres, Officers,
Messengers, &c.

MEN OF FRANCE.

KING CHARLES THE SIXTH.

THE DUKE OF BURGUNDY, *his Uncle, and Heir Presumptive to the Earl
of Flanders.*

THE DUKE OF BOURBON, *also Uncle to the King.*

SIR FLEUREANT OF HEURLÉE, *a Follower of the Duke of Bourbon.*

SIR OLIVER OF CLISSON, *Constable of France.*

SIR JOHN DE VIEN, *Admiral of France.*

THE LORDS OF SAIMPI, SANXERE, *and* ST. JUST; SIR RAOUL OF
RANEVAL; *the* LORD OF COUCY, *and many other Lords and
Knights belonging to the French King's Council.*

TRISTRAM OF LESTOVET, *Clerk of the Council.*

WOMEN.

ELĒNA DELLA TORRE, *an Italian Lady.*

CECILE, *her Attendant.*

DAME VOORST, *a Woman of Ypres.*

The SCENE is laid sometimes in FLANDERS and sometimes
in FRANCE.

PHILIP VAN ARTEVELDE.

ACT I.

SCENE I.—*An Ante-room to the State Apartments of the Grand Justiciary in the Royal Palace at Senlis, in France.—Several groups of Suitors holding Petitions in their hands. In front a Yeoman of Tournesis, and near him* SIR FLEUREANT OF HEURLÉE.

SIR FLEUREANT.

If I may be so bold, friend, whence art thou?
The times are stirring, and come whence thou may'st
Thou must bring news.

YEOMAN.

            So please your worship's grace
I come from this side Tournay; I am French,
And though I say it, sir, an honest yeoman.

SIR FLEUREANT.

And, honest yeoman, what's thine errand here?

YEOMAN.

I have a suit, sir, to my noble lord
The Duke of Burgundy.

P

SIR FLEUREANT.
                    Why, what ?—what suit ?

YEOMAN.
'Tis but for justice, sir ; I crave but justice.

SIR FLEUREANT.
Hast thou the price of justice in thy pocket ?

YEOMAN.
Nay, sir, I am poor.

SIR FLEUREANT.
Poor, and want justice ?—where was thy mother's thrift
To bring thee up in such a poor estate
And yet to lack such dainties !   Say wherein
Would'st thou be justified ? who is't hath wrong'd thee ?

YEOMAN.
Last Wednesday, sir, a troop of Flemings, led
By fierce Frans Ackerman, the frontier pass'd
And burn'd my homestead, ravaged all my fields,
And did sore havoc in the realm of France.

SIR FLEUREANT.
What say'st thou ? is it so ?   Ha, ha ! my friend,
This is high matter.   Thou'lt be heard on this.

Enter Usher.

USHER.
Depart ye, sirs ; his grace is with the king ;
He bids you all depart and come to-morrow ;
To-day his grace hath business with the king,
And will not be molested.   Clear the chamber.
Their graces and the king are coming hither,
And would be private ;—prithee, sir, depart.
                              [*To the* Yeoman, *who lingers.*

SIR FLEUREANT.

Take thou thy grievance to the outer hall,
But go no further hence.   Soft, Master Usher;
My friend shall have an audience of the duke.
Look he be carefully bestow'd without
Till he be call'd.   He is an injured man;
An injured man, and being so, yet welcome.
The grief he hath is worth its weight in gold.
Bestow him carefully without.

USHER.

This way.
[*Exit, with the* Yeoman.

Enter the DUKES *of* BURGUNDY *and* BOURBON.

BURGUNDY.

Good morrow, Flurry.   Not on us, good brother.
I grant you were we rashly to make war,
No council summon'd, no estates convened,
Then aught that should unhappily ensue
Might chance be charged on us, as natural guides,
And so reputed, of the youthful king.
But back'd by all the council,—yea, by all,
For I'll be warranty no voice dissents,—
Back'd by the council, wherein weighty reasons
Shall be well urged———

BOURBON.

Ay, brother, there it is!
That you have reasons of your own none doubts,
And Jacques Bonhomme will be bold to say
That reasons which are rank in Burgundy
Have been transplanted to the soil of France,
That fits them not.

P 2

BURGUNDY.

           In Jacques Bonhomme's throat
I'll tell him that he slanders me and lies.
No soil in Christendom but fits my reasons ;
No soil where virtue, chivalry, and honour
Are fed and flourish, but shall fit them well.
When honour and nobility fall prone
In Flanders, think you they stand fast in France?
Or losing ground in France, have hope elsewhere ?
This by no narrow bound is circumscribed :
It is the cause of chivalry at large.
Though heir to Flanders I am Frenchman born,
And nearer have at heart the weal of France
Than my far off inheritance.   Come, come ;
Lay we before the council the sad truth
Of these distractions that so rock the realm,—
Paris possess'd by Nicholas le Flamand
Where law's a nothing and the king a name ;
Armies with mallets but beginning there,
And gathering like the snow-wreaths in a storm
Before a man hath time to get him housed,
At Chalons on the Marne, Champagne, Beauvoisin,
At Orleans, at Rheims, at Blois, and Rouen,
And every reach of road from Paris south :
Then point we to the north, where Artevelde
Wields at his single will the Flemish force,
Five hundred thousand swords ; and ask what fate
Awaits our France, if those with these unite,
Bold villains both, and ripe for riving down
All royalty,—thereafter or therewith
Nobility !—Then strike whiles yet apart
Each single foe.

BOURBON.

But Philip speaks us fair.

BURGUNDY.

As fair as false.

SIR FLEUREANT.

My lords, there's proof of that
Here close at hand ; a yeoman from Tournesis,
But now arrived with news of ravage done
On the French frontier.

BURGUNDY.

There, good brother, there !
There's Flemish friendship, Flemish love of peace !
Shall we make nought of this ?

BOURBON.

We'll sift it, brother,
And find if it be true.

BURGUNDY.

Where is the man ?

SIR FLEUREANT.

I'll bring him in, my lord.   [*Exit.*

Enter the KING *with a Hawk on his hand.*

BURGUNDY.

How now, my royal cousin, have you done ?
Can you repeat the speech ?

KING.

O yes, good uncle.
' Right noble our liege councillors all, We greet you !
We have required your—'

BURGUNDY.

Presence here this day.

KING.

'We have required your presence here this day
On matters of high import, which surcharge
Our royal mind, that still affects the weal
Of our beloved lieges.   Much to peace
Our tender years incline us, but—but—but—'
I'll fly my hawk, good uncle, now; to-morrow
I'll say the rest.   Come, Jerry, Jerry, Jerry!
He is a Marzarolt, uncle, just reclaim'd;
The best in France for flying at the fur.
Whew!   Jerry, Jerry, Jerry!

BURGUNDY.
                              Cousin, stay.

Enter SIR FLEUREANT *with the* Yeoman.

Here is a worthy yeoman from Tournesis,
Who hath a tale to tell of ravage done
Upon the realm of France.   ·

KING.
                         A yeoman, uncle?
Here, worthy yeoman, you shall kiss our hand.
Get off there, Jerry.
                    [*The* Yeoman *kneels and kisses his hand.*

BOURBON.
                    Now, sir, from what place
In France or Flanders, com'st thou?

YEOMAN.
                         Please your highness,
'Twas a small holding from my lord of Vergues
Close to the liberties of Fontenoy.

BOURBON.
This side the bourn?   ⚡

YEOMAN.

Three miles, my lord, and long ones.

BURGUNDY.

Three miles in France.

BOURBON.

And what befell thee there?

YEOMAN.

My lord, my wife and I, on Wednesday night,
Saw fires to the north and 'westward, up by Orcq
And round to Beau-Renard, and knew by that
The Flemish commons had been there, that late
Have roam'd through Flanders, burning where they came
The houses of the gentlemen and knights.
Then said my wife (Pierilla, if it please you,)
' 'Tis well we're yeomen and of poor estate,
And that we're lieges of a mightier lord
Than was the Count of Flanders : 'tis God's mercy !
Or else might they that look from Beau-Renard
To the south and eastward, see this house on fire
To-morrow night, as we this night see theirs ! '
But hardly had she said it, when due south
The sky was all on fire ; and then we knew
The Flemings were in France, and Auzain burn'd.
We fled away, and looking back, beheld
Our humble dwelling flaming like a torch.
So, then, quoth I, we'll to my Lord the King,
And tell what's come to pass.

BURGUNDY.

Thou hast done well ;
Retire : His Majesty will bring thy case

Before the council.   Hold thyself prepared
To tell thy story there.
                              [*Exit* Yeoman.
I think my royal cousin, though he's young,
Bears yet a mind too mettlesome to brook
Such wrongs as these.   Your Majesty has heard :
The Flemish hordes lift plunder in your realm,
Driving your subjects from their peaceful homes,
Burning, destroying, wheresoe'er they reach,
And ever on nobility they fall
With sharpest tooth : let this have leave to grow,
And French insurgents shall from Flemish learn
The tricks of treason,—German boors from both ;
Till kings and princes, potentates and peers,
Landgraves, electors, palatines, and prelates,
Dukes, earls, and knights, shall be no more accounted
Than as the noblest and the loftiest trees,
Which the woodwarden as he walks the forest
Marks for the axe.   Our warlike cousin king
When once he takes the field shall make brief work
With the base Flemings, and with one sharp blow
Cut short by the head some twenty thousand treasons
Hatch'd lately, so to say, beneath the wings
Of this Van Artevelde, which chipp'd the shell
Two months agone when Paris grew too hot
To hold us, and that now are fledged and enter'd.
I would your Majesty were now in arms,
Leading your gallant troops.

                    KING.
                              To-morrow, uncle !
We will be arm'd and lead our troops to-morrow.
We'll ride the chestnut with the bells at his heels.
Let it be done to-morrow.

BOURBON.

            Should the council
Declare for war, your force can not so soon
Be drawn together as your highness thinks,
Though it lies mainly hereabouts.

BURGUNDY.

            No matter.
Speak boldly to the council as to us,
And if you'd presently be in the field
Be diligent to learn your speech—come in—
Both that you have and something I'll put to it
Touching this yeoman's grief—come in with me—
Ho! take away this hawk—and you shall have it.

        [*Exeunt* DUKE OF BURGUNDY *and the* KING.

BOURBON.

My brother, Fleureant, is all too hot
In this affair; he's ever taking starts,
And leaving them that he should carry with him.
He'll fright the council from their calmer sense,
And drive them to some rash resolve.

SIR FLEUREANT.

            My lord,
You shall perceive to-morrow at the board
How vast and voluble a thing is wit,
And what a sway a little of it hath
With councillors of state. My lord of Burgundy
Will blaze and thunder through a three hours' speech,
And stamp and strike his fist upon the board,
Whilst casements rattling and a fall of soot
Shall threaten direful war.

BOURBON.

         The constable,

The Earls of Ewe, and Blois, St. Poule, and Laval,
Guesclin, St. Just, the Seneschal of Rieux,
Raoul of Raneval,—all these and more,
Are to my certain knowledge clean against him.
They deem a mission should be sent to Flanders
Before the sword be drawn, and with my will
Nought else shall come to pass.

SIR FLEUREANT.
                              Van Artevelde,
Though obstinate at times, is politic too,
And lacks not understanding; he'll not brave
The wrath of France if he be well entreated.

BOURBON.
I spake with one last night who came from Bruges,
And on his way had sojourn'd in the camp
At Oudenarde, where, when the turbulent towns
Behind his back can spare him from their broils,
Van Artevelde o'ersees the leaguering force.
There was a market in the camp, he said,
And all things plentiful,—fruit, cheese, and wine,
All kinds of mercery, cloth, furs, and silks,
With trinketry, the plunder daily brought
By Van den Bosch's marauders.   Went and came
All men that chose from Brabant, Hainault, Liege,
And Germany; but Frenchmen were forbidden.
Van Artevelde, he said, in all things apes
The state and bearing of a sovereign prince;
Has bailiffs, masters of the horse, receivers,
A chamber of accompt, a hall of audience,
Off gold and silver eats, is clad in robes
Of scarlet furr'd with minever, gives feasts

With minstrelsy and dancing night and day
To damsels and to ladies,—whom amongst
Pre-eminent is that Italian minx
Late domiciled with me, the girl Elena.
To Bruges in company with me she came,
Where waiting till on my return from Liege
I could rejoin her, to the conqueror's hands
She fell when Bruges was taken.

SIR FLEUREANT.

Soh, my lord !
That lady hath a hook that twitches still.
If what I heard in Gascony be true
You claim'd her from Van Artevelde in vain,
Who answer'd not your missives.

BOURBON.

True it is ;
And he shall answer for so answering not,
If any voice of potency be mine
Touching this war.   But he may yet take thought
And make amends ; I'll send him once again
A message, and I know not who's so fit
To take it as thyself.

SIR FLEUREANT.

My lord, my tongue
Can utter nought with so much grace by half
As what you bid it speak ; I'll bear your message.

BOURBON.

Not that for foolishness and woman's love
I would do this or that, but you shall note
My honour is impawn'd.   Some half-hour hence
Come to my chamber, where in privacy

We'll further speak of this; and bring thou there
The yeoman of Tournesis; he must learn
How to demean himself before the Council.
He has been tamper'd with, I nothing doubt,
And what he's tutor'd to must we unteach.
Things run too fast to seed.

                                              [Exit.

SIR FLEUREANT.

                                    What soldier's heart
By dotage such as his was e'er possess'd
Upon a paramour! To win her back
Peace, war, or anything to him were good,
Nought evil but what works contrariwise.
And still his love goes muffled up for shame,
And masks itself with show of careless slights,
And giving her ill names of jade and minx,
Gipsy and slut.—The world's a masquerade,
And he whose wisdom is to pay it court
Should mask his own unpopular penetration,
And seem to think its several seemings real.

SCENE II.—*The Flemish Camp before Oudenarde. A Platform
in front of* VAN ARTEVELDE'S *Tent.*

Enter VAN ARTEVELDE *and* VAN RYK.

VAN RYK.

You seem fatigued, my lord.

ARTEVELDE.

Look to that horse; he coughs—I think I am;
The sun was hot for such a long day's ride.
What is the hour?

VAN RYK.

The moon has not yet risen,
It cannot yet be nine.

ARTEVELDE.

Not nine? well, well;

' Be the day never so long,
   At length cometh even-song.'

So saith the ancient rhyme. At eight o'clock
Or thereabouts, we cross'd the bridge of Rosebecque.

VAN RYK.

'Twas thereabouts, my lord.

ARTEVELDE.

Tell me, Van Ryk,
Was anything of moment in your thoughts
As we were crossing.

VAN RYK.

In my thoughts, my lord?
Nothing to speak of.

ARTEVELDE.

Well now it is strange!
I never knew myself to sleep o' horseback,
And yet I must have slept. The evening's heat
Had much oppress'd me; then the tedious tract
Of naked moorland, and the long flat road
And slow straight stream, for ever side by side,
Like poverty and crime—I'm sure I slept.

VAN RYK.

I saw not that you did, my lord.

ARTEVELDE.

I did;
Ay, and dream'd too. 'Twas an unwholesome dream,

If dream it was—a nightmare rather: first
A stifling pressure compass'd in my heart;
On my dull ears, with thick and muffled peal,
Came many a sound of battle and of flight,
Of tumult and distracted cries; my own,
That would have been the loudest, was unheard,
And seem'd to swell the chambers of my brain
With volume vast of sound I could not utter.
The screams of wounded horses, and the crash
Of broken planks, and then the heavy plunge
Of bodies in the water—they were loud,
But yet the sound that was confined in me,
Had it got utterance, would have drown'd them all!
But still it grew and swell'd, and therewithal
The burthen thicken'd on my heart; my blood,
That had been flowing freshly from my wounds,
Trickled, then clotted, and then flow'd no more:
My horse upon the barrier of the bridge
Stumbled; I started; and was wide awake.
'Twas an unpleasant dream.

VAN RYK.

                    It was, my lord.
I wonder how I mark'd not that you slept.

ARTEVELDE.

I must be wakeful now.   Who waits? who's there?
                    [*To an* Attendant, *who enters.*
The man I sent to Ypres with a letter—
Has he return'd?

ATTENDANT.

                    But now, my lord, arrived;
And with him Father John.

ARTEVELDE.

                    He come already!
With more alacrity he meets my wish
Than I deserve.   Prithee, conduct him hither.

ATTENDANT.

He comes, my lord.

ARTEVELDE.

               Then leave us—No, Van Ryk,
Not you; or if you will, lie down within,
And rest you till I call.
                [*Exeunt* VAN RYK *and the* Attendant.

          Enter FATHER JOHN.

My honour'd master, if a thousand welcomes
Could carry more than one, I'd say the word
More oft than you your Ave and your creed.
But welcome is enough.

FATHER JOHN.

                God's love, my son,
Be with you alway.   We have lately been
In outward act more strangers than we were,
But inwardly, I fain would hope, unalter'd.

ARTEVELDE.

Unalter'd, on my soul!   The storms of state
From time to time heave up some monstrous ridge,
Which each from other hides two friendly barks;
Nought else divides us, and we steer, I trust,
One course, are guided by one steadfast star,
That so one anchorage we may reach at last.
The cares and mighty troubles of the times
Have kept me company, and shut yours out.

FATHER JOHN.

It is your place, my son; private respects

Should be far from you—'tis no blame of yours.
But whence the present call?

ARTEVELDE.
                    To that at once.
France is in arms; the earl that was of Flanders
From Hedin went by Arras to Bapaume
On Wednesday se'nnight, if my scouts say true,
And there my lord of Burgundy he met,
And with him made a covenant; from thence
They came to Senlis, where the young king lies,
And there the dukes of Burgundy and Bourbon
Had gather'd from all parts a mighty force,
Some eighty or a hundred thousand men.
May that not startle me?

FATHER JOHN.
                    'Tis a large levy;
But yet you muster more.

ARTEVELDE.
                    Of men at arms
Not half the tale; and those for Senlis bound
Would double—so says fame—these now arrived.
It were a vain and profitless attempt
To disbelieve my danger, howsoe'er
I show a careless countenance to the crowd.
If Nicholas le Flamand call not back
The French king's force, as much I fear he will not,
There's one sufficiency of aid can reach
The measure of my need; one and no more;
And that is aid from England. This not sent,
Or else belated,—coming in the dusk
And sunset of my fortunes,—where am I?

FATHER JOHN.

At England's council-board in Edward's days
Sloth and delay had never seats; no paper
Lay gathering dust and losing its fresh looks,
No business lodged: would that it were so now!
Yet surely if King Richard deem it meet
And useful to his realm to send you aid,
'Twill come with speed.

ARTEVELDE.

          He knows not that despatch
Is now so all-important.   Nor from those
I sent him, will he learn it.   I myself
Thought not King Charles had crept so close upon me,
Else had I put your kindness then to proofs
Which I intend it now,—else had I ask'd
Your presence then in England.

FATHER JOHN.

            Nay, my son,
Six have you sent already—on their way
Our humble hospitality they shared
At Ypres.

ARTEVELDE.

      Then their quality you saw.
They were the best, methought, that I could spare
For foreign service, while thus press'd at home.
The first for state and dignity was named;
He whom Pope Urbayne, after Ghent rebell'd,
Appointed bishop to receive the dues
Which else had fallen to the see of Tournay,
Where Clement is acknowledged; for this end
Was he a bishop made, and to say truth

Q

He's equal to his function.   Next in rank
Comes our sagacious friend, John Sercolacke;
None better and none safer in affairs,
Were it but given to ponder and devise
Beforehand what at every need to say;
But should King Richard ask him on the sudden
What brought him there, confounded will he stand
Till livelier tongues from emptier heads have spoken;
Then on the morrow to a tittle know
What should have been his answer.

FATHER JOHN.
                                          Lois de Vaux
And master Blondel-Vatre have glib tongues.

ARTEVELDE.
Than Lois de Vaux there's no man sooner sees
Whatever at a glance is visible;
What is not, that he sees not, soon nor late.
Quick-witted is he, versatile, seizing points,
But never solving questions; vain he is—
It is his pride to see things on all sides
Which best to do he sets them on their corners.
Present before him arguments by scores
Bearing diversely on the affair in hand,
He'll see them all successively distinctly,
Yet never two of them can see together,
Or gather, blend, and balance what he sees
To make up one account; a mind it is
Accessible to reason's subtlest rays,
And many enter there, but none converge;
It is an army with no general,
An arch without a key-stone.—Then the other

Good Martin Blondel-Vatre—he is rich
In nothing else but difficulties and doubts;
You shall be told the evil of your scheme,
But not the scheme that's better; he forgets
That policy, expecting not clear gain,
Deals ever in alternatives; he's wise
In negatives, is skilful at erasures,
Expert in stepping backwards, an adept
At auguring eclipses; but admit
His apprehensions and demand, what then?
And you shall find you've turn'd the blank leaf over.

FATHER JOHN.

Still three are left.

ARTEVELDE.

Three names, and nothing more.
To please the towns that gave them birth they're sent,
Not for their merits.   Verily, Father John,
I should not willingly invade your leisure,
Or launch you on my now precarious fortunes;
But I am as a debtor against whom
The writs are out—I'm driven upon my friends;
Say, will you stead me?

FATHER JOHN.

With my best of service,
Such as it may be.   To King Richard's court
I will set forth to-morrow.

ARTEVELDE.

Ever kind!
Of all my friends the faithfullest, as the first.
Early to-morrow then we'll treat in full
The matter of your mission.   Now, good night.

Q 2

FATHER JOHN.

Adieu till then, and peace be with your slumbers.

[*Exit.*

ARTEVELDE.

Their hour is yet to come.   What ho! Van Ryk!

Enter VAN RYK.

You're sure, Van Ryk, it has not yet transpired
That I am in the camp?

VAN RYK.

Certain, my lord.

ARTEVELDE.

Then come with me; we'll cast a casual eye
On them that keep the watch;—though sooth to say,
I wish my day's work over,—to forget
This restless world and slumber like a babe;
For I am very tired—yea, tired at heart.

VAN RYK.

Your spirits were wont to bear you up more freshly.
If I might speak, my lord, my humble mind,
You have not, since your honour'd lady's death,
In such a sovereignty possess'd yourself
As you were wont to say that all men should.
Your thoughts have been more inwardly directed,
And led by fancies: should I be too bold
And let my duty lag behind my love,
To put you thus in mind, I crave your pardon.

ARTEVELDE.

That was a loss, Van Ryk; that was a loss.
The love betwixt us was not as the flush
And momentary kindling in warm youth;
But marriage and what term of time was given

Brought it an hourly increase, stored for Heaven.
Well—I am now the sport of circumstance,
Driven from my anchorage;—yet deem not thou
That I my soul surrender to the past
In chains and bondage;—that it is not so,
Bear witness for me long and busy days,
Which jostling and importunate affairs
So push and elbow, they but seldom leave
Shy midnight uninvaded.   No, Van Ryk;
At eve returning wearied to my tent,
If sometimes I may seem to stray in thought,
Seeking what is not there, the mood is brief,
The operative function within call,
Nor know I that for any little hour
The weal of Flanders (if I may presume
To hook it on my hours) is yielded up
To idle thought or vacant retrospect.
But now this body, exigent of rest,
Will needs put in a claim.   One round we'll take,
And then to bed.

VAN RYK.

                   My lord, you must be tired.
I am too bold to trouble you so late
With my unprofitable talk.

ARTEVELDE.

                   Not so;
Your talk is always welcome.   There within
You'll find a wardrobe, with some varlets' cloaks
For use at need; take one about yourself,
And meet me with another at the gate.
                              [*Exit* VAN RYK.

A serviceable, faithful, thoughtful friend,

Is old Van Ryk,—a man of humble heart,
And yet with faculties and gifts of sense
Which place him justly on no lowly level—
Why should I say a lowlier than my own,
Or otherwise than as an equal use him?
That with familiarity respect
Doth slacken, is a word of common use.
I never found it so.

ACT II.

SCENE I.—*The interior of the State Pavilion.*—VAN ARTEVELDE
seated at the head of his Council, with Attendants. *The*
French Herald *and* SIR FLEUREANT OF HEURLÉE. ARTE-
VELDE *rises to receive the* Herald *and reseats himself.*

ARTEVELDE.

France, I perceive, Sir Herald, owns at length
The laws of polity and civil use,
A recognition which I hardly hoped;
For when the messenger that late I sent
In amity, with friendly missives charged,
Was sent to prison, I deem'd some barbarous tribe,
That knew no usages of Christian lands,
Had dispossess'd you and usurp'd the realm.

SIR FLEUREANT.

My lord, you have your messenger again.

ARTEVELDE.

Ay sir, but not through courtesy I think,

Nor yet through love.

[*To the* Herald.

Sir, you have leave to speak.

HERALD.

My lord, I humbly thank you.   I entreat
That in my speech should aught offend your ears,
You from the utterer will remove the fault.
My office I obey and not my will,
Nor is a word that I'm to speak mine own.

ARTEVELDE.

Sir, nothing you can say shall be so gross,
Offensive, or unmannerly conceived,
As that it shall not credibly appear
To come from them that sent you; speak, then, freely.

HERALD.

Philip of Artevelde, sole son of Jacques,
Maltster and brewer in the town of Ghent,
The realm of France this unto thee delivers:
That forasmuch as thou, a liegeman born
To the Earl of Flanders, hast rebelled against him,
And with thy manifold treasons and contempts
Of duty and allegiance, hast drawn in
By twenties and by forties his good towns
To rise in fury and forget themselves,—
Thus saith the puissant and mighty lord,
The earl's affectionate kinsman, Charles of France:
Thou from before this town of Oudenarde
With all thy host shalt vanish like a mist;
Thou shalt surrender to their rightful lord
The towns of Ghent, and Ypres, Cassel, Bruges,
Of Thorout, Rousselart, Damme, Sluys, and Bergues,
Of Harlebeque, Poperinguen, Dendermonde,

Alost and Grammont; and with them all towns
Of lesser name, all castles and strong houses,
Shalt thou deliver up before the Feast
Of Corpus Christi coming, which undone
He the said puissant king, Sir Charles of France,
With all attendance of his chivalry,
Will raise his banner and his kingdom's force,
And scattering that vile people which thou lead'st
Will hang thee on a tree and nail thy head
Over the gates of Ghent, the mother of ill
That spawn'd thee;—and for these and sundry more
Just reasons and sufficient, thou art warn'd
To make thy peace betimes, and so God keep thee!

ARTEVELDE.

Sir Herald, thou hast well discharged thyself
Of an ill function.   Take these links of gold,
And with the company of words I give thee
Back to the braggart king from whom thou cam'st.
First, of my father:—had he lived to know
His glories, deeds, and dignities postponed
To names of barons, earls, and counts (that here
Are to men's ears importunately common
As chimes to dwellers in the market-place)
He with a silent and a bitter mirth
Had listen'd to the boast: may he his son
Pardon for in comparison setting forth
With his the name of this disconsolate earl.
How stand they in the title deeds of fame?
What hold and heritage in distant times
Doth each enjoy—what posthumous possession?
The dusty chronicler with painful search,
Long fingering forgotten scrolls, indites

That Louis Mâle was sometime Earl of Flanders,
That Louis Mâle his sometime earldom lost,
Through wrongs by him committed, that he lived
An outcast long in dole not undeserved,
And died dependent : there the history ends,
And who of them that hear it wastes a thought
On the unfriended fate of Louis Mâle?
But turn the page and look we for the tale
Of Artevelde's renown.   What man was this?
He humbly born, he highly gifted rose
By steps of various enterprise, by skill,
By native vigour to wide sway, and took
What his vain rival having could not keep.
His glory shall not cease, though cloth of gold
Wrap him no more, for not of golden cloth,
Nor fur, nor minever, his greatness came,
Whose fortunes were inborn : strip me the two,
This were the humblest, that the noblest, beggar
That ever braved a storm !

SIR FLEUREANT.

                My lord, your pardon ;
Nothing was utter'd in disparagement
Of your famed father, though a longer life
And better would he assuredly have lived,
Had it seem'd good to him to follow forth
His former craft, nor turn aside to brew
These frothy insurrections.

ARTEVELDE.

              Sir, your back
Shows me no tabard, nor a sign beside,
Denoting what your office is that asks

A hearing in this presence; nor know I yet
By what so friendly fortune I am graced
With your good company and gentle speech.
But we are here no niggards of respect
To merit's unauthenticated forms,
And therefore do I answer you, and thus:
You speak of insurrections: bear in mind
Against what rule my father and myself
Have been insurgent: whom did we supplant?—
There was a time, so ancient records tell,
There were communities, scarce known by name
In these degenerate days, but once far-famed,
Where liberty and justice, hand in hand,
Ordered the common weal; where great men grew
Up to their natural eminence, and none
Saving the wise, just, eloquent, were great;
Where power was of God's gift, to whom he gave
Supremacy of merit, the sole means
And broad highway to power, that ever then
Was meritoriously administer'd,
Whilst all its instruments from first to last,
The tools of state for service high or low,
Were chosen for their aptness to those ends
Which virtue meditates.   To shake the ground
Deep-founded whereupon this structure stood,
Was verily a crime; a treason it was
Conspiracies to hatch against this state
And its free innocence.   But now, I ask,
Where is there on God's earth that polity
Which it is not, by consequence converse,
A treason against nature to uphold?
Whom may we now call free? whom great? whom wise?

Whom innocent ?—the free are only they
Whom power makes free to execute all ills
Their hearts imagine ; they alone are great
Whose passions nurse them from their cradles up
In luxury and lewdness,—whom to see
Is to despise, whose aspects put to scorn
Their station's eminence ; the wise, they only
Who wait obscurely till the bolts of heaven
Shall break upon the land, and give them light
Whereby to walk ; the innocent,—alas !
Poor innocency lies where four roads meet,
A stone upon her head, a stake driven through her,
For who is innocent that cares to live ?
The hand of power doth press the very life
Of innocency out ! What then remains
But in the cause of nature to stand forth,
And turn this frame of things the right side up ?
For this the hour is come, the sword is drawn,
And tell your masters vainly they resist.
Nature, that slept beneath their poisonous drugs,
Is up and stirring, and from north and south,
From east and west, from England and from France,
From Germany, and Flanders, and Navarre,
Shall stand against them like a beast at bay.
The blood that they have shed will hide no longer
In the blood-sloken soil, but cries to heaven.
Their cruelties and wrongs against the poor
Shall quicken into swarms of venomous snakes,
And hiss through all the earth, till o'er the earth,
That ceases then from hissings and from groans,
Rises the song—How are the mighty fallen !
And by the peasant's hand !   Low lie the proud !

And smitten with the weapons of the poor—
The blacksmith's hammer and the woodman's axe.
Their tale is told; and for that they were rich,
And robb'd the poor; and for that they were strong,
And scourged the weak; and for that they made laws
Which turn'd the sweat of labour's brow to blood,—
For these their sins the nations cast them out,
The dunghills are their death-beds, and the stench
From their uncover'd carrion steaming wide,
Turns in the nostrils of enfranchised man
To a sweet savour.   These things come to pass
From small beginnings, because God is just.

SIR FLEUREANT.

Sir, you are bold in prophecy, but words
Will not demolish kingdoms.   This alone
Is clear, that we are charged to carry back
A warlike answer.

ARTEVELDE.

                You have caught my sense.
Let no more words be wasted.   What I said
Shall be engross'd, and render'd to your hands
To spare your memories ; and so farewell
Unto your functions.   For yourselves, I pray you
To grace our table with your company
At dinner time, and taste of what we have.
Meantime farewell.   And you, my honour'd friends
And councillors, I bid you to the board.
Adieu till then.   Good father, by your leave
I will detain you.

> [*The Council breaks up. The* Herald *and* SIR FLEUREANT *are
> conducted out, and only* ARTEVELDE *and* FATHER JOHN
> *remain. After a pause* ARTEVELDE *proceeds.*

                              Did I say too much?
What think you? was I rash?

                        FATHER JOHN.

                              My son, my son!
You've spoken some irrevocable words,
And more, in my weak judgment, than were wise.
Till now might accident have open'd out
A way to concord.   Casualties or care
Might yet have counsell'd peace, and was it well
To send this challenge?

                        ARTEVELDE.

                              Judge me not unheard.
We have been too successful to be safe
In standing still.   Things are too far afoot.
Being so high as this, to be no higher
Were presently to fall.   France will not brook
To see me as I am, though I should bear
My honours ne'er so meekly.   With bold words
I magnify my strength,—perhaps may dim
Their fire-new courage, their advance delay,
And raise the spirits of my friends.

                        FATHER JOHN.
                              My son,
These are the after-thoughts that reason coins
To justify excess, and pay the debts
Of passion's prodigality.

                        ARTEVELDE.
                        Nay, nay!
Something of passion may have mix'd with this,

Good Father, but I lost not from my thoughts
The policy I speak of.

FATHER JOHN.

Might I use
The liberty of former days to one
That's since so much exalted, I would tell
How it is said abroad that Artevelde
Is not unalter'd since he rose to power ;
Is not unvisited of worldly pride
And its attendant passions.

ARTEVELDE.

Say they so ?
Well, if it be so it is late to mend,
For self-amendment is a work of time,
And business will not wait.   Such as I am,
For better or for worse the world must take me,
For I must hasten on.   Perhaps the state
And royal splendour I affect, is deem'd
A proof of pride,—yet they that these contemn
Know little of the springs that move mankind.
'Tis but a juvenile philosophy
That strips itself and casts such things aside,
Which, be they in themselves or vile or precious,
Are means to govern.   Or I'm deem'd morose,
Severe, impatient of what hinders me ;
Yet think what manner of men are these I rule ;
What patience might have made of them, reflect.
If I be stern or fierce, 'tis from strong need
And strange provocatives.   If (which I own not)
I have drunk deeper of ambition's cup,
Be it remember'd that the cup of love

Was wrested from my hand.   Enough of this.
Ambition has its uses in the scheme
Of Providence, whose instrument I am
To work some changes in the world or die.
This hasty coming of the French disturbs me,
And I could wish you gone.

FATHER JOHN.

                              My horses wait
And I am ready.   I will bear in mind
With the best memory that my years permit,
Your charges ; and if nothing more remains,
God's blessing on your enterprise and you !
I go my way.

ARTEVELDE.

                    So long as lies the Lis
Between our hosts, I have the less to fear.
Say to King Richard I shall strive to keep
The passes of the Lis, and if his aid
Find them unforced, his way to France is straight
As that to Windsor.   I shall guard the Lis
With watch as circumspect as seamen keep
When in the night the leeward breakers flash.
But if he linger and the Lis be forced,
Tell him our days are number'd, and that three
Shall close this contest.   I am harping still
On the same string ; but you, my friend revered,
Will pardon my solicitudes, and deem
That they are for my cause, not for myself.
I keep you now no longer ; fare you well,
And may we meet again and meet in joy !
God grant it ! fare you well.

FATHER JOHN.
My horses, ho !

ARTEVELDE.

Let me attend you.

SCENE II.—*A Platform near Artevelde's Pavilion.*—VAN MUCK
is seated at some distance in the background.

Enter SIR FLEUREANT *and the* Herald.

SIR FLEUREANT.

Then be it as I said : the sun shall set
'Twixt seven and eight ; ere then I'll know my course ;
And if the Regent lend a willing ear
To the Duke's message, and this lady send
Upon his summons, merrily we go
Together, and who meets us on the road
Shall say, a goodly company, God bless them !
A man, a woman, and a pursuivant.
But 'twill not be so.

HERALD.'
Let us hope it may.

SIR FLEUREANT.

Assure yourself 'twill otherwise befall.
He will retain her, or herself hold back.
Then shall it be your prudence to depart
With your best speed, whilst I invent a cause
For lingering.   I will not take my answer,
But spin the matter of my mission out
Into such length as with that web to hide
My underworkings.   Be you gone from Flanders
Fast as you may and far, when this falls out,
And you shall tell the Duke with what good will

I hazard in his service loss of all
I have to lose,—my life.

HERALD.

        Loth should I be
To leave you so, but rest assured your zeal
Shall to the Duke be zealously commended.

SIR FLEUREANT (*discovering* VAN MUCK).

Whom have we here? a listener? God forbid!
And yet he seems attentive, and his ears
Are easy of approach, the cover'd way,
Scarp, counterscarp, and parapet, is rased.
Holloa, sir, are you there! Give you good-day!
What think you we were saying?

VAN MUCK.

I'm hard of hearing, sir, I ask your pardon.

SIR FLEUREANT.

Oh! we can pardon that; what, deaf—stone-deaf?

VAN MUCK.

No, sir, thank God! no deafer than yourself,
But slowish, sir, of hearing.

SIR FLEUREANT.

        What, snail-slow?

VAN MUCK.

No, sir, no slower than another man,
But not so quick of hearing, sir, as some,
Being a little deaf.

SIR FLEUREANT.

        Content thee, friend;
Thine ears are sharper than thine apprehension.
But wherefore want they flaps? who dock'd them thus?

R

VAN MUCK.

It is no trouble nor no loss to you,
Whoever did it.

SIR FLEUREANT.

Pardon me, my friend,
It troubles me and doth offend mine eyes
To see thee lack those handles to thy head.
Tell me who snipp'd them?

VAN MUCK.

'Twas my lord, the Regent.

SIR FLEUREANT.

The Regent? [*To the* Herald.] Upon this I go to work.
The Regent? and you wait upon him here?

VAN MUCK.

I wait to ask him for my company:
I was the captain of a company.

HERALD.

What, took he thy command away besides?

VAN MUCK.

Yea, sir.

HERALD.

And wherefore? what was thy offence?

VAN MUCK.

I was a little master'd, sir, with drink,
The night we carried Yerken, and a maid
Than ran upon me, sir, I know not how,
Forswore herself, and said I forced her will.

SIR FLEUREANT.

Well.

VAN MUCK.

And 'twas this that lost me my command.

SIR FLEUREANT.

Impossible! I've done as much myself
A thousand times.

VAN MUCK.

'Twas nothing, sir, but this.

SIR FLEUREANT.

Oh, monstrous! and you ask him to replace you?

VAN MUCK.

Yea, sir, to give me my command again.

SIR FLEUREANT.

And wilt thou ask him to replace thine ears?

VAN MUCK.

No, sir.

SIR FLEUREANT.

Why not? for you'll succeed as soon.
I've heard that never did he change his mind
But once, since he was Regent; once he did;
'Twas when he kindly pardon'd Peter Shultz:
He changed his mind and hung him.

VAN MUCK.

By our lady!
I would not ask him if I knew for certain
He would deny me.

SIR FLEUREANT.

What, deny thee? hang thee.
Take service with another lord—leave him;
Thou hast been foully dealt with. Never hope
To conquer pride with humbleness, but turn
To them that will be proud to use thee well.
I'll show thee many such, and to begin,
Here is myself. What lack'st thou? Money? See—

I am provided : hold me forth thy hand ;
The Regent left thee hands ; was that his skill ?
The injury that disables is more wise
Than that which stings—a hand he left to take—
And here's to fill it—and a hand to strike—
Look not amazed, I ask thee not to lift it ;
I ask thee but to carry me a letter
As far as Bruges.

VAN MUCK.

Sir, I'll be bound to do it.

SIR FLEUREANT.

And are there many men besides thyself
That have lost rank and service in the camp ?

VAN MUCK.

It was but yesterday two constables
Had their discharge.

SIR FLEUREANT.

And why were *they* dismiss'd ?

VAN MUCK.

'Twas by the Regent's order ; 'twas, he said,
Because they made more riots in the camp
Than they prevented.

SIR FLEUREANT.

He is hard to please.

What are they call'd ?

VAN MUCK.

Jan Bulsen and Carl Kortz.

[*Trumpets are heard at a little distance.*

HERALD.

Hark to the Regent's trumpets.

VAN MUCK.

He has finish'd
His daily rounds, and will be here anon.

SIR FLEUREANT.

Name me a place of meeting.

VAN MUCK.

The west dyke,
Behind the sutler Merlick's tent.

SIR FLEUREANT.

Do thou
And Kortz, and Bulsen, at the hour of nine,
Be there to take my orders.   Get thee gone,
And be not seen till then.   Go this way out,
That so the Regent meet thee not.   [*Exit* VAN MUCK.

That seed
Is sown, but whether I shall reap the fruits,
Is yet in Artevelde's arbitrement.
Let him comply, and those three hens shall meet
To hatch an addle egg.

HERALD.

'Tis more than time
That I were fairly on the road to France.
You're pushing on apace.

SIR FLEUREANT.

Our thrift lies there.
Spare time, spend gold, and so you win the day!

'For strongest castle, tower, and town,
The golden bullet beateth down!'

[*Trumpets again.*

Enter VAN ARTEVELDE.

ARTEVELDE.

You are equipp'd, I see, for taking horse;

I pray you have Sir Charles of France inform'd
It was your diligence with such speed dismiss'd you,
And not my lack of hospitality.

HERALD.

My lord, we surely shall report in France
That we were well and bounteously entreated.
Thankfully now, my lord, I take my leave :
Sir Fleureant follows, and ere night will reach
The hostel where we rest.   [*Exit* HERALD.

ARTEVELDE.

You are not, I will hope, so much in haste ?

SIR FLEUREANT.

My lord, I tarry but an hour behind,
And not for idleness.   My lord, I'm charged
With a strange mission, as to you 'twill seem,
But of great moment, from his grace of Bourbon.

ARTEVELDE.

Sir, I attend ; his grace has all my ears.
What would he ?

SIR FLEUREANT.

                    He has voices more than ten
In the king's council, and as they may speak
Touching this war, 'twill likely be resolved.
Now he is not implacably, as some,
Envenom'd, and if justice were but done him
He might be pacified, and turn the course
Of these precipitate counsels.

ARTEVELDE.

                    By mine honour,
If there be justice I can render him,
He should receive it from my ready hands,

Although his voice in council were as small
As a dog-whistle.   What may be his grief?

SIR FLEUREANT.

My lord, he sent you letters that pourtray'd
His grief in all its blackness.   To be short,
He wants his paramour; the damsel fair
Whom you surprised, sojourning at the court
Of Louis Mâle, the day that Bruges was taken.

ARTEVELDE.

Sir, he's thrice welcome to his paramour;
I never have withheld her.

SIR FLEUREANT.

                          Then to me,
A servant of the prince, 'tis his desire
She be consign'd, to take her to the palace
At Senlis.

ARTEVELDE.

                   To the hands of whom she will
I yield the lady, to go where she will,
Were it to the palace of the Prince of Darkness.
But at the lady's bidding it must be,
Not at the Prince's.

SIR FLEUREANT.

                    Do I learn from this
The lady is reluctant?

ARTEVELDE.

                    By no means.
The dangers of the journey have deterr'd her
From taking my safe conduct heretofore,
When, at the instance of the Duke of Bourbon,
I offer'd it; but, having come thus far

Toward the frontier, she may travel hence
In your protection safely.

SIR FLEUREANT.

May I learn

Her pleasure from herself?

ARTEVELDE.

I'll name your wish

To see her, and she doubtless will comply.
Attendance here!

Enter an Attendant.

Apprise the foreign lady,

That with her leave, at her convenient leisure,
I will entreat admittance for some words
Of brief discourse.   [*Exit* Attendant.

We'll walk towards her tent,

If that's your pleasure.

SIR FLEUREANT.

Still at your command.

SCENE III.—*A Pavilion richly hung and furnished.*

ELENA *and her Attendant* CECILE.

ELENA.

Art thou not weary of the camp, Cecile?

CECILE.

Oh no, my lady, it is always stirring;
There is good sport upon the market-days,
And women are much made of.

ELENA.

Well, I am.

Or rather I am weary of myself,

And carry dulness with me as the wind
Carries the cloud, and wheresoe'er I go,
An atmosphere of darkness and of storm
Girdles me round.   I wish that I were dead.

CECILE.

For shame, my lady! you that are so young
And beautiful, with all the world before you:
It is a sin to be so discontent.

ELENA.

Give me my lute, and I will answer that.

(*She sings.*)

Down lay in a nook my lady's brach,
     And said my feet are sore,
I cannot follow with the pack
     A-hunting of the boar.

And though the horn sounds never so clear
     With the hounds in loud uproar,
Yet I must stop and lie down here,
     Because my feet are sore.

The huntsman when he heard the same,
     What answer did he give?
The dog that's lame is much to blame,
     He is not fit to live.

Lo! some one comes.

Enter an Attendant.

ATTENDANT.

The Regent, madam, would attend your leisure
For some few moments' private conversation,
If it might please you to admit him.

ELENA.

                        Surely;
Acquaint him that I wait upon his pleasure.
                              [*Exit* Attendant.
What can he want! he never ask'd before

To speak with me in private.   It is strange;
But it will end in nothing.   Go, Cecile.
Stop; I've forgotten how my hair was dress'd
This morning; put it right.   Look, here he comes;
But there's one with him—said he not alone
He wish'd to see me?   I will go within
And thou canst say that I expect him there.

[Exit.

Enter VAN ARTEVELDE and SIR FLEUREANT.

CECILE.

My lady waits your pleasure, sir, within.

[VAN ARTEVELDE passes into the inner apartment.

Your servant, sir; would you too see my mistress?

SIR FLEUREANT.

If it so please your master.

CECILE.

Who's my master?

SIR FLEUREANT.

I cry you mercy, is it not the Regent?

CECILE.

The Regent is no master, sir, of mine.

SIR FLEUREANT.

No?

CECILE.

By no means.

SIR FLEUREANT.

But he is often here?

CECILE.

No oftener than it pleases him to come
And her to see him.

SIR FLEUREANT.

Which is twice a-day.

CECILE.

Who told you that?

SIR FLEUREANT.

A Cupid that brake loose
From the close service he was sent upon,
Which was to watch their meetings.

CECILE.

Said he so?

A runaway then told a fool a lie.

SIR FLEUREANT.

Nay but he had it from yourself.

CECILE.

If so
He gave it out, this was the great horse-lie
Made for the other to mount.

SIR FLEUREANT.

Come, then, the truth?

CECILE.

The well is not so deep but you may see it.
The Regent sometimes at the close of day
Has fits of lowness and is wearied much
With galloping so long from post to post,
And then my lady hath the voice of a bird
Which entertains his ears.

SIR FLEUREANT.

The live-long night?

CECILE.

An hour or two, no more.

SIR FLEUREANT.

Which being past—

CECILE.

Which being past, he wishes her good rest
And so departs.

SIR FLEUREANT.

And all the while he's there
Are you there too?

CECILE.

Never an instant gone.

SIR FLEUREANT.

Will you swear that?

CECILE.

Assuredly I will.

SIR FLEUREANT.

Or any thing beside.

CECILE.

I crave your pardon;
I would not swear that you had learnt good manners;
That you'd been whipp'd as often as need was
In breeding of you up, I would not swear;
I would not swear that what you wanted then
Has not been since made good; I would not swear—

SIR FLEUREANT.

Quarter, quarter!—truce to your would not swearing!
Here is the Regent.

Enter ARTEVELDE *with* ELENA.

ARTEVELDE.

Sir Fleureant, I have pled in your behalf
And gain'd you audience; for the rest, your trust
Is in your eloquence.

SIR FLEUREANT.

Alas! my lord,

In nothing better?   I had placed my trust
Not in the eloquence of rugged man,
But woman's fair fidelity.

ELENA.

Sir Knight,
I will not task your tongue for eloquence,
Though it be ne'er so ready.

ARTEVELDE.

I am here
But an intruder.   I will say no more,
Save that the lady's choice, be what it may,
Commands my utmost means and best good-will.

[*Exit.*

ELENA.

Stay, stay, Cecile; you will attend me here.
You come, sir, from my lord the Duke of Bourbon,
And why you come I partly can collect
From what the Regent spake.   The Duke's desire
Is that I join him presently in France.

SIR FLEUREANT.

Such is his—what?—his madness had I called it
Before I saw you,—but I call it now
Only his bitter fate, that nothing gay
In palaces or courts can win him off
From thoughts of you, that nothing high or great
In policy or war has power to move him,
Nothing which fame awaits, ambition woos,
Whilst you are absent entertains his mind.

ELENA.

I'm sorry if my absence vex the Duke.
Sorry if it offend him.

SIR FLEUREANT.

    'Tis a grief
More cutting as anticipated less;
For though the tie had not the Church's sanction,
He had not deem'd it therefore less secure.
Such faith was his in what he thought was faith
In her he loved, that all the world's traditions
Of woman's hollow words and treacherous wiles
Could not unfix him from his fast belief.
Moreover he has proffer'd deeds of gift
As ample as the dowry of a duchess,
Would you but meet his wishes and return
But for a day, and should you find thenceforth
Just cause of discontent, with this rich freight
Might you depart as freely as before.

ELENA.

The Duke has been most liberal of his offers,
And I have said I'm sorry to fall out
With what his grace desires :—that is not all—
His grace has been as liberal of reproaches;
But what, then, is his grief? Alas! alas!
The world's traditions may be true that speak
Of woman's infidelities and wiles,
But truer far that scripture is which saith
' Put not your trust in princes.'

SIR FLEUREANT.

     This is strange,
And would amaze him much. In what, I pray,
Has he deceived you?

ELENA.

    Men, sir, think it little;

'Tis less than little in a prince's judgment ;
In woman's estimation it is much.

SIR FLEUREANT.

I would entreat you to explain it farther.

ELENA.

So I design : thus tell the Duke from me :
I could have loved him once—not with the heat
Of that affection which himself conceived—
(For this poor heart had prodigally spent
Its fund of youthful passion ere we met)—
But with a reasonably warm regard.
This could I have bestow'd for many a year,
And did bestow at first, and all went well.
But soon the venomous world wherein we lived
Assail'd the prince with jocular remark
And question keen, importing that his soul
Was yoked in soft subjection to a woman ;
And were she of good life and conversation,
Insidious slanderers said, 'twere not so strange,
But he is vanquish'd by his paramour !
So the word went, and as it reach'd his ear
From time to time repeated, he grew cold,
Captious, suspicious, full of slights and cavils,
Asserting his supremacy in words
Of needless contradiction.   This I bore
Though not by such sad change unalienate ;
But presently there came to me reports,
Authentic though malignant, of loose gibes
Let fall among his retinue, whereby
His grace, to keep his wit in good repute
For shrewdness, and to boast his liberty,

Had shamefully belied his own belief—
For firm belief he had—that I was chaste.

SIR FLEUREANT.

Oh mischief! you gave credence to such tales!

ELENA.

This which I speak of, carry to the Duke;
'Tis therefore I relate it—he well knows
If it be true or false.   Say further this:
Finding his grace thus pitiably weak,
Alternate slave of vanity and love,
I from that moment in my heart resolved
To break the link that bound us: to this end
At Bruges I parted from his company,
And by the same abiding, I have made
This free deliverance of my mind to you.
Which task fulfill'd, (I'm sorry from my soul
If it offend) I wish you, sir, farewell.

[*Exit*, CECILE *following*.

SIR FLEUREANT.

'Tis a magnanimous harlot!   By my faith
Of all the queans that on my humble head
Have pour'd the vials of their wrath and scorn,
This is the prettiest, and I think, the proudest.
If one might bolt the bran from her discourse
I should take leave to guess her firm resolve
Was not fast clench'd till Artevelde took Bruges.
Whichever way it be, my path is plain
Though slippery, and forth I go upon it.

ACT III.

SCENE I.—*Night.   A Dingle in the Outskirts of the Camp,*
behind a Sutler's Tent.

VAN KORTZ, *to whom enter* VAN MUCK.

VAN KORTZ.

Who's there—Van Muck? halloa you, boy! what speed?

VAN MUCK.

Hush, hush! speak low; is no one here but you?

VAN KORTZ.

No jolly soul beside.

VAN MUCK.

Has the watch past?

VAN KORTZ.

By my permission, yes.   I drew a shaft
Chock to the steel, and from behind this tree
Aim'd it at Serjeant Laubscher's black old heart,
In quittance of an ancient debt I owe him ;
But pooh! I let him pass.

VAN MUCK.

Why, were you mad?
It would have baulk'd our meeting.

VAN KORTZ.

What care I?

VAN MUCK.

It is a matter of five hundred marks
White money down.

s

VAN KORTZ.

Aye, let me see it down,

And I'll believe you.

VAN MUCK.

He will soon be here,

And then you'll—here he is—no, 'tis but Bulsen.

Enter BULSEN.

BULSEN.

Well, is all right? 'tis close upon the hour.

VAN KORTZ.

Nothing is stirring; stand from out the trees

That he may see us, lest he miss the spot.

Art certain that he'll bring the money here?

VAN MUCK.

I saw it in his hands; doubtless he'll bring it.

VAN KORTZ.

Why, hark ye then—what need to go to Ghent,

Or Bruges, or Ypres, to get gold that's here?

VAN MUCK.

He gives it us for taking letters hence,

To Ghent, and Bruges, and Ypres.

VAN KORTZ.

Hold thy peace,

Thou nick-ear'd lubber; what have we to do

With whys and wherefores? Here he brings the gold,

And hence he takes it not, if we be men.

What say ye?

BULSEN.

Cut his throat!

VAN MUCK.

　　　　　　　　How now ! how now !
I would not for the world.

VAN KORTZ.

　　　　　　　Pluck up thy heart ;
Hast courage but for half a sin ?　As good
To eat the devil as the broth he's boil'd in.

VAN MUCK.

For mercy's sake do nothing to molest him !
'Twas I that brought him here, and God he knows
I did not go about to take his life.

VAN KORTZ.

Why, go thy way then ; two like me and Bulsen
Are men enough.

BULSEN.

　　　　　Enough to win the booty,
And by that token, friend, enough to share it.

VAN KORTZ.

Go to the devil with thy dolorous cheer ;
There is no manhood in thee.　Get thee gone,
Or I shall try six inches of my knife
On thine own inmeats first.

BULSEN.

　　　　　　　Thoud'st best be gone :
Thou art but in the way.

VAN KORTZ.

　　　　　　Go, pudding-heart !
Take thy huge offal and white liver hence,
Or in a twinkling of this true-blue steel
I shall be butching thee from nape to rump.

s 2

BULSEN.

Go thou thy ways, and thank thy prosperous stars
Thou art let live.

VAN MUCK.

I am rewarded bravely
For bringing this about; but ye shall see
If it be better for you.

BULSEN.

Hold, come back—
What, fast and loose—is that your game?—soho!
I see him coming.

SIR FLEUREANT (*without*).

Soft! was that the tent
He spoke of? surely then—or—nay, I know not—
Where am I going?

VAN KORTZ.

Come along, sir, come—
Where art thou going?—I will tell thee where,—
Going to grass, Sir Fleureant of Heurlée,
With thy teeth upward. May that serve thy turn?
Halloa, then, come along!

BULSEN.

Beware, beware.
Thou art the noisiest of all the cut-throats;
Will nothing stop thy tongue? This way, sir, here.

Enter SIR FLEUREANT OF HEURLÉE.

VAN MUCK (*passing between* SIR FLEUREANT *and the others*).
Your sword, Sir Fleureant! stand upon your guard;
We are not safe—there oft are men about
At such dark hours as this, that might surprise us—
Look to your guard—but we shall be a match
For more than one such?

BULSEN.

Never fear, Van Muck ;
If any such should break upon our meeting
We'd parley with them first, and see what good
Might come of fighting or of speaking fair.

SIR FLEUREANT.

Where is the danger? you are dreaming, friends!
Let me explain the matter I've in hand.

VAN KORTZ.

Come, come, Sir Hurly-Burly! where's your metal?
Write us the matter down in white and yellow.
No danger! but I say there shall be danger—
Out with this money—what if the Regent knew—
Are men like us to be entrapp'd and sold
And see no money down, Sir Hurly-Burly?
You are a knight and we are vile crossbow-men,
But steel is steel, and flesh is still but flesh,
So let us see your chinkers.

SIR FLEUREANT (*to* VAN MUCK).

Sure he's drunk?
Why brought you me a drunken knave like this?

VAN MUCK.

He is not drunk, sir; better that he were ;
If they are for foul play, so am not I,
Nor did I mean it.

SIR FLEUREANT.

Aye, is that their game?
Sirs, ye mistook our honest friend, Van Muck ;
I could not in hard money bring you here
More than a moiety of the sums you'll earn

By carrying of my letters; it is thus:
So much I'll pay you now, and as much more
You will receive in France from Hetz St. Croix,
King Charles's master of accompt.   The king
Gave orders for the payments.

BULSEN.

                             It is well;
We will convey your letters, sir, with speed.

VAN KORTZ.

We'll trust to meet you afterward at court
To see us justly paid.

SIR FLEUREANT.

                       Enquire for me
When you arrive at Senlis or at Lisle,
Or wheresoe'er the court may then abide.
Here are the letters and the skins of gold
I give with each.   The word is now 'Despatch!'
Speak not, nor eat nor drink with friend or foe,
But each man take his wallet on his back,
And steal away.   No lack of Frenchmen's friends
You'll find at Bruges or Ypres, and these letters
Will bring you to their knowledge; and at Ghent
Though France may find less favour with the many,
Still there are some that will befriend you.   Hence!
What noise is that?

VAN MUCK.

      It is the second watch.

SIR FLEUREANT.

Away then;—fare you well.
                    [*Exeunt* VAN MUCK, KORTZ, *and* BULSEN.
Now if one miscreant of the three play false

This head is worth the value of a potsherd.
Speed is my best safe-conduct, then, to France.

SCENE II.—*The Pavilion, as in Scene III. of Act II.*—ARTEVELDE
and ELENA. CECILE *attending in the background.*

ELENA.

On your way hither, then, you passed through Ghent,
The city which you saved.   How sweet a pleasure,
Revisiting a place which owes to you
All that it hath of glory or of ease!

ARTEVELDE.

Verily yes, it should have overjoyed me.
How diverse, how contrarious is man!
I know not wherefore, but I scarce was pleased
To see that town now wallowing in wealth,
Which last I saw, and saw with hearty courage,
Pinched like a beggar wintering at death's door.
Now, both the mart was full, and church; road, bridge,
River, and street, were populous and busy,
And money bags were toss'd from hand to hand
Of men more thriftless than a miser's heir.
I liked it not; my task, it seem'd, was done;
The arrow sped, the bow unbent, the cord
Soundless and slack.   I came away ill-pleased.

ELENA.

Perhaps you suffer'd losses in the siege?

ARTEVELDE.

Not in the siege; but I have suffer'd something.
There is a gate in Ghent—I pass'd beside it—
A threshold there, worn of my frequent feet,

Which I shall cross no more.   But wherefore thus
Divert me from my drift?   Look round; look on;
Think once again upon the proffer'd choice
Of French protection.   Though my army wear
This hour an aspect of security,
A battle must be fought ere many days.

ELENA.

You have been very kind to me, my lord,
And in the bounty of your noble nature,
Despite those ineradicable stains
That streak my life, have used me with respect.
I will not quit your camp,—unless you wish it.

ARTEVELDE.

Am I in life's embellishments so rich,
In pleasures so redundant, as to wish
The chiefest one away?   No, fairest friend;
Mine eyes have travell'd this horizon round,
Ending where they began; and they have roved
The boundless empyrean up and down,
And 'mid the undistinguish'd tumbling host
Of the black clouds, have lighted on a soft
And solitary spot of azure sky
Whereon they love to dwell.   The clouds close in,
And soon may shut it from my searching sight;
But let me still behold it whilst I may.

ELENA.

You are so busy all day long, I fear'd
A woman's company and trifling talk
Would only importune you.

ARTEVELDE.
                Think not so.

The sweets of converse and society
Are sweetest when they're snatch'd; the often-comer,
The boon companion of a thousand feasts,
Whose eye has grown familiar with the fair,
Whose tutor'd tongue, by practice perfect made,
Is tamely talkative,—he never knows
That truest, rarest light of social joy
Which gleams upon the man of many cares.

ELENA.

It is not every one could push aside
A country's weight so lightly.

ARTEVELDE.

                              By your leave,
There are but few that on so grave a theme
Continuously could ponder unrelieved.
The heart of man, walk it which way it will,
Sequester'd or frequented, smooth or rough,
Down the deep valley amongst tinkling flocks,
Or 'mid the clang of trumpets and the march
Of clattering ordnance, still must have its halt,
Its hour of truce, its instant of repose,
Its inn of rest; and craving still must seek
The food of its affections—still must slake
Its constant thirst of what is fresh and pure
And pleasant to behold.

ELENA.

                        To you that thirst,
Despite inebriating draughts of glory,
Despite ambition, power, and strife, remains;
But great men mostly lose the taste of joy
Save from such things as make their greatness greater:

Which, growing still, o'ershadows more and more
Of less enjoyments, until all are sunk
In business of the state.

ARTEVELDE,

'Tis otherwise,
And ever was with me.   It was not meant
By him who on the back the burthen bound,
That cares, though public, critical, and grave,
Should so encase us and encrust, as shuts
The gate on what is beautiful below,
And clogs those entries of the soul of man
Which lead the way to what he hath of heaven :
This was not meant, and me may not befal
Whilst thou remind'st me of those heavenly joys
I once possessed in peace.   Life—life, my friend,
May hold a not unornamented course
Wherever it shall flow ; be the bed rocky,
Yet are there flowers, and none of brighter hue,
That to the rock are native.   War itself
Deals in adornments, and the blade it wields
Is curiously carved and gaily gilt.
For me, let what is left of life, if brief,
Be bright, and let me kindle all its fires ;
For I am as a rocket hurled on high
But a few moments to be visible,
Which ended, all is dark.

Enter CECILE.

CECILE.

Gracious, my lady !
My lord, my humble duty to your highness.
If I might speak—

ARTEVELDE.
What hinders you, Cecile ?

ELENA.
Nought ever did, my lord, nor ever will ;
When she has breath you'll hear her.

CECILE.
                        Oh, my lady !
That frightful man I've told you of so oft
That comes for ever with his vows of love
And will not be denied,—I always said
Begone ! How dare you ! Get you gone forsooth !
To bring such tales to me !   But still he came,
And now to-night—

ARTEVELDE.
                  Who is it that she speaks of ?

ELENA.
His name is—nay, God help my memory !
What is his name, Cecile ?

CECILE.
                  Van Kortz, my lady.

ARTEVELDE.
Not he that once was marshalsman ?

CECILE.
                              The same.

ARTEVELDE.
I know him well—his quality at least,
And his career I know.   Right, right, Cecile ;
Deny him stoutly, for he means no good.

CECILE.
I did, my lord,—I heartily denied him ;
I said I never would so much as touch him.
I told him if he'd hang himself for love,
I'd love the rope that hang'd him,—nothing else.

ARTEVELDE.

And yet he comes again?

CECILE.

Even now, my lord,
He came as though it were to wreak his spite,
And show'd me bags of gold, and said that now
He was so rich that he could wed a countess,
Let pass a waiting wench, and from this time
He ne'er would look so low, but mend his fortune.
I told him he might seek his fortune far,
Ere he should find his match for pride and greed;
So with that word he set his spleen abroach,
And cursing all the camp, and most your highness,
Swore he could buy and sell the best amongst you.

ARTEVELDE.

What, said he so? and show'd you bags of gold?
He has been selling something. Ho, Van Ryk!
Van Ryk is waiting, no?

CECILE.

He is, my lord.

Enter VAN RYK.

ARTEVELDE.

Van Ryk, a word;
Thou know'st Van Kortz, the marshalsman that was—
He parted hence but now, and I have cause
To wish his person seized without delay
And brought before me with all scrips or scrolls
That may be found upon him. Take my guard,
And see it done.   [*Exit* VAN RYK.

ELENA.

What is it you suspect?

ARTEVELDE.

The gold is French.
He has not lately had the means to thrive
By Flemish gold.   He was a man disgraced.

CECILE.

You're right, my lord ; his talk was not of guilders,
'Twas still of crowns and francs.

ELENA.

Nay, but from whence
Hath he French gold ?

ARTEVELDE.

From him whom France sent here
Doubtless to bring it,—from the Knight of Heurlée.

ELENA.

Oh, surely, surely not,—a man who came
With sacred mission clothed, to seek for peace
Under protection of a herald's office !
It were but common honesty—

ARTEVELDE.

My friend,
Say in what time hath honesty been common ?
Soft ! silence, I beseech you ; here's Van Ryk,
And he has found his man.

Enter VAN RYK, *with* VAN KORTZ, *guarded.*

Whom hast thou there, Van Ryk, thus manacled,
And what is his offence ?

VAN RYK.

My lord, Van Kortz.

ARTEVELDE.

Van Kortz ! The gudgeon whom Sir Fleureant hired

To do French service, then betray'd, to save
His proper head!   Down, sir, upon thy knees,
And tell what wiles the crafty Frenchman used
To cheat thee of thy loyalty.

VAN KORTZ (kneeling).

My lord,

I tell the simple truth.   Sir Fleureant sware
The paper which he charged me with for Ghent
Was for his private ends, and nothing touch'd
The faith I owed your highness, and——

ARTEVELDE.

Van Ryk,

Bring me Sir Fleureant of Heurlée hither.
Soft ye awhile!—what found you on Van Kortz?

VAN RYK.

My lord, this paper, and a bag of money.

ARTEVELDE (reading the paper).

' *Worthy masters of Ghent,—this is to make it known unto
you, that we are hastily to come down into Flanders with a
hundred thousand men, and with God's help to replace our
worthy cousin, Lois of Flanders, in his ancient estate and
royalties, reducing to his obedience all that be rightfully bound
thereunto, and punishing the guilty. Wherefore we pray
and counsel you, that at the receiving hereof, you return to
your allegiance, and send to us in our army the heads of
these following: that is to say, Jacob Maurenbrecker, John
Stotler, and Ralph of Kerdell, which done, we shall receive all
others whatsoever to our friendship, and promise by these
presents that none, saving these only, shall be called to answer
what is past.*

> ' *Written and sealed with the broad seal of France, in
> our host before Senlis, the 2nd day of October, in the
> year of grace, 1382, by the king in his council.*'

Stay, what is here, an afterthought of mischief:

' You are to know that we have sent the like letters patent
to the good towns of Bruges and Ypres, to which lest they
reach not, we pray you to convey the contents hereof.'

Who are the messengers to Bruges and Ypres?

VAN KORTZ.

Van Muck, my lord, to Bruges ; to Ypres, Bulsen.
They have set forth.

ARTEVELDE.

             Convey him hence to prison.
Let fifty men be mounted—some pursue
Sir Fleureant of Heurlée, some Van Muck,
And others Bulsen, on the roads to France,
To Bruges and Ypres,—for the head of each
Proclaim a thousand florins,—haste, Van Ryk !

[*Exit* VAN RYK, *with* VAN KORTZ, *guarded.*

CECILE.

Oh Lord, the villain ! and he came to me
So proud and saucy ! Truly it is said
Give rope enough to rogues, they'll hang themselves.

ELENA.

And must he die, my lord ?

ARTEVELDE.

             What plea can save him ?

CECILE.

That he should jeopardise his wilful head
Only for spite at me !

ELENA.

      'Tis wonderful !

ARTEVELDE.

That Providence which makes the good take heed

To safety and success, contrariwise
Makes villains mostly reckless.   Look on life,
And you shall see the crimes of blackest dye
So clumsily committed, by such sots,
So lost to thought, so scant of circumspection,
As shall constrain you to pronounce that guilt
Bedarkens and confounds the mind of man.
Human intelligence on murders bent
Becomes a midnight fumbler ; human will
Of God abandoned, in its web of snares
Strangles its own intent.

ELENA.

How fortunate
Was this man's malice thus conceived to thee,
My good Cecile !   All woman as I am,
I can forgive thy beauty, that hath bred
This love-engender'd hate.

CECILE.

I thank you, madam.
The scornful knave ! to bring his gold to me
That never would have look'd upon him twice,
Though he'd been made of gold !

ELENA.

How came you first
To give him that authority and rank,
Which late you took away ?

ARTEVELDE.

Those are there here
That hardly will be govern'd save by men
Of fierce and forward natures.   He was known
For daring deeds from childhood ; in his youth,

Famed for his great desire of doing evil,
He was elected into Testenoire's troop
Of free-companions : so in field or forest,
Or in wall'd town, by stipend lured, or vill
Surprised and sack'd, by turns he lived at large,
And learn'd the vice indigenous to each.
Nought in dark corners of great cities done
Of lewdness or of outrage, was unknown
By him, or unpartaken ; nor the woods
Lodged in their loneliest caves a beast so wild.
The noise of strife and blows, the cry of murder,
Were to his ears indifferently common.
Thus grown at length more reckless than was safe
For his fraternity, they cast him off ;
And hanging loose upon the world what time
My name was noised abroad, he join'd my camp.

Enter SIR FLEUREANT OF HEURLÉE.

SIR FLEUREANT.

So, my lord Regent ! what is this I hear
Blown through the camp with trumpets ? what's my head,
That you should price it higher than the sum
Of good repute for honourable dealing,
Which you must part withal to take it ?   Much
I've heard of dangers in the Holy Land
Amongst the heathen and the infidel,
But never thought in Christendom to find
Such bloody breach of hospitable laws !

ARTEVELDE.

This is well spoken.

CECILE.

                Oh, my lord, for that,
He's free enough. . . . .

                                    T

ELENA.

Peace ! peace ! Cecile ; be silent.

ARTEVELDE.

What you have here deliver'd, sir, I say
Hath been well spoken : it remains to ask
If that which you have perpetrated here
Hath been well done.   Know you this writing ?

SIR FLEUREANT.

Yes.

I know it well ; 'twas by the King my master
Writ to the mayor and citizens of Ghent.

ARTEVELDE.

By you brought here ; by you to one Van Kortz
Deliver'd for despatch ; by him to me,
Upon his apprehension, yielded up.
Such is the story of these inky scratches
Which were to scribble out the loyalty
Of three good towns, to soil the faith and courage
Of my best friends, and finally to blur
The record of my glory in the page
Of history past, and blot me from the future !
This was a worthy business.

SIR FLEUREANT.

Aye, my lord ;
Who shall gainsay the King of France his right
To send what letters or what words he will
To the good towns of Flanders ?

ARTEVELDE.

Let him try ;
And gainsay those that can my privilege
To hang the bearers.   Thou, Sir Fleureant,

Hast by thy treachery betray'd thyself,
And unavoidably must suffer death.
Thou cam'st a sharer in a herald's office
Ensuing peace ; and cloak'd in that disguise,
With money for thy purposes provided,
Thou hast bought treason.   This may never pass ;
Else what security is mine that faith
Is not put up to auction in my camp,
Till each man sell his brother ?   Who provokes
Treason in others, to a traitor's death
Justly condemns himself.   Such is thy lot :
Yet do I rue the judgment I pronounce,
And wish it undeserved ; for you have colour'd
The darkness of your indirect attempts
With a more lively cheer and gallant bearing
Than most could brighten their best deeds withal.
Sir, I am sorry for you.

SIR FLEUREANT.

                         Spare your pity,
And use your power.   You see before you one
Who would more willingly confront the worst
Unpitying power inflicts, than cry for mercy !
I have been used to deem the loss of life
But as a dead man's loss, that feels it not.

ARTEVELDE.

You shall do well of mortal life to think
Thus slightly, and with serious thoughts prepare
For that which is celestial and to come.
'Twixt this and daylight is your leisure time
For such purgation as you need.   Cecile,
Send to St. Hubert's for some barefoot friar,

T 2

And bid him come so stored and with such speed
As on a death-bed summons.

[He steps to a door of the tent and calls some Soldiers of his guard.

CECILE.

Yes, my lord,
I'll go myself and say what work awaits him.

SIR FLEUREANT.

And prithee, wench, find me a merry friar,
Who shall beguile the time.

CECILE.

A merry friar !

SIR FLEUREANT.

Aye, wench ; if any in the camp there be
They will be known to thee ; a hearty man ;
For I have ever look'd on life and death,
The world which is and that which is to be,
With cheerful eyes, and hoped the best of both ;
And I would have death's usher wear a smile
As through the passage of to-night he leads me.
So send a merry friar.

ELENA.

Oh, sir knight !
If die you must so soon, for God's dear love
Take thought for your immortal soul's behoof !
Confess yourself and pass the night in prayer.

SIR FLEUREANT.

Confession will not hold us long ; I'm young,
And have not yet had time enough to act
Sins that are long in telling :

[Then to ARTEVELDE, *who returns with two Soldiers of the guard.*

You, my lord,

Cut short the catalogue betimes, I thank you.
To you, sweet lady, for your counsel kind
And monitory speech, my last poor prayers
I give,—more worth than thanks from dying men;
And in your supplications of to-night
When you lie down to rest, I humbly crave
To be remember'd in return.

ELENA.
                    Alas!
Would I could stead you more than with the prayers
Of such a sinful creature!

SIR FLEUREANT.
                    Soon, sweet lady,
You'll need them for yourself.   This fair array
Of warlike multitudes you see around you,
Will sunder and dissolve like wreaths of snow
Pelted and riddled with the rains in March.
Then should my Lord of Bourbon find you here,
'Twill be a rude rencounter; if at Bruges
You found a lover in an enemy,
The tables will be turn'd at Oudenarde,
And in a lover shall you find a foe.
I pray you think upon it.

ARTEVELDE.
                    Fare you well.
These will conduct you to your place of rest,
And all your needs or wishes may require
To make the night pass easily, supply.
Again, sir, fare you well.

SIR FLEUREANT.
                    My lord, farewell.

I hardly know what words should thank your bounty
That grants me every thing—except my life.

                                [Exit, guarded.

ELENA.

Oh, would, my lord, that you could grant him that !
He is a gallant gentleman.

ARTEVELDE.

                      He's stricken ;
Which makes the meanest hold his courage high
In presence of his lady : notwithstanding,
He is a brave and very noble knight,
And nothing moves me in his favour more
Than what he spake to you.   I'm grieved, in truth,
That stern necessity demands his death.
No more of that.——
The world declares us lovers, you have heard.

ELENA.

My lord ?

ARTEVELDE.

                The world, when men and women meet,
Is rich in sage remark, nor stints to strew
With roses and with myrtle fields of death.
Think you that they will grow?

ELENA.

                         My lord, your pardon ;
You speak in such enigmas, I am lost,
And cannot comprehend you.

ARTEVELDE.

                   Do I so?
That was not wont to be my fault.   In truth
There is a season when the plainest men

Will cease to be plain-spoken; for their thoughts
Plunge deep in labyrinths of flowers and thorns,
And very rarely to the light break through,
Whilst much they wander darkling.   Yet for once
Let love be marshall'd by the name of love,
To meet such entertainment as he may.

ELENA.

I have been much unfortunate, my lord;
I would not love again.

ARTEVELDE.

                    And so have I;
Nor man nor woman more unfortunate,
As none more bless'd in what was taken from him!
Dearest Elena,—of the living dearest,—
Let my misfortunes plead, and know their weight
By knowing of the worth of what I lost.
She was a creature framed by love divine
For mortal love to muse a life away
In pondering her perfections; so unmoved
Amidst the world's contentions, if they touch'd
No vital chord nor troubled what she loved,
Philosophy might look her in the face,
And like a hermit stooping to the well
That yields him sweet refreshment, might therein
See but his own serenity reflected
With a more heavenly tenderness of hue!
Yet whilst the world's ambitious empty cares,
Its small disquietudes and insect stings
Disturb'd her never, she was one made up
Of feminine affections, and her life
Was one full stream of love from fount to sea.
These are but words.

ELENA.

My lord, they're full of meaning.

ARTEVELDE.

No, they mean nothing—that which they would speak
Sinks into silence—'tis what none can know
That knew not her—the silence of the grave—
Whence could I call her radiant beauty back,
It could not come more savouring of Heaven
Than it went hence—the tomb received her charms
In their perfection, with nor trace of time
Nor stain of sin upon them ; only death
Had turn'd them pale.   I would that you had seen her
Living or dead.

ELENA.

I wish I had, my lord ;
I should have loved to look upon her much ;
For I can gaze on beauty all day long,
And think the all-day long is but too short.

ARTEVELDE.

She was so fair that in the angelic choir
She will not need put on another shape
Than that she bore on earth.   Well, well,—she's gone,
And I have tamed my sorrow.   Pain and grief
Are transitory things no less than joy,
And though they leave us not the men we were,
Yet they do leave us.   You behold me here
A man bereaved, with something of a blight
Upon the early blossoms of his life
And its first verdure, having not the less
A living root, and drawing from the earth
Its vital juices, from the air its powers :

And surely as man's health and strength are whole
His appetites regerminate, his heart
Re-opens, and his objects and desires
Shoot up renew'd.   What blank I found before me
From what is said you partly may surmise;
How I have hoped to fill it, may I tell?

ELENA.

I fear, my lord, that cannot be.

ARTEVELDE.

Indeed !
Then am I doubly hopeless.   What is gone,
Nor plaints, nor prayers, nor yearnings of the soul,
Nor memory's tricks nor fancy's invocations—
Though tears went with them frequent as the rain
In dusk November, sighs more sadly breathed
Than winter's o'er the vegetable dead,—
Can bring again : and should this living hope,
That like a violet from the other's grave
Grew sweetly, in the tear-besprinkled soil
Finding moist nourishment—this seedling sprung
Where recent grief had like a ploughshare pass'd
Through the soft soul and loosen'd its affections—
Should this new-blossom'd hope be coldly nipp'd,
Then were I desolate indeed ! a man
Whom heaven would wean from earth, and nothing leaves
But cares and quarrels, trouble and distraction,
The heavy burthens and the broils of life.
Is such my doom ?   Nay, speak it, if it be.

ELENA.

I said I fear'd another could not fill
The place of her you lost, being so fair
And perfect as you give her out.

ARTEVELDE.

'Tis true,

A perfect woman is not as a coin,
Which being gone, its very duplicate
Is counted in its place.   Yet waste so great
Might you repair, such wealth you have of charms
Luxuriant, albeit of what were hers
Rather the contrast than the counterpart.
Colour to wit—complexion ;—hers was light
And gladdening ; a roseate tincture shone
Transparent in its place, her skin elsewhere
White as the foam from which in happy hour
Sprang the Thalassian Venus : yours is clear
But bloodless, and though beautiful as night
In cloudless ether clad, not frank as day :
Such is the tinct of your diversity ;
Serenely radiant she, you darkly fair.

ELENA.

Dark still has been the colour of my fortunes,
And having not serenity of soul,
How should I wear the aspect ?

ARTEVELDE.

Wear it not ;
Wear only that of love.

ELENA.

Of love ? alas !

That is its opposite.   You counsel me
To scatter this so melancholy mist
By calling up the hurricane.   Time was
I had been prone to counsel such as yours ;
Adventurous I have been, it is true,
And this foolhardy heart would brave—nay court,

In other days, an enterprise of passion ;
Yea, like a witch, would whistle for a whirlwind.
But I have been admonish'd : painful years
Have tamed and taught me : I have suffer'd much.
Kind Heaven but grant tranquillity ! I seek
No further boon.

ARTEVELDE.

And may not love be tranquil ?

ELENA.

It may in some ; but not as I have known it.

ARTEVELDE.

Love, like an insect frequent in the woods,
Will take the colour of the tree it feeds on ;
As saturnine or sanguine is the soul,
Such is the passion.   Brightly upon me,
Like the red sunset of a stormy day,
Love breaks anew beneath the gathering clouds
That roll around me !   Tell me, sweet Elena,
May I not hope, or rather can I hope,
That for such brief and bounded space of time
As are my days on earth, you'll yield yourself
To such a love as mine, whose lamp of love
Is lighted at a funeral torch ?

ELENA.

Oh God !

Too great a destiny it were for me !
But say not that your days on earth are brief.
I see the long procession of your days
Through the far distant future streaming light,
Triumphal, crown'd with glory.

ARTEVELDE.

                              Crown'd with love.
Give to this day, this regal day, that crown ;
Let others run their course.   Give me this heart,
That beats itself to pieces . . . . .

ELENA.

                              No, I cannot,—
I cannot give you what you've had so long ;
Nor need I tell you what you know so well.
I must be gone.

ARTEVELDE.

                    Nay, sweetest, why these tears ?

ELENA.

No, let me go—I cannot tell—no—no—
I want to be alone—
Oh! Artevelde, for God's love let me go !

                                        [Exit.

ARTEVELDE (after a pause).

The night is far advanced upon the morrow,
And but for that conglomerated mass
Of cloud with ragged edges, like a mound
Or black pine-forest on a mountain's top,
Wherein the light lies ambush'd, dawn were near.—
Yes, I have wasted half a summer's night.
Was it well spent?   Successfully it was.
And yet of springs and sources taking note,
How little flattering is a woman's love !
Thrice gifted girl !   The conqueror of the world
In winning thee might deem he won a prize
More precious far, yet count the prize he won
As portion of his treasure, not his pride ;
For when was love the measure of desert ?

The few hours left are precious—who is there?
Ho! Nieuverkerchen!—when we think upon it,
How little flattering is a woman's love!
Given commonly to whosoe'er is nearest
And propp'd with most advantage; outward grace
Nor inward light is needful; day by day
Men wanting both are mated with the best
And loftiest of God's feminine creation,
Whose love takes no distinction but of gender,
And ridicules the very name of choice.
Ho! Nieuverkerchen!—what, then, do we sleep?
Are none of you awake?—and as for me,
The world says Philip is a famous man—
What is there women will not love, so taught?
Ho! Ellert! by your leave though, you must wake.

Enter an Officer.

Have me a gallows built upon the mount,
And let Van Kortz be hung at break of day.
No news of Bulsen, or Van Muck?

OFFICER.
                              My lord,
Bulsen is taken; but Van Muck, we fear,
Has got clear off.

ARTEVELDE.
                    Let Bulsen, too, be hung
At break of day.   Let there be priests to shrive them.
Who guards the knight, Sir Fleureant of Heurlée?

OFFICER.
Sasbout, my lord, and Tuning.

ARTEVELDE.
                              Very well.

Mount me a messenger; I shall have letters
To send to Van den Bosch upon the Lis.
Let Grebber wait upon me here.   Go thou
Upon thine errands.   [*Exit* Officer.]—So, Van Muck
    escaped!
And Ypres will receive its invitation.
I think, then, Van den Bosch must spare a force
To strengthen us at Ypres for a season.
I'll send him orders.   And Van Muck the traitor!
Stupidity is seldom soundly honest;
I should have known him better.   Live and learn!

SCENE III.—*The interior of a Tent.*—SIR FLEUREANT OF HEURLÉE
   is seated at a table, on which wine and refreshments are placed.
   Guards are seen without, walking backwards and forwards
   before the doors of the Tent.

SIR FLEUREANT.

I oft before have clomb to tickle places
But this will be the last of all my climbing.
Were it to do again, ten thousand dukes,
With all their wants of wit and wealth of folly,
Should tempt me not to such fool-hardihood.
Here is the end of Fleureant of Heurlée!
I know it; for my heart is dead already—
An omen that did cross me ne'er before
In any jeopardy of life.

CECILE *enters with a* Friar.

This wind
Is cold, methinks, that comes through yonder door.
I thought I had a cloak.

CECILE.

The friar, sir.

SIR FLEUREANT.

Well, this is strange ;—I surely had a cloak.

CECILE.

Sir, would you see the friar?

SIR FLEUREANT.

Eh? what? who?

CECILE.

The friar, sir.

SIR FLEUREANT.

What friar?—oh, your pardon !
What? is it time?

FRIAR.

This wench, my son, brought word
That you would fain confess yourself o'ernight ;
And then make merry, like a noble heart,
Till break of day that brings your latter end.

SIR FLEUREANT.

What is't o'clock?

CECILE.

An hour or two, no more,
Past midnight.

SIR FLEUREANT.

Yes, I wish'd myself confess'd ;
But, by your leave, not now ;—my eyes are heavy,
And I was fain to wrap me in my cloak,
And lay me down to sleep, as you came in.
I think I had a cloak.

CECILE.

'Tis here, sir, here.

SIR FLEUREANT.

Ah, there it is.   The air, I think, is chilly.

FRIAR.

'Tis a cold air, my son, a cold and dry ;
But here's an element that's hot and moist
To keep the other out.   I drink your health.

SIR FLEUREANT.

My health ! ha, ha ! I'll lie me down and sleep,
For I've a mortal weariness upon me.
My body's or my soul's health do you drink ?

FRIAR.

I drink, sir, to your good repose.

SIR FLEUREANT.

I thank you ;
I shall sleep sound to-morrow.

CECILE.

Put this cushion
Under your head.

SIR FLEUREANT.

Ah, you are kind, wench, now :
You're not so saucy as you were.   So,—there.

FRIAR.

And this I drink to your dear soul's salvation.

CECILE.

I'd tend you all night long, with all my heart,
If it might do you good.

SIR FLEUREANT.

Good night, good night.

FRIAR.

What, doth he sleep ?   Then sit you down, my maid,

And quaff me off this flask of Malvoisie.
Come sunrise and he'll lay his curly head
Upon a harder pillow—So it is !

> 'As a man lives so shall he die.
> As a tree falls so shall it lie.'

Take off thy glass, my merry wench of all ;
Thou know'st the song that Jack the headsman sings—

> 'Tis never to snivel and grovel
>   When a friend wants a turn of poor Jack's,
> But put him to bed with a shovel,
>   Having cut off his head with an axe—
>   Having
>   Cut off his head with an axe.'

CECILE.

Be not so loud, good friar, let him sleep.
He'll pass the time more easy.

FRIAR.
                    Let him sleep !
What hinders him to sleep ?—not I, my lass ;
I've shriven many a sinner for the gallows ;
There's nothing wakes them but a lusty tug.
I'd rather he should sleep than you, sweet wench ;
What, are you wakeful—Ah, you fat-ribs ! Ah !

CECILE.

Begone, you filthy friar ! At your tricks
With here a dead man lying, one may say,
Amongst one's feet !

FRIAR.
                    Who's dead, my merry soul ?
Not I, nor near it yet.

U

CECILE.

Out ! ancient blotch !

Enter ARTEVELDE.

ARTEVELDE (*stumbling against* SIR FLEUREANT, *who wakes and sits up*).

So, what is this? what wrangle ye about?
What mak'st thou, friar, with the wench?

FRIAR.

Who, I ?

CECILE.

Aye, tell his highness how you'd use a maid.

FRIAR.

Alack ! we churchmen, sir, have much ado !
We are but men, and women will be women.
Fie, they are naughty jades !—sluts all ! sluts all !
Fie, how they steal upon our idle hours !

CECILE.

Thou liest, thou scandalous friar——

ARTEVELDE.

Soft you, Cecile !

FRIAR.

Oh, she's a light-skirts !—yea, and at this present
A little, as you see, concern'd with liquor.

CECILE.

A light-skirts !   If it were not for thy cowl
I have that lesson at my fingers' ends
Should teach thee how to lay thy carrion's sins
Upon a wholesome maid.

ARTEVELDE.

Peace, peace, I say !

I would discourse some matters with this knight.
Leave us together.   Friar, go thy ways ;
Thy hands are not too clean.   I know the wench ;
She would not tempt thee.   Get thee gone, I say.

FRIAR.

My lord, the peace of God be with your highness,
And with this knight, and with that sinful woman.

[*Exit.*

CECILE.

I thank your highness—Oh the mouldy villain !
I thank you, sir.   Good even to your highness.

[*Exit.*

ARTEVELDE.

Good night, Cecile.—Sir, I disturb'd your rest ;
I saw not that you lay there.

SIR FLEUREANT.

Oh, my lord,
It matters not ; to-morrow I shall lie
Where you will not disturb me.

ARTEVELDE.

So you think.

SIR FLEUREANT.

So you, my lord, have said.

ARTEVELDE.

You stand condemn'd.
Yet 'tis a word that I would fain unsay.

SIR FLEUREANT.

You are most kind, my lord ; the word went always
You were a merciful man and fearing God,
And God is good to such and prospers them ;

v 2

And if my life it please you now to spare,
You may find mercy for yourself in straits
According as you show it.

ARTEVELDE.

                    Nay, thy life
Is justly forfeited : and if I spare thee
It is not that I look for God's reward
In sparing crime ; since justice is most mercy.
Thou hast an intercessor, to whose prayers
I grant thy life, absolving thee, not freely,
But on conditions.

SIR FLEUREANT.

                    Whatsoe'er they be
I will be bound most solemnly by oath,
So God be my salvation, to fulfil them.

ARTEVELDE.

'Tis but to pay thy debt of gratitude
To her whose charity redeems thy life,
That I would bind thee.   At the supplication
Of thy lord's sometime lady thou art spared.

SIR FLEUREANT.

I'm bound to her for ever.

ARTEVELDE.

                    Sometime hence
Mischances may befall her.   Though I trust,
And with good reason, that my arms are proof,
Yet is the tide of war unsteady ever ;
And should my hope be wreck'd upon some reef
Of adverse fortune, there is cause to fear
Her former lord, thy master, who suspects

Uneasily her faith, in victory's pride
Would give his vengeance and his jealousy
Free way to her destruction.   In such hour,
Should it arrive, thou might'st befriend the lady,
As in thy present peril she doth thee.

SIR FLEUREANT.

I were ungrateful past all reach of words
That speak of baseness and ingratitude,
Should I not hold my life, and heart, and service,
Purely at her behest from this time forth.
And truly in conjunctures such as those
Your highness hath foreseen, to aid her flight,
Were service which no Fleming could perform,
How true soe'er his heart,—and yet to me
It were an easy task.

ARTEVELDE.

I trust the day
Will never come, that asks such service from you ;
But should it so, I charge you on your faith
And duty as a knight, perform it stoutly.
Prudence, meantime, demands that you remain
In close confinement.

SIR FLEUREANT.

As you please, my lord.

ARTEVELDE (*after a pause*).

What, watch there, ho !

Enter two Guards.

You will give passage to Sir Fleureant
To go at large.   My mind you see is changed :
It ever was my way, and shall be still,

When I do trust a man, to trust him wholly.
You shall not quit my camp; but that word given,
You are at large within it.

SIR FLEUREANT.

Sir, your trust
Shall not appear misplaced.

ARTEVELDE.

Give you good rest!
And better dreams than those I woke you from.

SIR FLEUREANT.

With grateful heart I say, my lord, God keep you!

ACT IV.

SCENE I.—*Ypres.*—*The* Burgomaster *of Ypres, with several*
Burghers *of the French Faction, and* VAN MUCK.

BURGOMASTER.

Well, well, God bless us! have a care—oh me!
Be careful how you speak; wear a white hat;
And ever, mind'st thou, when thou see'st Vauclaire,
Uncover and stand back.

VAN MUCK.

I will, your worship.

BURGOMASTER.

Nay, but you must.   And Roosdyk—speak him fair:
For give him but a saucy word, he's out,

And twinkling me his dagger in the sun,
Says, "take you that," and you are dead for good.

VAN MUCK.

I'll speak him fair.

BURGOMASTER.

Nay, but I say you shall.
'Tis a good rule to be more civil-spoken
Than wantonly be cut and stabb'd for nothing.

VAN MUCK.

'Tis so, your worship.

BURGOMASTER.

Cast not away your life.

VAN MUCK.

'Tis as your worship pleases.

FIRST BURGHER.

But if Vauclaire, or Roosdyk, or the captains
Should ask him whence he comes, or what's his craft,
Being strange-looking for a citizen,
What should he answer?

BURGOMASTER.

Say thou com'st from Dinand—
From Dinand, say, to sell Dinandery,
Pots, pitchers, mugs and beakers and the like.

VAN MUCK.

Suppose I'm question'd where they are?

BURGOMASTER.

You've sold 'em.
Say you praise God.   Say you're a thriving man.

FIRST BURGHER (*aside to second*).

This matter will be out.

SECOND BURGHER.

Why so?

FIRST BURGHER.

                    Good friend,
Did'st ever know a secret to lie close
Under a goose's wing?

SECOND BURGHER.

                    I think 'twill out.
'Twill surely out.

FIRST BURGHER.

          The frighten'd fox sits fast;
Folly with fear will flutter still and cackle.
[Aloud].   This will be known.   I am for rising now,
Slaying Vauclaire and Roosdyk in their beds
Before they nose it, sounding through the streets
King Charles's pardon and the town's submission,
And so to present issue with it all.

BURGOMASTER.

Mercy! what foolishness will young men talk!

FIRST BURGHER.

Under your favour—old men too at times.

THIRD BURGHER.

De Vry, a word.   I marvel at thy rashness;
We are not ripe for action: in a week,
Perchance a day—nay, it may be this hour,
Or Van den Bosch will conquer at Commines,
Or the French force the passage.   If the first,
In vain were this revolt, for Van den Bosch
Would quell us in a trice; and if the second,
Then were the time to rise, for all the town
Would then rise with us.

SECOND BURGHER.
　　　　　　In good time, Verstolken;
The axe's edge is turn'd towards us now,
And what shall save us, if this mooncalf here
Should let his errand out?

VAN MUCK.
　　　　　　Call you me mooncalf?
I am an honest man; I dare you, sir,
To signify me other.

SECOND BURGHER.
　　　　　Hold thy peace.
Whilst the French king is look'd for at Commines,
Too wise is Van den Bosch to break his strength
With sending soldiers hither.　He but counts
Nine thousand men.

FOURTH BURGHER.
　　　　　The double were too few
To be divided.

FIFTH BURGHER.
　　More than some two thousand
Would hardly march on Ypres, should we thrive;
And if they did, we'd bowl them down like nine-pins.

SECOND BURGHER.
He'll never waste his forces upon us
Whilst the French king's to come; and then the news
Of Ypres fallen off, will cheer the French,
Sicken the White-Hoods, and make sure the loss
Of that famed passage, which shall magnify
Our merits with King Charles.

Enter a Sixth Burgher.

SIXTH BURGHER.

Away, away!
Vauclaire has word of all you do ; a troop
Despatch'd by Van den Bosch to give him aid
Is riding into town.   Van Muck's commission
Is whisper'd of, and loudly.

BURGOMASTER.

There now, there!
I told you so—I told you this would come ;
But still you talk'd of rising.   Run, Van Muck,
Thou villain run, and be not seen abroad
With honest citizens.

SECOND BURGHER.

Aye, get thee hence ;
Best quit the town, and make thy way to France.

VAN MUCK.

I will, your worships.   [*Exit, but returns immediately.*
Please you, sir, the street
Is full of men-at-arms that come this way.

BURGOMASTER.

I said so ; there! and still you hearken'd not!
Oh Time and Tide! Oh wala-wa! Oh me!

THIRD BURGHER.

What shall we do?

SECOND BURGHER.

Van Muck, stand fast ; they come :
It is Vauclaire himself.

BURGOMASTER.

Say you sell pots.

Enter VAUCLAIRE *and* ROOSDYK *followed by a troop of*
Men-at-arms.

VAUCLAIRE.

Ah, Master Burgomaster, here you are !

ROOSDYK.

Make fast the doors.

VAUCLAIRE.

And thou, Verstolken—nay !
Here's Goswin Hex, and Drimmelen, and Breero !
And thou, De Vry—Van Rosendaal, and thou !
How rare a thing is faith !   Alas, my masters !
Here is a work you put me to !

ROOSDYK.

Stand forth,
Master Van Muck ! where are you ?—which is he ?

THIRD BURGHER.

What is it, sirs, you charge us with ?

ROOSDYK.

What think ye ?
Say treason, and I'll call you conjurors.

VAUCLAIRE.

I have my orders—stand thou forth, Van Muck—
And I must needs obey them.   Say, what art thou ?

ROOSDYK.

A villain.

VAN MUCK.

No, sirs, I am not a villain.
I am a travelling trader ; I sell pots.

ROOSDYK.

Thyself—thou sell'st thyself—a precious vessel !
Where is the provost marshal ?   Hark you, sir !

Put irons on them all, and give Van Muck
A taste of what you have.

BURGOMASTER.

               Hold off! what's this?

I am your master.

ROOSDYK.

             Knock him on the head ;

Bid him be patient.

VAUCLAIRE.

           I am amazed at this !

So sweetly as you all demean'd yourselves !
A guileful world we live in ! God forgive us !
Make fast the gyves and take them off to prison.

BURGOMASTER.

Sirs, hear me, oh !

ROOSDYK.

          Gag me this grey-beard !

BURGOMASTER.

                           Oh !

FIRST BURGHER.

Thank God !

VAUCLAIRE.

        The Stadt-house.   You shall all be heard
Except Van Muck, whose treason is too rank
To be excused.   I must obey my orders ;
First to the rack they doom him, then to the gallows.

VAN MUCK.

Sirs, grant me mercy ; I am not a traitor ;
I'll tell it all.

ROOSDYK.

       That shall you, or the rack
Is not so good a singing-master now
As it was wont to be.

VAN MUCK.

Oh Lord ! oh Lord !

[He is taken out.

VAUCLAIRE.

Bring them away : we'll hear them at the Stadt-house,
Each by himself.   Bring them away at once ;
Keep them apart, and let them not have speech
One of another.

ROOSDYK.

            If any man make signs,
Despatch him on the spot.   Master Vauclaire,
We follow you.

SCENE II.—*The French Court at Arras.—An Antechamber in the
Maison de Ville.* TRISTRAM OF LESTOVET, *Clerk of the Council,
and* SIR FLEUREANT OF HEURLÉE.

SIR FLEUREANT.

When I forgive him, may the stars rain down
And pierce me with ten thousand points of fire !
His whore ! his leman !

LESTOVET.

             Had she been his wife,
A small transgression might have pass'd.   Learn thou
To keep thy hands from meddling with men's whores ;
For dubious rights are jealously enforced,
And what men keep for pleasure is more precious
Than what need is they keep.

SIR FLEUREANT.

              He'll be the worse,
And knows it.   When I fled I left behind
A notion of my purpose.   There's none here
Can know like me his weakness and his strength.

Let but the council hear me ; I shall tell
What shall be worth to them ten thousand spears.

LESTOVET.

'Tis now their time to meet ; but the young king
Lies long a-bed.   Here comes my Lord of Burgundy.

Enter DUKE OF BURGUNDY.

BURGUNDY.

Good-morrow, sirs, good-morrow !   So, your stars,
They tell me, are your good friends still, good Flurry ;
You always come clear off;—well, I'm glad on't.

SIR FLEUREANT.

I give your highness thanks.

BURGUNDY.

Well, Lestovet,
My brother of Bourbon keeps his mind, they say ;
He is for Tournay still ; 'tis wonderful,
A man of sense to be so much besotted !

LESTOVET.

His grace of Bourbon, sir, is misdirected ;
He is deluded by a sort of men
That should know better.

BURGUNDY.

They shall rue it dearly.
To turn aside ten leagues, ten Flemish leagues,
With sixty thousand men ! 'tis moonish madness !

LESTOVET.

Sir Fleureant here, who left the rebel camp
No longer past than Wednesday, says their strength
Lies wholly eastward of the Scheldt.

SIR FLEUREANT.

                                The towns
Betwixt the Scheldt and Lis, your grace should know,
Are shaking to their steeple-tops with fear
Of the French force ; and westward of the Lis
You need but blow a trumpet, and the gates
Of Ypres, Poperinguen, Rousselaere,
And Ingelmunster gape to take you in.

BURGUNDY.

They are my words, they are my very words ;
Twenty times over have I told my brother
These towns would join us if he would but let them ;
But he's as stubborn as a mule ; and oh !
That constable !   Oh, Oliver of Clisson !
That such a man as thou, at such a time,
Should hold the staff of constable of France !
Well ! such men are !

LESTOVET.

                          My lord, I crave your pardon
For so exorbitantly shooting past
My line of duty as to tender words
Of counsel to your highness ; but my thoughts
Will out, and I have deem'd that with his grace,
Your royal brother, you have dealt too shortly.
The noble frankness of your nature breaks
Too suddenly upon the minds of men
That love themselves, and with a jealous love
Are wedded to their purposes : not only
His grace of Bourbon, but full many lords
Who bear a part against you in the council,
Would yield upon a gentle provocation,
That stiffen with a rougher.

BURGUNDY.

That may be ;
But, Lestovet, to sue to them to turn !
I cannot do it.

LESTOVET.

May it please your grace
To leave it in my hands.   With easier ear
They listen to a man of low condition ;
And under forms that in your grace to use
It were unseemly, I can oft approach,
And with a current that themselves perceive not
Can turn the tenour of their counsels.

BURGUNDY.

Nay ;
But how can I be absent from the board
At such a time as this ?

LESTOVET.

A seizure, say,
Of sudden illness.   They'll be here anon,—
I think I hear them now.

SIR FLEUREANT.

There is a sound
Of horses' feet.

BURGUNDY.

Then try it, Lestovet ;
You are a wise and wary man ; this day
I leave the field to you ; say that the gout
Confines me to my chamber.

LESTOVET.

Hark, my lord,
They come.

BURGUNDY.

Farewell to you ; improve your time. [Exit.

LESTOVET.

Ha! ha! the council! they are men of spirit.
Arouse their passions, and they'll have opinions;
Leave them but cool, they know not what to think.

SIR FLEUREANT.

You'll tell them I am here.

LESTOVET.

Before they rise
You shall be heard at large; but leave to me
To choose the fitting moment.   Hide without
Until the Usher have a sign: the mace
Shall trundle from the board, which he shall hear:
Then come at once as one that from his horse
Leaps down, and reeking hurries in to tell
A tale that will not wait.

SCENE III.—*The Council Chamber.—The* KING *is brought in by
the* DUKE OF BOURBON, *and seated on a Chair of State at
the head of the Board; three seats are placed below, on two of
which the* DUKES *of* BOURBON *and* BERRY *place themselves.
The other* Councillors *then enter, and take their seats in suc-
cession, to the number of twelve; to wit,* SIR OLIVER OF
CLISSON, *Constable of France;* SIR JOHN OF VIEN, *Admiral
of France; the* LORD OF COUCY, SIR WILLIAM OF POICTIERS,
SIR AYMENON OF PUMIERS, *the* BASTARD OF LANGRES, SIR
RAOUL OF RANEVAL, *the* LORD OF ST. JUST, *the* LORD OF
SAIMPI, SIR MAURICE OF TRESSIQUIDY, SIR LOIS OF
SANXERE, *and the* BEGUE OF VILLAINES. *A desk is placed
opposite the lower end of the Board, at which is seated*
TRISTRAM OF LESTOVET, *Clerk of the Council.*

BOURBON.

My brother of Burgundy is sick to-day;
Your majesty excuses his attendance.

x

THE KING.

We do.

BOURBON.

Save him, our number is complete.
Sir Oliver of Clisson, unto thee,
By virtue of thine office, appertaineth,
More than to any here, to point the course
Of the king's armies : wherefore he desires
Thou open this day's business.

THE KING.

'Tis our will.

THE CONSTABLE.

May it please your majesty—my lords, and you!
So much was said on Friday of the choice
'Twixt Lille and Tournay—that the more direct
And this, 'tis justly held, the safer road—
That I should waste your patience and your time,
Did I detain you long.   To Lille, my lords,
Were two days' journey ; thence to Warneston
Were one day, let or hindrance coming none ;
But should the rains continue, and the Deule—

THE KING.

What ails my Lord of Burgundy, good uncle ?

BOURBON.

The gout, sweet cousin.   May it please your grace
To hearken to the Constable.

THE CONSTABLE.

My lords,
If with these luckless rains the Deule be flooded,
As there is cause to think it is already,
From Armentières to Quesnoy, and the Marque

Be also fuller than its wont, what days
Should bring us to the Lis were hard to tell.
But grant we reach so far, all over-pass'd
Without mishap the intervenient waters,
The bridges on the upper Lis, we know,
Are broken down; and on the further shore
Lies Van den Bosch—and where are we to pass?
I put it to you, where are we to pass?
How do we cross the Lis?

LORD OF SAIMPI.

May it please your grace,
I would be bold to ask the Constable
Hath not the Lis a source?

SIR LOIS OF SANXERE.

Yea, one or more.

LORD OF SAIMPI.

Why, then it may be cross'd.

THE CONSTABLE.

My Lord of Saimpi,
Surely it may be cross'd, if other ways
Present no better hope.   My lords, ye all
Have voices in the council; speak your minds,
And God forefend that any words of mine
Should blind your better judgments.

SIR AYMENON OF PUMIERS.

Higher up,
A few leagues south, by Venay and St. Venant,
The Lis is fordable, and is not kept.

SIR RAOUL OF RANEVAL.

Not kept, my lords! why should it? Van den Bosch

Were doubtless overjoy'd to see us strike,
Amidst the drenching of these torrents, deep
Into the lands of Cassel and Vertus;
An English force, for aught we know, the while
Borne like a flock of wild geese o'er the seas,
And dropp'd at Dunkirk.   On the left are they,
The Flemings on the right, strong towns in front;
And so we plunge from clammy slough to slough,
With fog and flood around us.

SIR LOIS OF SANXERE.

Yea, wet-footed.

SIR RAOUL OF RANEVAL.

What say you?

SIR LOIS OF SANXERE.

For the love of God, my lords,
Keep we dry feet.   Rheumatic pains, catarrhs,
And knotty squeezings of the inward man,
Thus may we fly the taste of.

SIR RAOUL OF RANEVAL.

Soft, Sir Lois;
Spare us thy gibes; I've stood more winters' nights
Above my knees in mire, than thou hast hairs
Upon the furnish'd outside of thy skull.

SIR LOIS OF SANXERE.

I say, my lords, take heed of mists and swamps;
Eschew rain water; think on winter nights;
Beware the Flemish on the Lis; beware
The English, that are in much strength—at London.
Ye've brought the king to Arras in November,
And now ye find that in November rain
Is wont to fall; ye find that fallen rain

Swells rivers and makes floods ; whereof advised,
Take the king back with all convenient speed,
And shut him up at Senlis.

THE KING.

                    Hold, Sir Lois ;
I will not go.

SIR LOIS OF SANXERE.

            I crave your Grace's pardon ;
I little dream'd you would ; you are a man.

SIR RAOUL OF RANEVAL.

Lois of Sanxere, I ask thee in this presence,
Fling'st thou these girds at me ?

THE CONSTABLE.

                        My lords, my lords !
I do beseech you to bethink yourselves.
Remember where ye are.

SIR RAOUL OF RANEVAL (*drawing off his glove*).

            Lois of Sanxere—

[*Here* TRISTRAM OF LESTOVET, *in arranging some parchments,
touches the mace, which rolls heavily from the table, and falls
close to the feet of* SIR RAOUL OF RANEVAL. *He starts up.*

LESTOVET.

No hurt, my lord, I hope ? Thank God ! thank God !
Most humbly do I sue to you, my lord,
To grant me your forgiveness.

SIR RAOUL OF RANEVAL.

                        Nay, 'tis nothing ;
It might have been a bruise, but——

Enter an Usher, *followed by* SIR FLEUREANT OF HEURLÉE.

USHER.

                    Please your Grace,

Sir Fleureant of Heurlée waits without,
Hot from the Flemish camp, which he but left
Two days agone, and he can tell your Grace
How all things stand in Flanders.

BOURBON.

Now we'll see!

This is an apt arrival; welcome, sir!
What is the news you bring us?

SIR FLEUREANT.

Please your Grace,
The letters patent I sought means to send
To Ypres, Ghent, and Bruges; but to the first
Only they reached in safety, though from thence
Doubtless the terms have spread.   The Regent, warn'd
Of what was machinated, as I hear,
Sent orders to the Lis for Van den Bosch
To split his power, and throw a third to Ypres
To fortify Vauclaire; whilst he stood fast,
But held himself prepared, if Bruges should rise
Or Ghent, to drop adown the Lis to Heule,
Or Desselghem, or Rosebecque, there to join
The Regent's force, that then should raise the siege
Of Oudenarde, and gather on the Lis.

BOURBON.

These are good tidings; yet I deem the Lis
Is still too strongly guarded for our force
There to make way.

THE CONSTABLE.

Your Grace is ever just
In all your views.

THE BEGUE OF VILLAINES.

　　　　　　　Sir Constable, some thought
Let us bestow on tidings whence we learn
The fears o' the adverse, and the slide this way
Of Ypres, Ghent, and Bruges.

SIR RAOUL OF RANEVAL.

　　　　　　　　　　Should these towns turn,
A larger force the Regent were constrain'd
To keep i' the west; and passing down the Scheldt
By Tournay, we are less opposed.

SIR LOIS OF SANXERE.

　　　　　　　　　Not so.

SIR RAOUL OF RANEVAL.

I say we meet with opposition less
Upon the Scheldt at Tournay.

SIR LOIS OF SANXERE.

　　　　　　　　I say, no.
Turning our faces from these doubting towns,
What can they but fall back?

SIR RAOUL OF RANEVAL.

　　　　　　　　　Wilt have it so?
Methinks, my lords, if turning and backsliding
And lack of loyalty——

LESTOVET (*to* SIR FLEUREANT OF HEURLÉE).

　　　　　　　　Hilloa, sir, ho!
You cannot go, you must not quit the board;
My lords will further question you anon.
Spake you not of the Scheldt? doubtless my lords
Would hear you upon that.

BOURBON.

Aye, aye, the Scheldt;
What say'st thou of the Scheldt?

SIR FLEUREANT.

My lords, your pardon;
With my own eyes I have not view'd the Scheldt
Higher than Oudenarde; yet what I know
More sure than common rumour I may tell,
That reach by reach from Elsegem to Kam,
At sundry stations, say Kerckhoven first,
'Twixt Berkhem and Avelghem, where the Ronne
Its tide contributes elbowing Escanaffe,
At Pontespiers and Pecq, and divers points
Betwixt them interposed, strong piles are driven
Deep in the belly of the stream athwart.
Thus neither up nor down can make their way
Boat, raft, nor caravel.

BASTARD OF LANGRES.

We see, my lords,
The Scheldt is no purveyor of our victual
Should we proceed by Tournay.

LORD OF SAIMPI.

I surmise
We shall find spears as thick upon the banks
As stakes within the stream.

SIR RAOUL OF RANEVAL.

Then let us find them!
Who is it now that flinches and postpones?
I say, once pass'd the Scheldt, and better far
We should confront the Flemish spears; so be it!

We'd give the villains such a taste of France
That thence for evermore 'Mount Joye St. Denis'
Should bo a cry to make their life-blood freeze
And teach rebellion duty.

SIR LOIS OF SANXERE.

Fee, faw, fum !

LESTOVET.

Sir John de Vien would speak ; Sir John de Vien
Hath not yet spoken.

SIR JOHN DE VIEN.

Here we lie, my lords,
At Arras still, disputing.   I am a man
Of little fruitfulness in words ; the days
That we lie here, my lords, I deem ill spent.
Once and again the time of year is told,
That we are in November : whiles we vex
This theme, what follows ?—why, December ! True,
The time of year is late, my lords ; yea truly,
The fall of the year, I say, my lords, November,
Is a late season when it rains, my lords.
I have not, as you know, the gift of speech,
But thus much may a plain man say,—time flies ;
The English are a people deft, my lords,
And sudden in the crossing of the seas ;
And should we linger here with winter coming,
We were not call'd good men of war, forsooth.
So truly, sirs, my voice, with humbleness,
Is for short counsel ; in good truth, my lords—

THE KING.

Dear uncle, what's o'clock ?

BOURBON.

        'Tis noon, sweet cousin.

THE KING.

I want my dinner.

BOURBON.

        Presently, fair cousin.

SIR LOIS OF SANXERE.

Your majesty is of the admiral's mind;
You love short counsel; marry, and of mine;
I love it too; more specially I love it
With mallets at our backs and winter near.
We talk so long that what is said at first
What follows sponges from our memories.
Pass to the vote, my lords, nor waste your breath
In further talk.

BOURBON.

        Then pass we to the vote.

THE CONSTABLE.

So be it; to the vote.

OTHERS.

        Agreed: to the vote.

LESTOVET.

My lords, may it please you, ere your votes I gather
That briefly I rehearse what each hath said,
As noted with a hasty pen, or writ
In a weak memory.

BOURBON.

        So do, so do.

LESTOVET.

First, my lord constable: he bade you think
What length of way and waters lay between

Ere you could reach the Lis ; where when you come
You find no bridge, and on the further bank
The Flemish power : then spake my Lord of Saimpi,
Touching a passage nearer to the springs
By Venay and St. Venant : whereunto
My Lord of Raneval made answer meet,
That though the Lis were fordable above,
Yet in the lands of Cassel and Vertus
There dwelt a dangerous people, sulking boors,
Who, when we straggled, as perforce we must,
Through bye-ways sunder'd by the branching waters,
Should fall upon us, founder'd in the sloughs,
And raise the country round :—thus far, my lords,
Had you proceeded, when the tiding came
Of Ypres, Ghent, and Bruges upon the turn,
Repentant of their sins and looking back
For their allegiance ; with the sequel fair
Of much diminish'd squadrons at Commines.
Then though my lord of Raneval spake well
Of clearance on the Scheldt, through direful need
That now must westward suck the Flemish force,
Yet in abatement came the shrewd account
Of how the Scheldt was grated, gagg'd, jaw-lock'd,
With here a turnpike and with there a turnpike,
And Friesland horses.   Said the Knight of Langres,
How shall our victual reach us ?   To which adds
Sir Hugh of Saimpi, that the banks are kept.
Whereat my Lord of Raneval rejoin'd
That he, as best became him, took no heed,
So it were soon, to whereabouts he faced
The Flemish scum in arms, or on the Scheldt,
Or on the Lis——

SIR RAOUL OF RANEVAL.

        Permit me, sir, the Lis
I spake not of.

LESTOVET.

        I humbly crave your pardon;
My memory is but crazy, good my lords;
It oft betrays me vilely. Sir Raoul,
I do beseech you pardon me; I deem'd
(Misled perchance by that so rife renown
Which plants you ever foremost) that your voice
Was mainly raised for speed.

SIR RAOUL OF RANEVAL.

                I grant you that;
No man is more for speed, my lords, than I,
So we outrun not wisdom.

BOURBON.

        Next—proceed.

LESTOVET.

My lord the admiral was next, and last
The Souldich of Sanxere; the English fleet
Expected shortly; winter distant now
But few days' journey; mallets at your backs,—
These were their fruitful topics: on the last,
An't please your lordships to vouchsafe me audience,
Some tidings have I gather'd, here and there,
Which haply not unworthy of your ears
You might, when heard, pronounce.

BOURBON.

                Say on, sir; well!

LESTOVET.

At Paris, when the Commons and vile people
Beat in the prison doors, ye know, my lords,

That Aubriot their friend, the sometime provost,
Who lay in prison then, made good his flight
To Arc in Burgundy ; from thence, I learn,
He look'd abroad, and journeying up and down,
He practised with the towns upon the Marne,
With Rheims and Chalons, Toul, and Bar-le-Duc,
With sundry villages in Vermandois,
And Brieche and Laon ; so he moved the poor
(Through help, as I believe, of something evil,
From which God shield good men !) that straight they
    slew
The chatelains and farmers of the aids.
They next would raise a power and march to Paris :
But Nicholas le Flamand bade them wait
Until the Scheldt were 'twixt the king and them,
Which shelter found, he trusted with their aid
To bring the castle of the Louvre low,
And not of Paris only, but of France
And Burgundy, to make the mean-folk lords.
This have I gather'd from the last that left
Champagne and Beauvoisin.

BOURBON.

                    Something of this
Reach'd me last night.

THE CONSTABLE.

              I had some tidings, too.

SIR JOHN DE VIEN.

And I.

BOURBON.

      I think, my lords, this matter asks
A further inquest.   If the whole be true,

We were not wise in council to o'erlook it.
Let us take order so to sift the truth
That clearer-sighted we may meet to-morrow;
Till when I deem it prudent we should hang
In a free judgment.

LORD OF ST. JUST.

Till to-morrow, then.

THE CONSTABLE.

One day's delay will hurt us not.

SIR LOIS OF SANXERE.

To-morrow.

LORD OF SAIMPI.

To-morrow be it, then.

SIR JOHN DE VIEN.

At noon, my lords?

BOURBON.

To-morrow noon.   Sir Oliver of Clisson,
Wilt please you ride?

THE CONSTABLE.

Your highness does me honour.

THE KING.

Dear uncle, is the council up?

BOURBON.

It is.

THE KING.

Take that, old Tristram.

BOURBON.

Soberly, fair cousin;
You do not well to toss about the parchments.

Ho! tell my serving men we ride to Vis,
The constable and I.   Adieu, fair sirs.

[*Exeunt the* King *and the* Lords *of the Council.* *Manent* TRISTRAM
of LESTOVET *and* SIR FLEUREANT *of* HEURLÉE.

LESTOVET.

Go to the duke; tell him the point is carried.

SIR FLEUREANT.

But is it so?

LESTOVET.

It is as good.

SIR FLEUREANT.

They seek
Some further knowledge.

LESTOVET.

Tut! they know it all;
They knew it ere I told them; but my mind
As touching it, they knew not of till now.
Run to the duke; pray him to keep his chamber;
Let him but stand aloof another day,
And come the next, we march upon Commines.

SCENE IV.—*The Market-place at Ypres. In front,* VAN WHELK,
*a Householder, driving the last nails into a Scaffolding erected
against his House.* VAN STOCKENSTROM, *another, looking
on. A* Woman *is scouring the Doorstead of the next House.
At some little distance six Gallows-trees are seen, opposite the
Stadt-house.*

VAN WHELK.

Room for five ducats at a groat a head.

VAN STOCKENSTROM.

'Twill be a piteous spectacle!   Good day,
How do you, mistress?

WOMAN.

Thank you, how's yourself?

VAN STOCKENSTROM.

'Twill be a sight most piteous to behold!
A corporation hung!

WOMAN.

Alack a day!

VAN WHELK.

'Twill be a sight that never yet was seen
Since Ypres was a town.   A groat is cheap;
A groat is very reasonable cheap.

VAN STOCKENSTROM.

The burgomaster was confess'd at seven;
He is the first.

VAN WHELK.

Van Rosendael the next,
And then comes Drimmelen, Verstolken then,
And Goswin Hex, and Breero, and De Vry.

VAN STOCKENSTROM.

This ancient corporation!

WOMAN.

Wo's the day!
Poor gentlemen! alas, they did not think,
Nor no man else, the Regent would take life
So hastily.

VAN WHELK.

The like was never seen,
Nor ever will be after.

VAN STOCKENSTROM.

Hold you there;

Come the French king, and we shall see this square
More thick with gallows than with butchers' stalls
Upon a market day.

WOMAN.

Nay, God forbid!
Master Van Stockenstrom, you will not say so?

VAN STOCKENSTROM.

It is not saying it that hangs them, dame:
I tell you it is true.

WOMAN.

There's some have said,
How that King Charles was mighty tender-hearted;
The dukes his uncles likewise; and that none
Were lother to shed blood.

VAN STOCKENSTROM.

Those burghers said it,
Whom yonder gallows wait for; and if lies
Were worthy hanging, they deserved their doom.

WOMAN.

Well, sirs, I know not.

VAN STOCKENSTROM.

Tut! King Charles, I say,
The dukes his uncles, and his councillors all,
Are of one flesh and follow after kind.
There are humane amongst them! how humane?
Humane to lords and ladies, kings and counts.
Humane to such as we?   Believe it not.

VAN WHELK.

The Earl of Flanders is the French king's cousin.

VAN STOCKENSTROM.

His majesty, to show his cousin kindness,

Y

Would canter over acres of our bodies.
His cousin is in what he calls distress;
To succour the distress'd is kind and good;
So with an army comes the good King Charles,
And kindly to his cousin cuts our throats.
And that is their humanity, and such
Is man's humanity the wide world through!
Men's hearts you'll find on one side soft as wax,
Hard as the nether mill-stone on the other.

VAN WHELK.

How is it with your own, Dame Voorst?

WOMAN.

God save us!

I would not hurt a hair upon the head
Of any man alive.

VAN STOCKENSTROM.

Look you, the earl—
But hearken to a tale: Once in my youth—
Ah, Mistress Voorst! years, years, they steal upon us!
But what! you're comely yet,—well, in my youth,
Occasion was that I should wend my way
From Reninghelst to Ronques, to gather there
Some monies that were owing me; the road
Went wavering like jagged lightning through the
     moors,—
For mind, Van Whelk, in those days Rening Fell
Was not so sluiced as now; the night was near
And wore an ugly likeness to a storm,
When I, misdoubting of my way and weary,
Descried the flickering of a cottage fire
Thorough the casements; thither sped my feet:

The door was open'd by a buxom dame
That smiled and bade me welcome, and great cheer
She made me, with a jocund, stirring mien
Of kindly entertainment, whilst with logs
Crackled the fire, and seem'd the very pot
To bubble in a hospitable hurry
That I might sup betimes.   Now say, Dame Voorst,
Was not the mistress of this cottage lone
A kind good soul ?

WOMAN.

Yea, truly was she, sir.

VAN STOCKENSTROM.

Master Van Whelk, what think you?

VAN WHELK.

Let me see ;
Did she take nothing from you?

VAN STOCKENSTROM.

Not a stiver.

VAN WHELK.

Why, that was charitable ; that was kind;
That was a woman of the good old times.

VAN STOCKENSTROM.

Now mark, Van Whelk ; now listen, Mistress Voorst.
The seething-pan upon the fire contain'd
Six craw-fish for my supper: as I stood
Upon the ruddy hearth, my unlaced thoughts
Fall'n to a mood of idle cogitation,
My eyes chanced fix upon the bubbling pot:
Unconsciously awhile I gazed, as one
Seeing that sees not ; but ere long appear'd
A tumbling and a labouring in the pot

More than of boiling water ; whereupon,
Looking with eyes inquisitive, I saw
The craw-fish rolling one upon another,
Bouncing, and tossing all their legs abroad
That writhed and twisted, as mix'd each with each
They whirl'd about the pan.   God's love! quoth I,
These craw-fish are alive ! Yea, sir, she answered,
They are not good but when they're sodden quick.
I said no more, but turn'd me from the hearth,
Feeling a sickness here ; and inwardly
I cried heigh-ho ! that for one man's one supper
Six of God's creatures should be boil'd alive !

WOMAN.

Lord help us, sir !   You wail about the fish
As they were Christians.

VAN STOCKENSTROM.

                    Look you, Mistress Voorst ;
The King will be as kind to Louis Mâle
As this good wife to me : of us mean folk
He will take count as of so many craw-fish ;
To please his cousin 'twere to him no sin
To boil us in a pot.—Back, back, Van Whelk !
Here be the captains !

                              [*They retire.*

Enter VAUCLAIRE, ROOSDYK, *and* VAN DEN BOSCH's Lieutenant.

VAUCLAIRE.

Shrewd news ! whence cam'st thou last ?

LIEUTENANT.

                              From St. Eloy.

ROOSDYK.

On Monday was it that the French pass'd over ?

LIEUTENANT.

All Monday night 'twould seem that they were crossing
By nines and tens ; the craft would hold no more.

ROOSDYK.

Were there none watching of those jobbernowls
That follow Van den Bosch ?

LIEUTENANT.

     The night was dark ;
The most part of our men were sent to sleep
In quarters at Commines, that they might rise
Fresh on the morrow, when the French, 'twas thought,
Would try the passage by the bridge.   The rest
Kept guard upon the causeway.   Two miles down
The river crankles round an alder grove ;
'Twas there they brought the boats ; strong stakes were
  driven
In either bank, and ropes were pass'd betwixt
Stretching athwart the stream ; by aid of these
Hand over hand they tugged themselves across,
And hid within the thicket; when day dawn'd
They still were crossing, but the constable,
Who always kept his ground, made show to force
The passage of the bridge, and brought us there
To handy-strokes, which so misled our eyes
That nothing else was seen.

ROOSDYK.

     Ha, ha ! I love you !
Set you to watch the cat !

LIEUTENANT.

     When first we knew
Their stratagem, six banners could we count,
And thirty pennons on the hither bank,

The Lord of Saimpi leading them : were there
Sir Herbeaux of Bellperche, Sir John of Roy,
The Lords of Chaudronne, Malestroit, Sanxere,
All Bretons, with Sir Oliver of Guesclin,
The Lords of Laval, Rohan, Belliers, Meaulx,
Sir Tristram de la Jaille, and to be short,
The flower of all their host, from Poictou, Troyes,
Artois and Hainault, Burgundy and France,
That had their station marshall'd in the van.

VAUCLAIRE.

And there they stood ?

LIEUTENANT.

      As yet they had not fought,
When I was order'd thence ; for Van den Bosch
Upon the eminence beside the bridge
Awaited them as on a vantage ground,
Whilst they abode below to gather force
From them continually that cross'd the stream.

VAUCLAIRE.

Then went you to the good towns near.

LIEUTENANT.

        To Bergues,
To Poperinguen, Rolers, Warneston,
To Mesiers and Vertain, with strict command
From Van den Bosch to muster all their men
And send him succour ; thence I hasten'd here
To pray you do the like.

ROOSDYK.

      Oh rare ! I love you !
Didst ever see one beggar dropping alms
Into another's hat ?

LIEUTENANT.

My master sware,
If he should lose the day the cause should lie
In that misfortunate wasting of his strength
By sending aid to Ypres.

VAUCLAIRE.

Send it back,
And we shall lose the town, and he the battle,
Ere it shall reach him : from the nearer towns
He may be timeously recomforted.
Meanwhile lest ill betide him, which, when here
It should be known, would bring a wild destruction
On us and ours, behoves us send forthright
Unto the Regent, to advise his Highness
Of what hath come to pass.   Christoffel Waal,
Mount thee thy horse and hie to Oudenarde,
And bid the Regent know the Lis is pass'd.
That said is all said : he shall know by that
We shall have much ado with this good town
Ere many days be gone, or many hours.
If he can help us, so.

ROOSDYK.

Aye, mount thy nag,
And make his heels strike fire ; away, begone !

VAUCLAIRE.

Know'st thou thy message ?

WAAL.

Sirs, from point to point. [*Exit.*

[*A bell tolls. Muffled drums are heard, and the head of a Procession
appears, entering the Market-place. The Procession is formed
chiefly by* Friars *and* Guards; *and lastly appear the* Burgomaster *and* Aldermen *of several Guilds as Malefactors, with
their arms pinioned. They form a line between the Gallows and
the Stadt-House. The Market-place suddenly fills with the
Populace.*

VAUCLAIRE.

This folk looks strangely! guess you what's toward?
Is the news known?

ROOSDYK.

          I see no women here;
There is a mischievous intent.

VAUCLAIRE.

                  Go you
And get our men of battle under arms;
We shall have fighting; this must mean a rescue.

ROOSDYK.

Let the clerks hold the culprits in confession
Some fifteen minutes, and I'll bring you here
The most I can, and till I come again
Let no thief swing, for that should be their sign
Doubtless for rising. I'll be here anon.

                                [*Exit.*

Enter a Pricker.

VAUCLAIRE.

Thy spurs are bloody—what, from Commines, ha!
A battle lost?

PRICKER.

          'Tis so, sir. Van den Bosch
With what remains of us is flying hither,
And wills you arm.

VAUCLAIRE.

          We shall be arm'd anon:
And some of us you see.

        [*He beckons to the* Captain of the Guard, *who has charge of
the prisoners.*

                 Sir, draw your men
More close upon their charge, and look about you,
For here's foul weather.

        [*Cries begin to be heard and stones are thrown, one of which
hits the steel cap of* VAUCLAIRE.

                    Said I not? look here!
These drops fore-run the storm.

[A cry is heard at the opposite corner of the Market-place, and
VAN DEN BOSCH's Page is seen approaching.

                              Lo,—stand aside;
There is a face I'll swear I've sometime seen
Attending Van den Bosch.

PRICKER.

            His Page, sir, surely.

PAGE.

My master, sir, is near—

VAUCLAIRE.

                Say'st thou! how near?

PAGE.

Close on the town.   He enters now.

VAUCLAIRE.

                        What force
Comes with him?

PAGE.

            It is hard to say; they ride
So scatter'd and so broken, wounded most,
And mile by mile, now one and now another,
They tumble from their horses.   He himself
Is sorely piked and gash'd, and of his hurts,
One, the leech deems, is mortal.

VAUCLAIRE.

                Christ forbid!

PAGE.

They bear him in a litter, and each jog
They give him, when the bearers change their hands,
Makes him to bleed afresh.

PRICKER.

See, there he comes!

[*The tumult which had been increasing, is in some measure stilled
as* VAN DEN BOSCH *is borne across the Market-place to the
front of the scene.*

VAN DEN BOSCH (*raising himself in the litter*).

Who's that? Vauclaire?   We're ruin'd, sir, we're lost!
How stand ye here?

VAUCLAIRE.

The worst is what I see.
Yet hath the town an evil inclination,
And we shall feel it suddenly.

VAN DEN BOSCH.

Send forth—
Be still thou jumping villain, with thy jolts!
Thou grind'st my bones to powder.   Oh! oh! oh!
I would thou hadst my shoulder.—Send abroad,
And bid the Commons to the market-place.

VAUCLAIRE.

Nay, here they are, as thick as they can stand.

VAN DEN BOSCH.

Are they?   My eyesight fails me.   And is this
The market-place?   Oho! then lift me up
Upon some cart or tumbril or the like
That I may make a preachment to the people.

VAUCLAIRE.

Leave that to me: betake thee to thy bed;
Roosdyk is making muster of our force,
And what is instant to be cared for here
We will perform.

VAN DEN BOSCH.

Not whilst I live, Vauclaire.

The leech, I think, has patch'd me up this body
To last a season.   Hoist me—have a care—
Mount me upon this scaffolding : up, up—
Smoothly and altogether—there we go—
Oh ! oh ! that's thou again, uneasy whelp !
Hast the string-halt ?   Now set me down ;—so—so.
Let silence be commanded.

> [*The soldiery fall back, so as to admit the people to the space imme-
> diately in front of the scaffolding.   Sundry officers pass to and
> fro, vociferating ' Silence!' which is obtained.*]

                            Friends, sirs of Ypres !
Dear friends of Ypres ! we have lost a battle.
This once, by evil hap, the day is theirs :
Which is no fault of mine ; for, sirs, I'll tell you
How this hath chanced.
By the Black Art (which Frenchmen dare to use
For lack of godlier courage)—by this art
They brought a cloudy film upon the eyes
Of half our host, the half that should have watch'd ;
Which was on Monday night : and thus ere dawn
They cross'd the Lis.   Then, sirs, what force had I,
Without advantage to affront the flower
Of the French van ?   Solely twelve thousand spears !
Yet, like a hedge-pig, tuck'd I up my power
The softer parts within ; and when Sanxere
Came nuzzling like a dog to find some flesh
Whereon to fix and turn me inside out,
I'll warrant you I prick'd his snout a little !
Well, sirs, we might have conquer'd, but that then
The Commons of Commines—bell, book, and candle
Curse them that pass for Flemings and are none !—
They of Commines, that call'd themselves so stout,
Show'd such a fear and faintness of their hearts

As makes me sweat with shame to think upon ;
And, traitors in their flight, they fired the town,
To stay the following French.   From that time forth
Seeing we had no holding-place behind,
The best began to falter ; and, in brief,
Ye see us here.—Fellow, some wine ; I tire ;
I've lost some blood.

VAUCLAIRE.

Prithee go in-a-doors,
And let thy hurts be tended.

VAN DEN BOSCH (*a cup of wine is brought, which he drinks off*).

Fair and softly !
There's more to say.

[*An arrow, shot from the crowd, strikes the scaffolding close to*
VAN DEN BOSCH, *whereupon loud cries are heard from both
parties and some blows pass between them, followed by great
uproar and confusion.*

Who hinders my discourse
With shooting cross-bow shafts?   Oh, there you are !
See you yon villain there that gapes and shouts ?
Send me an arrow down his throat.—I say,
This battle lost is nothing lost at all.
For thus the French are wiled across the Lis,
Which ne'er shall they repass.   Inveigled on
By wheedling fortune, they shall thus be snared :
For hither comes the Regent from the Scheldt,
And hither come the English, that are now
Landed at Dunkirk—landed now, I tell you ;
The news was brought me yesterday ; which heard,
Verily I was glad I lost this battle,
Although it cost me something—(for ye see
How I am troubled in my head and shoulder)—

Yea truly I rejoiced that thus the French
Should run upon a pit-fall, whilst we sweep
A circle round them, so that none——more wine——

[Sinks suddenly back in the litter.

Here is a bandage loose—stauuch me this blood—
Look ye, I bleed to death—oh, doctor vile!
Oh treacherous chirurgeon!—endless fire
Crumble his bones in hell!—I die, I die!

VAUCLAIRE (*helping to re-adjust the bandage*).

Another plie; now draw it tight; anon
Roosdyk will come and give us escort hence;
Meanwhile defend yourselves and shoot again
If you be shot at.

VAN DEN BOSCH.

Now the trumpets sound!
Chains for the King! The trumpets sound again!
Chains for the knights and nobles! Victory!
Thou gaoler, shut the doors. 'Tis very dark!
Whose hand is this?—Van Artevelde's?—I thank you:
'Twas Fortune favour'd me. Chains, chains and death!
Chains for the King of France!—You've shut me in.
It is all over with me now, good mother.
Let the bells toll.

VAUCLAIRE.

Bring him behind these boards;
The arrows now come quickly. Send a flight——
They've loosed the prisoners. See, they bear this way;
Shoot well together once and then fall back,
And force a road to Ghent with Van den Bosch
Alive or dead. I follow if I can.

Well shot !—they're flutter'd : steadily, my friends ;
Take forth the litter first ; now close your ranks ;
Show a back front ; so—off ye go—well done !

ACT V.

SCENE I.—*Van Artevelde's Tent, in the Flemish camp before Oudenarde.*

ELENA *and* CECILE.

ELENA (*singing*).

Quoth tongue of neither maid nor wife
    To heart of neither wife nor maid,
Lead we not here a jolly life
    Betwixt the shine and shade.

Quoth heart of neither maid nor wife
    To tongue of neither wife nor maid,
Thou wag'st, but I am worn with strife,
    And feel like flowers that fade.

There was truth in that, Cecile.

CECILE.
                         Fie on such truth !
Rather than that my heart spoke truth in dumps,
I'd have it what it is, a merry liar.

ELENA.
Yes, you are right ; I would that I were merry !
Not for my own particular, God knows !
But for his ease ; he needs to be enliven'd ;
And for myself in him ; because I know
That often he must think me dull and dry,
I am so heavy-hearted, and at times

Outright incapable of speech.　Oh me!
I was not made to please.

CECILE.

　　　　　　Yourself, my lady;
'Tis true to please yourself you were not made,
Being truly by yourself most hard to please;
But speak for none beside; for you were made
Come gleam or gloom, all others to enchant,
Wherein you never fail.

ELENA.

　　　　　Yes, but I do;
How can I please him when I cannot speak?
When he is absent I am full of thought,
And fruitful in expression inwardly,
And fresh and free and cordial is the flow
Of my ideal and unheard discourse,
Calling him in my heart endearing names,
Familiarly fearless.　But alas!
No sooner is he present than my thoughts
Are breathless and bewitch'd, and stunted so
In force and freedom, that I ask myself
Whether I think at all, or feel, or live,
So senseless am I!

CECILE.

　　　　　Heed not that, my lady;
Men heed it not; I never heard of one
That quarrell'd with his lady for not talking.
I have had lovers more than I can count,
And some so quarrelsome, a slap in the face
Would make them hang themselves if you'd believe them;
But for my insufficiencies of speech

They ne'er reproach'd me : no, the testiest of them
Ne'er fish'd a quarrel out of that.

ELENA.

                                        Thy swains
Might bear their provocations in that kind,
Yet not of silence prove themselves enamour'd.
But mark you this, Cecile : your grave and wise
And melancholy men, if they have souls,
As commonly they have, susceptible
Of all impressions, lavish most their love
Upon the blithe and sportive, and on such
As yield their want and chase their sad excess
With jocund salutations, nimble talk,
And buoyant bearing.   Would that I were merry !
Mirth have I valued not before ; but now
What would I give to be the laughing fount
Of gay imaginations ever bright,
And sparkling fantasies !   Oh, all I have,
(Which is not nothing though I prize it not,)
My understanding soul, my brooding sense,
My passionate fancy, and the gift of gifts
Dearest to woman which deflowering Time,
Slow ravisher, from clenched'st fingers wrings—
My corporal beauty, would I barter now
For such an antic and exulting spirit
As lives in lively women.   Who comes hither?

CECILE.

'Tis the old friar ; he they sent to England ;
That ancient man so yellow !   By our Lady !
He's yellower than he went.   Note but his look ;
His rind's the colour of a mouldy walnut.

Troth! his complexion is no wholesomer
Than a sick frog's.

ELENA.

Be silent ; he will hear you.

CECILE.

It makes me ill to look at him.

ELENA.

Hush! hush!

CECILE.

It makes me very ill.

Enter FATHER JOHN OF HEDA.

FATHER JOHN.

Your pardon, lady,

I seek the Regent.

ELENA.

Please you, sit awhile ;

He comes anon.

FATHER JOHN.

This tent is his?

ELENA.

It is.

FATHER JOHN.

And likewise yours.—(*Aside.*)   Yea, this is as I heard ;
A wily woman hither sent from France.
Alas! alas! how frail the state of man!
How weak the strongest!   This is such a fall
As Samson suffer'd.

CECILE (*aside to Elena.*)

How the friar croaks!

What gibbering is this?

ELENA.

May we not deem

z

Your swift return auspicious?   Sure it denotes
A prosperous mission?

FATHER JOHN.

What I see and hear
Of sinful courses, and of nets and snares
Encompassing the feet of them that once
Were steadfast deem'd, speaks only to my heart
Of coming judgments.

CECILE.

What I see and hear
Of naughty friars and of——

ELENA.

Peace, Cecile!
Go to your chamber; you forget yourself.
Father, your words afflict me.

[*Exit* CECILE.

Enter VAN ARTEVELDE.

ARTEVELDE (*as he enters*).   .

Who is it says
That Father John is come?   Ah! here he is.
Give me your hand, good Father!   For your news,
Philosophy befriend me that I show
No strange impatience; for your every word
Must touch me in the quick.

FATHER JOHN.

To you alone
Would I address myself.

ARTEVELDE.

Nay heed not her;
She is my privy councillor.

FATHER JOHN.

My lord,
Such councillors I abjure.   My function speaks,

And through me speaks the Master whom I serve :
After strange women them that went astray
God never prosper'd in the olden time,
Nor will he bless them now.   An angry eye
That sleeps not, follows thee till from thy camp
Thou shalt have put away the evil thing.
This in her presence will I say—

ELENA.

Oh God !

FATHER JOHN.

That whilst a foreign leman—

ARTEVELDE.

Nay, spare her ;
To me say what thou wilt.

FATHER JOHN.

Thus then it is :
This foreign tie is not to Heaven alone
Displeasing, but to those on whose firm faith
Rests under Heaven your all ;—
It is offensive to your army—nay
And justly, for they deem themselves betray'd,
When circumvented thus by foreign wiles
They see their chief.

ELENA.

Oh ! let me quit the camp.
Misfortune follows wheresoe'er I come !
My destiny on whomsoe'er I love
Alights !   It shall not, Artevelde, on thee ;
For I will leave thee to thy better fortune,
And pray for thee aloof.

FATHER JOHN.

Thou shalt do well

z 2

For him and for thyself; the camp is now
A post of danger.

ELENA.

Artevelde! Oh God!
In such an hour as this, then, must I quit thee?

FATHER JOHN.

As thou wouldst make his danger more or less
So now demean thyself—stay or depart.
I say again the universal camp,
Nay more—the towns of Flanders are agape
With tales of sorceries, witcheries, and spells,
That blind their chief, and yield him up a prey
To treasons foul.   How much is true or false
I know not, and I say not; but this truth
I sorrowfully declare,—that ill repute
And sin and shame grow up with every hour
That sees you link'd together in these bonds
Of spurious love.

ELENA.

Father, enough is said.
Clerk's eyes nor soldier's will I more molest
By tarrying here.   Seek other food to feed
Your pious scorn and pertinent suspicions.
I am a sinful and unhappy creature:
Yet may be injured; there is room to wrong me,
As you will find hereafter.   I will go,
Lest this injustice done to me work harm
Unto my lord the Regent.

ARTEVELDE.

Hold, Elena;
Give me a voice in this.   You, Father John,
I blame not, nor myself will justify;

But call my weakness what you will, the time
Is past for reparation.   Now to cast off
The partner of my sin were further sin ;
'Twere with her first to sin, and next against her.
And for the army, if their trust in me
Be sliding, let it go ; I know my course ;
And be it armies, cities, people, priests,
That quarrel with my love, wise men or fools,
Friends, foes, or factions, they may swear their oaths,
And make their murmur—rave, and fret, and fear,
Suspect, admonish—they but waste their rage,
Their wits, their words, their counsel : Here I stand
Upon the deep foundations of my faith
To this fair outcast plighted ; and the storm
That princes from their palaces shakes out,
Though it should turn and head me, should not strain
The seeming silken texture of this tie.—
To business next.—Come hither, my Elena ;
I will not have thee go as one suspect ;
Stay and hear all.   Father, forgive my heat,
And do not deem me stubborn.   Now at once
The English news ?

FATHER JOHN.

                      Your deeds upon your head !
Be silent, my surprise—be told, my tale.
No open answer from the English king
Could we procure, no honest yea or nay,
But only grave denotements of good-will,
With mention of the perils of the seas,
The much tempestuous season, and the loss
Unspeakable that England suffer'd late
In her sea-strengths ; but not the less, they said,

By reason of good love and amity,
The king should order reckonings to be made,
By two sufficient scholars, of the charge
Of what we sought; his parliament then sitting
He would take counsel of, and send you word
What might be done.

ARTEVELDE.

A leisurely resolve.
The king took council of his own desires,
Ere of his lords and commons.   Had he wish'd
To do this thing, he had not ask'd advice.
In the pure polity of a monarch's mind
The will is privy-councillor to the judgment.
When shall his answer reach us?

FATHER JOHN.

In my wake
Sir Richard Farrington, I found, had follow'd;
And sped by favourabler winds than mine,
Reach'd Dunkirk with me.   Letters seal'd he brought;
But hearing how far forth the French had fared,
He halted, and would neither bring nor send
His letters, nor their purport would disclose.

ARTEVELDE.

Have you no guess of their contents?

FATHER JOHN.

A shrewd one.
They promised, doubtless, largely; but were meant
To be deliver'd should you thrive—not else.
The English nobles, though they'd use your arms
If victory crown'd them, to encumber France,
Much in their secret minds mislike your cause.
Jack Straw, Wat Tyler, Lister, Walker, Ball,

That against servage raised the late revolt,
Were deem'd the spawn of your success : last year
Has taught the nobles that their foes at home
Are worthier notice than the French.   In truth
They should not be displeased at any ill
That might befall you.

ARTEVELDE.

Father, so I think.
Lo ! with the chivalry of Christendom
I wage my war—no nation for my friend,
Yet in each nation having hosts of friends !
The bondsmen of the world, that to their lords
Are bound with chains of iron, unto me
Are knit by their affections.   Be it so.
From kings and nobles will I seek no more
Aid, friendship, nor alliance.   With the poor
I make my treaty, and the heart of man
Sets the broad seal of its allegiance there,
And ratifies the compact.   Vassals, serfs,
Ye that are bent with unrequited toil,
Ye that have whiten'd in the dungeon's darkness
Through years that knew not change of night and day—
Tatterdemalions, lodgers in the hedge,
Lean beggars with raw backs and rumbling maws,
Whose poverty was whipp'd for starving you,—
I hail you my auxiliars and allies,
The only potentates whose help I crave !
Richard of England, thou hast slain Jack Straw,
But thou hast left unquench'd the vital spark
That set Jack Straw on fire.   The spirit lives ;
And as when he of Canterbury fell,
His seat was fill'd by some no better clerk,

So shall John Ball that slew him be replaced ;
And if I live and thrive, these English lords
Double requital shall be served withal
For this their double-dealing.——Pardon me ;
You are but just dismounted, and the soil
Of travel is upon you; food and rest
You must require. Attendance there ! what ho !

Enter two Serving-men.

These will supply your wants. To-morrow morn
We will speak more together. Father John,
Though peradventure fallen in your esteem,
I humbly ask your blessing, as a man
That having pass'd for more in your repute
Than he could justify, should be content,
Not with his state, but with the judgment true
That to the lowly level of his state
Brings down his reputation.

FATHER JOHN.

                 Oh, my son !
High as you stand, I will not strain mine eyes
To see how higher still you stood before.
God's blessing be upon you ! Fare you well.

                               [*Exit.*

ARTEVELDE.

The old man weeps. Let England play me false :
The greater is my glory if the day
Is won without her aid. I stand alone ;
And standing so against the mingled might
Of Burgundy and France, to hold mine own
Is special commendation ; to prevail
So far as victory were high renown ;
To be foredone no singular disgrace.

Enter an Attendant, *followed by a Man-at-arms.*

Whom have we here, Rovarden?

ATTENDANT.

                    Please your highness,
A scout from Van den Bosch.

ARTEVELDE.

                  And with ill news
Thy face would say.   What is it?

SCOUT.

                  With your leave,
My master bids you know that yesterday
Some cunning Frenchmen stole across the Lis
In boats and rafts, a league below Commines,
And now they press him hard upon his rear;
Wherefore he warns you that you look to Ypres,
Which he can do no longer.

ARTEVELDE.

                  The Lis past!
Mischief, be welcome, if thou com'st alone!
Is that the worst?

SCOUT.

        'Tis all, my lord, I know.

ELENA.

Is it so very bad?

ARTEVELDE.

         No, no, 'tis not.
Let him have food and wine; he has ridden hard,
And lacks refreshment.   Go, repair thy looks,
And make me no such signals in my camp
Of losses and mishap.   Speak cheerily
To whomsoe'er thou seest.

               Exeunt Attendant *and* Scout.

        No, 'tis untoward,

Luckless, unfortunate ; but that is all.
If Ypres bear as stoutly up against it
As I can do, we're not so much the worse.

Enter VAN RYK, *followed by a* Messenger.

VAN RYK.

A messenger, my lord, arrived from Ypres.

ARTEVELDE.

Here is another ugly face of news !
What now ?

MESSENGER.

My lord, sure tidings came last night
That Van den Bosch was worsted on the Lis,
And with a broken force was falling back
On Ypres for protection.

ARTEVELDE.

Is that all ?

MESSENGER.

It is, my lord.

ARTEVELDE.

It is enough.   What news
Had ye of Menin, Werwick, and Messines ?

MESSENGER.

The bells were rung in each, and they were bid
To send all aid that they could muster straight
To Van den Bosch ; but little went, or none.

ARTEVELDE.

And doubtless now the Frenchman has them all ?

MESSENGER.

I know not that, my lord.

ARTEVELDE.

But I do.   Go ;
Thou art a wofuller fellow than the last,
Yet cheerfuller than what is like to follow.
Get thee to dinner, and be spare of speech.

MESSENGER.

My master bade me to entreat your highness
To send him instant succour.

ARTEVELDE.

What, to Ypres ?
He's mad to think it!   How should aid get there,
With all the Upper Lis, as past a doubt
It must be now, from Warneston to Courtray,
O'errun with French?   I will not send a man.
It were but to lose more.

MESSENGER.

My master, sir,
Was fearful of the burghers.

ARTEVELDE.

So he might,
And I am troubled at his jeopardy ;
Far liefer would I part with this right hand,
Than with Vauclaire, his service and his love.
I think the burghers will hold off awhile
To see the issue of my personal arms.
If not, I cannot help him.   If they do,
That which is best for all is best for him.
Go ; keep thy counsel ; talk not in the camp.

[*Exit* Messenger.

VAN RYK.

My lord, the rumour in the camp goes further
Than where his story stops.

ARTEVELDE.
                    Aye, does it; how?

VAN RYK.

Ypres revolted; Van den Bosch, Vauclaire,
And Roosdyk slain or taken.   So it runs.

ELENA.

Oh, this is worse and worse!

ARTEVELDE.
                    Go in Elena.
These are not matters for a feminine council.

ELENA.

Oh, let me stay with you.

ARTEVELDE.
                    Go in, my love.—
                              [*Exit* ELENA.

Worst rumours now will still be likest truth;
And yet if Ypres truly had revolted,
Undoubted tidings of so great a matter
Had surely reached us.

VAN RYK.

                    If you mark, my lord,
Mostly a rumour of such things precedes
The certain tiding.

ARTEVELDE.

                    It is strange, yet true,
That doubtful knowledge travels with a speed
Miraculous, which certain cannot match.
I know not why, when this or that has chanced,
The smoke should come before the flash; yet 'tis so.
Why who comes here?   Vauclaire himself!

Enter VAUCLAIRE, *in disordered apparel, and covered with the soil of travel.*

Vauclaire,
Thy coming speaks; it tells of Ypres lost;
Perhaps of worse; and thou art welcome still!
Can friendship speak thee fairer?

VAUCLAIRE.

Thanks, my lord.
You have lost Ypres, 'tis no worse nor better.

ARTEVELDE.

I can spare Ypres so I keep Vauclaire.
Let the town go.   How came you off alive?

VAUCLAIRE.

The rascal burghers tied me hand and foot,
And like a thief upon a hurdle trailed me
Toward King Charles's camp upon the mount;
Half way to which some twenty of my guard,
With Roosdyk at their head, brake in upon them,
Crying a rescue, and ere aid could come
We were safe mounted upon chosen nags
That distanced all pursuit.

ARTEVELDE.

Why that is well.
Where's Roosdyk?

VAUCLAIRE.

Eating, I'll be sworn, and drinking.

ARTEVELDE.

And Van den Bosch?

VAUCLAIRE.

That is a sadder story;
I fear he lives no longer.

ARTEVELDE.

Aye, Vauclaire!

VAUCLAIRE.

Much wounded from Commines he came to Ypres,
Whence we despatch'd him, less alive than dead,
Upon the road to Ghent.   I hardly think
That he can live the journey through.

ARTEVELDE.

Farewell!
Brave Van den Bosch! and God assoile thy soul!
Vauclaire, we must be stirring; to the dead
An after time will give the meed of mourning;
Our present days are due to them that live.
Let us to council with my officers;
And sit by me; for in my host henceforth
Thou shalt be next me in authority.

VAUCLAIRE.

Deep are my debts to your good-will, my lord;
More than my life can pay.

ARTEVELDE.

Nay, say no more;
You owe me nothing; what I have to give
Is held in trust and parted with for service.
Value received is writ on my commissions,
Nor would I thank the man that should thank me
For aught as given him gratis.   Let's to council;
I'll lie no longer here at Oudenarde
To hear of towns betraying me.   Our camp
We must break up to-morrow and push on
Boldly to Courtray and the Lower Lis.
The towns to the North and West will falter else

And Frenchify their faith.   It is God's mercy
That some seven thousand citizens of Bruges
Are in my host, whose heads will pledges be
For what might fail me there.   From Damme and Sluys,
From Dendermonde, the Quatre-Metiers, Ghent,
From Ardenburgh and Grammont and Alost,
We'll bring the rear-guard up.   The Lis, the Lis!
Let me but reach the Lis before King Charles!

VAUCLAIRE.

The Upper Lis were easily regain'd
Could we but keep the Lower.

ARTEVELDE.

             Now to council.

Enter VAN RYK.

VAN RYK.

A countryman, my lord, arrived from Heule
Says that King Charles is on his march to Rosebecque.

ARTEVELDE.

To Rosebecque let him come!   With God's good-speed
I shall be there before him.   Sirs, to council.

SCENE II.—*The French Camp at Winkel St. Eloy.*

Enter from opposite sides the DUKE OF BURGUNDY *and* TRISTRAM
OF LESTOVET.

BURGUNDY.

Another town come in, I hear; that's ten.
Now they will own I knew my way to Flanders.
Ypres, and Dunkirk, Cassel, Thorout, Bergues,
Make five wall'd towns, and Poperinguen six;

And then there's Werwick, Vailant, and Messines,
And now comes Rousselaere, which rounds the tale.
Anon they'll say that I had reason, ha?

LESTOVET.

They will, my lord.   Success will couch the blind.
The wise by speculation know to trade,
And give their wits long credit and they thrive;
A scrambling wit must live from hand to mouth
On issues and events.   Prosperity
Is warranty of wisdom with the world;
Failure is foolishness.   Now all will prize
Your grace's judgment at its worth.

[*A cry within,* ' Place ho!'

Enter the KING, *with the* CONSTABLE, *the* LORDS OF SAIMPI *and*
    SANXERE, *and others, and lastly, somewhat apart from the*
    rest, SIR FLEUREANT OF HEURLÉE.

THE KING.

Well uncle, here we are!   Get supper ready.
How fast you rode!   I gallop'd half a mile—
But then St. Poule, he blew—oh he's too fat!
Is not the bastard of St. Poule too fat?

LORD OF SAIMPI.

May't please your majesty he's grossly fat.

THE KING.

I gallop'd—uncle, what is this? Lo me!
A span-new sword—by God, of Spanish steel,
And longer than mine own—uncle, by God,
A king's sword should be longer than a duke's;
I must have this; this is a royal sword.

BURGUNDY.

Cousin, you are not tall enough to wear it.

THE KING.

Not tall enough indeed!   Is supper ready?
When shall we get to Rosebecque?   Here's St. Poule.

Enter ST. POULE.

So, here you come, you broken-winded bastard,
You're always left behind.   How far to Rosebecque?
Tell me, my lords, shall we be there to-morrow?

THE CONSTABLE.

Your majesty, with weather to your wish,
Might lodge at Rosebecque with your vanguard force
To-morrow night.

THE KING.

And when shall come the rear?

THE CONSTABLE.

On Wednesday morning.

THE KING.

And on Thursday night
The bastard of St. Poule.   Hurrah for Rosebecque!
Remember, uncle, when the armies meet,
I am to make the knights; four hundred of them;
The constable himself will tell you so.
Four hundred fire-new knights there should be made
Before the battle joins, and I'm to make them:
My lord of Clisson am I not?   Thwack, thwack,
Thwack, thwack, thwack, thwack, will go my sword,
        thwack, thwack.
You Lestovet, you Tristram, kneel you down
And I will—thwack—I'll try my hand—thwack, thwack.

BURGUNDY.

Come, cousin, come, you're wanton.   Go within
And eat your supper.

A A

THE KING.

What, is supper ready?
Lights, lights here, ho!   Come, bastard, come along.

The first of a feast and the last of a fray,
Has been a wise word for this many a day!

[Exit, followed by all but the DUKE OF BURGUNDY
and LESTOVET.

BURGUNDY.

Yon southern sky is black; were rain to fall
Our van could hardly, in but one day's march,
Arrive at Rosebecque; or if press'd so far,
'Twould tell against their strength upon the morrow,
And stop them there.

LESTOVET.

My lord, that there they'll stop
I doubt not; for I'm inmostly assured
That we shall find upon the Lower Lis
The total Flemish host: the Lower Lis
They to the utterance will dispute; for there
Their chief, who lacks not capability,
Will justly deem their all to be impledged.
'Twere not amiss to slack the vanguard's pace
And quicken up the rear, that like a worm
The army's tail should gather to its head
Before it move again.

BURGUNDY.

It may be well.
Your thought is mine touching the Flemish host;
It will be found at Rosebecque, and, God willing,
It shall be left to feed the vultures there.
Where'er tis met, that such will be its fate
I am as sure as that this glove is steel,
And I am Duke of Burgundy.

LESTOVET.

                 My lord,
That this vile Flemish scum, with coats of mail
Not worth three folds of cloth, should hold at bay
The spear-heads of Bourdeaux, were doubtless strange :
And yet such things have happen'd. In their chief
Resides the spell which makes this herd so mad
To brave the chivalry of France in arms.
Their chief is either leagued with hell himself,
Or hath some potent necromancer's aid ;
If he be not the devil's feudatory,
He holds in soccage of a fiend that is.
You'll see a hundred thousand spell-bound hearts
By art of witchcraft so affatuate,
That for his love they'd dress themselves in dowlas
And fight with men of steel.

BURGUNDY.

                 At Bruges, 'tis true,
They dared but little less.

LESTOVET.

               Methinks, my lord,
The Knight of Heurlée is of late much alter'd.

BURGUNDY.

It may be so ; what, since he join'd us last ?

LESTOVET.

He hath a dirty, wild, neglected favour ;
Is careless of his garb, gets drunk alone,
Lies late a-bed, as skulking from the day,
Curses his serving-men, avoids his friends,
Is quarrelsome and very meagre-witted
To what he was, save only in his gibes,

                      A A 2

And them less savoury season'd; what was once
An ounce of venom to a pound of mirth
Apportion'd t'other way.   In truth, he's changed;
A moody, heavy, sad-condition'd man,
That had from nature a most mounting heart,
And revell'd formerly in joys to him
As native and as unsolicited
As to the lark her song.

BURGUNDY.

> Whence comes this change?

LESTOVET.

In truth, my lord, I know not.

BURGUNDY.

> Hear you nothing?

Is nothing said, surmised? what think you, ha?
Some secret discontent?

LESTOVET.

> Not that, my lord.

More likely that he finds his knightly name
Something bedimm'd, and held in less esteem,
By reason of his flight from Oudenarde:
For though he will not own it, 'tis believed
He was at large upon his honour's pawn
To keep within the Flemish camp, and fled
Leaving the pledge behind him.

BURGUNDY.

> Nothing more?

LESTOVET.

That is one wound; but there is yet another;
Whether by word, or blow, or both, 'twas dealt,

I know not, for he's reticent and shy
To a close question; but this much I know,
That in the sleeping-chamber of a maid
(So called for courtesy) he was caught at night,
Concealed for no good purpose, whereupon
The Regent (so by courtesy again—
As much a regent he as she a maid)
Who entertain'd the damsel for himself,
Moved by his anger, offer'd to the knight,
In act or threat, some dire indignity,
That ever since hath poison'd all the springs
At which his spirit drank, and is the cause,
If my conjecture err not, that he stands
The wither'd, blacken'd, and disfigured stump
We see him now.

BURGUNDY.

If that be all, his grief
Toucheth not us.

LESTOVET.

The contrary, my lord;
It touches more the enemy.   Your grace
Has possibly had read to you the tale,
Long chronicled, of an Earl of Conversana,
Who in the day of battle met his death,
Not from his opposites in the field, though brave,
But from the hand of one who rode beside him.
An ancient grudge had treasured been till then
When death were doubly bitter, bringing down
Defeat and overthrow and loss of lands
And ruin to his friends.   'Twere strange, my lord,
If such a fate befel Van Artevelde.

BURGUNDY.

Yes, it were very strange.

LESTOVET.

Your grace was right!
We shall have rain; the sky looks wondrous heavy.
I know not if your grace gave heed to it,
But yesterday at noon or thereabouts
I heard some grumblings up amongst the clouds
That much resembled thunder: Pish! quoth I,
The year is too far wearing from its prime
To speak in thunder now.

BURGUNDY.

Who was that earl?
The Earl of Conversana?

LESTOVET.

He, my lord.
But yet again I heard it, and more plain;
And then, quoth I, if this be aught but thunder,
The God of thunder keeps a mocking bird,
And it is that we hear.

BURGUNDY.

Upon what ground
Deem'd you the Earl of Conversana's fate
Should figure forth Van Artevelde's?

LESTOVET.

My lord?

BURGUNDY.

What mean you by this history of that earl?
How doth it typify Van Artevelde's?
How lights the one the other?

LESTOVET.

Nay, my lord,

"Twas but a stumbling comment of my thought.
When we have strain'd our foresight past its power
Fantastic flashes oft will come across it,
And whence we nothing know.

BURGUNDY.

Come, Lestovet,
Let us be open and direct.   Thy drift?
What did thy thought contain, that being stirr'd
Sent to the top this story of a murder?

LESTOVET.

The honest truth to tell, my lord, a dream,
Whether by good or evil spirit drawn
Upon the vacant canvass of my sleep,
Your grace shall be the judge,—a dream it was
Showed me Van Artevelde upon his horse—
Though whether mounted to survey the ground,
Or to array his host, or lead the charge,
I saw not,—but there sitting as he gazed
Upon an undistinguishable blank
Of anything or nothing—what I know not—
Struck from behind he fell—and with his fall
Vanish'd his host.

BURGUNDY.

This was a waking dream.

LESTOVET.

I mused upon it waking.

BURGUNDY.

And this dream
Thou think'st will peradventure come to pass?

LESTOVET.

If fate so orders it, my lord.

BURGUNDY.

                              And fate
Will find some human furtherance; is it so?

LESTOVET.

Were it a thing well warranted, my lord,
It might be well attended.

BURGUNDY.

                              Truly fate
Should do the King a singular good service
If this should happen.

LESTOVET.

                    Destiny, my lord,
Is oft-times worked upon by mighty names
Of dukes and regal potentates, whose power
May currently avouch her doubtful deeds,
If haply called in question.

BURGUNDY.

                              Six o'clock
Were not too soon to be afoot to-morrow,
If, as is likely, there be waters out
Upon our lines of march.

LESTOVET.

                    There's light at six.
Two words, my lord, were warranty enough.

BURGUNDY.

Why, very well then; six is late enough.
Tell my lord constable before he sleeps
To let the trumpets sound us a reveillée
Some half an hour to six.

                                        [*Exit.*

LESTOVET.

                    Well said, my lord.

Your grace's scruples master not your heart,
But serve your reputation.   This is conscience ;
A herald marshalling each act its place
By its emblazonry and cognisance.
My Lord of Burgundy, your grace is wary ;
So, by your leave, is humble Lestovet.
If policy stick fast, be tried revenge ;
And what revenge more sharp, my Lord of Bourbon,
Than what is sprung of jealousy.   That bites.
My lord, I'll pluck your jealousy by the ear,
And if it wake not, why your grace's bosom
Is not the serpent's nest I take it for.

SCENE III.—*The Flemish Camp on the Eastern Bank of the
Lis, between Desselghem and Rosebecque.*—VAN ARTEVELDE'S
Pavilion.

VAN ARTEVELDE *and* ELENA.

ELENA.
What is it that disturbs you ?

ARTEVELDE.
Nothing, dearest ;
I am not disturb'd.

ELENA.
You are not like yourself.
What took you from your bed ere break of day ?
Where have you been ? I know you're vex'd with some-
    thing.
Tell me, now, what has happen'd.

ARTEVELDE.
Be at rest.
No accident, save of the world within ;
Occurrences of thought ; 'tis nothing more.

ELENA.

It is of such that love most needs to know.
The loud transactions of the outlying world
Tell to your masculine friends : tell me your thoughts.

ARTEVELDE.

They stumbled in the dusk 'twixt night and day.
I dream'd distressfully, and waking knew
How an old sorrow had stolen upon my sleep,
Molesting midnight and that short repose
Which industry had earn'd, so to stir up
About my heart remembrances of pain
Least sleeping when I sleep, least sleeping then
When reason and the voluntary powers
That turn and govern thought are laid to rest.
Those powers by this nocturnal inroad wild
Surprised and broken, vainly I essay'd
To rally, and the mind, unsubjugate,
Took its direction from a driftless dream.
Then pass'd I forth.

ELENA.

                    You stole away so softly
I knew it not, and wonder'd when I woke.

ARTEVELDE.

The gibbous moon was in a wan decline,
And all was silent as a sick man's chamber.
Mixing its small beginnings with the dregs
Of the pale moonshine and a few faint stars,
The cold uncomfortable daylight dawn'd ;
And the white tents, topping a low ground-fog,
Show'd like a fleet becalm'd.   I wander'd far,
'Till reaching to the bridge I sate me down
Upon the parapet.   Much mused I there,

Revolving many a passage of my life,
And the strange destiny that lifted me
To be the leader of a mighty host
And terrible to kings. What follow'd then
I hardly may relate, for you would smile,
And say I might have dream'd as well a-bed
As gone abroad to dream.

ELENA.

      I shall not smile ;
And if I did, you would not grudge my lips
So rare a visitation. But the cause,
Whate'er it be, that casts a shadow here,
[Kissing his brow.
How should it make me smile ? What follow'd, say,
After your meditations on the bridge ?

ARTEVELDE.

I'll tell it, but I bid you not believe it ;
For I am scarce so credulous myself
As to believe that was, which my eyes saw—
A visual not an actual existence.

ELENA.

What was it like ? Wore it a human likeness ?

ARTEVELDE.

That such existences there are, I know ;
For whether by the corporal organ framed,
Or painted by a brainish fantasy
Upon the inner sense, not once nor twice,
But sundry times, have I beheld such things
Since my tenth year, and most in this last past.

ELENA.

What was it you beheld ?

ARTEVELDE.
To-day?

ELENA.
Last night—
This morning—when you sate upon the bridge.

ARTEVELDE.
'Twas a fantastic sight.

ELENA.
What sort of sight?

ARTEVELDE (*after a pause*).

Once in my sad and philosophic youth—
For very philosophic in my dawn
And twilight of intelligence was I—
Once at this cock-crow of philosophy,
Much tired with rest and with the stable earth,
I launch'd my little bark and put to sea,
Errant for geste and enterprise of wit
Through all this circumnavigable globe.
I cavilled at the elements—what is earth?
A huge congestion of unmethodised matter
With but a skin of life—a mighty solid
Which Nature, prodigal of space, provides
For superficial uses: and what air?
A motion and a pressure: fire, a change;
And light the language of the things call'd dumb.

ELENA.

I have been told the studies of your youth
Were strangely thought of, but I'm well assured
They never were unlawful.

ARTEVELDE.
You are right.

My meditations in their outset wore
The braveries of ignorance and youth,
But cast them, and were innocent thenceforth ;
For they were follow'd with a humble heart,
Though an inquisitive ; and humbler still
In spirit wax'd they as they further went.
The elements I left to contemplate.
Then I considered life in all its forms,
Of vegetables first, next zoöphytes,
The tribe that dwells upon the confine strange
'Twixt plants and fish ; some are there from their mouth
Spit out their progeny, and some that breed
By suckers from their base or tubercles,
Sea-hedgehog, madrepore, sea-ruff, or pad,
Fungus, or sponge, or that gelatinous fish
That taken from its element at once
Stinks, melts, and dies a fluid ;—so from these,
Through many a tribe of less equivocal life,
Dividual or insect, up I ranged,
From sentient to percipient—small advance—
Next to intelligent, to rational next,
So to half-spiritual human-kind,
And what is more, is more than man may know.
Last came the troublesome question—what am I ?
A blade, a seedling of this growth of life
Wherewith the outside of the earth is cover'd ;
A comprehensive atom, all the world
In act of thought embracing ; in the world
A grain scarce filling a particular place !
Thus travell'd I the region up and down
Wherein the soul is circumscribed below ;
And unto what conclusion ?

ELENA.

                     Nay, your promise !
Tell what you saw ; I must not be denied
After a promise given ; tell me of that.

ARTEVELDE.

I say to what conclusion came I then,
These winding links to fasten ?

ELENA.

                     I surmise
To none ; such ramblings end where they begin.

ARTEVELDE.

Conclusions inconclusive, that I own ;
Yet, I would say, not vain, not nothing worth.
This circulating principle of life
That vivifies the outside of the earth
And permeates the sea ; that here and there
Awakening up a particle of matter,
Informs it, organises, gives it power
To gather and associate to itself,
Transmute, incorporate other, for a term
Sustains the congruous fabric, and then quits it ;
This vagrant principle so multiform,
Ebullient here and undetected there,
Is not unauthorised, nor increate,
Though indestructible.   Life never dies ;
Matter dies off it, and it lives elsewhere,
Or elsehow circumstanced and shaped ; it goes ;
At every instant we may say 'tis gone,
But never it hath ceased ; the type is changed,
Is ever in transition, for life's law
To its eternal essence doth prescribe

Eternal mutability: and thus
To say I live—says, I partake of that
Which never dies.   But how far I may hold
An interest indivisible from life
Through change (and whether it be mortal change,
Change of senescence, or of gradual growth,
Or other whatsoever 'tis alike)
Is question not of argument, but fact.
In all men some such interest inheres ;
In most 'tis posthumous ; the more expand
Our thoughts and feelings past the very present,
The more that interest overtakes of change
And comprehends, till what it comprehends
Is comprehended in eternity,
And in no less a span.

ELENA.

Love is eternal.
Whatever dies, that lives, I feel and know.
It is too great a thing to die.

ARTEVELDE.

So be it !

ELENA.

But, Artevelde, you shall not lead me off
Through by-ways from my quest.   Touching this sight
Which you have seen.

ARTEVELDE.

Touching this eye-creation ;
What is it to surprise us?   Here we are
Engender'd out of nothing cognisable.
If this be not a wonder, nothing is ;
If this be wonderful, then all is so.
Man's grosser attributes can generate

What is not, and has never been at all;
What should forbid his fancy to restore
A being pass'd away?   The wonder lies
In the mind merely of the wondering man.
Treading the steps of common life with eyes
Of curious inquisition, some will stare
At each discovery of nature's ways,
As it were new to find that God contrives.
The contrary were marvellous to me,
And till I find it I shall marvel not.
Or all is wonderful, or nothing is.
As for this creature of my eyes——

ELENA.

                    What was it?
The semblance of a human creature?

ARTEVELDE.

                    Yes.

ELENA.

Like any you had known in life?

ARTEVELDE.

                  Most like;
Or more than like; it was the very same.
It was the image of my wife.

ELENA.

               Of her!
The Lady Adriana?

ARTEVELDE.

My dead wife.

ELENA.

Oh God! how strange!

ARTEVELDE.

         And wherefore?—wherefore strange?

Why should not fancy summon to its presence
This shape as soon as any?

ELENA.

Gracious Heaven!

And were you not afraid?

ARTEVELDE.

I felt no fear.

Dejected I had been before: that sight
Inspired a deeper sadness, but no fear.
Nor had it struck that sadness to my soul
But for the dismal cheer the thing put on,
And the unsightly points of circumstance
That sullied its appearance and departure.

ELENA.

For how long saw you it?

ARTEVELDE.

I cannot tell.

I did not mark.

ELENA.

And what was that appearance

You say was so unsightly?

ARTEVELDE.

She appear'd

In white, as when I saw her last, laid out
After her death; suspended in the air
She seem'd, and o'er her breast her arms were cross'd:
Her feet were drawn together pointing downwards,
And rigid was her form and motionless.
From near her heart, as if the source were there,
A stain of blood went wavering to her feet.
So she remain'd inflexible as stone

B B

And I as fixedly regarding her.
Then suddenly, and in a line oblique,
Thy figure darted past her, whereupon,
Though rigid still and straight, she downward moved,
And as she pierced the river with her feet
Descending steadily, the streak of blood
Peel'd off upon the water, which, as she vanish'd,
Appear'd all blood, and swell'd and welter'd sore,
And midmost in the eddy and the whirl
My own face saw I, which was pale and calm
As death could make it:——then the vision pass'd,
And I perceived the river and the bridge,
The mottled sky and horizontal moon,
The distant camp, and all things as they were.

ELENA.

If you are not afraid to see such things,
I am to hear them.   Go not near that bridge ;—
You said that something happen'd there before—
Oh, cross it not again ; for my sake do not.

ARTEVELDE.

The river cannot otherwise be pass'd.

ELENA.

Oh, cross it not !

ARTEVELDE.

                That were a strange resolve,
And to the French most acceptable : yes,
You will be held of council with King Charles,
Opposing thus my passage.

            Enter VAUCLAIRE *and* VAN RYK.

                        Sirs, good day !
You're soon astir for men that watch'd so late.

VAUCLAIRE.

And you, my lord.

ARTEVELDE.

For me, my eyes untask'd
Close with the owl's and open with the lark's ;
Almost have they forgotten the use of sleep.
Have any scouts come in.

VAN RYK.

Yes, two, my lord.

ARTEVELDE.

Ah ! and with tidings ?   Nothing good, I know :
But let me hear.

VAUCLAIRE.

In truth, it is not good.
They say that Poperinguen, Rousselaere,
And Thorout have declared for France.

ARTEVELDE.

Three more !
That is a heavy falling-off, my friends,
And arrantly ill-timed.   Despatch ! despatch !
The cure for these defections must be found
At any hazard.   Forward must we press,
And try our fortune ere another town
Can find occasion to play foul.   ·

VAUCLAIRE.

To-night,
If I mistake not, they would reach us here ;
And better were it, in my mind, the stream
Should be betwixt us, than as much dry land.

ARTEVELDE.

We will to council, and consider there

B B 2

What may be best.   If they be here to-night,
We may abide them.   Whither away, Vauclaire?

VAUCLAIRE.

You'll wish, my lord, to have the scouts, and others
That are inform'd, before you.

ARTEVELDE.

It were well.

[*Exit* VAUCLAIRE.

And thou, Van Ryk, go round, and fetch to council
The captains of the host.

[*Exit* VAN RYK.

This troubles me.
Three towns, and two before !—a deadly blow !

ELENA.

Oh say not so ; when once they know you're near,
The towns will all hold out—all will be well.
Your presence ever righted your affairs,
Whatever was amiss.

ARTEVELDE.

Two months ago
My presence was a spell omnipotent
That seem'd of power to win me all the world.
But now my fortune wears a faded beauty ;
And as some dame, her hour of conquest past,
Repairs her ravaged charms, and here a tooth
Replaces, where the flesh had else fallen in
Making a wrinkle in the rounded cheek,
And there the never more redundant locks
Replenishes—so do I waste my pains
In patching fortunes which are past their prime.
It is a useless trouble ; by my faith,

A most unprofitable, idle charge.
So soon as my advance made Courtray sure,
Thence sent I with all speed to Rousselaere
My best of chatelains, Walraven.   Nay !
Labour in vain !   Precautions and endeavours
Null, fruitless all !

ELENA.

Too anxious, Artevelde,
And too impatient are you grown of late.
You used to be so calm and even-minded,
That nothing ruffled you.

ARTEVELDE.

I stand reproved.
'Tis time and circumstance that tries us all ;
And they that temperately take their start,
And keep their souls indifferently sedate
Through much of good and evil, at the last
May find the weakness of their hearts thus tried.
My cause appears more precious than it did
In its triumphant days.

ELENA.

You prize it more
The more it is endanger'd.

ARTEVELDE.

Even so.
A mother dotes upon the reckling child
More than the strong ; solicitous cares, sad watchings,
Rallies, reverses, all vicissitudes,
Give the affection exercise and growth.
So is it in the nursing a sick hope.

Enter VAUCLAIRE's Lieutenant.

LIEUTENANT.

The captains are in council met, my lord,
And wait upon your leisure.

ARTEVELDE.

I am coming.

LIEUTENANT.

My master, sir, has heard, he bade me say,
That Cassel has revolted.

ARTEVELDE.

What of that?

LIEUTENANT.

He wish'd that you should know it first, my lord,
And judge if it were fit to be disclosed
Before the council.

ARTEVELDE.

Fit to be disclosed!
Pooh! Tell the council I am coming. No;
I'll have no secrets. And for this forsooth,
What is it but that we are in the moult,
And here's a feather fallen? Say I come.

[*Exit* Lieutenant.

Another stab, and in a vital part!
For Cassel's defalcation is no less.
'Twere hard to keep a secret that is shared
By yonder ape; my nose took note of that,
Admonished by the musk upon his beard
As up and down his salutations tost it,
Like a hen drinking. Well, it matters not.
The battle now is all, and that to win

Were to win back my losses; that to lose
Were to make all that I had lost before
Into one sum of loss.

ELENA.

I feel assured
That you will win the day!

ARTEVELDE.

You choose to say so.
Elena, think not that I stand in need
Of false encouragement. I have my strength,
Which, though it lie not in the sanguine mood,
Will answer my occasions. To yourself,
Though to none other, I at times present
The gloomiest thoughts that gloomy truths inspire,
Because I love you. But I need no prop;
Nor could I find it in a tinsel show
Of prosperous surmise. Before the world
I wear a cheerful aspect, not so false
As for your lover's solace you put on;
Nor in my closet does the oil run low,
Or the light flicker.

ELENA.

Lo now! you are angry
Because I try to cheer you.

ARTEVELDE.

No, my love,
Not angry; that I never was with you;
But as I deal not falsely with my own,
So would I wish the heart of her I love
To be both true and brave; nor self-beguiled,
Nor putting on disguises for my sake,
As though I falter'd. I have anxious hours,

As who in like extremities hath not?
But I have something stable here within
Which bears their weight.

Enter VAN RYK.

               I keep the council waiting?
Here comes Van Ryk to tell me so.

ELENA.

                 'Twas I,
Master Van Ryk, that stay'd him: 'tis my fault,
And lest I make it more, I'll take me hence.
                                [Exit.

VAN RYK.

The council can abide your time, my lord.
There waits without a stranger just arrived
Whom it were well you speak with ere you go.
He will not lift his beaver save to you,
But boldly calls himself an arrant traitor
That left the French last night, and seeks your camp
To sell you what he knows.

ARTEVELDE.

                 Desert to me!
I thought desertion look'd the other way.
What is he like?

VAN RYK.

               I think he is of rank.
In his deportment knightly eyes might see
What they would gladly imitate.

ARTEVELDE.

                 Of rank!
This is the very madness of desertion!
Go, fetch him in.
                       [Exit VAN RYK.

Thorout and Poperinguen !
Cassel and Rousselaere !   And who, I wist,
Can keep a town's allegiance on its legs,
If not Walraven ?

Re-enter VAN RYK, *conducting* SIR FLEUREANT OF HEURLÉE
in armour, with his vizor closed.

Give us leave, Van Ryk.

[*Exit* VAN RYK.

Well, sir ! your pleasure ? and say first by whom
My camp is honour'd thus.

SIR FLEUREANT.

By one, my lord,
Known to your host by all reproachful names
Of miscreant, perfidious traitor, knave,
Caitiff, and cur.

ARTEVELDE.

These, sir, are shrewd additions,
And not, I hope, deserved.

SIR FLEUREANT.

They have been so ;
Had not contrition wash'd desert with tears,
They were so still.   I am that perjured knight,
Fleureant of Heurlée.

ARTEVELDE.

Art thou he indeed ?
What brings thee hither ?

SIR FLEUREANT.

That which brings the proud
To crave a low equality with dust ;

Which arms the lover lorn, the suitor cast, the sinner
    caught,
The courtier supplanted, with the knife,
Or bowl, or halter—for their several griefs
The sovereign cures.   My lord, what brings me here
Is of that grain—a loathing of my life;
And, to come closer, such a sort of grief
As wrung Iscariot's heart when forth he went
And hung himself upon the field of blood,
Has made me thus (in my Aceldama
The sin of self-destruction partly spared)
To run upon your sword.

ARTEVELDE.

               I am not bound
To find thee in a hangman.   Go thy ways!
Thou art a slight, inconstant, violent man.

SIR FLEUREANT.

My lord, I come prepared for your disdain,
And slender were I in my penitence
If I should not confess it well bestow'd.
But light and fickle as you justly deem me,
To one fix'd purpose am I wedded now
For better and for worse—'tis to repair
The wrong that I have done you, and to die.

ARTEVELDE.

Sir, you may live or die, as likes you best.
It is your own affair; to me all's one.
The hurt your treachery has done to me
Can neither be repeated nor repair'd.
No further harm can follow from your life,

Save in the sundering my time and thoughts
From matters of more moment.

SIR FLEUREANT.

                    Pause, my lord,
Ere you pronounce me as inept for good
As I am harmless.   Slight me as you may,
You cannot cast me in mine own esteem
More low than where I lie; I scorn myself
With such a bitterness as bars all taste
Of others' scorn.   But from this bitter tree
Good fruitage, if so please you, you may pluck.
I have been well esteem'd for soldiership,
And none can better know your enemy's host,
Where soft, where hard, where rotten, and where sound,
Their hopes and fears, the order of their march,
Their counsels and intents.   If all I know
With what small service I by deeds might render,
May be accepted as a sacrifice
My conscience to appease, I die content.

ARTEVELDE.

Methinks I barely comprehend your conscience;
For sicken'd with one treasonable poison,
'Twould seem to seek another for a cure.
What says your conscience on your king's behalf?

SIR FLEUREANT.

It says, my lord, that there all claims are cancell'd,
All ties dissolved; for never was a knight
Of prowess known, more thanklessly repaid,
More scurvily entreated, than by him
And by his ingrate uncles and his court
Was Fleureant of Heurlée.

ARTEVELDE.

Are you there!
Ah! now I understand you.   Come this way.
My council is awaiting me.   Ere night
I will speak further with you.   Until when——

SCENE IV.—*The Royal Pavilion in the French Camp at Mount
Dorre, on the western bank of the Lis, at the distance of a
league from Rosebecque.   The* KING *is discovered rising from
supper and bidding adieu to his* Uncles, *the* ADMIRAL OF
FRANCE, *the* LORD OF COUCY, *and a number of other* guests
who are leaving the Pavilion.   SIR GUY OF BAVEUX *is in
attendance, and the* DUKE OF BURGUNDY *remains behind the
others.*

THE KING.

My lords, we wish you all a sweet good night.
Sir Constable—he's gone—Sir Constable—
Run after him, Sir Guy, and bring him back.
                              [*Exit* SIR GUY OF BAVEUX.
Uncle of Burgundy, what says your grace?
Shall it be now?

BURGUNDY.

Fair cousin, now or never.
                                             [*Exit.*
THE KING.

He will be mightily displeased!   I swear
I have no heart to speak it!   Me!   I quake.

Re-enter SIR GUY OF BAVEUX *with the* Constable.

We call'd you back, Sir Oliver; you heard not.

THE CONSTABLE.

Your grace shall pardon me; my ears are dull;
A blow was dealt upon my head at Nantes
That something stunn'd my hearing.

THE KING.

Sir, the love
We bear you is well known; and for this night
And for the morrow, out of love and grace,
We would that you should tarry by our person,
And give your baton to my Lord of Coucy.

THE CONSTABLE.

Most gracious sir! I am amazed at this!
I do beseech you hear me. Well I know
No greater honour can your servant share
Than to help guard your person; but, dear sir,
Think how the van should marvel, first to miss me
At such a time! Sir, do not shake them so;
Nor do not, I entreat your majesty,
Unsettle what advisedly was fixed
To be for your advantage. Be assured
(I say it with all deference to such counsel
As may have moved your majesty to this)
The parting from your purposes thus late
Will put you in much peril. For myself
I have perform'd my function with such zeal
As doth not, I am bold to say, deserve
That I should be degraded.

THE KING.

Constable,
I know that you have well discharged your office
In my time and my father's; 'tis the great trust
And sure affiance that both he and I
Have ever placed in you, which makes me speak
To have you still beside me in this business.

CONSTABLE.

Most noble sir, you are so well begirt

With valiant men, and all is so well order'd,
That nought can be amended.   Wherefore, sir,
You and your council ought to be content.
I pray you, sir, maintain me in mine office,
And if I err not, you will find no cause
To-morrow to repent it.

THE KING.

By St. Denis,
Good constable, your pleasure shall be mine ;
So exercise your office at your will,
And I will say no more : for by St. Denis,
You have seen further into this than I,
Or they that moved me in the matter first.
To-morrow come to me at mass.

THE CONSTABLE.

Kind sir,
Most willingly I will.   God keep your grace !
All has been well disposed.   The rear is up,
Save only skeletons of squadrons dropp'd
Upon our line of march : with tents and fires
They make a show of forces left behind,
So to beguile the Fleming, who will deem
We are not whole.   God give your grace good rest !

THE KING.

Good night, sir constable.   To bed, to bed !

SCENE V.—VAN ARTEVELDE's *Pavilion, in his camp, on the
eastern side of the Lis, as in the last Scene but one.   It is
night.* VAN ARTEVELDE *is discovered sleeping upon a low
couch beside the embers of a fire.* ELENA *enters.*

ELENA.

My lord—Van Artevelde—up, up, my lord !

I never knew him to sleep sound before !
Awake, my lord, awake !

ARTEVELDE.

Charge once again !

ELENA.

Awake, Van Artevelde !

ARTEVELDE.

Fall back ! all's lost !
Not by the bridge—no, no, no, no, no, no.

ELENA.

Arouse yourself, Van Artevelde, awake !

ARTEVELDE (*awaking*).

Elena, love, fly, fly !   Eh ! what's the matter ?

ELENA.

Nay, start not—it is only my surmise ;
But I could deem the Frenchman was afoot.

ARTEVELDE.

Why think you so ?   Van Ryk ! what ho ! Van Ryk !

ELENA.

I could not sleep, and sate without the tent,
And sudden from the river seem'd to rise
A din of battle, mix'd with lengthen'd shouts
That sounded hollow like a windy thaw.
I look'd, and in the cloudy western sky
There was a glow of fire, and then the cries
Were less confused, and I believed I heard
' Mount Joye, St. Denis ! '   ' Flanders and the Lion ! '
With that I came to waken you.

ARTEVELDE.

Van Ryk !—

I'll go myself and hearken.   Where's my page?
Send for Van Ryk, I say.

[He passes to the door of the tent.

ELENA.

Courage, my soul!
Play thou the heroine's part for one half hour,
And ever after take thy woman's way.

ARTEVELDE (*returning*).

Who is within?

Enter an Attendant.

Bid them to sound my trumpet.

[Exit the Attendant, *and soon after a reveillée is sounded without.
Then* VAN RYK *enters.*

ARTEVELDE.

What watch is this we keep?   Here's battle join'd
And none of us astir!

VAN RYK.

Not so, my lord.

ARTEVELDE.

Heard you not war-cries coming from the river?

VAN RYK.

'Tis true, my lord, both they that had the watch,
And I myself, believed we heard a fight,
With shouts and hootings on the river's marge;
But sending there, nought was there to be seen,
Nought to be heard, nor was a Frenchman stirring.
This thus made sure, we deem'd to rouse yourself,
Or waken up the host, should bring us blame!
Wherefore we let it pass.

ARTEVELDE.

'Tis very strange.

VAN RYK.

It was as much a battle to the ear
As sound could make it.

ELENA.

                              Saw you not besides
A redness in the sky ?

VAN RYK.

                              Yes, a red light ;
But that was cast from fires beneath the hedges
Upon Mount Dorre.

ARTEVELDE.

                              This is a phantom fight.
The ghosts of them that are to fall to-morrow
(To-day I might have said, for day is breaking)
Rehearse their parts. Van Ryk, we'll sleep no more.
My trumpet hath been sounded, and by this
The host is arming. We will sleep no more
Till we have tried our fortune. Bid Vauclaire
And Ukenheim and Roosdyk, when they're arm'd,
Meet me below beside the willow-grove.
Bid silence to be kept through all the host.
What think'st thou of the day ? Will it be bright ?

VAN RYK.

A mist is spreading from the river up :
I think, my lord, it shall not clear away
Till sunrise, or it may be not till noon.

ARTEVELDE.

That is all well. Send me the captains there.
                                        [*Exit* Van Ryk.
I go, my fairest ! Should I not return,
There's nothing here that I shall leave with pain

                                        c c

Except thyself, my beautiful Elena !
What strange forgetfulness appears it now
So many mis-spent moments to have given
To anything but love !   They're gone for ever
With all their wasted sunshine !   Now is left
One moment but to spare, one word to speak;
Farewell, my dearest love !

ELENA.

Farewell, my lord.

ARTEVELDE.

And if we meet no more, a heart thou hast,
Though heretofore misled, and like mine own
Bedarken'd in the gloom of devious ways,
Yet surely destined from the first by Heaven
To issue into light.   My shade removed,
The radiance of redeeming love shall shine
Upon thine after-life, and point the path
Thro' penitence to peace.   Pray for me then,
And thou shalt then be heard.

ELENA.

Farewell, my lord.

ARTEVELDE.

And is it thus we part ?   Enough, enough ;
Full hearts, few words.   But there is yet another
I would not leave unsaid.   If time be short
To seek for pardon of my sins from Heaven,
To thee and for my sins against thyself,
I shall not in the shortest sue in vain.
For reparation of one fatal fault
I would that I might be preserved to-day ;
If not, I know that I shall fall forgiven.

ELENA.

Try me no further, Artevelde; go, go;
If I should speak to thee one word of love
I should not hold myself on this side reason.
Go whilst I have my senses, Artevelde;
Or stay and hear the passion of my heart
Break out,—and not in words; if throes and shrieks
Thou wouldst be fain to witness, stay; if not
Content thee with one bitter word, adieu!

ARTEVELDE.

This fair hand trembles.   Dearest, be thou calm;
Calm and courageous.   I commend thy silence.
Yonder's the Knight of Heurlée; he is coming
To summon me away.

ELENA.

Oh God! I hate him!
Why is he with thee wheresoe'er thou goest?
It sends a very horror to my heart
To see his fiendish face!   Why is it he
That comes to bring thee?

ARTEVELDE.

Dearest, what imports it?
Nay—what is this? Elena—Sweet Elena—
She hears me not—What ho! Cecile!

Enter CECILE.

There, take her.

CECILE.

She will be better soon, my lord.

ARTEVELDE.

Say worse:
'Tis better for her to be thus bereft.

c c 2

One other kiss on that bewitching brow,
Pale hemisphere of charms!   Unhappy girl!
The curse of beauty was upon thy birth,
Nor love bestow'd a blessing.   Fare thee well!

SCENE VI.—*The western side of the Lis.—A watch-fire in advance
of the French Encampment.   Two* Soldiers *of the Watch.*

FIRST SOLDIER (*sings*).

Four stakes and a mat
  Make a very good house:
'Tis ill found, quoth the rat;
  Not a whit, said the louse.

SECOND SOLDIER.

The devil catch thy breath and mar thy singing!
The trumpets of the Flemish host may sound,
And nothing to be heard for thy fond ballads.

FIRST SOLDIER (*still singing*).

More happy are we than the count and the earl,
More happy are we than the gold-hatching churl,
Than the squire and friar, and seller and buyer,
Than he that is high, who still sees something higher.
    Your ear and I'll tell you
      The why and the wherefore—
    He that hath nothing
      Hath nothing to care for.

SECOND SOLDIER.

Be still, I say; I hear a trumpet now.
Hark! hush! now—there—a trumpet clear as day!
Be brisk and handy; bundle up your blankets,
And hie we to the captain of the watch.

SCENE VII.—*The eastern side of the Lis.*

VAN ARTEVELDE, *his* PAGE, *and* SIR FLEUREANT OF HEURLÉE.

ARTEVELDE.

They gather on the left.   Fly to Vauclaire,
And bid him when he sees me pass the bridge,
To drive his force along as though the devil
Were at his heels.

      [*Exeunt* VAN ARTEVELDE *and* Page.

SIR FLEUREANT.

   He is at yours, my lord.

SCENE VIII.—*A rising ground, entrenched and strongly guarded,
in the rear of the French Host.—The* KING, *attended by the*
LORDS OF COUCY *and* POICTIERS, *the* BASTARD OF ST. POULE.
&c. Messengers *arriving and departing.*

THE KING.

Here comes another—well, sir—tell me—what?

MESSENGER.

Sire, when Van Artevelde had cross'd the bridge——

LORD OF COUCY.

What! cross'd the bridge alive?

THE KING.

      Well, well; what then?

MESSENGER.

He poured himself upon the Breton flank,
Which stumbled back a step, but rallied soon,
Spurr'd by the Lords of Saimpi and St. Just,

Who hasten'd to the spot; and there it is
That now the battle rages.

THE KING.

　　　　　　　　　Ho! my horse!
My lords, do you your pleasures; it is mine
To get upon my horse and take what's going.

LORD OF POICTIERS.

Your majesty should bear in mind——another!

Enter a second Messenger.

THE KING.

Whence com'st thou? speak.

SECOND MESSENGER.

　　　　　　　　　Sire, I was sent to say
Van Artevelde was kill'd; so went the cry
Where I was—on the right; but coming hither
The knight of Saimpi did I jump withal
Borne wounded to the rear, and learnt from him
That Artevelde was living, proof whereof
He bore upon his body, for his wounds
Were got in fighting with him hand to hand.

THE KING.

My horse! I'll fight him hand to hand myself!
Stay you, my lords, or go; I mount my horse.

LORD OF COUCY.

Have with your grace! I cannot blame you much,
Though you shall fret your uncles.

THE KING.

　　　　　　　　　By St. Denis
Rather than stay I'll fight my uncles too.

SCENE IX.—*A part of the Field on the western side of the Lis.*—
VAN ARTEVELDE, *attended by several* Officers *and* Pages.

ARTEVELDE.

Who's here? Fly, Sibrand, to the further left;
Bid Eversdyk and Alphen wheel their force
To prop me on my flank.

[*Exit* SIBRAND.

Enter a Messenger.

Run thou, De Roo—

MESSENGER.

Vauclaire, my lord, is slain.

ARTEVELDE.

Is slain—hah—slain—
Thou to the rear, De Roo, and bid Van Ryk
Keep open passage on the bridge. Thou, Paul——

Enter a second Messenger.

SECOND MESSENGER.

Roosdyk, my lord, is dying of his wounds.

ARTEVELDE.

I cannot help it. Keep the causeway clear,
And summon Reehorst to my aid. We shake.
The cry is, still, Van Artevelde is slain.
Go make it known I live. Up with my cry!

SCENE X.—*Another part of the Field, still on the western side
of the Lis.*—*The* DUKE OF BURGUNDY, SIR FLEUREANT OF
HEURLÉE, *and* Followers.

BURGUNDY.

Another charge like that—ill-sorted knaves!

They stumbled on each other, each by each
Pegg'd in and pinion'd.   Now they're loose enough.
Another charge—they scurry to Mount Dorre.
We'll drive them up the hill, and from the top
Like a staved cask shall they be trundled down.
What wait we for?

SIR FLEUREANT.

Truly the cask rings hollow:
Yea, sir, the wine is spilt that made them bold.
Lo! yonder goes the King.

BURGUNDY.

What! breaking bounds!
He must not be before us.   Scale the hill.

SCENE XI.—*Another part of the Field, on the same side of the Lis, near the Bridge.*

VAN ARTEVELDE *and* VAN RYK.

ARTEVELDE.

I bleed, Van Ryk.   Can anything be done?
For if there can, my spirit's sight is dimm'd,
And I discern it not.

VAN RYK.

To fly, my lord,
Is what remains.

ARTEVELDE.

To fly!   Then mount my horse,
And make away before the general flight
Chokes up the bridge.

VAN RYK.

Not I, my lord.   Your horse
Should bear his proper burthen: mount yourself.

ARTEVELDE.

Never, Van Ryk.   My errand upon earth
Ends in this overthrow.   Bind up my wound;
Give me but strength again to reach the field,
And I will carve myself a nobler death
Than they design'd me.   God would not permit
That I should fall by any hand so base
As his who hurt me thus.

VAN RYK.

Whose hand was that?

ARTEVELDE.

Sir Fleureant's : he stabb'd me on the bridge,
And fled amongst the French.

VAN RYK.

Oh, monstrous deed!

ARTEVELDE.

I hid it whilst I could, which was not long;
And being seen so tottering in my seat,
The rumour ran that I was hurt to death,
And then they stagger'd.   Lo! we're flying all!
Mount, mount, old man; at least let one be saved!
Roosdyk! Vauclaire! the gallant and the kind!
Who shall inscribe your merits on your tombs?
May mine tell nothing to the world but this :
That never did that prince or leader live,
Who had more loyal or more loving friends!
Let it be written that fidelity
Could go no farther.   Mount, old friend, and fly!

VAN RYK.

With you, my lord, not else.   A fear-struck throng
Comes rushing from Mount Dorre. Sir, cross the bridge.

ARTEVELDE.

The bridge! my soul abhors—but cross it thou;
And take this token to my Love, Van Ryk;
Fly for my sake in hers, and take her hence;
It is my last command.   See her convey'd
To Ghent by Olsen or what safer road
Thy prudence shall descry.   This do, Van Ryk—
Lo! now they pour upon us like a flood!—
Thou that didst never disobey me yet,
This last good office render me.   Begone!
Fly whilst the way is free.

VAN RYK.

My lord, alas!
You put my duty to the sternest test
It ever yet endured; but I obey.
I do beseech you come across the bridge;
This rush of runaways——

ARTEVELDE.

Farewell, Van Ryk.

VAN RYK.

Fellows, stand back!   What! see you not my lord?
Stand back, I say!

ARTEVELDE.

Ho! turn ye round once more!
Cry Artevelde! and charge them once again!
What! courage, friends!   We yet can keep the bridge.
Three minutes but stand fast, and our reserves
Shall succour us.   Heigh, heigh, sir! who are you
That dares to touch me?

VAN RYK.

Nay, sirs, nay, stand back.

[VAN RYK *is forced off by the crowd.*

ARTEVELDE.

Shame on you, cowards! what! do you know me! back!
Back, villains! will you suffocate your lord?
Back, or I'll stab you with my dagger.　Oh!
Give me but space to breathe!　Now God forgive me!
What have I done?—why such a death?—why thus?—
Oh! for a wound as wide as famine's mouth,
To make a soldier's passage for my soul.

[*Exit, borne along in the rout towards the bridge.*

SCENE XII.—*The same.　Enter the* DUKES OF BURGUNDY *and*
BOURBON *with* Followers *on the one side, and* SIR LOIS OF
SANXERE *with* Followers *on the other.*

SIR LOIS OF SANXERE.

Halt ye a space, my lords, ye cannot pass:
The bridge has broken down beneath the weight
Of them that fly.

BURGUNDY.

　　　　A lath should bear up us,
We are so light of heart, so light of heel!
It was the leaden spirit of defeat
That brake the bridge.　Shoot me a plank across,
And see if I shall strain it!

SIR LOIS OF SANXERE.

　　　　　　Stay, my lord;
They're pushing beams athwart the shatter'd arch,
And presently the passage shall be safe
For all the host; but farther down the stream

There are some boats, though but a few, for those
Who would be foremost.

BURGUNDY.
              I am of them.   Who follows?

SCENE XIII.—*A part of the Field on the eastern side of the Lis.
It is strewn with the dead and wounded and other wreck of the
Battle. In front is the Body of* VAN ARTEVELDE. ELENA
is kneeling beside it. VAN RYK *and one of* VAN ARTEVELDE'S
*Pages are standing near. Trumpets are heard from time to
time at a distance.*

VAN RYK.
Bring her away.   Hark! hark!

PAGE.
                        She will not stir.
Either she does not hear me when I speak,
Or will not seem to hear.

VAN RYK.
                  Leave her to me.
Fly, if thou lov'st thy life, and make for Ghent.
                                            [*Exit* Page.
Madam, arouse yourself; the French come fast:
Arouse yourself, sweet lady; fly with me.
I pray you hear; it was his last command
That I should take you hence to Ghent by Olsen.

ELENA.
I cannot go on foot.

VAN RYK.
              No, lady, no,
You shall not need; horses are close at hand.
Let me but take you hence.   I pray you, come.

ELENA.

Take him then too.

VAN RYK.

The enemy is near
In hot pursuit; we cannot take the body.

ELENA.

The body!

VAN RYK.

Hush!

Enter DUKE OF BURGUNDY.

BURGUNDY.

What hideous cry was that?
What are ye? Flemings? Who art thou, old sir?
Who she that flung that long funereal note
Into the upper sky? Speak.

VAN RYK.

What I am,
Yourself have spoken. I am, as you said,
Old and a Fleming. Younger by a day
I could have wish'd to die; but what of that?
For death to be behind-hand but a day
Is but a little grief.

BURGUNDY.

Well said, old man;
And who is she?

VAN RYK.

Sir, she is not a Fleming.

Enter the KING, *the* DUKE OF BOURBON, *the* EARL OF FLANDERS.
SIR FLEUREANT OF HEURLÉE, *the* Constable, TRISTRAM OF
LESTOVET, *the* LORD OF COUCY, *and many other* Lords *and*
Knights, *with* Guards *and* Attendants.

THE KING.

What is your parley, uncle; who are these?

BURGUNDY.

Your majesty shall ask them that yourself;
I cannot make them tell.

THE KING.

                              Come on, come on !
We've sent a hundred men to search the field
For Artevelde's dead body.

SIR FLEUREANT.

                              Sire, for that
You shall need seek no further ; there he lies.

THE KING.

What, say you so ?   What ! this Van Artevelde ?
God's me ! how sad a sight !

BURGUNDY.

                              But are you sure ?
Lift up his head.

                    THE CONSTABLE.

                    Sir Fleureant, is it he ?

SIR FLEUREANT.

Sirs, this is that habiliment of flesh
Which clothed the spirit of Van Artevelde
Some half an hour ago.   Between the ribs
You'll find a wound, whereof so much of this
                              [*Drawing his dagger.*
As is imbrued with blood, denotes the depth.

THE KING.

Oh me ! how sad and terrible he looks !
He hath a princely countenance.   Alas!
I would he might have lived, and taken service
Upon the better side !

BURGUNDY.

And who is she?

[ELENA *raises her head from the body.*

BOURBON.

That *I* can answer: she's a traitress vile,
The villain's paramour.

SIR FLEUREANT.

Beseech you, sir,
Believe it not; she was not what you think.
She did affect him, but in no such sort
As you impute, which she can promptly prove.

ELENA (*springing upon her feet*).

Tis false! thou liest! I WAS his paramour.

BOURBON.

Oh, shameless harlot! dost thou boast thy sin?
Aye, down upon the carrion once again!
Ho, guards! dispart her from the rebel's carcase,
And hang it on a gibbet.   Thus and thus
I spit upon and spurn it.

ELENA (*snatching* ARTEVELDE'S *dagger from its sheath*).

Miscreant foul!
Black-hearted felon!

[*Aims a blow at the* DUKE OF BOURBON, *which* SIR FLEUREANT
intercepts.

Aye, dost baulk me! there—
As good for thee as him!

[*Stabs* SIR FLEUREANT, *who falls dead.*

BURGUNDY.

Seize her! secure her! tie her hand and foot!

What ! routed we a hundred thousand men
Here to be slaughter'd by a crazy wench !

> [*The* Guards *rush upon* ELENA ; VAN RYK *interposes for her defence ; after some struggle, both are struck down and slain.*

BOURBON.

So ! curst untoward vermin ! are they dead ?
His very corse breeds maggots of despite !

BURGUNDY.

I did not bid them to be kill'd.

CAPTAIN OF THE GUARD.

                                 My lord,
They were so sturdy and so desperate
We could not else come near them.

THE KING.

                                 Uncle, lo !
The Knight of Heurlée, too, stone dead.

SIR LOIS OF SANXERE.

                                 By Heaven
This is the strangest battle I have known !
First we've to fight the foe, and then the captives.

BOURBON.

Take forth the bodies.   For the woman's corse,
Let it have Christian burial.   As for his,
The arch-insurgent's, hang it on a tree
Where all the host may see it.

BURGUNDY.

                                 Brother, no ;
It were not for our honour, nor the king's,
To use it so.   Dire rebel though he was,
Yet with a noble nature and great gifts

Was he endow'd,—courage, discretion, wit,
An equal temper and an ample soul,
Rock-bound and fortified against assaults
Of transitory passion, but below
Built on a surging subterranean fire
That stirr'd and lifted him to high attempts.
So prompt and capable, and yet so calm,
He nothing lack'd in sovereignty but the right,
Nothing in soldiership except good fortune.
Wherefore with honour lay him in his grave,
And thereby shall increase of honour come
Unto their arms who vanquish'd one so wise,
So valiant, so renown'd.   Sirs, pass we on,
And let the bodies follow us on biers.
Wolf of the weald and yellow-footed kite,
Enough is spread for you of meaner prey.
Other interment than your maws afford
Is due to these.   At Courtray we shall sleep,
And there I'll see them buried side by side.

THE END.

D D

NOTES.

Preface, page xv.

" Lord Byron's conception of a hero is an evidence, not only of scanty materials of knowledge from which to construct the ideal of a human being, but also of a want of perception of what is great or noble in our nature."

I WILL beg to extract here, as an Appendix to my Preface,* three or four stanzas from the conclusion of a poem written above six years ago, which will support the assertion that some of the opinions I have expressed, obnoxious as I am afraid they may at first sight appear to the charge of presumption, are not hastily hazarded, or now first adopted. The poem from which the extracts are taken, was written in anticipation of the accomplishment of the work now published, and was intended as a proem or poetical introduction to it. But writing then with no more than a distant and indistinct prospect of publication, I was betrayed into a sort of domestic egoism, which, now that the time comes to print, I do not venture to present to public notice. The stanzas which follow, are, I trust, unobjectionable on this score; and they contain (besides the expression of opinion to which I have adverted) an acknowledgment of intellectual obligations which I am unwilling to omit, and a tribute of respect and admiration which I confess that it is a pleasure to me to pay in public; and which is not improperly so paid, because the person spoken of is one with whom it cannot be said that the public have no concern.

*   *   *   *   *

Then learn'd I to despise that far-famed school
Who place in wickedness their pride, and deem

* Dated in 1834.

DD 2

Power chiefly to be shown where passions rule,
    And not where they are ruled: in whose new scheme
    Of heroism, self-government should seem
A thing left out, or something to contemn,—
    Whose notions, incoherent as a dream,
Make strength go *with* the torrent, and not stem,
For 'wicked and thence weak' is not a creed for them.

I left these passionate weaklings: I perceived
    What took away all nobleness from pride,
All dignity from sorrow; what bereaved
    Even genius of respect; they seemed allied
    To mendicants that by the highway side
Expose their self-inflicted wounds, to gain
    The alms of sympathy—far best denied.
I heard the sorrowful sensualist complain,
If with compassion, not without disdain.

```
    *       *       *       *
    *       *       *       *
    *       *       *       *
    *       *       *   two friends
```
    Lent me a further light, whose equal hate
On all unwholesome sentiment attends,
Nor whom may genius charm where heart infirm offends.

In all things else contrarious were these two:
    The one, a man upon whose laurell'd brow
Grey hairs were growing! glory ever new
    Shall circle him in after years as now,
    For spent detraction may not disavow
The world of knowledge with the wit combined,
    The elastic force no burthen e'er could bow,
The various talents and the single mind
Which give him moral power and mastery o'er mankind.

His sixty summers—what are they in truth?
    By Providence peculiarly blest,

aaaassist . ok

With him the strong hilarity of youth
  Abides, despite grey hairs, a constant guest.
  His sun has veer'd a point toward the west,
But light as dawn his heart is glowing yet;
  That heart the simplest, gentlest, kindliest, best,
Where truth and manly tenderness are met
With faith and heavenward hope, the suns that never set.

*　　*　　*　　*　　*

Thus nurtured and thus disciplined in thought
  By kindred and associates, strange it were
If work of mine, though faint, should not have caught
  Some colour of transmitted light, some stir
  Of congruous emotion.　If I err
In deeming that some portion of my tale
  Impersonates the virtues I aver
To hold in admiration,—if I fail
In this, then what is writ will be of no avail.

But if from time to time upon the page
  Some token of these higher aims be traced,
Some fair ideal, borrow'd from an age
  Of ruder but of less emasculate taste,
  Some nook whence Nature hath not been displaced
For Fashion's sake; if mine it be to feed
  To a robust complexion, not to waste
With idle stimulation them that read,
Then forth upon my way I go with God to speed!

Preface, page xiii.

"Poetry of which sense is not the basis, &c.

Till this moment, when recurring for another purpose to
Mr. Wordsworth's preface to his poems, and to Mr. Coleridge's
remarks upon them in his "Biographia Literaria," I was not
aware for how many of my tenets I was indebted to those

admirable specimens of philosophical criticism. The root of the matter is to be found in them.

In the first and second editions this note ended here. I have since been informed by a friend who was once a visitor at Rydal Mount at the same time with myself, that some parts of my preface have been borrowed from Mr. Wordsworth's conversation. I daresay this is the case. I can only wish that my mind and writings were as much enriched as they ought to be, by the abundant opportunities I have enjoyed of drawing from the same source.

Preface, page xiii.

" He (Lord Byron) was in knowledge merely a man of belles lettres."

I am aware that Lord Byron made out a long catalogue of books read in his early youth. I cannot help feeling persuaded that there must be mistakes in the enumeration. I have too high an opinion of Lord Byron's natural capacity, to allow myself to believe that he could have read some of the profound and philosophical works mentioned in his catalogue without deriving benefit from them as a writer.

Part I., Act I., Scene I., page 5.

" For truly there are here a sort of crafts
So factious still and obstinate," &c.

It is curious to observe in these trade unions of the fourteenth century, compared with those of the present day,* the tendency of society, from time to time, in conjunctures when the influences of physical force, commercial wealth, and prescriptive polity, reach certain approximations to an equipoise, to throw itself into something like the same forms and divisions. Our own political unions, and the effects which they are calculated to produce, have never been described in a more philosophic spirit and temper, or more forcibly, than in the speech from which the following extract is taken :—

---

* The year 1834.

"That Political Unions are an evil, no one is readier to declare
than I. I do not hesitate to say that such institutions are
fraught with destruction more than can be calculated, destruction to all government, destruction to all property, destruction
to all freedom, destruction to the very nature and characters of
Englishmen. I should hate to live in a country in which such
institutions predominated, (and predominate they must if they
exist at all,) as I should hate to live in a country in which great
measures were concerted silently and executed speedily; in
which men should meet together in multitudes, to agree upon
secret schemes and spread them abroad secretly and put them
in operation secretly; in which all individual liberty, and all
individual responsibility, without which no man can be good or
wise or strong or happy, should be bowed into uniformity with
the general will, (if through fear, bad enough—if willingly, still
worse,) should be merged and melted down and mingled up
into that great mass of ordered and digested opinion, in which
alone consists the much-boasted strength of these much-boasted
Political Combinations; as I should hate, in short, to live in a
land where men should act in multitudes, and think in multitudes, and be free in multitudes. . . . . . . I do not deny that
such a nation might triumph over every outward obstacle; I do
not deny that, in such a nation, commerce might flourish and
wealth increase, that she might be full, even to fatness, with
the glory of political wealth and political conquest and political
independence. But I do deny that any one of these things, of
all these things together, make up one item in the happiness,
the virtue, the wisdom, or the real freedom of a nation. I do
deny that, for all these things, I would consent to make England
a nation of politicians; say rather of political instruments, of
men, that the whole together might be powerful, consenting to
be each man a slave. I say, I do deny, that for centuries of
such wealth, such glory, and such independence, I would consent
to barter one hour of that domestic comfort, and domestic
freedom, household strength, and household virtue, with which
it is our boast to have been blest above other nations, and which
all come of the sacred inheritance of *individual freedom*, the

free thought of the free soul, for which the worst of *occasional* convulsions and calamities are not too dear a price to pay."

After some account of the manner in which these unions are generated, he proceeds :—

"And there are not wanting men wiser in their generation, with other and further views, whose game it is to excite and inflame these discontents; men who, if they can get any hold by which to sway this 'huge and fiery mass of passion,' from being the outcasts of society can make themselves its terrors; and there is no lack of meaning and stirring phrases which spread anger and disobedience like wildfire from eye to eye and from mouth to mouth. And then begins the vast and vital disorder; for as yet we have traced it only to its beginnings; then begins the fearful and ever-widening breach between the very rich and the very poor; the poor looking on the rich with hatred springing from sense of wrong; the rich upon the poor, first with cold and distant pride, then with the angry and jealous alarm of pride frightened from its propriety."

I have quoted these passages from an anonymous pamphlet, published by Ridgway in 1832, entitled "Substance of a Speech against Political Unions, delivered in a Debating Society in the University of Cambridge." It is a singular trait of the times, that a speech containing so much of sagacity and mature reflection as is to be found in this exercitation, should have been delivered in an academical debating club, and should have passed away in a pamphlet, which, as far as I am aware, attracted no notice. Time and place consenting, a brilliant Parliamentary reputation might be built upon a tithe of the merit.

Part I., Act I., Scene III., page 19.

This description of Launoy's fate is little more than a versification of the following account of it :—

"When the Earl of Flanders came to the minster, and saw them of Ghent fly into the church, he commanded the minster to be set on fire, which was quickly done, and the fire soon mounted to the covering of the minster. There they of Ghent died in great pain, for they were burnt alive, and such of them as issued out were slain, and cast into the fire again. John Launoy, who was in the steeple, seeing himself about to be burnt, cried to them without, 'Ransom! Ransom!' and offered his coat, which was full of florins, to save his life; but they without did but laugh at him, and said, 'John, come out at some window and speak with us, and we shall receive you: make a leap, as you have made some of us leap within this year; it behoveth you so to do.' When John Launoy found he could not escape and that the fire came so near him, he thought he had better be slain than burnt, and so he leaped out at a window among his enemies, and was there received on spears and swords, and cut to pieces, and cast into the fire again. Thus ended John Launoy."—*Froissart*, vol. ii., chap. cix.

Part I., Act I., Scene VII., page 35, and Part I., Act II., Scene I., page 58.

The history of Jacques Van Artevelde, the father, is more generally known to the English reader than that of Philip, the son; for his power lasted longer, and he was in close political connection with Edward the Third of England. "To speak properly," says Froissart, "there never was in Flanders, nor in any other country, prince, duke, or other, that ruled a country so peaceably, so long, as this James D'Arteville ruled Flanders." His downfall was brought about by an attempt to stretch his power to the extent of substituting the issue of Edward the Third for that of the Earl of Flanders, in the inheritance of that territory. The good town of Ghent had long supported him in usurping the Earl's actual authority and dominion; but they revolted against the idea of altering the legitimate descent. "When he returned, he came into Ghent about noon; they of the town knew of his coming, and many were assembled together in the street as he was to pass, and when they saw him they began to murmur, and said—'Behold yonder Great Master who would order all Flanders after his pleasure, which is not to be suffered.' They also whispered through all the town that James D'Arteville had received for nine years all the revenues of Flanders, without giving any account, and thereby hath maintained his dignity, and also sends great riches out of the country, into England privately. These expressions fired them of Ghent, and as he rode through the street he perceived that they were incensed at him, for such as had formerly made reverence to him as he passed, now turned their backs to him and entered their houses: then he began to be alarmed, and as soon as he had entered his house, he fastened his gates, doors, and windows; this was scarcely done before the street was full of men, and especially those of the smaller crafts. There they assailed his house both behind and before, and broke it open: he and his people within defended themselves for a long time, and slew and wounded many without; but finally he could not sustain it, for three parts of the townsmen were at the assault. When James saw that he was so severely oppressed, he came to a window with great humility, bareheaded, and said, with fair language—'Good people, what ails you? why are you so much incensed against me? how have I displeased you? inform me, and I shall make you amends:' Then those who heard him answered all with one voice—'We desire an account of the great treasure of Flanders that you have sent away, without any reason.' Then James answered meekly, and said—'Certainly, sirs, I never took any of the treasure of Flanders; withdraw quietly into your houses, and return in the morning, and I will give you so good an account, that you should reasonably be satisfied.' Then they all answered —'Nay, we will have an account immediately; you shall not escape us so; we know that you have sent great riches into England without our knowledge, therefore you shall die.' When he heard this, he clasped his hands, and weeping said—'Sirs, such as I am you have made me, and you have sworn to me before this to defend me against all persons, and now you would slay me without reason; you may do it if you please, for I am but one man among so many; for God's sake take better advice, and remember the time past, and consider the great favours and courtesy that I have done you and your town: you know that commerce was nearly annihilated in this country, and by my means it is recovered; I have also governed you peaceably; for during my government ye have had all things as you could desire; corn, riches, and all sorts of merchandise.' Then they all exclaimed as with one voice, 'Come down to us, and talk not so high, and give us an account of the great treasure of Flanders, that you have controlled so long without accounting for, which is unbecoming an officer to do, to receive the goods of his lord, or of a country, without accounting.' When James saw that he could not appease them, he drew in his head and closed his window, and so thought to steal out by the back door, into a church that adjoined his house, but four hundred persons had entered into his house; and finally there he was taken and slain."—*Froissart*, vol. i., chap. cxv.

Part I., Act I., Scene X., page 50.

" *Nor heeds the weltering of the* PLANGENT *wave.*"

I have adopted this (as it sounds to my ears) very euphonous epithet, from a little poem called " The Errors of Ecstacie," by Mr. Darley—a poem which is full of this sort of euphony, and remarkable on other accounts.

Part I., Act I., Last Scene, page 53.

" *Lives, lives, my lord, take freely ;*
But spare the lands and burgages and moneys.
The father dead shall sleep and be forgotten ;
The patrimony gone, that makes a wound
That's slow to heal ; heirs are above-ground ever."

It would be difficult to find in the works of Machiavelli a more characteristic passage than that from which the above is taken: "Deve nondimeno il principe farsi temere in modo che, se non acquista l'amore e' fugga l'odio; perche può molto bene star insieme, esser temuto e non odiato; et quando pure gli bisognasse procedere contro al sangue di qualcuno, farlo quando vi sia giustificatione conveniente, et causa manifesta; ma sopra tutto astenersi dalla robba d' altri, perche gli uomini dimenticano più tosto la morte del padre, che la perdita del patrimonio."—*Principe*, cap. xvii.

Part I., Act I., Last Scene, page 55.

" You know, my lord, the humour we of Ghent
Have still indulged."

A hundred years produced little change in the humour of the
people of Ghent, whose dispositions towards peace and a dutiful
demeanour appear to have been as equivocal under the House
of Burgundy in the fifteenth century, as under that of Flanders
in the fourteenth. An indication of this is to be found in a
whimsical proceeding of theirs related by Commines as having
taken place upon the accession of Charles the Bold. Ghent had
been in rebellion against his father, Philip, but had been brought
to terms, and had never, whilst most disaffected to his father,
shown any unfriendly dispositions towards himself; for it was
indeed a proverb, that " Ceulx de Gand aymoient bien le filx de
leur Prince, mais le Prince non jamais."   Charles, relying upon
his former relations with Ghent, and upon the assurances of the
magistrates and rich citizens that he would be received with the
utmost joy and good-will, made a solemn entry into the town,
on the morning of the 28th of June, 1467. He was, to all
appearance, exceedingly well received ; the streets were hung
with the most beautiful tapestries, stages were erected from
place to place on which mysteries were performed, the chimes
were rung out from all the steeples, and there was every possible
demonstration of loyalty and respect. One of the chief grievances of the people had been a certain tax upon corn, which
had been levied to pay the expenses of a former rebellion, and
which was continued though the people were persuaded that
all those expenses had been long since paid. Even this complaint, however, was scarcely heard, or but very softly uttered,
in the universal happiness which appeared to prevail upon the
entry of the Duke into his good town of Ghent. The day of his
entry happened to be that of the celebration of the martyrdom
of St. Liévin, who was the favourite saint of the mean crafts.
According to their use on this day they carried him in procession
in his shrine to the village of Holtheim, the spot of his martyrdom, where they passed the night with him, taking him back

the next day to the Church of St. Bavon, which was his ordinary place of abode. Directly on their way back through the Market-place to the Church, stood the house which had been erected for the purpose of levying there the obnoxious gabelle upon corn. They knocked the shrine against the wall of the house, and then, alleging that the Saint would not turn out of the straight road, they forthwith levelled the building to the ground, and carried him over the ruins. The indignation of Charles the Bold may easily be imagined; but for once he was brought to feel the necessity of placing his temper under restraint, and after incurring some danger by giving way to the first burst of anger, he betook himself to dissimulation and fair words, and departed from the city ostensibly in peace.—*Commines*, lib. ii., chap. iv., and *Barante*, vol. ix., p. 7.

Part I., Act II., Scene I., page 59.

" And wenches who were there said Artevelde
Was a sweet name and musical to hear."

I have thought it expedient to confine to the female portion of the White-Hood party this motive for placing themselves under the command of Van Artevelde; though the historian relates, without any such limitation, that he was chosen for the reason, amongst others, that his name was " Le mieulx seant à prononcer."

Part I., Act II., Scene III., page 68.

" And thou who wert a gentle-hearted man,
Must lead these monsters where they will !"

It is a remark of Cicero that, "bellorum civilium ii semper sunt exitus, ut non ea solùm fiant quæ velit victor, sed etiam ab iis mos gerendus sit, quibus adjutoribus parta sit victoria."

Part I., Act II., Last Scene, page 99.

" Think of your mariners."

The relatives of the Earl's bailiff, who had been slain by the White-Hoods, as Froissart says, "*somewhat* revenged the death

of their cousin, by seizing the crews of forty ships belonging
to Ghent, and putting out their eyes." — *Froissart*, vol. ii.,
chap. lxxxviii.

Part I., Act IV., Scene I., page 88.

I have borrowed, in this place, a line from a poem by a near
relative, who died several years ago, at an early age.   I will take
this opportunity of printing that poem, persuaded that by those
who can appreciate the strain of thought and feeling which
pervades it, the indulgence of a natural wish to preserve it will
not be thought unreasonable :—

MONOLOGUE.   SCENE, IN THE MOUNTAINS.

(*The Speaker above one hundred years old*)—*Time, early Morning.*

Dawn smiles ; around the golden isle of heav'n
Break the white-rushing clouds in paler spray ;
Till down among the eastern heights she sets,
And night, a second night, a paler shade,
Van-courier of the morn, is on the skies.
Twilight with trembling fingers sketches there
Vast outlines, mountains summitless, grey wastes,
Now caught against the clouds, and now all dark.
Forth from the bosoms of those shadowy mounds
Launch the fresh breezes on their early voyage,
And the dark eaglets from their aëries watch
The nearing sun .... Sounds, that are gathering round me,
And the half-distinguish'd landscape's glimmerings,
Rouse in my heart the waning thoughts of times
That have past far away .... a concourse strange
As haunts that eve when charnels give to air
Their white-robed tenantry ;—worn out Remembrance
Puts forth her light, that, like the eternal lamps
Of tombs, burns only to illuminate
Sepulchral gloom, and cheer cold isolation.
These oaks have waved here for a hundred years
Since I first knew this vale, and they which flung

Around, below, a wide and rustling shade,
A green pavilion, broad and beautiful,
Have wither'd into leafless stocks ; . . . . alas !
There is no blessing in so long a life; . . . .
I left this valley yet a little child,
And have return'd beneath a load of years ;
Men with grey beards look up to me; yea dotards
Ask of their ancestry from me ; and dames
Pray in their folly that their infants reach
Such age as mine ; and the babes gaze with awe
At the old Gaffer's long white beard, and ask
Who in the valleys is so old as he ?
Men have seen changes—mighty changes wrought—
And in few years—and over potent states—
Have not the raven and the vulture dwelt
Among the empty stones of Judah's towers ?
Have not the desert rushes waved in Tyre ?
Babes held the princedom of Jerusalem ?
Slaves worn the purple of most mighty Rome ?
Aye, and the growth of yonder mountain firs
Where I was wont to have my gay expanse
Of garden-ground, gives me a deeper sadness
Than mournful tales of ruin'd monarchies,
Dismantled cities, nations past away.—
Morn of white front and pearly eye ! that now
Thy kindly salutations giv'st to all,
I cannot win one joyful thought from thee.
I view thy roseate chaplettings of cloud
With an untemper'd fancy, the cold spleen
And heartless weariness of extreme age,
A weak recoil from all that's gay and fair ;
For the young mind clings at the first approach
Of Pleasure's magnet; but we travel on,
Creep to the further pole, and are repell'd.
Life's earliest fountain-gush is pure from heaven,
And all the after-stream with earth-sprung taints,
And gathering lutulence, made foul : and mine

Hath spread into a dank, unhealthful marsh ;
An obstinate stagnation.—They are all,
All gone ;—with whom how fondly once I loved
To seek this height and wander through yon dells—
None left upon the earth ; all laid beneath ;—
Death, like a kindly shepherd, came to them,
When they were straying in the vale of years,
And took them to their fold, and bade them sleep ;
But he hath been to me a jealous master ;
Hovering for years around me ; with approach
Enfeebling, but forbearing still to touch,
He tempts with outstretch'd hand, and disappoints.
'Tis hard—to feel cheeks wrinkle-plough'd like these
Wetted with tears—Not yet ! I have not yet,
Old as I am, reach'd second infancy ;
My soul hath lost her fire, but not her force.
Dry up, thou sun, these drops ! Remembrance struck
This arid rock, and they have gush'd unbidden.—
But that is o'er ; and high Resolve hath set
Her seal upon the heart ; and I will gaze,
With a clear eye and steady lip, around,
On hill and heath, that are the cenotaphs
Of those I will not name again.—'Tis day . . . .
Back to the vale ; to men ; to life ! I bear
Within me warm and urgent thanksgivings
For the gifts left me ; the time-scorning power,
And constancy of thought ;—the unchanged command,
And might of the invulnerable mind.

He died within two or three days after he had completed his
twentieth year. If a powerful reasoning faculty and an ardent
and affluent imagination be, as I believe, the constituents of
true genius, he was possessed of it.

Part I., Act V., Scene VIII., page 177, *et seq.*

It is impossible to represent the Earl's adventures upon his defeat at Bruges, with more of dramatic effect than belongs to them, as related by Froissart :—

. "In the mean time that the Earl was at his lodging, and sent forth the clerks of every ward from street to street, to have every man to draw to the market-place to recover the town, they of Ghent pursued their enemies so fiercely, that they entered into the town with them of Bruges; and as soon as they were within the town, the first thing they did they went straight to the market-place, and there set themselves in array. The Earl had then sent a knight of his, called Sir Robert Mareschault, to the gate, to see what they of Ghent did; and when he came to the gate he found it beaten down, and the enemy masters of the passage: and some of them of Bruges met with him and said—'Sir Robert, return and save yourself if you can, for the town is in the possession of our enemies.' Then the knight returned to the Earl as fast as he could, who was coming out of his lodging on horseback, with a great number of cressets and torches with him, and was going to the market-place; and as he was entering, such as were before him, seeing their enemies all ranged in the place, said to the Earl—'Sir, return again; if you go any farther you will be killed or taken by your enemies, for they are ranged in the market-place, and wait for you.' They showed him truth. And when the conquerors saw those clear lights coming down the street they said—'Yonder cometh the Earl, he will fall into our hands.' And Philip D'Arteville had commanded from street to street, as he went, that if the Earl came among them no man should do to him any bodily harm, but take him alive, and then have him to Ghent, and so to make their peace as they pleased. . . . . . The Earl, who hoped to have recovered all, came near to the place where they of Ghent were. Then divers of his men said—'Sir, go no further, for your enemies are lords of the market-place and of the town; if you enter into the market-place, you are in danger of being taken or slain : a great number of your enemies are going from street to street seeking their enemies; they have certain of them of the town to conduct them from house to house, where they would be; and, sir, you cannot issue out of any of the gates, for the

E E

enemy is possessed of them; nor can you return to your own
lodging, for your enemies are going thither.' And when the
Earl heard those tidings, which much distressed him, as may be
imagined, he was greatly alarmed, and considered the danger he
was in. Then he believed the counsel, and would go no farther,
but endeavour to save himself; and so he took his own counsel.
He commanded all the lights to be put out; and said to them
that were about him—'I see well there is no recovery; let
every man depart, and save himself as well as he can.' And it
was done as he commanded; the lights were quenched and cast
into the street, and every man departed. The Earl then went
into a back lane, and made a varlet of his to unarm him, and
cast away his armour, and put on an old cloak of his varlet's,
and then said to him—'Go thy way from me, and save yourself
if you can; and have a good tongue if you fall into the hands of
your enemies; and if they ask anything of me do not acknow-
ledge that I am in the town.' He answered and said—'Sir, I
had rather die than betray you.' . . . . . Thus about the hour of
midnight the Earl went from street to street and by back lanes,
so that at last he was fain to take a house, or else he had been
taken by his enemies; and so, as he went about the town, he
entered into a poor woman's house, which was not fit for such
a lord: there was neither hall, parlour, nor chamber; it was a
poor smoky house; there was nothing but one poor place, black
with smoke, and above a small room with a ladder of seven
steps to go up to it; and in that room was a mean couch, where
the poor woman's children lay. Then the Earl, much alarmed
and trembling, said as he entered—'O good woman, save me! I
am thy lord, the Earl of Flanders; but now I must hide myself,
for my enemies pursue me; and if you do me a service now, I
shall reward you for it hereafter.' The poor woman knew him
well, for she had been often at his gate to fetch alms, and had
often seen him going and returning from sporting; so she immediately consented; for if she had made any delay, he had been
taken talking with her by the fire. Then she said—'Sir, mount
up this ladder, and lay yourself under the bed you find there,
where my children sleep.' And in the mean time the woman

sat down by the fire with another child that she had in her arms. So the Earl mounted the ladder as well as he could, and crept between the couch and the straw, and lay as flat as possible. And immediately some of his enemies entered the house, for some of them said they had seen a man enter the house before them; and so they found the woman sitting at the fire with her child. Then they said—'Good woman, where is the man we saw enter this house before us, and shut the door after him?' 'Sirs,' quoth she, 'I saw no man enter here this night: I went out just now, and cast out a little water, and shut my door again. If any were here I could not hide him; you see all my house at once; here is my bed, and up this ladder lie my poor children.' Then one of them took a candle and mounted up the ladder, and looked and saw only the poor couch where the children lay asleep; and so he looked all about, and then said to his company —'Let us go hence, we are losing time: the poor woman speaks the truth, here is no creature but she and her children:' and then they departed out of the house. After that, there was none entered to do any hurt. All these words the Earl heard well, while he lay under the couch: you may suppose he was in great fear for his life. He might well say— 'I am now one of the poorest princes in the world: how uncertain are the affairs of this world!' Yet it was fortunate he escaped with his life : howbeit this dangerous adventure might well be to him a memorial all his life after, and an example to all others."—*Froissart*, vol. ii., chap. cxxxi.

The Earl's final escape is thus told :—

"I was informed, and I believe it to be true, that on the Sunday at night the Earl of Flanders issued out of the town at Bruges, by what means I cannot say, but I believe he was assisted. He issued out all alone on foot, in an old simple cloak; and when he came into the fields he was glad, for then he thought he had escaped great danger; so he went forth at a venture, and stopped at a thick bush, to see what way he might take, for he knew not the ways, nor was he accustomed to travel on foot : and as he stood under the bush, he heard by chance a man speak as he came by, and it was a knight of his.

called Sir Robert Mareschault, who had married his bastard daughter. The Earl knew him by his voice, and as he passed by he said—'Robert, are you there?' The knight, who knew the Earl by his speech, said—'Ah, sir, I have been seeking for you this day in many places about Bruges: how did you get out?' 'Let us go our way,' quoth the Earl, 'it is not time to tell our adventures; I pray you let us endeavour to get a horse, for I am greatly fatigued with going on foot, and I pray you let us take the way to Lisle, if you know it.' 'Yes, sir,' replied the knight, 'I know it well;' and so they travelled till the next morning without being able to get a horse; but they found a mare, which they took from a poor man in a village, and on which the Earl rode without saddle or pannel, and at night came to Lisle, where the greatest part of his knights had arrived who fled from the field, some on foot and some on horseback."—*Froissart*, vol. ii., chap. cxxxii.

Notwithstanding the orders which Froissart relates to have been given by Van Artevelde to take the Earl alive and not do him any bodily harm, he says, in another place, that had he been taken his life would have been in danger. If any danger was to be apprehended, it was probably rather from the accidents of tumult and disorder than from any deliberate purpose to put him to death. About a century later the people of Ghent are thus spoken of by Commines:—"Après le peuple du Liège, il n'en est nul plus inconstant que ceulx de Gand. Une chose ont ils assez honneste, selon leur mauvaistie: car à la personne de leur Prince ne toucherent jamais."—Lib. ii., chap. iv.

Part I., Act V., Last Scene, page 184.

"*As ye were brave, so be ye temperate now.*"

" No people ever acted more mildly with their enemies than they of Ghent did with them of Bruges; for they did no injury to any man of the small crafts of the town, unless he was greatly accused. When Philip d'Artevelde and the captains of Ghent saw that they were lords of Bruges, and all was at their command, then they made proclamation that every man, on pain of death, should draw to his lodging, and not plunder, or make any disturbance, unless they were commanded." — *Froissart*, vol. ii., chap. cxxxii.

Note to the Sixth Edition.—Part II., Dramatis Personæ.

ELĒNA.

This accentuation is said to be erroneous, and nothing was more likely than that I should commit an error of this kind. But a friend more learned than myself supplies me with an old prosodial rule, which takes the distinction of " meretrix Helĕna sed sancta Helēna," whence it may be inferred that in the middle ages the name was, sometimes at least, accented on the second syllable.

Part II., Act I., Scene I., page 213.

" Enter the King with a hawk on his hand."

The partiality of this boy-king for hawking, may be inferred from his dreams :—

" It happened while the King lay at Senlis, one night as he was asleep in bed, he had a vision. It seemed to him clearly that he was in the city of Arras, where he had never been before, and with him were all the most valiant men of France; and he thought that there came to him the Earl of Flanders, and presented him with a fine falcon pelerin, saying to him—'Sir, I give you this falcon, as the best that ever I saw, for pursuing and destroying of fowls.' Of this present the king thought he had great joy, and said—'My dear cousin, I thank you.' And therewith he thought he regarded the Constable of France, Sir Oliver Clisson, and said unto him—'Sir Oliver, let us two go into the fields to prove this excellent falcon that my cousin of Flanders hath given me.' And then he thought the constable said to him —'Sir, let us go when it pleases you.' And so then he thought that they took their horses, they two alone, and went into the fields and found plenty of herons to pursue. Then the King said—'Constable, let the falcon fly, and we shall see how she will pursue her game.' Then the Constable cast off the falcon, and she mounted so high into the air that they could hardly see her, and the King thought that she proceeded directly towards Flanders. Then the King said—'Let us ride after my bird, I should be sorry to lose her.' And so he thought they rode after her till they came to a great marsh and a thick wood; which being unable to pass on horseback, they alighted: and then he thought that servants came to them and took their horses. And so the King and the Constable entered into the wood with great difficulty, and travelled so long that they came to a fine piece of land; and there the King thought he saw his falcon chasing herons, and fighting with them, and they with him; and it appeared to the King that his falcon pursued the herons till at last he lost sight of her, wherewith he thought he felt much disappointed, seeing that he could not follow his hawk; and he thought he said to the Constable—'Ah, I fear I shall lose my falcon, whereof I am sorry, and I have nothing to allure her back.' While in this difficulty, the King thought there appeared before him a great hart with wings, and inclined himself before him, whereof he had great joy, and thought he said to his Constable—'Remain here, sir, and I will mount on this hart, and so follow my falcon.' And so the King thought he mounted this flying hart, which, according to his desire, bore him over all the great woods and trees, and there he saw his falcon beating down a vast number of fowls; and then it appeared to the King, when his falcon had destroyed many herons, that he called her, and the falcon immediately came and settled on his hand; and then the hart flew again over the woods, and brought the King to the same land where the Constable tarried for him, who was very glad of his return: and as soon as he was alighted, he thought the hart departed, and then he never after saw him. And so there the King thought he told the Constable that the hart had borne him more easily than ever he had ridden before; and also he thought he told him of the success of his falcon. And therewith it seemed to him that his servants came to them and brought them their horses, and they mounted and took the highway, and so returned to Arras. And therewith the King awoke, and was much amazed at that vision, and he remembered every thing thereof perfectly well, and he showed it to them of his chamber that were about him. And the figure of this hart pleased him so much, that all his imagination was set thereon. And this was one of the first circumstances that occasioned him, when he went into Flanders to fight against the Flemings, to bear in his arms the flying hart."—*Froissart*, vol. ii.. chap. cxxxvii.

Part II., Act II., Scene I., page 237.

" We have been too successful to be safe
In standing still."

When Vespasian was so favourably situated that no one would believe him to be without designs upon the purple, Mucianus explained to him, in a few words, the dangers of moderation : "Abiit jam, et transvectum est tempus, quo posses videri concupisse: *confugiendum est ad imperium.*"—*Tac. Hist.*, ii. 76. Machiavelli, who studied Tacitus for his philosophy as diligently as he consulted Livy for his facts, generalises the observation : " Ne possono gli uomini che hanno qualità eleggere lo starsi, quando bene lo ellegessino veramente, et senza alcuna ambitione ; perche non é loro creduto ; tal che se si vogliono star loro, non sono lasciati stare da altri."—*Discorsi*, iii. 2.

Hobbes would seem to have had this passage in his memory when he wrote as follows : " Because there be some that taking pleasure in contemplating their own power in the acts of conquest which they pursue farther than their security requires ; if others, that otherwise would be glad to be at ease within modest bounds, should not by invasion increase their power, they would not be able, long time, by standing only on their defence, to subsist. And by consequence, such augmentation of dominion over men, being necessary to a man's conservation, it ought to be allowed him."—*Leviathan*, part i., chap. 13.

Part II., Act II., Scene II., page 244.

" The injury that disables is more wise
Than that which stings."

In the preceding note I have cited one instance in which
Machiavelli has developed, in a general maxim, the philosophy
with which Tacitus seldom fails to impregnate the speeches
which he represents to have been delivered on particular occasions. I am here tempted to quote another example. When
the Belgic provinces rose against Vocula, and placed him in
such extremity that he was urgently counselled to flight, the
view of the matter which was taken by that severe and intrepid
commander is expressed in these words: "Nunc hostes, quia
molle servitium : cùm spoliati, exutique fuerint, amicos fore."—
Machiavelli, in his exposition of the various means for retaining
conquered and distant territories in obedience, makes a maxim
of the same policy: "Si ha à notare, che li uomini si debbono, ò
vezzeggiare, ò spegnere; perche si vendicano delle leggieri offese,
delle gravi non possono."—*Principe*, cap. iii.

Part II., Act III., Scene II., pages 272-3.

" In his youth
Famed for his great desire of doing evil
He was elected into Testenoire's troop
Of free companions."

"Geoffrey Testenoire," says Froissart, "was a cruel man, and
void of feeling, and *would as soon kill a knight or squire as a
villain.*"—Vol. ii., chap. clxxi. Testenoire, however, was in the
regular service of the English king, and it is perhaps doing him
some injustice to represent him as the leader of a free company.
Of the manner in which such a company was formed, and the
qualifications required in its captain, the following is a lively
account. The parties are certain English and Gascon auxiliaries
of the king of Portugal, and their pay was in arrear :—" Then
they began to speak, and make their complaints to each other;
and among them there was a knight, a bastard brother of the
king of England, called Sir John Sounder, who was very bold

in speaking, and said, 'The Earl of Cambridge hath brought us hither; we are always ready to venture our lives for him, and yet he withholdeth our wages; I counsel, let us all be of one accord, and let us among ourselves raise up the banner of St. George, and be friends to God and enemies to all the world : for unless we make ourselves feared, we shall get nothing.'— 'By my faith,' quoth Sir William Helman, 'you speak well, and so let us do.' They all agreed with one voice, and so considered among themselves who should be their captain. Then they agreed that in this case *they could not have a better captain than Sir John Sounder, for he had then great desire to do evil, and they thought him more competent thereto than any other.*"—*Froissart,* vol. ii., chap. cxxiv.

Part II., Act III., Scene II., page 280.

" *Pain and grief*
Are transitory things no less than joy,
And though they leave us not the men we were,
Yet they do leave us.   You behold me here
A man bereaved, with something of a blight
Upon the early blossoms of his life
And its first verdure, having not the less
A living root, and drawing from the earth
Its vital juices, from the air its powers:
And surely as man's health and strength are whole,
His appetites regerminate, his heart
Re-opens, and his objects and desires
Shoot up renewed."

The mixed state of feeling which is expressed or implied in this and other passages in the same scene, has been characteristically treated by South, in his comments upon "Sorrow for Sin."—"As Solomon says, 'in the midst of laughter the heart is sorrowful,' so in the midst of sorrow here, the heart may rejoice : for while it mourns, it reads, that those that mourn shall be comforted ; and so while the penitent weeps with one eye, he views his deliverance with the other.   But then for the external expressions and vent of sorrow, we know that there is a certain pleasure in weeping ; it is the discharge of a big and swelling grief, of a full and strangling discontent ; and therefore he that never had such a burthen upon his heart as to give him opportunity thus to ease it, has one pleasure in this world yet to come."

Reading this with the free mind and easy acceptation which should be brought to the perusal of what concerns the moral affections, no one can fail to understand what it means, and feel the truth as well as the liveliness of the remark. It may be worth while, however, to take the exception to it to which it is logically liable, for the sake of the metaphysical proposition which it involves. If the matter be stated strictly, then, the admixture of better feelings with the sorrow can only be so far a recommendation, as the sorrow is thereby not so bad as it might be; but so far as the thing is taken as an individual entity and properly called a sorrow, it must be qualified by the term which belongs to the balance of its constituent feelings, and called painful. In a series of sensations whereof the first is the *most* painful, and the rest follow in constantly mitigated succession, the first only may be as a pain, and the rest as pleasures, to the patient or sentient; *these* being felt as pleasures relatively to *that* the foregoing excess of pain; though all *absolute* pains, *i. e.* pains relatively to a state of indifference—all and singular of them substantive pains—all as comprehending that first excess in virtue of which only any pass for pleasures—each singularly taken, because, taken without relation to its antecedents, the object of comparison with each is of course a state of indifference. In the reversal of this order of succession, the feelings passing from less to more intense, instead of from more to less, is to be found the root of the distinction between the pains of sorrow and those of anxiety, and the cause of the preference to be given, *cæteris paribus,* to the former. Whilst I am upon such subjects, I shall easily be excused for presenting the reader with another extract from South—an extract of so much as relates to joy and sorrow, from that writer's admirable description of the affections of man such as they were before his fall from a state of innocence:—"In the next place for the lightsome passion of *Joy.* It was not that which now often usurps this name; that trivial, vanishing, superficial thing, that only gilds the apprehension, and plays upon the surface of the soul. It was not the mere crackling of thorns, a sudden blaze of the spirits, the exultation of a tickled fancy or a pleased appetite. Joy was then a masculine and a severe thing; the recreation of the judgment, the jubilee of reason. It was the result of a real good suitably applied. It commenced upon the solidities of truth, and the substance of fruition. It did not run out in voice, or undecent eruptions, but filled the soul as God does the universe, silently and without noise. It was refreshing but composed; like the pleasantness of youth tempered with the gravity of age; or the mirth of a festival managed with the silence of contemplation. And, on the other side, for *Sorrow*. Had any loss or disaster made but room for grief, it would have moved according to the severe allowances of prudence, and the proportions of the provocation. It would not have sallied out into complaint or loudness, nor spread itself upon the face, and writ sad stories upon the forehead. No wringing of the hands, knocking of the breast, or wishing oneself unborn; all which are but the ceremonies of sorrow, the pomp and ostentation of an effeminate grief: which speak not so much the greatness of the misery, as the smallness of the mind. Tears may spoil the eyes, but not wash away the affliction. Sighs may exhaust the man, but not eject the burthen. Sorrow *then* would have been as silent as thought, as severe as philosophy."

Part II., Act IV., Scene II., page 303.

——" and oh!
That constable! Oh, Oliver of Clisson!
That such a man as thou, at such a time,
Should hold the staff of constable of France."

I have represented Sir Oliver of Clisson according to the impression which his conduct in this campaign certainly appears to be calculated to convey. I have made him pliant and irresolute. It should be observed, however, that the history of other wars in which he bore a most conspicuous part, ascribes to him no such weaknesses; and to his character for vigour of one kind his soubriquet of 'Oliver the Butcher' bears testimony.

Part II., Act V., Scene III., page 364.

" *Once in my sad and philosophic youth—*
For very philosophic in my dawn
And twilight of intelligence was I—
Once at this cock-crow of philosophy,
Much tired with rest and with the stable earth,
I launch'd my little bark and put to sea,
Errant for geste and enterprise of wit
Through all this circumnavigable globe."

I have represented Van Artevelde, in this scene principally, and incidentally also elsewhere, as not forgetful of the studies of his earlier years ; and although such studies were not common in the age in which he lived, and though in every age, men but rarely carry such remembrances along with them after they have embarked in public life, yet the peculiar course of the life led by Van Artevelde, and the almost compulsory character of the exchange which he made of a meditative privacy for a military and political career, has appeared to me to render not unnatural the combination, in his case, of thoughtfulness with the activity which his public station required of him.   I revert to the subject here, chiefly for the purpose of quoting a passage from Mr. Landor's " Imaginary Conversations,"—a work, in my estimation, more rich in thought and brilliant in expression than any that has been published of late years.   " How many," says Sir Philip Sidney, one of the imaginary collocutors, "How many, who have abandoned for public life the studies of philosophy and poetry, may be compared to brooks and rivers, which in the beginning of their course have assuaged our thirst, and have invited us to tranquillity by their bright resemblance of it, and which afterwards partake the nature of that vast body into which they run, its dreariness, its bitterness, its foams, its storms, its everlasting noise and commotion ?   I have known several such, and when I have innocently smiled at them, their countenances seemed to say,—' *I wish I could despise you : but alas! I am a runaway slave, and from the best of mistresses to the worst of masters ; I serve at a tavern where every hour is dinner-time, and pick a bone upon a silver dish.*' "   I never recur to Mr. Landor's volumes without renewed admiration of his abilities, nor without the wish that his writings could be cleared from the tone of uncalled-for defiance and unnecessary self-assertion which lowers them.

Part II., Act V., Scene III., page 373.

" *A mother dotes upon the reckling child*
 More than the strong: solicitous cares, sad watchings,
 Rallies, reverses, all vicissitudes,
 Give the affection exercise and growth.
 So is it in the nursing a sick hope." .

This either is casually concurrent with the following passage in Madoc, or was unconsciously borrowed from it :—

" Have I not nursed for two long wretched years
 That miserable hope, which every day
 Grew weaker, like a baby sick to death,
 Yet dearer for its weakness day by day."

Part II., Act V., Scene V., page 383.

"ELENA.

I could not sleep, and sate without the tent,
And sudden from the river seem'd to rise
A din of battle, mixed with lengthen'd shouts
That sounded hollow like a windy thaw.
I look'd, and in the cloudy western sky
There was a glow of red, and then the cries
Were less confused, and I believed I heard
' Mount Joye, St. Denis!' ' Flanders and the Lion!'
With that I came to waken you."

I will extract here the picturesque and romantic passage in Froissart, upon which the above is founded :—

"Thus when the Flemings were at rest in their lodgings, (howbeit they knew well their enemies were on the hill not more than a league from them), Philip d'Arteville had brought a damsel with him out of Ghent; and as Philip lay and slept on a couch, by the side of a little fire of coals in a pavilion, this said damsel, about midnight, went out of the pavilion to take the air, and to see what time it appeared to be, for she could not sleep; she looked towards Rosebecque, and saw in the sky

smoke and fire (it was the reflection of the fires the French made
under hedges and bushes); this damsel hearkened, and thought
she heard much noise between the two armies, and the French
crying 'Mountjoy! St. Denis!' and other cries; and this she
thought was on Mount Dorre, between there and Rosebecque;
of this thing she was much afraid, and so entered the pavilion,
and suddenly awaked Philip. and said—'Sir, rise and arm yourself quickly, for I have heard a great noise on the Mount Dorre;
I believe it is the French coming to attack you.' With these
words he rose and cast on his gown, took his axe in his hand,
and issued out of the pavilion to see what it was; and he heard
the same noise the damsel had told him of, and it seemed to
him that there was a great tournament on the said hill: then
he immediately entered his pavilion, and caused his trumpet to
be blown, when every man rose and armed himself. They of
the watch immediately sent to Philip d'Arteville, to know why
he stirred up the host, seeing there was no cause, for that they
had sent to the enemy's host, and there was nothing stirring.
'What then,' said Philip, 'was that noise on Mount Dorre?'
'Sir,' said they, 'we heard the same, and sent to know what it
was, but they that went said that when they went they heard
nor saw nothing; therefore, sir, we did not rouse the army, for
we should have been blamed if we had done so without a cause.'
And when they of the watch had told Philip this, he appeased
himself and all the host, but yet he was astonished at this
phenomenon. Some said it was fiends of hell, who played
there where the battle was to be the next day, for joy of the
great prey they were likely to have there."—*Froissart*, vol. ii.,
chap. cl.

Part II., Act V., Scene XI., page 395.

" Oh for a wound as wide as famine's mouth,
To make a soldier's passage for my soul."

"So these men of arms pressed so close upon the Flemings,
that they could not defend themselves; so there were many
that lost their strength and breath, and fell upon each other,
and were pressed to death, without striking any stroke: and

there was Philip d'Arteville wounded and beaten down among his men of Ghent; and when his page with his horse saw that his master was defeated, he departed and left his master, for he could not render him any assistance, and so rode to Courtray, on the way to Ghent. . . . . . Thus when the battle was ended, they at last left the pursuit, and trumpets sounded the retreat. . . . . . Then the King said to them that were about him, 'Sirs, I wish to see Philip d'Arteville, whether he be alive or dead.' They answered that they would do their best to gratify him. And then it was proclaimed through the host that whoever could find Philip d'Arteville should have a hundred francs for his labour. Then many went among the dead bodies, who were most all stripped of their clothes; at last there was such search made that he was found and known by a varlet who had served him long before, and he recognised him by many tokens; so he was brought before the king's pavilion, and the king and all the lords beheld him for some time; and the body was examined, to see what wounds he had, but they could see none that appeared to be mortal; but it was judged that he fell into a little dike, and many of them of Ghent upon him, and was so pressed to death."—*Froissart*, vol. ii., chap. cliii., cliv.

Part II., Act V., Scene last, page 401.

" Wolf of the weald and yellow-footed kite,
Enough is left for you of meaner prey."

"More bodies were left on the field for the yellow-footed kite and the eagle, and the grizzly wolf of the weald, than had fallen under the edge of the sword in any battle since the Angles and Saxons first came over the broad sea," is the account given by an Anglo-Saxon poet, of the carnage at the battle of Brunnaburgh, A.D. 938. It is quoted by Mr. Southey, whose unequalled command of the materials which poetry supplies for the elucidation of history, is nowhere more apparent than in the work in which this quotation occurs, the Naval History of England.

www.ingramcontent.com/pod-product-compliance
Lightning Source LLC
Chambersburg PA
CBHW022021110726
47901CB00006B/1613